Whisper INTO THE Night

Whisper into the Night

The Rainbow Brigade - Book One

JAY LEIGH

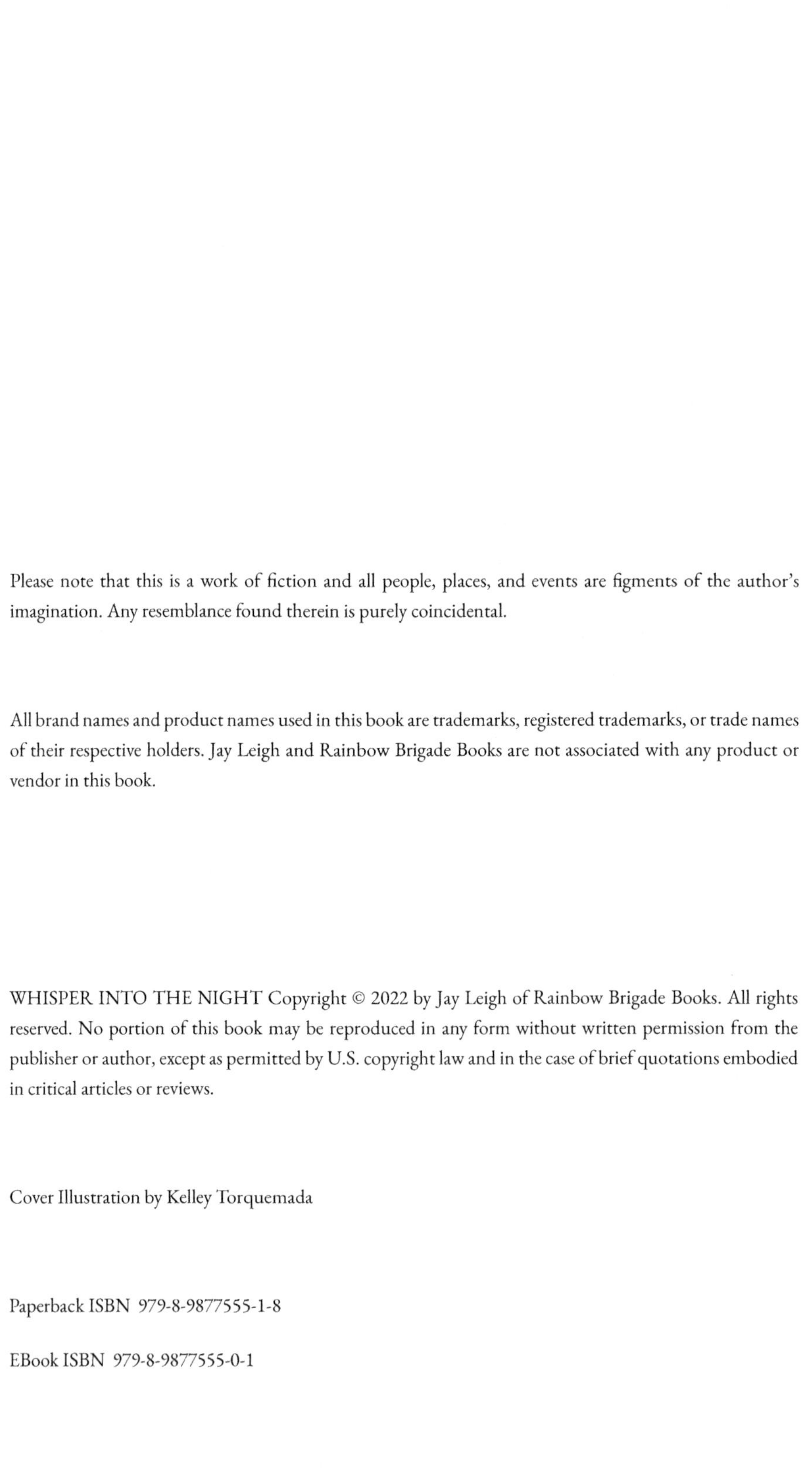

Cover Illustration by Kelley Torquemada

Paperback ISBN 979-8-9877555-1-8

EBook ISBN 979-8-9877555-0-1

To those who hold true the belief that love is love and comes with no conditions—and the one who taught me this with hers.

Author's Note

Dear Reader,

Whisper into the Night is intended for a mature audience. The characters in this story deal with numerous obstacles, both internal and external, throughout the narrative. Sometimes the events that take place might be hard to experience. Sometimes it will be violent. Sometimes it will be heart-wrenching. From misogyny to right-wing extremism, hospitalizations, mental health struggles, and harrowing situations involving kidnapping and death, at times the journey might be difficult. You can find a comprehensive list of content warnings on my website.

But this is also a story of resilience, strength, and most of all, the power of love.

Additionally, while I spent countless hours researching to provide an accurate depiction of the lives of these characters, I also had to make certain narrative choices that might stray from how things work outside a fictional setting. This is not intended to be an accurate account of how certain federal agencies work but an exploration of the myriad types of people who work in them.

This is a love story. And love stories have an expected conclusion that will be hard-won. Despite this, your experience as a reader is paramount, so please do what is right for your mental health.

All my love,

Jay

CHAPTER ONE

Theo

Inauguration Day started early, the end of the marathon still a distant dream. Things in the White House had devolved into a standoff at high noon as the trio of First Children stood opposite a cadre of Secret Service agents. The atmosphere bristled with hair-trigger tension, and Theodore Moreau had run low on energy and patience, which meant his younger siblings Tobias and Annalise were likewise done with the day. Blood loyalty ran deep in the children of President Adelaide Montgomery, and the younger two were looking to Theo for his first move. It would be the moment that would define the next four years of their new life in the People's House they now called home, but he lost the advantage when a dirty blond bear of a man stepped toward the invisible line in the sand.

"Miss, misters. I'm Agent Connor O'Brien. On behalf of your security detail, allow me to welcome y'all home." Shots fired; it was a low blow sending the eye candy to parley, especially when that voice dripped with a honeyed Southern drawl.

"Call me Theo. This is Toby and Anna. And this isn't our home." He crossed his arms over his chest. Toby mirrored the action with a brooding, prepubescent attitude, and Anna followed suit with the whip-crack sass that seven years of life experience gifted her. Theo found it difficult to be excited about moving into the White House, not when the place resembled a museum turned prison state, and the decor left so much to be desired. Nevertheless, Theo was an adult and had to be a role model. "Thanks, though. I guess."

"Of course, Sir. Agents Fornell and Mitchell here are assigned to Miss and Mister Montgomery, and I'll be with you through the rest of the evening. At the balls."

"He said balls." Toby snickered, as one does when one is twelve.

"Theo's getting balls tonight!" Anna's voice chirped with a giggle.

Connor's grin must have been some sort of breach of protocol with how it lit up his entire face compared to the somber expressions of the stony sentinels behind him. Naturally, he had glorious dimples. It was just one more thing that added to Theo's mounting frustrations.

"God. Toby, Anna, that's enough." Theo covered his face with his hands, muffling the admonishment but likely doing nothing to hide the blush he could feel warming his cheeks. "Just go and do whatever it is you two do. Try not to burn the place down. Wait at least a week before the arson, yeah?"

"Have fun with your balls!" Anna sprinted up the steps to the residential area before Theo could respond, which left him sputtering swear words under his breath at Toby. The snickers of the latter had turned into hysterical laughter that echoed down the stairwell as he left the scene. Finally, Theo thought in vain, a moment's peace. Of course, it wasn't long-lived.

"Theo! There you are. We have to go now if we are going to keep to the schedule. Stop being difficult."

All business, just like always. Mom burst into view like a tornado of sequins and silk from somewhere within the confusing tangle of rooms filled with random antiques and dated furniture. Mom was probably the wrong title, though. She carried herself in full President Montgomery mode, and Theo exhaled a resigned sigh.

"I just don't understand why I have to be your escort tonight, mom. I'm literally the worst choice for this. I know it, you know it, everyone knows it." Stress caused his voice to waver and crack as Theo shifted anxiously, tugging at the ridiculous bowtie in a futile attempt to relieve some of the tension. Compared to his mother's designer-chic sheath dress, all glitter and pomp, his off-the-rack tux made for a comical contrast that left him uncomfortable in his own skin.

"Mn, too late. We already had this argument. Agent, have him at the motorcade in two." Without so much as a by-your-leave, President Mom disappeared up the stairwell the kids had just climbed, her entourage of agents waiting in formation at the base.

"Reckon we ought to get on it, then?" Connor was still grinning like a cat that had just eaten the last living canary in the world, and Theo couldn't help but scowl. No one should be that damn happy all the time.

"Whatever."

Anxiety and dread crept up Theo's spine as Connor led him through the maze of halls. Not one, not two, not even three, but four official inaugural balls awaited him, and each step felt more and more like a march toward his execution as the reality of it sunk in. He wasn't aware they had arrived at the motorcade until he was already climbing into the backseat, his reluctant limbs moving on autopilot as the unease caused his chest to grow tighter with every breath in and out. When the door thunked closed behind him, he felt like a caged animal.

He knew this evening would be chaos. Everything about this presidency was unprecedented, and Theo hated how much attention followed his family because of it. His mom had arrived on the scene with the force of a hurricane. Her career trajectory soared from her start as a struggling single mother to a well-respected politician, and the press just loved to devour every little detail, including unsavory ones that were pure speculation.

What they loved the most was her tragic love story. Her marriage to a decorated Marine might as well have been plucked straight out of a fairy tale. Her two younger children had even inherited their father's golden curls and blue eyes. But his stepfather's sudden passing overseas right after Anna had been born propelled his mom even deeper into politics as a coping mechanism for her grief. Dark-haired, moody, and anxious, Theo didn't fit into that storybook chapter. Something his nerves tried to remind him of at this moment.

The feeling only got worse as the night went on. Theo barely made it through the motions as they navigated the first appearance. Camera flashes left him blind. The din of the crowd vying for his mother's attention split his skull in half. He stumbled three times during the requisite dance, with every eye and numerous camera crews catching every misstep. His smile felt weak and artificial as he stood aside while she gave her thanks and other social niceties to the nameless faces that pressed in closer every time they turned around. Politicians, supporters, lobbyists, and socialites crowded them all night, everyone dressed in the finest designer evening wear and desperate to capture the newly-minted President's attention.

Despite the clamoring crowds, they made it back to the motorcade. His mother was ushered into the official limousine, and Theo, in all his non-presidential mediocrity, had been shuffled into a smaller SUV nearby. He all but collapsed into the seat, the vice around his chest impossible to ignore as he fumbled with shaking hands in the pockets of the unbearable tuxedo jacket. With a shallow, desperate gasp, he felt the inhaler burn at the back of his throat, the exhalation tasting medicinal as he struggled to regain control over his breathing. He hung his head low, pointedly ignoring the whiskey-gold eyes glancing back at him in the rearview mirror.

"Y'all right, Sir?" Connor's voice slipped into his ears, soft and slow, and Theo bristled at the attention.

"Yep." He huddled against the car door, thankful for the privacy afforded by the blacked-out windows. The last thing he needed was another gossip magazine scandal or terrible paparazzi shot.

The second appearance had been a carbon copy of the same torture. Halfway through the third appearance, Theo really started to slip as anxiety slowly morphed into something closer to panic. *Don't make a scene, don't make a scene.* The words had become a mantra that Theo clung to like a life preserver as he hung at his mother's heels, tossed around the crowd like a passenger thrown overboard at sea.

"Mom? Mom, I need to... mom?" Theo tried to get the President's attention, but she was already being pulled in so many different directions that the words didn't even register. All smiles and soft laughs, she remained completely unaware of just how badly Theo struggled right beside her. Anger, resentment, fear, and sadness hit Theo all at once, and that, combined with his current mental state, became a heady concoction. He gasped in surprise as a hand landed on the small of his back.

"Sir?" Connor's one-word question cut through the noise like a lifeline. A ray of sunshine that sliced through the tempest-tossed sea of chaos threatening to drown Theo.

"I need a minute. Please?"

Theo's face must have said everything else he couldn't articulate. Connor guided him through the crowd and toward a service hall as if he knew the layout of the building by memory. If Theo had the energy, he would have laughed at the way the Secret Service agent made a show of clearing the hall before pulling Theo in, but he could barely put one foot in front of the other. Sighing, he slid down the wall and landed with a thud, his elbows finding his knees and his head falling into his hands. The air sent a shiver down his spine, considerably cooler in the empty hallway, and the perpetual hum of noise and chatter became muffled by the separation, easing the prickling tension that crawled over his skin.

After a while, Theo had gathered enough of his wits to sit up straighter. He stretched his legs out as he pulled a sandwich bag from where he'd stashed it in his pants pocket. Emotional support cookies, his first meal of the day, not that it counted as anything remotely nutritional. The problem with anxiety was that it led to nausea, and nausea led to not eating, and not eating led to more nausea, and that led to more anxiety. The result? Theo usually found himself sitting on the floor eating sad emotional support cookies. As if today wasn't already the worst.

Sidelong glances from the intrepid agent still hovering nearby pulled Theo out of the spiral of his wandering thoughts. There wasn't anything judgmental in his gaze. If anything, it appeared to be earnest curiosity, and again, Theo felt himself blushing when he realized how ridiculous the scene must look to this stranger. After admiring this handsome stranger with the whiskey eyes and honey voice from afar during the weeks leading up to this moment, a niggling, vain part of Theo wanted to make a good impression. Instead, he looked like a trainwreck personified. Warily, Theo extended the bag of cookies, and Connor surprised him by flashing another grin, deadly dimples on full display, before fishing a cookie from the flimsy plastic bag.

"Mmm. They're warm." Connor paused before taking another bite as if sampling a fine wine or artisanal cheese. "Tasty."

"Wow. Way to make it awkward, O'Brien."

"Yeah, I get that a lot. But..." Connor popped the last of the cookie in his mouth and held his hand out toward Theo. "... it made you smile."

Theo let out a little huff as Connor hoisted him to his feet with little effort. He tried to conceal his smile with a scowl but went slack-jawed instead when Connor winked. The man had no shame. None whatsoever. A smug grin and the realization that his cheeks were freckle-dusted had every synapse in Theo's brain misfiring as he stood there, entirely too close and still holding onto Connor's hand.

"Who's making it awkward now, Moreau?" Connor whispered, his lips still curled and a mischievous crinkle at the corners of his eyes.

Theo snapped back to reality as he tore his hand out of Connor's calloused grip. "God. You're ridicul—"

"Ridiculously awesome. Yeah, I get that a lot, too."

Theo resorted to muttering swear words under his breath as he stepped back, suddenly desperate to put some much-needed space between himself and this incorrigible man.

Flustered and floundering, Theo shoved the baggy of cookies back in his pocket and fussed over his tux in an attempt to recover his composure. Temptations like freckled southern boys who were off-limits to people like him could quickly become a dangerous and slippery slope, so he did the only thing he could think to save himself from further embarrassment. He moved toward the door leading back into the convention center. With any luck, the chaos of too many people pressing in too close would distract him from this suddenly overwhelming hallway.

Of course, Agent Connor O'Brien appeared right on his heels. Theo didn't mind at all when a hand ghosted over his lower back again, an anchor in the stormy sea of presidential enthusiasm, and for a moment, he finally felt like he could breathe.

CHAPTER TWO

Connor

THE CHAOS OF THE convention hall assaulted Connor's senses, a sobering reminder that he still had a job to perform. He really should not have let himself get as carried away as he did. Flirting with the protectee is probably most definitely written somewhere in the long list of what not to do on the job. His mentor told him the worst part was how boring it could sometimes be, but Connor quickly realized that wouldn't be the case as soon as he had the chance to interact with Theo one-on-one. The weeks leading up to tonight were a tease of admiration from afar. Now, he finally had a chance to be up close and personal, and he had to remind himself to behave.

Connor spent months doing copious amounts of research under the pretense of preparing for his new role on the protective detail. Paparazzi photos and newspaper articles couldn't hold a candle to Theo's actual appearance. Long dark curls, sparkly hazel eyes, skin so pale it appeared nearly luminescent, cheekbones that would make any model weep with envy. Theo, the physical embodiment of every fantasy novel book boyfriend Connor had allowed himself to daydream over for the last decade. Coming face to face with Theo's wary, smoldering attitude made the situation much more alluring. He carried himself with the enigmatic wariness of a mystical being, practically elven in elegance and disdain both. Connor was definitely in over his head. Something he found rather exhilarating.

Also quite thrilling was the fact that Theo retracted his claws, at least a little, after their brief detour to the service hallway. The whole exchange left Connor eager to learn more about the mystery that is Theo Moreau. The gossip magazines and divisive political articles weren't very kind to Theo during the campaign. Still,

Connor knew better than to believe any of the hot air that came out of those questionable publications. Theo was complex, and Connor felt the magnetic pull to unravel those layers more and more with every glimpse of the man behind the reputation.

Theo's brief vulnerability earlier in the hallway ignited the protective desire that had driven Connor to work toward the promotion to personal detail in the first place. The fact that Theo didn't mind him standing closer only fueled those flames higher. Yeah, Connor knew he was being ridiculous. He couldn't really find it in himself to care much, though. Not when he caught yet another glance sneaking his way as the two maneuvered through the crowds in search of the President Theo was supposed to be escorting tonight. That stereotype of the somber, stone-faced Secret Service agent? Not him. Connor's cheeks ached from how much he found himself smiling. This job wasn't going to be even remotely boring.

By the time Connor and Theo rejoined the presidential entourage, the group had already neared the exit, and Connor fell into stride with the other agents with practiced ease. He had to be at peak performance. Protective detail work is about constant vigilance, but controlled spaces like the convention hall were not nearly as risky as moving the protectees to the motorcade. Despite this, Connor took a moment to note how easily he fell in sync with Theo as he stepped closer, moving as if he were Theo's shadow tethered to every movement. They were so close Connor could feel Theo flinch as the doors swung open, and the first camera flash blinded them both. Only the pressure of Connor's palm against Theo's lower back kept them moving forward as the flashing lights and shouts swiftly rose in intensity.

The vehicles were only about twenty paces from the exit, an inconsequential distance. The bite of the cold air washed over his skin, refreshing after the oppressive heat of the convention center. He kept them moving, never pulling his hand from where it fit too easily in the curve of Theo's spine. Moving from point A to point B would be an operation that ran as smoothly as silk. But the hair on the back of Connor's neck stood up as a sound cut above the cacophony of eager reporters crowding against the barriers at either side of their egress route.

The sound echoed to the left and grew louder on the right until it became the only thing Connor could hear. People were howling like wolves. Connor's blood became ice in his veins.

Time slowed as instinct took over. Something wasn't right. Screams rose abruptly on either side as the path narrowed, barriers falling to the crush of bodies as reporters toppled over like pins on a bowling alley.

"Get the President to the Beast! Go, go, go!" Connor didn't recognize the voice in his headset, but they all already knew what they needed to do. Countless exercises and drills had prepared Connor for all manner of scenarios. The adrenaline flooding his system further honed his actions as he grabbed Theo's body and bent him over at the waist, curling his frame over Theo's back like a shield. They sprinted through the quickly narrowing gap that led toward the line of vehicles. Glass shattered somewhere nearby, too close. A bloom of orange light and the acrid smell of gasoline assaulted Connor's senses as the ground to the left ignited in flames. He couldn't hear anything over the screaming, and then he could only hear a high-pitched whine as a sharp pain suddenly erupted at the back of his skull.

Undeterred and working on muscle memory and training, Connor heaved Theo's body into the backseat of the SUV and leapt in to cover him, the vehicle speeding into motion as soon as the door closed behind them. The interior wasn't silent as the engine roared, but it might as well have been in contrast to the shouting and chaos they had just escaped. Connor's chest heaved with every deep breath he took, his arms framing Theo's body beneath him in the vehicle's back seat. The sound of his pulse in his ears and the shrill whine that had robbed him of his sense of hearing just moments ago finally subsided, only to be replaced by the chatter over his headset and the shouting from the agent in the driver's seat of the SUV.

"O'Brien! Report! Do you copy? What's the status on Whisper?" The crackle of the voice over the audio snapped him back into action.

"Christ, O'Brien, move!" The driver's words were terse, spoken through a clenched jaw as he whipped the SUV around a tight corner. The motion sent Connor reeling back against the car door, freeing Theo where he remained plastered to the seat, curled into the fetal position, and quaking from head to toe. Now that the fog had lifted, Connor's hands flew to Theo's body without a second thought. His cursory check for physical injuries had Connor recalling his basic first aid training from his days in the Marine Corps. Satisfied that Theo was unharmed, Connor keyed up the mic at his wrist to respond.

"Whisper is secured, en route to White House. Will report to medical. Over."

Connor's quick assessment had only checked for apparent physical injury, but the lack of any outward signs of damage didn't mean he was all right. Theo appeared to be anything but all right as he curled even tighter around himself, whimpering with a soft keening sound muffled by the upholstery of the seat where he remained huddled.

"Sir? Sir! Theo!" Connor resorted to physically manhandling Theo into an upright position, grunting with the effort. Despite being lithe and lean, Theo was still a six-foot-tall man, just a couple of inches shy of Connor's height. The stiffness of his limbs made it even harder to move. Once Connor had managed to pry him off the seat, Theo shifted with astonishing speed to latch onto Connor's jacket with an iron grip. Despite his height, Theo made himself remarkably small as he clung to Connor's chest, still trembling and not speaking a single word. His breaths came in ragged, shallow gasps against Connor's neck, and all he could do in response was wrap his arms around Theo's shoulders and pull him even closer.

By the time they reached the White House and crawled from the back of the SUV, Theo had become fused to Connor's frame and moved only by Connor's direction as they navigated the passageways toward the medical center. The White House buzzed with frenetic activity as agents stalked the halls, and the chatter over the headset was just as chaotic. Nevertheless, Connor ignored most of it as he steered Theo through the center's office, down a small hall, and into an exam room of the on-site medical facility. The Physician to the President was, naturally, not in the medical unit. Instead, a younger doctor swiftly moved into action as Connor more or less hoisted Theo onto the table at the center of the room.

"I reckon it's shock. He's had a rough go with anxiety today. Prolly a panic attack. I seen him use his inhaler, too. Asthma, I reckon." After he finished his report, Connor realized how thick his accent had become, the subsiding adrenaline leaving him shaky and too tired to worry about tempering his Texan drawl.

The young lady didn't reply to Connor directly, but her voice came out soft and soothing when she spoke to Theo. "Theo, I'm Dr. Lily Ward. You're all right now. I'm going to check you over real quick, and then we'll get you out of here, okay?"

Connor hovered, likely a bit too close, but with the way Theo refused to loosen his grip on the lapel of his jacket, he didn't have much choice. After a short time and numerous little lights, instruments, and beeping gadgets, the physician's assistant exhaled with a soft hum at the back of her throat.

"Theo. Theo, your oxygen levels are too low, and your blood pressure is elevated." She cocked her head to the side and tried again when Theo didn't respond, his eyes staring unfocused at some distant nothing. "Theo. I'm going to grab an inhaler."

"Here, lemme." Connor reached into the pocket of Theo's tuxedo jacket where he'd watched him stow the little blue-grey canister earlier that evening. Holding the item before Theo's face, Connor whistled shrilly with his free hand's middle finger and thumb tucked between his lips. With a startled gasp, Theo's eyes snapped back to life as he snatched the inhaler from Connor and made quick work of taking the medication. Connor couldn't help but exhale a sigh of relief. While Theo still trembled, he became somewhat more aware and responsive as he administered another dose of the inhaler, eyes frantically darting around the room with a confused expression.

With another soft inhalation of surprise, Theo suddenly turned to stare at Connor with a frown, his eyebrows bunching with a furrow of the brow. "You," he murmured, his voice quivering as he reached a shaky hand out to turn Connor's face to the side, the fingertips cold on his jaw but the touch surprisingly tender in a way that sent a little shiver down Conner's spine. "Y-you're hurt."

That got the young doctor's attention as she tore her gaze from the pulse oximeter she studied on Theo's fingertip.

"Ah, it's nothing. Just a bump, yeah?" Connor tried to flash a reassuring grin, but he realized it looked like a feeble attempt when the young woman's lips flattened into a thin line. Donning a fresh set of gloves, she jockeyed into position to examine the back of Connor's head, fussing with gauze and liquid that soaked into his hair, far too cold for Connor's liking and stinging with a medicinal burn.

"A laceration, but it's small. I'd like both of you to stay in the medical unit for a while longer. He needs an O2 monitor, and you need observation for a concussion. This way, please."

"Today really sucks." Theo's petulant muttering sounded breathy, tinged with the essence of his earlier attitude, although his voice still shook and his hands continued to tremble. Whether from relief over the return of the grouchy Theo he had come to expect or amusement over how true the statement was, he wasn't sure, but Connor burst into laughter. Theo's scowl was just an added balm for his frayed nerves. They were all right. Everything was all right, for now, and they'd made it through the most chaotic and unexpected Inauguration Day the country had ever seen.

CHAPTER THREE

Adelaide

ADELAIDE HEAVED A POINTED sigh as she pressed her fingertips to her temples and waited not so patiently for Dr. Anand Desai, the Physician to the President, as he took her blood pressure readings for the third time. The Situation Room was in a frenzy all around her and getting more crowded by the moment as advisors continued to trickle in to handle the aftermath of the disaster they'd just escaped. Newscasters on the small monitors lining one wall were already dubbing it the Inaugural Insurrection. The headlines crawled along the bottom of the screens, each displaying shoddy cell phone footage of an event that felt surreal, even though she had just been there in person.

"Dr. Desai, with all due respect, the reading will not change anytime soon. I'm not dying. I'm stressed. If you want to be helpful to my blood pressure, go check in on my son."

"Perhaps it is time for me to go, but I will return, Madam President." Dr. Desai made a point to level his gaze with hers before he continued. "If only to bring news of your son, yes? And you will indulge me in rechecking your vitals when I do."

Adelaide responded with a vague humming noise as she reached out to take the sweatshirt someone was offering her. She needed to concentrate, but everyone wanted her to focus on them, not the situation that had them all gathering in the aptly named room. She waited for the doctor to leave, an agent shutting the door behind him as she pulled the sweatshirt over her head and took a seat at the head of the table. Emblazoned on the front of the garment was a star-shaped decal, something from one of her Secret Service agents, most likely. Worn over the evening gown, it made for quite an interesting look. She was glad there were no paparazzi there to capture the style.

"All right, someone, please tell me what we know so far." Back to business, she scanned the faces around the room and avoided the headlines on the monitors. The various stations had only just gotten the footage within the hour, and she was already tired of watching the grainy images playing in a nightmarish loop from numerous angles.

"Agents from our uniformed division were able to apprehend numerous suspects at the scene, Madam President. They're being processed as we speak. I've spoken with Director Fields from the FBI about running this as a joint investigation." Adelaide swung her gaze toward the source of the voice, coming face to face with James Locke's soft grey eyes and stern expression. She'd met with the Special Agent in Charge of the Presidential security detail numerous times, and she was glad he broke the silence first. Calm, confident authority was precisely what everyone in the room needed right now, herself included.

"Thank you, Agent Locke. Do we have any information about casualties?" Adelaide felt a tightness in her chest as she said the words. So far, all she'd heard about Theo was that he had been brought to the medical unit on the premises, and the other bits and pieces she'd heard from her agents were not at all reassuring.

"Seventeen civilians injured, four agents, two law enforcement, but we'll have a better idea in a few hours as things settle down."

Before Adelaide could open her mouth to ask another question, a loud rapping at the door stole everyone's attention, another Secret Service agent poking his head in with a short nod.

"Agents Garcia and Williams from the FBI, ma'am."

More names, more faces. Adelaide wanted to scream. Nevertheless, she nodded and sat back in her chair, covertly toeing her high heels off under the table. When she looked up again, she gave each agent a quick once-over. Agent Williams was easy to identify. He was a cousin of her long-time friend and current Chief of Staff, and the family resemblance was instantly recognizable, especially given the shared surname. Light brown hair, tall, almost unremarkable until she noticed the eyes. His were just like Elias', a blue so pale they looked almost silver, the pupils stark in contrast to such light coloring. Beside him stood a young woman that looked prepared to fight anyone who glanced at her wrong. Impeccable tailoring on her black suit highlighted her athletic curves. Her deep brown hair had been pulled up in a tight bun, the color complementing her rich bronze complexion. Adelaide found herself briefly covetous of the woman's presence. If she could look half as imperious as this woman, she'd never have to deal with another accusation of being too soft for the job.

"Madam President, we were sent by Director Fields to take statements and provide our intelligence reports for the joint investigation." Agent Garcia's voice carried just the barest hint of an accent, the melodic lilt tinging her crisp, dauntless delivery.

With another nod, Adelaide turned back to the room. "What is the next step? Was this an isolated event, or are we expecting more?"

No one answered. With another glance around the room, Adelaide found James' gaze again, arching a single brow to drive home the fact that she'd asked a question.

"Unfortunately, ma'am, we don't really know at this point. We've increased security, and law enforcement has increased its visible presence on the streets. Once we have the statements and preliminary interviews, I think we'll better understand what we're working with."

"Understandable." Adelaide sighed before standing up at the head of the table, her movement inspiring the others to do the same. "I want a call as soon as anyone learns anything, no matter how insignificant. In the meantime, if you believe everything is under control, I'd like to go see my son."

James stepped around the table as the remaining advisors and attendees started filtering out of the cramped space, moving closer to Adelaide before clearing his throat softly. "Madam President, if I may?"

"Yes, Agent Locke?"

"Your son is fine." James tapped the earpiece tucked in his left ear before smiling, a startling expression given how severe and stern he'd always been in all their prior meetings. "One of my agents is with him in the medical unit and just gave me the full report. He's sleeping soundly. Unharmed. Apparently, they want him to stay the night to watch his oxygen levels?"

"Ah, yes. I'm not surprised. He has asthma, and stress is one of the triggers. What about your agent? Is it the same agent that was... " Adelaide had a hard time finishing the question. She'd seen the looping footage on the nearby screens, the news programs obsessively replaying the image of her son being dragged through the riot by a Secret Service agent. The bodies as the reporters fell to the ground. The fire from the molotov cocktail. The projectiles as they flew through the air.

"Yes, ma'am. Agent O'Brien is still with him. He's under observation to rule out a concussion but swears he's fit as a fiddle. His words, not mine." James reached out to give her shoulder a gentle squeeze, the gesture paternal and warm, the effort soothing her rattled nerves. "He's a good kid, one of my best. Your boy's in good hands, ma'am."

Adelaide couldn't help but smile at that. James' pride over his team could be heard in every word he spoke, and she found that to be quite moving. Despite his stern nature, he cared about them like they were his children.

"Thank you, Agent Locke. And please tell the rest of your agents I said thank you?"

"Just doing our job, Madam President. With pleasure, I might add. Your Theo's fast asleep. The other kids are snug up in the residence with agents on standby. The situation is being handled. Go, get some rest. You earned it."

At that, Adelaide laughed, the sound surprising her as it spilled unbidden from her lips. "Rest? Mn. I can already see the doctor waiting to pester me again in the hall, and I'm pretty sure there is still a mountain of things to be read before we can call this day a wrap. The sentiment is appreciated, regardless. Goodnight, Agent Locke."

She didn't linger to hear his reply as she padded barefoot into the hall, the doctor and her protective agent falling into step behind her. It felt like the night was never going to end at this point. *Welcome to the White House.* She laughed at the thought under her breath. It sounded like something her Theo would say, sarcastic tone and all.

Another hour had passed before she was finally on her way back to the residential area of the White House. Doctor Desai had eventually left, satisfied her blood pressure was from stress and not an impending heart attack. He reassured her Theo was sleeping, aided by a mild sedative his doctor had suggested, and having his oxygen levels routinely monitored. She gave her official statement to the FBI agents as well as one of the Secret Service's field officers. Now, she was climbing the staircase with her arms full of folders and reports. But by the time she got halfway down the hallway, all thoughts of working through the night evaporated. The flicker flash of a television caught her attention from the nearby sitting room, the blue glow illuminating the otherwise dark room.

There, curled up together on the couch, Toby and Anna were fast asleep. Adelaide's heart sank as she realized that the television had been tuned to a news channel, the same looping images she had left behind in the Situation Room still replaying, images curated to highlight the best angles of the chaos. The children were huddled under a mountain of throw blankets and surrounded by dozens of used tissues. She tossed the folders onto a side table and hurried for the remote, quickly mashing the buttons to find anything other than the nightmare currently playing on the screen.

"Mnnf. Theo? Is that you?" Toby's voice rasped heavy with sleep and emotion, but his eyes were wide as he glanced up. Suddenly, all signs of drowsiness were gone. "Mom! Anna, wake up!"

"Huh? Wha— Mom! You're okay!" Anna tumbled from the couch, but it didn't matter. Adelaide appeared there in a millisecond, her arms gathering up the two children as they assaulted her with a barrage of words, each talking over the other as they fell into the embrace.

"Where's Theo?"

"Are you okay?"

"Is he okay?"

"When can we go home?"

"I don't wanna stay here!"

"Tell me! Where's Theo?!"

"Shh, shh, my loves. Oh, my babies. I'm okay. Theo's okay. I promise. Everything is all right. Shh, I'm here now." Adelaide managed to keep her voice level and calm, but inside, she felt anything but. Here, in the privacy of their new home, on the floor of this foreign sitting room, she felt the cracks forming in her resolve. The reality of the night she had endured seeped into those cracks, and she squeezed her two youngest children even closer. "I'm here now, my loves."

Toby was trying hard not to cry, his blue eyes shimmering with unshed tears. Anna made no such attempt at restraint, tiny sobs quaking through her body as she burrowed into Adelaide's side, her tears dampening the collar of the baggy sweatshirt.

"Mom? If Theo's okay, why's he not here?" Toby whispered, his eyes round with fear. Adelaide pressed her forehead to his as she recognized that fear for what it was. She wasn't looking at the gaze of her twelve-year-old son. She had been transported back in time to the moment when she had struggled with how to tell a six-year-old boy that his father was never coming home again. Burgeoning tears escaped, falling over his lashes, and Adelaide felt her own emotions break through as her tears fell into Anna's curly blonde hair.

"Baby, I swear, Theo is fine. He's sleeping somewhere safe and sound, and I promise, I swear to you, you'll see him first thing in the morning."

Jaw tense and eyes scrunched closed, Toby nodded, swallowing the lump in his throat as he leaned back into the embrace. Adelaide shut her eyes, too, utterly overwhelmed by the sheer magnitude of everything she was feeling. She desperately wished Theo was here with them, that she had gone to see him herself, and the knowledge that he was so close and yet so far overwhelmed her. The distance crushed her, almost too heavy to bear.

CHAPTER FOUR

Abriella

DESPITE SPLITTING UP TO get the initial statements from the Secret Service agents and available witnesses, it still took Abriella and Tristan over two hours to get through the majority. That didn't mean they had finished by any means. Abriella had left the remaining interviews for last intentionally, hoping she would be able to shake her partner beforehand.

"Williams, return to the Secret Service headquarters on-site, and I will handle the last two interviews in the medical unit. I know O'Brien, so I already have the rapport. It will not take long."

Tristan's eyebrow arched, the expression comical on his otherwise expressionless face. "Works for me, Garcia. It's just the same damn story over and over again."

He was right, too, as much as she hated to admit when Agent Tristan Williams was right. Something about the man had never sat well with her. She'd chalked it up to his striking eyes and basic features paired with his caustic personality, though she couldn't ignore the fact that he had an enviable poker face. Partnering with him had been an exercise in patience for the last six months, so she often took any opportunity to split their efforts. It was never a hard sell when she advertised it as working more efficiently.

On top of wanting to avoid extra time with Tristan, she didn't want to linger in the Secret Service on-site headquarters any longer than she needed. It smelled somehow worse than a locker room. While she was used to the stench of unwashed men and neglect of basic housekeeping from years in the Marines and

FBI, it didn't mean she had to subject her senses to it more than was absolutely necessary.

She lingered for a moment, watching Tristan pivot and stride away, pursing her lips once she no longer had to school her expression. *Adios*, she thought to herself. Better he stared unnervingly at someone else for a while. There was absolutely no way she was going to subject her best friend to this disconcerting and cold FBI agent. She turned once she lost sight of Tristan to a corner, making her way toward the medical unit. It was late enough now that the frenetic activity of the halls had disappeared, and her heels echoed with a soft sound only somewhat muffled by the carpet underfoot.

She tapped the door to the medical unit with her knuckle and slipped in without waiting for an answer, only to be met by yet another eyebrow arched at her. This one, at least, was perfectly shaped and belonged to one of the most attractive women Abriella had met in a while. She looked like a dancer, all lean frame and long limbs on display as she stood up behind the desk. Wavy hair the color of burnt umber was held in place by a claw clip that allowed loose strands to frame her face. The dainty pair of reading glasses perched on her nose complemented the clinical white coat and the stethoscope around her neck. The whole aesthetic had Abriella thinking thoughts that were not at all appropriate in a matter of seconds.

"Can I help you?"

"I'm sure you can." Abriella paused, straightening her spine and smoothing her suit jacket before pulling out her badge. "Agent Abriella Garcia, FBI. I need to speak with two witnesses. I was told I could find them both here."

"You do realize how late it is and that this is the medical ward, correct?" she responded, light brown eyes narrowing as she leveled her gaze over the rim of the glasses.

Abriella said a silent prayer to the angels above for her training because it was the only thing keeping her from making an absolute fool of herself in front of this woman. "Yes. I would not be here if it were not important to get the statements in a timely fashion. Name?"

"Lilien Ward, MD. Wait here. I will see if my patients are available to speak with you." Lily made a point to stress the word "my" as she removed her glasses, tucking them into the breast pocket of her coat before disappearing farther into the medical ward. Abriella's nerves were grateful for the reprieve. The parting view was also something she appreciated, making a mental note to go to confession as soon as she had the free time available.

It wasn't very long before the tap of Lily's heels on the floor heralded her return. She leaned through the doorway before beckoning with a curling motion of her index finger, and Abriella volleyed a slew of silent Spanish expletives at herself for where her mind went with the visual. Without a word, she followed the young woman down a narrow hall, soon finding herself in a room that appeared to be set up as some sort of passage-turned-waiting room. It was hard to miss the giant sitting on the couch, but before Abriella could greet her best friend, Lily turned abruptly, causing her to stop short. Up close, the scent of rubbing alcohol mixed with hydrangeas nearly became her undoing.

"Badge number?"

"Excuse me?"

"I want your badge number. If you disturb my patients in any way, I will contact your supervisor." Lily's clipped tone left no room for argument, and Abriella reached into her suit jacket to pull out one of her cards.

"That would be Director Luke Fields. But I won't be disturbing anyone. Just a few routine questions, ma'am."

"Agent O'Brien has agreed to speak with you. You are not to bother Mr. Moreau. He is unavailable." With that, Lily brushed past Abriella, disappearing back into the office they'd just come from. Connor started chuckling behind her, and Abriella turned, laughing as she joined him on the couch.

"Dios mio, ella es muy bonita!" Abriella whispered as she leaned in to press a kiss on Connor's cheek. "How are you, Biggs?"

"Eh, I'm fine. How're you, Smalls?" Connor stretched before slouching into the couch.

"Tired. Are you getting out of here soon?"

"Yeah, I reckon she just wants to flash her little light in my eyes and ask me the same questions a couple more times before she'll believe me when I say I'm fit as a fiddle." Despite the late hour and the obvious signs of exhaustion lining Connor's face, he still managed to smile, his country boy charm as unflappable as always.

"You are a stubborn ass. I'm glad she is giving you a hard time." Abriella bumped his brawny shoulder with her far smaller one, settling beside him to pull out her notebook and get the information she had come here to get. The same questions she'd repeated half a dozen times so far that evening were over and done with in short order, and she reluctantly slid back to her feet.

"Hey, Smalls, you doing anything tomorrow night?" Connor lifted his eyes to look up at her, the hopeful expression on his face reminiscent of a puppy and reminding Abriella why she adored this man.

"If we get the interrogations done quickly, no. I won't be chasing leads after nightfall. This case already feels like it will be a pain in my ass. Why, mi sol? You miss me already?" Abriella patted Connor's cheeks with her fingertips, matching the wattage of his brilliant grin with a smile of her own.

"Yep, you know it! Jim told me to take twenty-four once Miss Lily lets me leave. Wanna watch the game at my place?"

"Are you making something delicious?"

"Duh. Ribs. You in?"

"Ribs? Si! Of course." Abriella leaned down to press another kiss to Connor's cheek, landing it square on the bull's eye of his dimple. He chuckled, the sound a predictable reaction just like his kiss in return, pressed in with a loud smack.

"Get home safe, sugar. I'll see you tomorrow, 'round six or so."

Abriella paused in the hallway. She smoothed her suit jacket once more, puffing out her chest before stepping through the door. Lily paused her paperwork, angling her gaze over the rim of the glasses that had found their way back onto her nose.

"You left Mr. Moreau alone, correct?" she asked with a clipped tone.

"Yes, ma'am. I have a few questions for you if you have the time?" Abriella responded, stopping before the desk to look down on the young woman whose gaze was currently burning into her soul with a level of impatience Abriella found exciting and annoying in equal measure.

"I might have answers. It depends on the question." Lily slowly sat back in the desk chair, loosely crossing her arms over her chest. "But I will not share patient information."

"God, so serious." Abriella exhaled with a breath of awe.

"Of course. I take my job seriously."

"I just wanted to ask if you had any information you could share, as a medical professional, about the injuries sustained tonight."

"I've only treated Agent O'Brien and Mr. Moreau. The latter was not injured in the incident, but I will not share details about my patient's private medical information." Again, Lily made a point to emphasize the "my" in her statement, and Abriella couldn't help but marvel at this wisp of a woman's aggressive possessiveness and her overly protective nature.

"Of course, I would never pry. I'm just trying to do my job, which I also take seriously. So any information you can spare to shed some light on the whole picture would be beneficial, Miss Ward."

"I have your number if anything comes to mind. Will that be all?" Lily raised her eyebrow again as if daring Abriella to say more on the matter. If she were a more reckless person, she'd have played the back-and-forth game all night, but as it was, everything about this woman already had her feeling off-balance. Abriella needed to recalibrate and find her center before she did something stupid. Something like snatching the cell phone she spied on the corner of the desk and putting her number in it or asking the young woman when she got off and inviting her for coffee or drinks or something equally ridiculous.

With a short nod, Abriella moved away from the desk. "Thank you, Miss Ward. We'll be in touch." Walking away from Lily's critical gaze felt like tearing her hair out at the root with how the woman made her skin crawl in the worst best way. But walk away, she did.

She met up with Tristan outside the Secret Service's headquarters. He lounged against the doorframe, playing that irritating slots game he played on his phone whenever he could steal the time. The clang-clang-jingle sound of the app's atrocious sound effects grated on Abriella's nerves before she was even close enough to make eye contact.

"Williams, I hate you almost as much as I hate that app."

"Mutual on the hate front, Garcia. You finally done with your little muscle bear leather jock daddy muffin? Or whatever labels you guys toss around?" Something in Tristan's tone sent ice down Abriella's spine, and her jaw tensed.

"Excuse me, Williams?" Her response came whipcrack sharp, spat through grit teeth.

Tristan lifted his gaze from his phone with a lax expression, straightening with a languid roll of the shoulders. "Joking, Ella. Jesus, you're wound tight."

Abriella didn't trust herself not to make a scene, so she just narrowed her eyes, hoping the warning was evident enough. She would throw down if anyone ever stepped a hair out of line when it came to Connor. He got the hint and pocketed the phone before stepping into stride with her, the two of them blissfully silent as they wound through the hallways that made up the underbelly of the White House before spilling into the underground garage.

They continued their monk-like vow of silence as they slipped into the SUV, Abriella angling her torso to look out the passenger side window as the engine rumbled into life. She had been stuck with the shotgun seat since the first day they got assigned as partners, a battle she didn't bother fighting. The warzone that their contentious partnership within the FBI had become was delicately balanced. Sometimes, she had to pick her battles.

Tristan eventually broke the silence, something she ticked on the side of winning. "Pretty much twelve carbon copies of the same story and those stories don't leave us with much evidence. How are we going to run the interrogations tomorrow?"

"Director Fields texted me earlier. At least half the suspects in custody are going through withdrawals right now, so I'm not expecting we'll get much from the interviews tomorrow."

"Wait, you're telling me a bunch of junkies and tweakers started a damn insurrection on Inauguration Day, and not a single Secret Service agent was aware of the risk potential?" Tristan whistled a soft, low sound that cut surprisingly loud through the confines of the vehicle. "They're worse than I thought they were."

"Watch it, Williams!" Abriella's head snapped around so fast she almost gave herself whiplash.

Tristan briefly pressed the brakes as he glanced to the side with a scowl aimed at her glaring expression. "I don't know why you have such a hard-on for these guys, and I don't know what your problem is with me, but can you just chill?"

"Drop me on the corner. I'll walk the rest of the way." Abriella's tone sliced through the air, cold as ice.

"Look, whatever it is, I'm sorry. Okay?" Tristan clenched his jaw. She could see the ripple of the facial muscles in her periphery, but she didn't care if he was angry or not. She just wanted to get out of the car.

"Corner, Williams."

The car stopped short at the corner, the tires chirping on the asphalt.

"I'll meet you at the lock-up at eight tomorrow." Abriella didn't even wait for the response, slamming the door behind her as she started down the street. Her apartment was only two blocks away, and the cold January night air kissing her skin felt like salvation. She inhaled deep breaths, the frigid winter temperature acting as a buffer to the urban scents of exhaust and asphalt and so much humanity squished into such small square footage. Everything about Tristan's attitude grated like nails on a chalkboard, so she found herself grateful for the quiet that the late hour had brought to her familiar neighborhood. But she wasn't alone. Not yet. The SUV remained unmoving, idling near the corner behind her, and the hair on her arms stood on end. She wouldn't look back. She couldn't bring herself to give that smug man the pleasure.

CHAPTER FIVE

Theo

THE KITCHEN IN THE residential area of the White House had turned into a warm cocoon of vanilla-scented air. It wasn't as large a space as he'd expected, but that had been the case for many of the rooms Theo had explored. Still, it had more space than the kitchen he had called home in their old apartment, and he'd fallen into the serenity of baking with practiced ease. His cookies were cooling on racks as he wiped down the surfaces, the hazy film of powdery flour disappearing with every methodical swipe of the paper towel. Lost to his thoughts and the music blaring in his earbuds, Theo wasn't aware of his mother's arrival until she bumped his hip with hers.

"What the—" Theo whirled around, tearing the earbuds from his ears as he stumbled backward, stopping short as his lower back hit the edge of the refrigerator. "God, mom. Don't... don't do that."

His mother held her hands up, palms outstretched as though she were approaching a wild animal. "I'm sorry, baby. I smelled emotional support cookies baking and came to investigate."

She let her hands fall slowly, and the air between them became charged with static electricity. They had neither seen nor spoken to one another in almost two days, not since the chaos of the riot. By the time he'd returned to the residential area the following day, she had already left, likely before dawn. The kids were ecstatic when he woke them up before their alarms could, the three sharing tears, hugs, and pancakes before the Secret Service agents arrived to ferry Toby and Anna to school for the day. She worked late that night and left early again the following morning. They had become like ships passing in the night.

"Where have you been? I never see you anymore." Theo hated how his voice cracked, his hands restless as he fidgeted with the earbuds in the pockets of his hooded sweatshirt.

"I go down to the Oval Office early. I can't sleep, and there is just so much to do." She nodded toward the racks of cookies. "These smell delicious. May I?"

Theo bobbed his head, reaching for the paper towel where it lay abandoned on the counter, if only to give his hands something to do. Everything between him and his mother felt even more strained than usual, and the tension crawled higher up his spine with every stilted syllable they exchanged. So much had gone left unsaid over the years, and Theo didn't know where to start, especially not in the aftermath of the attack at the Inauguration Ball. An event that haunted his nightmares.

"I'm glad you're okay, baby. I was so worried the other night."

"Were you, though?" The words came out mumbled as Theo mindlessly wiped the counters, his hand making small circles over the same section with a repetitive motion.

"Theo… " Adelaide stepped closer, letting her forehead rest on his shoulder as she sighed. "Of course I was worried. You're my baby. I love you."

"You didn't come. You didn't call. You didn't even send a text, mom."

"Theo, you aren't being fair. Agent Locke and Dr. Desai both promised me you were fine, and you know that I had to be there to handle the situation."

"Fair? Nothing about this is fair!" Theo's hand curled into a fist around the paper towel as his temper began to flare, fueled by the awkward tension and rising anxiety. "I didn't even want to go to the stupid appearances. I begged you for weeks. But I went anyway, and it all went sideways, and you couldn't even bother to send a damn text to let me know you thought about me for even two seconds!"

"Oh, come on! You were sedated and asleep by the time I was free. Would it have even mattered? I'm here now, Theodore," she snapped, her voice rising to echo off the hard surfaces of the kitchen. Her temper often became worse than Theo's when they were at odds. Despite the distance and tension between them, Theo and his mother were far too alike in all the wrong ways.

"Did you even bother asking why I had to be sedated, mom?" he barked with a scowl, turning to face his mother head-on. He watched as a variety of emotions played over the features of her face, her fingers shaking as she tucked a strand of wavy, dark chestnut hair behind her ear. Her lips parted, but she didn't reply. "Yeah. That's what I thought."

He turned away, throwing the ruined paper towel into the trash before moving to the other side of the kitchen island. Despite how his hands trembled, he managed to package his cookies into two plastic storage containers without breaking any. He didn't bother looking back as he grabbed the containers and moved toward the door.

"Theo, wait."

"Just go back to work, mom. I'm sure your country needs you."

....

After waiting in his room until the sound of his mother's high heels disappeared through the hall and down the stairs, Theo felt calm enough to continue his mission for the day. Doubt began to gnaw at his resolve as he paused at the top of the stairs, unease returning with a vengeance. He barely resisted the urge to return to his room. Closing his eyes, he inhaled to the count of four and held it for the same count, slowly exhaling in a mirrored pattern. *This shouldn't be this hard*, he thought to himself as he opened his eyes. He needed another deep breath in and out before he managed to take the first step down the stairs. One step forward after the night of the riot had set him countless steps backward.

He didn't have to go too far to find his mission's first target. Standing on duty at the base of the stairs was Agent Connor O'Brien, caught red-handed trying to slip his cell phone back into the pocket of his suit pants. He grinned lopsidedly, only one dimple showing, the guilty expression giving Theo just enough confidence to traverse the last half of the staircase.

"Hi." Juggling two containers of cookies, Theo couldn't stuff his hands into his pockets, so he settled for scuffing the toes of his Converse.

'Y'all right, Sir?" Connor's voice sounded just as smooth and slow as Theo had remembered. This was a stupid idea, and he briefly contemplated turning right around and climbing back up the stairs.

"Yeah. You should call me Theo. Really. Please?"

"Of course, Sir." Connor's smile grew even wider in response to Theo's scowl. "Whatcha got there?"

He regretted his plan more and more with every second he failed to come up with a response that didn't sound weak and ridiculous. He made it worse by not saying anything at all, shoving one of the containers of cookies toward Connor so fast it thunked against the center of his chest.

"Shit, sorry! I didn't mean... sorry. It's for you." Theo exhaled in a rush, mentally berating himself for being such a wreck. "I should go."

"Why?" Connor wrapped his hands around the container and Theo's hand, halting his escape while simultaneously throwing his balance even more off-kilter.

"I don't know. Maybe this was a dumb idea. I just... I just wanted to say thanks."

Connor tutted, sliding the container from Theo's hand before prying it open. "You don't have anything to thank me for. And cookies are never a bad idea, so you should prolly take that back."

Theo huffed a soft breath through his nose, pursing his lips before leveling his gaze with Connor's. "Dude, you took a brick to the head for me. I think that deserves at least a thank you."

"I reckon. Did you make these?" Connor had already managed to down a whole cookie and was starting in on a second.

"Yeah. It's supposed to be like a vanilla latte in cookie form." Theo briefly marveled as Connor tucked into a third cookie. "I could send you the recipe if you have a phone or email or something?"

Connor hesitated for a split second, his whiskey-gold eyes dancing between Theo's as he leaned in a little closer. For the briefest of moments, Theo held his breath.

"Was this all a ploy to get my number, Theodore?" Connor winked, a wolfish grin plastered on his cheeks. He was so close that his breath ghosted over Theo's cheek. "If you think you can buy me with cookies, well..." Shrugging, Connor straightened again, putting some much-needed distance between himself and Theo before he popped another cookie into his mouth. Once Connor's hand was free, he held it out, fluttering his fingertips with a beckoning motion.

"You're ridiculous," Theo muttered, eyes narrowing as he fished his phone from the back pocket of his jeans. Once the face ID registered and he had a new contact card open, he dropped the phone into Connor's outstretched palm. Despite the size of his hands, Connor added his information and sent himself a text in a matter of seconds, one-handed, before returning it to Theo.

"Since you have to anyway, do you wanna come with me while I bring these to the doctor?" Theo tapped the top of the container he still held.

"Doc Lily? Of course. She's real sweet, ain't she?"

"She deserves thanks too. For putting up with my shit the other night."

Connor tutted once more, glancing sideways down at Theo's profile as they started down the hall. "None of that nonsense, Sir."

Theo didn't respond, already mentally preparing himself for the next social call as they moved through the busier sections of the White House. Ever since that night, his anxiety had skyrocketed to unbearable levels, and he was getting antsier and antsier with every person who passed them in the hall. On top of that, the bits and pieces that had filtered back into his consciousness from that evening left him not only paranoid but also embarrassed to face the doctor. After the initial shock had worn off, he had found himself in a strange room, on a strange bed, with a strange woman checking his pulse, and the panic attack that had followed was one of the worst he'd ever experienced.

By the time they reached the medical unit, he had become so nervous that he once again regretted his decision to come, inching closer to Connor as soon as he knocked on the door. A man called them in from the other side, and he took a deep breath before grasping the handle. Connor's hand slid over his lower back, the simple act giving him just enough encouragement to push the door open and step inside. There, sitting side by side behind the desk in the office of the medical ward, were Lily and Dr. Desai.

"Mr. Moreau, is everything all right?" Lily rose to her feet as she pulled the reading glasses from her nose, setting them atop the folders spread out on the surface of the desk.

"Oh, yeah. Am I interrupting? I can come back or just leave these..." Theo huffed, trying to expel the nerves.

"No interruption, none at all. Come from the door. Let us see what you have brought." Dr. Desai's voice was bright and melodic, his hands animated as he made a sweeping gesture like he had invited them into a palatial estate. He appeared to be on the higher end of middle age, his dark eyes adorned with laugh lines, though his hair remained nearly jet black, complementing his deep, rich complexion.

"He brought vanilla latte cookies. Made them himself." Connor's sultry, musical voice ran interception for Theo, something he was grateful for as he leaned forward to set the container near Lily.

"You bake?" Lily's typically crisp and clinical tone carried an air of surprise as she cocked her head at Theo.

Theo's defenses bristled. "Yeah, that's not weird. Lots of people do."

"I'm aware, Mr. Moreau. I also bake," she replied, amusement coloring her expression as she folded her arms over her chest.

"Sorry. I didn't mean to—"

"It's fine, Mr. Moreau. But I'd like to schedule follow-up appointments while I have you both here."

"What? Why?" Theo's eyes went round as he shoved his hands deep into the pockets of his hoodie. "I'm fine, really. I didn't get hurt or anything."

"That's true, but there are other things I believe we need to discuss." Lily glanced between Connor and Dr. Desai. The latter had reclined in his desk chair, steepling his fingers as he followed the conversation around the room with keen eyes.

"Things? Is something wrong? You can't just say that and not explain!" Theo's face twisted into a scowl, and he wanted to crawl out of his skin.

Dr. Desai chuckled, the sound bouncing around the small room. "Are you comfortable with Agent O'Brien hearing the purpose of the follow-up, Mr. Moreau?"

"Yeah, whatever. Just tell me. Please?"

Connor, to his credit, had assumed a blank expression as he stood at attention near Theo's side, but Theo caught the subtle, sidelong glance as he scuffed the sole of his shoe against the floor.

"I apologize, Mr. Moreau. My delivery was indelicate, and I didn't mean to cause concern. I merely wish to discuss some options for better managing your pre-existing conditions. Agent O'Brien, I'd like to see you to follow up on your head injury."

"I really wish all you people would call me Theo. Seriously." Theo grimaced internally, sounding more like an irritable teenager and not an adult. He inhaled deep before blowing the breath through pursed lips, trying in vain to take the edge off his nerves before he grew even snappier. Connor was trying hard not to smile beside him, not entirely successful in the endeavor. Dr. Desai appeared to be delighted, and even Lily's fleeting look of amusement had returned. Theo wanted the ground to open up and swallow him whole.

"How does next Tuesday sound? I can text you both with appointment times." Ever efficient, clinical Lily had returned, clearly not intending to drop the issue.

Theo had already started inching backward toward the door. "Yeah, works for me. I should— oh! The cookies! Thanks. Thank you for putting up with me the other night. That's why I came. And now I'm gonna go."

Connor had to jog to catch up with Theo in the hall. All Theo wanted was to be somewhere that people weren't.

CHAPTER SIX

Connor

The pounding of Connor's sneakers as they struck the pavement rivaled the volume of the music blasting in his earbuds, each long stride matching the heavy bass beat of the fast-tempo EDM. Despite the winter's chill in the early light of dawn, sweat poured off of him from the distance he'd already covered. Still, despite all this, he couldn't manage to clear his head.

Giving Theo his cell phone number was a huge mistake, but Connor didn't regret it. The turmoil this wreaked on him had kept him up for most of the night. As did texting with Theo. He wasn't even sure if Theo would text at all, but the buzz of his cell shortly after he had finished his dinner the night before was the beginning of what would surely be the end. He had to be breaking all sorts of rules, but at this point, he wasn't too eager to look into the protocols to confirm his suspicions.

For all Theo's grouchiness and short answers in person, their conversation last night had been a complete one-eighty flip. Sure, it had started out awkward and unsure, but they had soon settled into a back-and-forth volley of texts that went on for hours, sharing likes and dislikes and favorites and jokes. Connor assumed Theo's wary attitude in person had something to do with the anxiety of talking face to face. But behind the safety of the screen, Theo had a wicked sense of humor, all sharp wit, and banter. And he was smart, regaling him with little flashes of knowledge across a broad range of topics that left Connor feeling in over his head at times. He had been smitten before, but by the time his eyelids had started to droop, well past when he would typically go to sleep, he had realized he was diving headfirst into full-on infatuation.

When his alarm had gone off this morning, it became the warning bell of all his poor decisions regarding Theo. Connor had never had an issue keeping himself professional, whether in the Marines or when working the Secret Service investigations on the field. Now, less than a couple of months into the protective detail assignment, he was turning into a fool over a pair of hazel eyes that he could never look into and call his own. Not if he still wanted to have a job after he slid down this slippery slope.

By the time he'd finished his circuit of the neighborhood, Connor had come to a stop at the entrance of his building, winded, exhausted, and covered in sweat. Bent at the waist, hands braced on his knees, he panted to catch his breath, each exhalation huffing out as a cloud of visible steam in the cold winter air. His phone buzzed where he had it clipped into the band around his bicep, and he willed himself not to check it. Apparently, the iron will and determined grit he'd relied on to get him through everything he'd seen over his numerous years in the service meant nothing when it came to resisting the temptation of an attractive man with a sharp-as-tacks attitude. There on the screen was a picture of a box of cereal spilled over the kitchen floor.

Theo: Ugh, there is not enough coffee in the world today.

Despite admonishing himself over opening the text, Connor was grinning and typing a reply as he climbed the stairs to his third-floor apartment.

Connor: Uh oh. What'd you do that for?

Theo: Me?! Blame Anna. You'd think seven years old was old enough to handle cereal for breakfast but NOOOO apparently I was wrong.

Connor: Make her clean it.

Theo: Ha, you're funny.

Connor: Sarcastic, much?

Theo: You like it ;)

Connor: :P Maybe a little, I reckon.

His phone clattered against the countertop as he pushed it away. Twenty-seven years old, and he had turned into a bumbling teenager with a high school crush, flirting through text messages. He pushed the power button on the coffee maker and escaped to the bathroom so he could get ready for the day, putting distance between himself and his phone before he could send any more ridiculous text messages. He needed to get this runaway train back on track before it turned into a wreck his career might not survive. His only hope at this point was a cold shower.

Sufficiently dressed and still shivering from the icy water he'd stood under while reminding himself of his responsibilities, Connor returned to the kitchen and poured himself a giant mug of black coffee. His cell phone taunted him from the opposite edge of the counter, but he was stronger than that. Better than that. Worthy of trust and confidence. The Secret Service motto. He could do this. He knew he could. He only lasted five minutes.

Theo: Work today?

Connor: Duh. I'm on the school rotation with Mitchell.

Theo: God save you. It's art day for Anna and I didn't wash Toby's gym bag. RIP your fancy car.

Connor: lol not my car. I'll bring Febreeze.

It was too easy to keep texting back and forth, but the time on his watch put a stop to it. He had to leave now if he wanted to make it to the White House during the early morning rush hour in time to meet up with Agent Mitchell and escort the kids to school. He poured himself a travel mug of coffee after he flicked the power button off, grabbed his suit jacket, and locked the apartment behind him before descending the stairs two at a time. Once he hit the seat of his SUV, he couldn't get the phone out of his pocket. It was a small blessing since he had no restraint anymore.

Agent Thomas Mitchell pulled into the parking garage under the White House right behind Connor. They walked into the headquarters together, sharing friendly jabs and making promises to visit the shooting range together the next time they both had a day shift off at the same time. Even if he was still wet behind the ears, Mitchell was a good agent. He was shorter than Connor, lean muscled compared to Connor's build. Where Connor had spent his youth on the football field, Mitchell had wiled away his teenage years cycling. The Marines had taken Connor's bulk and honed it into something suitable for military service, but Mitchell had gone straight from school into law enforcement before making the jump to the Secret Service.

Nevertheless, they were an even match on the firing range and had a running competition over who could punch out the center of the bull's eye most accurately every time they met up to practice their firearms training. Connor had a soft spot for Mitchell. After one too many beers watching a football game at Mitchell's rundown townhouse, they'd formed a bond while complaining about growing up with absentee fathers and struggling single mothers. The guy needed a mentor and, similar to how James had stepped up for him, he tried to be there for Mitchell.

"School rotation is my least favorite. I hate these days." Mitchell's accent was straight from New York City, the words tumbling over themselves in a hurry, as if the bustle of the Big Apple had somehow engrained itself into his DNA and came out through his mouth.

"I reckon it's not my favorite, but I don't hate it. The kids are pretty funny." Connor was mindful to temper his southern drawl when he was with the guys. Too many taunts about being a slow hick had followed him from the service into the agency. A little temperance went a long way, even if his speech pattern would never match Mitchell's rapid-fire talk.

"Yeah, no. I don't do kids. No thanks. I'm here for the hours and the experience." Mitchell flashed a crooked smile, his blue-grey eyes crinkling at the corners. "Give me door duty any day."

"You're in the wrong industry then, Mitch. Maybe the mall is hiring?" Connor nudged his partner's shoulder with his own as he flashed a grin, the two donning earpieces and radios, checking their tactical belts, and gathering the rest of their equipment before heading toward the residential area of the White House. With any luck, the kids would be ready in time. They would be in the thick of the morning rush hour on the way to the private school the Montgomery children attended. While they waited at the bottom of the stairs, Connor snuck a peek at his cell. Another new text alert. He unlocked the screen to read the message, Mitchell conveniently sneaking one last glance at his phone at the same time.

Theo: Good luck. Anna's in rare form today.

Connor held his phone close against his thigh, firing back a message typed with just his thumb to avoid getting caught texting on the job.

Connor: The chaos doesn't stop at cereal? Lord help us all.

Theo: It was nice knowing you, wish we had more time. Rest in peace. With the cereal. Demon spawn incoming.

Connor: It's okay to move on. What we had was special, but I just want you to be happy.

Theo: You're ridiculous.

....

The school day passed without incident, allowing Connor plenty of time to sit with his thoughts. His stubbornness finally worked in his favor, and he resisted the urge to check his phone for the entire time, but once they got back to the White House and he was standing on duty near the residence, he chanced a peek. He tried to ignore his disappointment when there were no new text alerts, even though he knew that was for the best and had promised himself he wouldn't initiate any more flirtatious exchanges. Still, he had to admit it stung a little.

His thoughts continued to wander as he waited for the end of his shift, idle plans for what he'd make for dinner, what book he'd read tonight, and contemplations of what he would do on his next day off. Shopping lists, to-do lists, and bucket list fantasies filled the mindless minutes that crawled by as the afternoon wound into the evening. He was torn from his musings when screams became audible from the residence, the shrill cries echoing down the stairs and setting Connor's protective urges into overdrive.

"No, stop! Get off! Let me go!"

Despite the distance, he instantly recognized it as Theo's voice and acted on pure instinct, flying up the stairs two at a time, his hand reaching to the gun holstered at his hip. He flew down the hall toward the direction the screams had come.

"Get away from me! Don't you dare!" Theo's shout was clearer now, coming from the nearest sitting room. Connor sprinted faster, unfastening the clasp of his holster as he neared the doorway. He was about to pull it out when Theo himself came barreling through the door, crashing face-first into Connor's chest with a loud grunt.

Connor instinctively wrapped his arms around Theo's frame, stumbling as the force pushed him backward three steps. Behind him, Anna and Toby stopped dead in their tracks, eyes wide with a mixture of surprise and terror. Still surrounded in Connor's arms, Theo was breathless and likewise stunned, cheeks flush and eyes sparkling as he stared slack-jawed up at Connor's face.

"Is everything all right here?" Connor was utterly confused, unable to figure out what he had interrupted. "It sounded like trouble."

"Oh, God. I'm so sorry! I didn't realize you could hear! Shit, I'm sorry!" Theo's already flushed cheeks turned nearly magenta as he blushed, and the children behind him were still frozen in shock.

"Everything is all right, though? You sounded like something serious was going on."

"Yeah, yup, totally fine. Nothing to see here."

Connor searched Theo's face, the few inches difference between their heights bringing their faces entirely too close as time seemed to slow and stretch. Theo's arms had settled around Connor's waist during their collision. It was a frustratingly perfect fit, and Connor froze like a deer in the headlights of an oncoming semi-truck. The solid warmth of Theo in his arms, breaths that smelled like coffee and vanilla dusting over his lips, the intoxicating scent of aftershave and laundry detergent, and so much Theo crashing into him at full speed. He was dumbstruck until Anna's voice cut through the moment.

"Oh my God, Toby, look..." Her whisper slowly increased in volume until it was a shrill little squeal. "It's just like in my movies, oh my God! Kiss!"

Theo and Connor's heads snapped up as they turned toward Anna, speaking the word "what" simultaneously. He didn't want to let go, he wanted to sink into the moment and let time run away from them both, but a seven-year-old girl who loved romance films ruined the mood. She really was in rare form today. Despite how much he wanted to cling tighter, Connor let go. He would always have to let go. He knew that. But letting go of Theo stung much more than he realized it would. The ghost of Theo's arms around his waist stayed with him, and Theo made it even worse when he glanced sideways at Connor, chewing his lower lip.

"No, you're supposed to be kissing! Like in the movies!" Anna scowled and stamped her foot as her arms crossed over her chest.

"God, Anna, please," Theo muttered, the blush on his cheeks growing incrementally darker as he tousled the messy curls on his head and tried to avoid Connor's eyes.

"Ain't you a bit young for kissing movies, Miss Montgomery?" Connor cleared his throat and tried to straighten his suit jacket and tie, his hands itching to do something.

"Pssh, whatever. You're both doing it wrong. Toby, hold him down so I can tickle him again!"

"Think we could make him scream louder?" Toby sounded dangerously serious as he started to inch forward.

"Don't you dare!" Theo leapt like a cat, scurrying to slide behind Connor's frame where he stood. "He probably has a gun or a taser or something! Stay back!"

"He does have a gun! He showed me when I asked. But he won't shoot us. Right, Mr. Connor?" Anna batted her lashes with a grin that would rival the wattage of a football stadium light. Connor could do nothing but burst into laughter that bordered on crazed.

"No, no, I won't, miss. But let's leave Theo alone now, yeah? Or I might have to report you to the boss."

"And if you surrender, I'll let you watch that new movie on my Netflix. Popcorn for promises?" Theo was hovering so close against Connor's back as he bartered with the children that his breath brushed over the whorls of Connor's ear. It sent a shiver through his body from top to toe.

"Sounds like a good deal. I reckon I'll leave you all to it." Connor couldn't escape fast enough. It wasn't a casual departure as he clattered down the stairs, but it didn't matter how quickly he fled. Connor was definitely entirely captivated by Theodore Moreau, and there was no escaping that now.

CHAPTER SEVEN

Lily

"JASPER, PLEASE. I JUST fed you. You're going to make me late again. Shoo." Lily scrambled around her apartment, frantically grabbing her things as she did a swing dance around the long-haired calico that continued to wind around her stockinged feet. She was halfway out the door with her high heels in hand when she remembered she had forgotten the container of cookies on the counter. Reentering the apartment resulted in a desperate meowing as Jasper pounced. Lily bit back a curse as his claws nicked her ankles and nearly tripped her.

"Sometimes, I wish Desiree hadn't left you behind. You should be torturing her instead of me." Scooping up the container, she hopped over the cat just as he pounced again, fleeing toward the door like a gazelle running from a lion across the African plains. "I love you, babykins! I'll see you tonight!"

She slammed the door before the demon of a cat could escape and make her even later than she already was. Fumbling with her keys, shoes, bag, and a container of cookies, she jogged down the stairs before struggling to put the shoes on. A faint dusting of snow had fallen overnight, and her day had been miserable the last time she had run to her car without them on after a snowfall. With an exasperated huff, she tossed the remaining things in the passenger seat and started the car, nosing the front fender into the stop-and-go of the lunchtime traffic. With any luck, she'd only be a few minutes late. Dr. Desai never said anything, but she hated it nevertheless.

At the White House, she pulled into her parking place behind the Old Executive Office Building and tried to make more sense of the belongings she had tossed in the front seat. Her white coat, stethoscope, and identification badge had become tangled when she'd shoved them in the bag the night before. Making another useless pledge to get her life in order, she abandoned the task of untangling the items in favor of getting into the office relatively close to her scheduled shift. No one paid her any attention as she navigated the busy halls of the OEOB and continued onward toward the White House and through the even busier halls within.

Taking a deep breath to recenter herself, she nudged the door to the medical ward open with her hip and slipped inside, nodding to Dr. Desai at the desk with a faint smile. "Good afternoon, Doctor. How're you today?"

"Miss Lily, my dear girl. I am delightful. You look radiant. So vibrant today! How are you?" Dr. Desai's smile was a bright flash of brilliant white, his jovial tone causing Lily to smile wider in response. Dr. Desai was the only reason she had applied for this position in the White House. Once she had learned he was leaving the clinic to take on the role of Physician to the President, she knew she'd do anything to follow behind. Her mentor for almost a decade was the silver lining of most of her days. And the only person her introverted self could tentatively call a friend.

"I'm very well. Did you need anything before I head back to pull charts?"

"Oh no, my darling girl. Just knowing you are here is all I need today. I will send your patient back when he comes."

Lily squeezed the doctor's shoulder as she passed, continuing deeper into the medical unit housed in the heart of the White House's twisting hallways. She'd been here for about three weeks, so the floorplan that had once confused her finally made sense, and the space felt more and more like theirs as they settled into the new routine. Nerves over her first official patient at the White House caused her to fuss needlessly over trivial details. It was one thing to handle walk-ins and the minor bumps and bruises that wandered in throughout the day, and Dr. Desai typically dealt with the more senior ranking officials and cabinet members. Lily was claiming the First Son as her own.

Something about his wary, nervous energy reminded her so much of herself that she felt compelled to take him on as a patient. Dr. Desai had agreed heartily, and they'd spent several days going over his records and medical charts, discussing options and potential treatment plans for the conditions they found in them. When she had explained what had happened on the night of the insurrection, he was even more adamant about creating a plan that could help comprehensively. Of all the doctors Lily had worked under over the years, in her mind, Dr. Desai was the most passionate about treating the whole patient and not just the condition. It was a trait she admired in him and another reason she'd uprooted herself from the clinic where they had worked together and came with him to serve the new administration within the White House. Hopefully, her newest patient would understand.

She didn't have long to fuss, though, as she heard Dr. Desai's melodic voice coming down the hall. She had all her charts and laptop set up in her most comfortable room. She took a brief second to smooth her white coat into place, thankful for the wrinkle-resistant fabric. She really needed to apply the same attention to detail to her own life and not just the lives of her patients.

"And here we are, Mr. Moreau! Miss Ward awaits you. Please make yourself comfortable."

Theo edged through the door, his shoulders hunched and his hands shoved into the pockets of his zippered hoodie. Lips pursed and eyes evasive, Lily could instantly tell he wanted to be anywhere but here. Thankfully, she'd assumed that would be the case, so she'd converted the room into something closer to a sitting room, trying to erase as much of the clinical nature as possible. The exam table was pushed against the wall, and two small chairs occupied the center, with an end table between them. She'd poached it from an office elsewhere in the White House with the help of one of the ushers who had come in to get a sprained wrist looked at. The effect was almost homey, charming in a mismatched way. Her container of cookies sat on the end table alongside two paper cups of hot tea.

"I'm glad to see you made it, Theo. Do you want the door closed or open?"

Blinking in confusion, Theo took in the surroundings before snapping his eyes back toward her. "Finally, someone got the memo."

"Excuse me?"

"You called me Theo. No one ever listens when I ask them to call me Theo."

Lily couldn't help but giggle at the comment. She thought she was pushing too many boundaries to bridge the gap between herself and her surly patient. At least she had found one way to put him at ease.

"Please come sit with me. I wasn't sure if you drank coffee or tea, so I went with tea."

"Am I dying or something? Cut the crap and give it to me straight because all of this—" Theo gestured to the furniture arrangement before pushing his hair back from his eyes, "—is making me really nervous."

"You're not dying, Theo. I wanted to talk and get to know you as a patient. I thought making the setting a little more casual would make it easier. For both of us." Lily crossed her arms over her chest, defenses rising.

"Oh. I guess... I'm sorry, I'm not used to this. Any of this." He moved away from the door, leaving it open to the hallway outside, before sliding into the farthest chair, both hands firmly planted back in the pockets of the sweatshirt. Doctors and medical professionals learned to read body language almost before they learned to read vitals, and Theo's screamed, "Everyone leave me alone!"

"My grandmother taught me never to return a container empty, so I made cappuccino cookies. Your latte ones were delicious. Thank you again."

There it was, a flicker of a smile and a brief moment of eye contact. It felt like the professional win of the decade as she eased herself into the chair and pulled her bag closer.

"Maybe we could swap the recipes? I'm always looking for new ones, and the ones off the internet are usually so bad." Theo finally pulled his hands from his pockets to reach for the container of cookies, settling it in his lap to pry the lid open. He held the container out toward her as he continued, "And I don't really know anyone else who likes baking."

"Me neither. My grandmother taught me. Did you pick up the hobby from someone, too?"

"There was a program at the YMCA when I was kid, real young. All the other programs were loud and crazy crowded, but there was this little old lady who would teach baking. I loved it."

"I'd like to talk about that while we sit, if that's all right with you, Theo? How long has the anxiety been an issue?"

Sitting up a little straighter, she watched as Theo took a deep breath, releasing it slowly. He glanced at her again, the wariness returning to his features with a scowl. He nodded, nibbling the cookie he held in his hand like a mouse, brushing crumbs from his sweatshirt every third bite.

"I'm sure you're aware that all your medical records have been forwarded to us here, so we can continue any treatments you were undergoing without interruption. But I'd like to hear your version, the personal version."

"I guess for a while. I'm not sure. It just became a thing over time?" He shifted in his seat, his body angling ever so slightly away from her as he crossed one leg over the other at the knee. "I mean, it's manageable. It's whatever. I'm fine."

"If I may, Theo, I might suggest that you think it's fine, but maybe it could be a little better. Would you agree?"

"I tried the therapy thing, and it worked for a while, but things got too busy, so that doesn't work now. And I don't want to go back on those pills mom had me on. That definitely didn't work. Really, it's fine. I can handle it."

"We don't have to discuss medication until you're comfortable with the idea. However, there are many different options, including a number of newer ones. What you were on in high school isn't the only thing available on the market. What about a support system? Would you say you have supportive friends or family who are understanding and can help?"

Theo didn't answer. So Lily didn't push. She'd been in his seat before, the roles reversed. Patience was vital when dealing with patients, especially ones as closed off as Theo currently was. She settled back in her chair, selecting another cookie from the container and gathering her tea in her free hand. The silence in the room was nearly deafening. Eventually, he cracked under the pressure.

"I'm not some science project, okay? I'm not some pathetic wimp who can't handle his shit and needs a savior to come to the rescue. I've been handling it, all of it, for a long time. Got it?"

"What do you mean by handling all of it, Theo?" She'd learned the leading with questions from her work as a therapist, so the query came out before she even had a chance to realize what she was doing.

"The kids, school, work, all this political campaign stuff, the stress. All of it. I'm not gonna crack or whatever, okay? Is that what this is? Did mom pull strings and get you to drag me in here?"

"No, Theo. I asked you to come in today because I asked Dr. Desai if I could take on your care. If I can be honest with you, I've never even met your mother, not personally, and we both agreed that, as an adult and an individual, it would be best if you had someone other than your mother's physician to work with."

Lily leaned forward, leveling her gaze with Theo's when he glanced to follow the movement. "And for the record, I think you're the farthest thing from pathetic or wimpy. I understand how strong you need to be to handle anxiety daily because I've been in your shoes before. I can't fathom how hard that must be with all the other responsibilities you also carry. So yes, I want to help, but I'm not here as a knight in shining armor or looking for a science project. I'm here because I'm a doctor and want to help my patient. Is that so wrong?"

Theo went slack-jawed, his eyes wide as he shifted in his seat before heaving a sigh and ducking his head. A soft mumble that sounded like an apology came from his lips as he pressed his palms to his face, rubbing vigorously before dropping his hands back into his lap.

"I do that a lot. Get snappy with people. I don't mean to, but sometimes, it's just..."

"Too much?" Lily volunteered the words quietly.

"Yeah. Everything gets so intense, and I snap. I feel bad as soon as it happens, which makes it worse. I guess that part I'm not handling well."

"Would you be willing to do this regularly? You and me, just sitting to talk about things like this? I think one thing you might lack, please correct me if I'm wrong, is an understanding support system, and we can work together to find better coping mechanisms. If that doesn't work, we can explore other options."

"So what, like, pretend therapy and cookies?" Theo's voice carried a tinge of doubt as he pulled at the cuff of his sweatshirt.

"Real therapy, and yes, cookies. I'm personally invested in having a baking friend." Lily hid her smile behind her tea, taking a long sip as Theo processed the offer.

"Yeah, okay. Deal. Weird, but okay." Lily couldn't stop her giggle in response. It was an odd arrangement, but she had assumed working in the White House would be peculiar. She hadn't imagined it would involve swapping recipes with the First Son of the United States. By the time they finished the remainder of the appointment, exchanging phone numbers between checking vitals and refilling prescriptions for his asthma medications, he seemed just a bit more relaxed. He even made a promise of mocha chip cookies as he scheduled another appointment for the same time the following week. Lily was high on her professional win for the remainder of the day.

CHAPTER EIGHT

Elias

"DAD, DO YOU TINK Uncle Teo will let me put extra cheese on my pizza tonight?" Parker's voice was barely a whisper, so quiet Elias almost missed it over the sound of their feet as the Secret Service agent led them through the halls of the White House.

"I think Uncle Theo will let you put whatever you'd like on your pizza, Park. He's cool like that." Elias gave Parker's hand a gentle squeeze as they climbed the stairs leading up to the First Family's residential quarters. Hopefully, the agent wouldn't linger too close. Parker's shyness had returned in full force when faced with the stranger, and Elias wanted him to have a good time with his friend. It'd been months since they'd been able to have one of their pizza party nights, and Parker had been talking about it for weeks.

"Hello, hello?" Elias called down the hall once they reached the top of the stairs, not sure where to go once they'd reached the top and getting no direction or indication from the stone-silent agent who lingered at their side like they were suspected shoplifters casing a department store. He could hear pop music blasting, but he had no idea where it was coming from.

"Parker, my man! You made it!" Theo jogged into the hall, his black sweatshirt and skinny jeans covered in streaks of flour, the neon green socks on his feet a gaudy contrast to his typical uniform of all-black everything. "Elias, dude. I'm so happy to see you guys. Anna has not stopped talking about tonight."

"Parker's been the same. You'd think they didn't see each other every day at school." Elias leaned in, sharing a cheek kiss with Theo. It was good to see him again, and he was confident the feeling was mutual with the smile that spread over

Theo's face. Theo's smile had always been rare and fleeting in the six years that Elias had known him. He stood back as Theo crouched down, bringing himself eye-level with Parker, whose shell had vanished as he danced back and forth on the balls of his feet.

"Let me guess, extra cheese tonight?" Theo winked as Parker nodded so hard Elias worried his glasses might fall off. "Anna's through that hall, the door on the right. Can you follow the sound of the music, or do you want me to sho—"

And with that, Parker was gone. Theo and Elias both laughed, shaking their heads. Theo reached out to take the jackets Elias was holding, turning to the agent who still lingered nearby.

"You don't have to stay, Agent ... um, was it Mitchell? Sorry, you all kind of look the same." Theo couldn't help but flush as he scuffed the toe of his sock against the carpeting.

"Yes, Sir, Agent Thomas Mitchell. I'll be on standby just outside the residence to escort the Williams' out when your visit is over." Mitchell's voice was rapid-fire fast, his movements equally hurried as he nodded and strode on long legs toward the stairwell they'd just ascended.

"How strange is it? With the agents and the security and everything?" Elias kicked his shoes off and hoisted his backpack higher on his shoulder before following Theo into the kitchen. It was warm and smelled of yeast, little bowls covered in towels sitting on the counter near the oven. On the island at the center of the kitchen, two empty wine glasses and a wine key stood sentinel, their pizza night tradition waiting for them to begin.

"It's all a damn nightmare, Eli. I knew it would be bad, but not like this. How're you settling in with the Chief of Staff thing?" Theo hopped onto the island, his neon socks dangling as he grabbed the wine key and reached out toward Elias. The bottle of red he'd smuggled into the White House in his backpack popped with a soft sound, the familiar glug glug of the liquid filling the glasses reminding him of so many other pizza party nights he and Theo had shared. Theirs was an unlikely friendship, born of Elias' lengthy friendship with the newly-minted President of the United States, but he wouldn't change a thing about it.

"I think I'm mostly starting to get a handle on it. My assistant has already saved my ass a few times, but we're hanging in there. How about you? How's the internship working out with all of this?" Elias met Theo's glass halfway with a tiny clink of glass meeting glass as they settled into their familiar pattern in the unfamiliar locale, Theo sitting on the counter and Elias leaning nearby.

"Yeah. It's not. I had to give up the internship." The flicker of disappointment on Theo's face weighed heavy on Elias' heart. He'd worried this would happen.

"What happened? You were so excited about that."

"Well, between the kids, the security stuff, the Secret Service. It just isn't the right time, I guess." Theo heaved a sigh as he took a sip of his wine, licking the liquid from his lips before he continued. "Mom won't let me refuse the Secret Service detail because I'm with the kids all the time, and the tech company was sketched out by the background checks and the stipulations for the software on my computers, so they pulled the plug on it."

"Damn, man. I'm sorry. You're still working, at least?"

"I have a few clients of my own, but it's all boring stuff. Website updates, sysadmin stuff. Little things I can do even if my computer is practically a brick at this point with all the security protections. It's whatever. I can figure it out in a couple of years." Theo shrugged as if he hadn't just admitted he lost the internship opportunity he'd cried with joy over when he told Elias about it eight months ago.

"Theo, I'm sorry. Really. I know how important that was to you."

"It's whatever, Eli. I'm fine, really. Should we call the troops? I'll grab the toppings and start rolling." Theo hopped off the counter, already moving toward the refrigerator. Diversionary tactics were his forte, something Elias had learned over the years. Once he got too close to a sore spot, Theo shifted the conversation. They'd been dancing around this minefield together since Theo was fifteen, so Elias knew to let it go.

"Want me to holler while you get everything sorted?"

"Sounds good, but yell extra loud for Toby. He had his headphones on last I checked."

Laughing, Elias set down his wine glass and returned to the hallway, retracing his steps until he could follow the sounds of the peppy pop music. Inside the room that was the source of the music, he found Anna and Parker tangled together in the center of a massive pile of throw pillows, chatting away at a mile a minute as they painted one another's toenails.

"Well, well, well. What do we have here? A spa day, and I wasn't invited?"

"I can do yours at home, Dad. Anna says I can have the blue one if you tink it is okay for me to have it. Uncle Teo gets dem on Amazon." Parker's silvery-blue eyes were wide with excitement behind the round rims of his glasses. Elias' heart melted at the sight of them.

"I think that sounds like a great plan. We can shop for some to bring next time we come for pizza night, too. Wrap it up in five, though. It's time to make the pizzas."

Elias left as the cheers erupted behind him, catching a glimpse of Toby in the room across the hall from Anna's. He sat slumped in a bean bag chair with a gaming console in his hands, chunky teal headphones pushing his short blonde curls into a tousled halo over his head. Elias knocked on the door jam before calling out to him, the gaming console sliding from Toby's hands as he jumped in surprise.

"Hey, bud. Theo's rolling out the pizza dough, so get in the kitchen in less than five unless you want Parker to steal all the cheese again."

"Let me finish this level, Uncle Eli. Don't let Spiderman steal all my cheese. I'll be right there." Toby had Theo's smile. A bright, albeit scarce thing. Elias didn't realize how much he'd missed them all until they were together again, something he was pondering as he returned to help in the kitchen. He stopped at the door, not meaning to snoop but startled to spy Theo taking a selfie with his wine glass and the discs of dough arranged behind him on the island. His smile was radiant, cheeks growing pink as he ducked his head and put down the glass to type something out on the screen. Elias was afraid to move lest he disturb the moment, watching for a few seconds as Theo stared at his screen before typing again, the smile growing wider as his thumbs flew over the keyboard. Elias noted that the screen was turned face-down on the counter when he put the phone down.

"So..." Elias slipped into the kitchen and tried to play it casual as he gathered his wine glass in his hand. "What's his name?"

Theo jumped, shoving his hands into the pockets of his sweatshirt, leaving behind more smudges of white flour as he did so. "Shit, dude. Don't do that."

"I asked you a question, Theodore." Elias couldn't hold back his grin as he watched Theo's cheeks turn from pink to red.

"I don't know what you're talking about, Eli."

"Bullshit. I know that look. So what's his name?"

"It's nothing. I mean, it's stupid. It's just a thing. It's not serious." The phone buzzed on the counter, and Theo's eyes snapped toward it instantly.

"Yeah, looks pretty not serious to me. Stop lying to me, Theo, or I'll tell Anna, and we know she's ruthless."

"Okay, shots fired. That's just rude, Elias."

"Three, two, on—"

"It's not going to go anywhere because it can't. You can't tell anyone, all right? I don't wanna get him in trouble with his job." Theo grabbed his wine glass, spinning it between his index finger and thumb as he glanced up at Elias through his eyelashes, worry etched on his expression.

"I'm not going to tell anyone, man. Explain what's going on, and maybe we can figure it out?" Elias kept his voice low, the babbling voices of the excited children coming down the hall.

"Okay, yeah. Once we get these in the oven. But hush for now."

At that point, all hell broke loose in the kitchen. It was a modestly sized space, but it suddenly felt overcrowded as the five of them pushed in around the island, the two youngest chattering nonstop as sauce, shredded cheese, and various toppings exploded over the discs of dough and every inch of the counter in between. Elias, used to the calm quiet of an only child with a penchant for shyness, was overwhelmed by the lack of volume modulation. Theo, on the other hand, seemed to take it all in stride as he cajoled Anna with praise over her smiley face pepperoni pizza, averted disaster by materializing more cheese as if by some sleight of hand magic, and reminded Toby he hadn't brought his homework agenda to get checked. Amid all that, he still managed to make a pizza for himself and Elias, catching a bowl of sauce just seconds before Parker's elbow knocked it to the floor.

Just as swiftly as the chaos had erupted, it was gone. Theo hollered at the kids to be back in fifteen if they wanted to eat, sliding the pizzas into the oven and reaching for the paper towels to start the clean-up process. Elias jumped forward, swatting Theo's hands out of the way.

"I can handle the cleaning. You did the hard part. Why haven't you considered becoming a teacher anyway? You're like the kid whisperer."

Theo made an incredulous sound as he ignored Elias and helped with the cleanup, but not before snapping a quick picture of the aftermath of pizza making. He almost got away with it, slipping the phone into his back pocket when he caught Elias smirking at him.

"Spill the tea, Theo. Who's got you grinning like a schoolgirl with a crush?"

"You're too old to be talking about spilling the tea, Eli. Sorry to break it to you."

"Hi, sorry, did you say something? I couldn't hear you over all that bullshit."

Theo laughed at that, a breathy sort of giggle that devolved into a soft chuckle. "Okay, fine. Jesus. His name's Connor. He's one of the Secret Service agents. The one who was with me on inauguration night. We're just texting, mostly. It's not going to go anywhere serious."

"Why not?"

"Duh, because he's an agent, and I'm the protectee, and that's like, against the rules or something."

"You know that sounds ridiculous, right?" Elias stopped wiping down the counters to take a sip of wine, setting it out of the way before continuing. "I'm not saying you guys should go hit the nightclubs or move in together, but I don't want to see you sacrifice something that could be good over some technicality."

"It's super unprofessional, and he could get in trouble. I'm not worth all that. Trust me."

"Theodore Moreau, what in the fresh hell did you just say?"

Theo blinked once, his expression going lax as his mouth fell open.

"Yeah. Bold of you to assume I'd let that one slide." Elias huffed as he tore the paper towel out of Theo's hand and tossed it in the trash alongside his own.

"Again, as I said, you don't have to shack up or tear up the gayborhood, but don't you dare push this away before you even give it half a chance. If he's texting, roll with it. He's a big boy. Let him worry about the technicalities and just enjoy it."

"Shit, dude. That was a little savage. I approve." Theo's voice was awed, a smile flickering over his lips as he chewed his lower lip. "You think I should 'roll with it' then?"

"Stop your worrying. I think you think too much." Elias refilled their glasses and held his up with a grin. "You're young. So act young for once."

The heart-to-heart abruptly ended as the timer went off, and the stampede of hungry kids descended on the kitchen. The subtle smile that played over Theo's face exponentially improved Elias' mood as they all gathered around the island, the familiar voices of their motley crew filling the space with a warmth that rivaled that of the oven.

CHAPTER NINE

Theo

THEO SAT UP STRAIGHTER in his bed, his spine cracking in three different places as he groaned with relief. He'd been glued to his laptop for hours, making edits to the user interface on a website until the alarm on his phone finally gave him a reason to put the work aside for the day. The kids would be crashing up the stairs to the private residence any minute now. He still couldn't bring himself to call the place home, but their routines were still very much the same as they had always been. First came the chaos, then the snacks, finally homework, and then dinner. The White House staff kept insisting that he could order the food made in the kitchens elsewhere on the property, but he wasn't eager to let go of even more control over his life. His whole reason for being here in the first place was to maintain normalcy for the kids. He wasn't about to lose what little normal they still had left.

As if on cue, the clatter of shoes raced down the hallway toward his room, Anna giggling as Toby shouted something behind her. Theo had barely enough time to move his laptop from the mattress to the nightstand before Anna's tiny form jettisoned through the air to land with an oomph on the comforter.

"Theo, Theo! I got a special sticker for my art today! Mrs. Addison said it was 'remarkable.' Do you wanna see?"

"Of course, bug. I knew you'd do awesome. Hey Tob! How was practice?" Theo shimmied to the edge of the mattress, another crunch coming from his lower spine as he stood up.

"I made the line-up to start the game tomorrow. Do you think you guys will be able to come and watch?" Toby hovered near the door, scuffing the toe of his sneaker against the carpeting. "It's a home game, but I understand if it's too complicated."

"Pssh, dude. We're going to make it work. Anna even got pompoms." Theo smiled to himself when Toby's face lit up. He was at that awkward age between adolescence and teen, still such a kid even when he tried to be grown-up and serious.

"Yeah! I got pompoms, and Theo said we could do face paints and nail polish to be like the cheerleaders. You're gonna be so embarrassed. It's awesome." Anna looked smug as she pulled out her art portfolio from her backpack, simultaneously dumping what looked like fifty papers all over Theo's bed. Chaos incarnate goes by the name Annalise Montogomery.

"Come on, Tob. Let's see Anna's remarkable art." Toby dumped his gym bag on the floor outside Theo's room before coming closer—something Theo silently counted as a huge blessing. Febreeze was a godsend when dealing with Toby's gym bag.

Anna made a spectacle of opening her portfolio, turning with a flourish as she held up her latest masterpiece. Surprisingly, it actually was quite remarkable. He knew her art class was working on portraits this month, but he'd expected something akin to a Picasso or Dali, given that she was seven and not the next international art sensation. Instead, he found a detailed colored pencil sketch of one of their mother's campaign photos. He remembered the day Anna had clipped it off the cover of one of the gossip magazines. Their mom had been traveling for almost a month on the campaign trail. A photographer had snapped a picture of her on the stage somewhere in Wisconsin. Anna said she looked like a princess and whined until Theo bought the magazine at the grocery store check-out. Her artistic rendering of the familiar picture was vivid and colorful, the background awash in pinks, blues, and purples that contrasted the orangey brown hue of their mother's windblown hair.

"Jesus, Anna. That's actually really amazing. You did this all by yourself?" Theo tousled Anna's tangled curls with his fingertips before looping his arm over Toby's shoulders. "Don't you think it looks great, Tob?"

"It does look great. Want me to hang it on the fridge for you?"

"I was wondering if we could go show mommy?" Anna reached for more of the papers that had managed to spread themselves over the bed's surface. "I got a hundred on my spelling test, too. And Toby, you got an A on your paper. You could show her."

Theo glanced from Toby to Anna and back again. He could already feel his tension rising at the prospect of navigating the White House during the busiest time of day, but the hopeful look on both kids' faces won the battle. "Yeah. Yeah, I guess we can do that. They can't tell us no, I don't think."

As an afterthought, Theo bent down and dug under the bed for the Amazon box he'd stashed there. With a flourish of his own, he pulled out the pompoms he'd ordered in the school colors. If they were doing this, they might as well make it a fun event for the two of them. "Let's go before it gets too late."

The walk through the halls of the White House was just as long as Theo had dreaded, but when he slowed his pace, Anna silently reached out to slip her hand into his. She squeezed gently and smiled up at him before tugging him forward.

"I get nervous too, Theo. But it's okay. I got you." Theo wanted to grab her up and give her the biggest hug. Seven years old and already wiser than he was at that age.

Once they got near the Oval Office, Theo had concerns over executing their impromptu plan. The door was closed, and the secretary said they'd have to wait. So wait, they did. Theo pulled his phone out to send their mother a text, but the woman behind the desk, her face pinched in all the wrong places, reminded him there was no personal cell phone use allowed in the West Wing. So they waited some more. They waited until the kids started getting antsy, and then they waited even after that. By the time the doorknob to the Oval Office turned, and the door slid open, he thought Anna and Toby both were about to combust on the spot.

"Mom! Surprise!" Anna waved her pompom over her head, Theo vaguely shaking his with a crooked smile. Toby crossed his arms over his practice jersey, looking like he wanted to leave ages ago.

"Oh, my babies! What a surprise! Andrew, you remember the kids, right?" Their mother looked exhausted. Theo felt a pang of remorse over interrupting her at work. Her hair was in a messy bun, and the circles under her eyes were bruise-dark. She really needed to figure out this work-life balance thing before she passed out from the weight of it.

"Of course, I remember. How could I forget such angels? Tobias, you've gotten taller. Annalise, pretty girl! Theodore." Vice President Andrew Evans nodded to each of them in succession, his tone patronizing with Anna and Toby and clipped with Theo. Theo hadn't bothered trying to hide his disapproval when his mother had picked Andrew as her running mate. It was a political move and not about platforms. Andrew's stance was just barely enough left of the line to be considered a Democrat but moderate enough to curry favor with the Republicans. Theo had told his mother he was a fake with a farce for a party declaration. It was the last time he and his mother had discussed politics. Especially since he had said it at a McDonald's, and it hit the press the following morning.

"Mom, the kids wanted to come steal you for a few minutes to share all their good news." Theo edged closer to his mother's left side, trying to get her attention off the phone she was typing on and back on the children.

"One second, sorry. I only have five minutes." She sent the message and dropped the phone into her jacket pocket. "So what do we have here, my babies?"

The room became more chaotic as Toby and Anna tried to talk over one another, words flying back and forth as the small room began to fill with even more people, presumably for the crucial meeting that left his mother with only a few minutes to spare for her children. Theo's skin began to crawl with the press of bodies and prying eyes, and he wanted to sink into the corner or the floor and disappear. Between Secret Service agents, the Vice President, the cabinet members, and their assistants, Theo felt like they'd breathed too much oxygen out of the air too quickly.

"Mom, mom, look at my drawing too!" Anna's shrill excitement cut through Theo's spiraling thoughts and brought him back from the edge. He held the drawing out for their mother to see.

"It's lovely, my darling. So lovely. I'm going to try to make it home to say good night tonight, okay? You hurry along and be good." His mother was already somewhere else. Theo knew his face was saying a lot of things it shouldn't, even if his mouth was silent. Until it wasn't.

"Mom, I'm taking Anna to Toby's game tomorrow. Do you want me to text you pictures?" Theo heard the edge in his voice too late to do anything about it.

"What game? Are you sure that's the best idea?"

"I sent you the information. Toby just told you about the starting line-up. Plus, I sent it to your secretary. And yeah, we're going. For Toby."

"Now's not the best time, but I really don't think this is a good idea."

"Whatever, mom. If you wanna talk about it, come home once in a while. Let's go, guys. Mom has work. We can make mac and cheese." Theo grabbed Anna's hand and nodded to Toby, taking a shaky breath as he tried to weave through the bodies that were crowded into the room around them.

"Can we still go, Theo? I wanted to cheer for Toby." Anna sounded like she had just watched someone kick a puppy. Theo's jaw tensed so hard he felt the pain in his molars.

"We're going. And it's going to be great, bug." People parted to clear the way as Theo sped up, desperate to flee the claustrophobic quarters that threatened to overwhelm him at any moment. Anger plus anxiety are never a good mix, and he wanted to scream, cry, or maybe both.

By the time they made it to a quieter section of the West Wing, Theo was trembling from head to toe, and Anna was tugging at his hand. Toby was worryingly silent and sulking behind them. With a sigh, Theo sagged against the nearest wall and rocked his head back to stare at the ceiling.

Anna squeezed his hand again, and Toby sighed a soft, melancholy sound. "Theo, you guys don't have to come. It's okay."

"Damn it, Toby. I told you. We're doing this, okay? I've got your back, and we'll be there, in the stands, cheering for you. Got it?"

"Thanks, Theo. It means a lot." Suddenly, Toby's arms wrapped around him. Startled, Theo froze in place with the shock of it. Toby wasn't free with his displays of physical affection. Recovering, Theo pulled Anna closer, and together, they all joined in a group hug.

"I love you guys, you know that?" Theo hated how weak and emotional his voice sounded, but at that moment, he couldn't be bothered trying to hide it.

"I love you too, Theo."

"Yeah, same," Toby mumbled, but he hugged Theo even tighter, saying more with his actions than he did with his words. They might have been standing in a public hallway, government officials and White House staff passing by on every side while the stoic Secret Service agents lingered nearby, but Theo's entire world existed in the space between the three of them.

CHAPTER TEN

Connor

CONNOR'S PHONE BUZZED OFF and on all day, pictures of face paint, nail polish, and pompoms splashing over the screen in between texts counting down the hours and reminding Connor he should try to come to the residence early if he could manage it without getting in trouble. Naturally, he could not resist the temptation and was on his way up the service elevator a full hour before their planned departure time. Not that the texts were out of the realm of what was normal for them now. What started as a sporadic thing throughout the day and often into the night became almost a perpetual, never-ending conversation.

He shifted as the elevator came to a stop at the top, nervous excitement filling him with jitters. Not about their upcoming sporting event, but about a bit of stolen time with Theo. They rarely saw each other without other people milling around. The flirtation that had insinuated itself into their regular conversations made Connor feel like he was a teenager sneaking into his crush's house when his parents weren't home. Yeah, he was being ridiculous. He also didn't care.

The doors slid open with a swoosh, and Connor stepped into the hall, pulling out his phone.

Connor: I'm here. Are you decent?

Theo: What if I said no?

Connor: Teasing isn't fair. ;) Where are you?

Theo: Kitchen.

His cheeks already ached from grinning. He was in so much trouble today. Tucking his phone back into his pocket, he navigated the halls to the kitchen and was just about to slip in, but he stopped dead in his tracks when he caught a glimpse of Theo. Gone was the typical baggy sweatshirt, replaced by an undersized t-shirt from the kids' private school. The shirt paired with the skinny jeans and bright blue socks, his curls pulled back in a messy half-up, half-down style completely transformed Theo's appearance. The narrow strip of skin visible above the low waistband of the jeans wasn't helping Connor's reserve one bit.

"Oh, hey! You're here."

"Hi." Connor tried not to stare. He failed.

Theo arched his eyebrow, a smirk playing over his lips. "What?"

"I like this better than the sweatshirt. This—" Connor gestured head to toe at Theo's wardrobe, "—is not fair."

"Shut up, you're ridiculous." The rosy flush beneath the red and white face paint of Theo's cheeks was going to be Connor's undoing. "Question; can you wear face paint, or is that against the whole Men in Black thing you guys have going on?"

"I, uh ... honestly, I don't know. Should be fine if I keep it subtle, I reckon?" Connor licked his lips, trying to get his brain to filter words around the distracting vision of Theo's hip bones.

"Subtle. I can do subtle. Okay, hold still."

Suddenly Theo was right there, right in front of him, and it was torture. He clasped his hands behind his back to resist the temptation standing just inches away from him in a t-shirt that was so tight it taunted him with ten different imagined scenarios involving how he could tear it off. Theo busied himself dabbing Connor's cheeks with a small paintbrush, concentrating his efforts on the dimples he knew were growing deeper with the increasing intensity of his grin. Their eyes kept meeting in the close space between them as if they had a gravitational pull toward one another.

"You keep smiling like that, you're gonna get kissed," Theo groused.

"Promise?" Connor's reply was barely a whisper. Time did that funny thing it always seemed to do when they were close, stretching, distorting, and freezing. He tracked the motion as Theo's tongue swept over his lower lip, but neither of them made a move to close the narrow gap. The moment disappeared in a flash as Anna came careening into the room with a squeal.

"Let's do this thing!"

Connor burst into laughter as Theo's forehead thunked against his chest with a muffled groan.

"You two are ridiculous. Get out of my way, Mr. Connor. It's my turn!" Anna pushed him aside with no qualms, jockeying into place for her turn with the face paint.

"Y'all really like that word. Ridiculous." Connor stepped aside, leaning against the counter to observe the team spirit coming to life.

"Yes, because Theo says we aren't allowed to use the words 'dumb', 'crazy,' or 'stupid.' So ridiculous is our word."

"It's a good word. I like it. Theo's a smart one."

"Shush." Theo snuck a glance toward him, his scowl fading into a smile before he turned back to his pep rally face paint project.

Before long, the three of them were suitably decorated and hurrying toward the parking garage, pompoms in hand. Connor waved Mitchell's incredulous expression away with a grunt when he noticed the face paint, unable to bite back his smile. "Don't be jealous, Mitch."

The levity of the occasion was interrupted once they made it to the sports complex on the grounds of the private school. The Secret Service team had run through the contingencies numerous times in a round table meeting this morning, but the reality was always a different experience from the theoretical one. The crowds were challenging to navigate, and the small group became a spectacle as the agents cleared a path to get them to the seating the school had managed to rope off for the First Family. Theo scooped Anna up, perching her on his hip as they hustled through the bodies, the hushed murmurs and chatter accompanied by cell phone camera clicks and people pointing from every angle. Public appearances were always a nightmare.

Finally, they managed to slide into their section of the bleachers, but the buzz of the crowd didn't get any calmer. Out of the corner of his eye, Connor caught Theo's tense jaw and measured breathing. Without thinking, he slid in even closer, stooping to whisper in Theo's ear.

"Y'all right? It'll settle once the game starts. Just ignore them, yeah?"

"Yeah. I'm fine, really. It's just … a lot." Theo tried a smile as he looked up at Connor, the tension in his expression noticeable around his hazel eyes. Connor wanted to smooth away every last crease with the pad of his thumb. Once the game started, though, he didn't have to worry. Theo managed to channel his nervous energy into cheering for the home team, with Anna shrieking at his side. They were both on their feet every time Toby was on the court, shouting and cheering and generally making fools of themselves at their brother's expense.

"Hey, you like sports. Help me understand what the hell is going on?" Theo's words brushed over Connor's ear with a warm breath that somehow always smelled like vanilla. He was keenly aware of how close Theo had leaned, and he chuckled as one of the pompoms was pressed into his hand.

"Well, cheer louder when the ball is closest to that net, and I reckon you'll be in good shape. Cheer loudest when Toby has it in his hands. Boo when it goes in the other net." Connor flounced his pompom over Theo's face with a grin before taking up the cheer. Toby scored another basket, Anna squealing with delight as she bounced up and down on the bleacher seat in front of them. Connor was overwhelmed by a peculiar sense of nostalgia over something he'd never experienced. There was a strange sort of domesticity in cheering at a middle school basketball game, side by side with Theo, as Anna danced in front of them, all three garishly adorned with school colors and growing hoarse with their rabid support.

Time sped up, another funny thing it seemed to do when he was around Theo, and before he realized it, the game was over. The sports center erupted with cheers as the last buzzer grated through the charged air. Toby's team had claimed the victory, and he jogged toward them on the bleachers as soon as the teams dispersed.

"Here, lemme get a picture of you three." Connor beamed as he lined up the shot, the trio of smiling faces on the screen needling at something deep in his subconscious. The glitter-bright twinkle of Theo's eyes seemed to zero in on that prickling sensation, and it grew in intensity as he looked up from the screen and met the eye contact directly. He really was ridiculous. It was the only way to explain how electric everything felt.

They lingered in the security of their roped-off section until most of the crowd had departed before they made their escape. Another movement the Secret Service had run through earlier in the day to ensure it all went smoothly. As an afterthought, Connor shucked his suit jacket off with a fluid movement, tucking it around Theo's shoulders and holding it in place as he slipped his arms into the sleeves.

"Thanks, O'Brien." Theo's hushed voice was tinged with the smile he flashed to Connor. With a grunt at the effort, Theo bent to scoop Anna up, perching her on his hip again before they started to move toward the exit. With the agents in formation, they managed to part the thinning crowd, moving in closer as they slipped through the exit and made their way to the waiting SUV. It would be crowded in the backseat, but it was easier for all three of the First Family to leave together. Connor breathed a sigh of relief as he climbed into the front passenger seat, grinning ear to ear as he caught Theo's eyes in the rearview mirror.

··········

Back at the White House, Theo herded the kids to their rooms to shower and start their homework, reappearing long enough to grab Connor by the hand and pull him roughly down the hall and into a sitting room. Connor stumbled behind him, stunned by the unexpected change in scenery. With a kick, Theo shut the door, pushing Connor against it with trembling hands.

"Tell me, Connor, please. Am I imagining this, or are you serious?" Theo's voice seemed on the verge of cracking, the breathy waver matching the uncertainty in his eyes as they flicked back and forth between Connor's.

"What? What are you talking about?" Connor's hands moved with a mind of their own, his palms landing on the hips that had been a distraction to him all evening long.

"This, this thing. The flirting and the texts and the... all of it. Are you being serious, or are you playing with me?"

"You think this is a joke?" Connor rested his forehead against Theo's, tightening his hands around Theo's hips as he shut his eyes. It was all too intense, too overwhelming, and he needed to close his eyes before it drowned him. "It's the farthest thing from a joke. If you need me to spell it out for you, I reckon I'd start by saying I can't get you out of my head. This is torture. You're torturing me."

"Connor." Theo's breath against his lips threatened to turn him inside out. His resolve crumbled, the sound of his name on Theo's lips like a sledgehammer. He didn't need to open his eyes to close the distance between them, their lips crashing together as if they'd done this a thousand times before. Theo tasted exactly like Connor had found himself imagining, vanilla, mint, and something distinctly Theo turning into the ambrosia he'd tried in vain to deny himself despite the magnitude of his growing attraction.

This was a terrible idea, but Connor cared exactly zero percent about that. With a rapid spin, he switched their positions against the door, sandwiching Theo against the flat plane with his body as he slid his hands over Theo's sides and under that t-shirt that had taunted him for hours. Theo's muffled groan was all the reward he needed to justify how many rules he was surely breaking. As if someone had taken a match to a tinder box, desire engulfed them, Theo's hands finding their way into Connor's hair as their lips parted, tongues dancing in competition to see who could learn the taste of the other faster.

It was Connor's turn to groan, a sound he tried to smother deep in his chest as Theo rolled his hips. Alarm bells sounded deep in Connor's brain, but he ignored every last one of them as his hips responded with an instinctual answer to Theo's writhing frame. The battle of their kiss became an all-out war as they tugged at clothing and hair and whatever their fingers could find purchase on, minutes, hours, days, weeks of building tension trying to rush out all at once until the world came crashing down around them.

He could feel Theo's phone buzz in his back pocket where he was groping at Theo's ass. His own started buzzing in his suit pants. Then his earpiece crackled to life.

"Base to O'Brien."

"God damn it!" Connor swore, something he seldom did, before he keyed up the mic at his wrist, trying desperately not to sound as out of breath as he was. "Go for O'Brien."

"We have a situation. Do you have Whisper, Willow, and Wiggle secured?"

"Three Ws secured in residence. What's going on?"

"Check the newsfeed. Stay with the Ws. Standby."

Theo was still panting as Connor dropped his forehead to rest on Theo's shoulder, taking a moment to breathe before he pulled his phone out. When he saw the headlines, he swore again. Theo went pale while watching Connor scroll through the images and headlines. His gut dropped like a broken elevator, the high of finally, finally getting a taste of the man he'd dreamed of for days crashing as he watched that man's life begin to fall apart on a live news stream.

CHAPTER ELEVEN

Abriella

THE WHITE HOUSE WAS chaotic, not that it was ever actually quiet, but it was pure frenetic energy as Abriella and Tristan navigated the halls tonight. Advisors, assistants, and secretaries were sprinting from one place to another, most juggling two phones and numerous conversations as they barreled around the agents. Par for the course when press exposés hit the headlines and protests broke out nationwide.

She was fortunate that Connor was still with Theodore Moreau. A quick text, and she was headed straight for the target of her most pressing investigative interview. Press releases and gossip magazines are usually nothing more than a bunch of garbage in a pretty package, but something about this one did not sit right with her. The timing, the photographs, and the quotes from "people close to the First Family" all seemed too conveniently curated. It made her uneasy, but she kept her concerns to herself as she glanced to the side at Tristan. His face was already irritating her simply because it existed near hers. He was the last person she would share her conspiracy theory with until she was sure.

Abriella already had her badge pulled out as they rounded the corner and neared the stairs leading into the residence of the First Family. On the other hand, Tristan walked right up to one of the agents on duty and clasped his shoulder, pulling him in close to whisper something in his ear.

"Williams, what are you doing?" she spat the words out, annoyance hanging on every syllable.

"Chill, Garcia. Agent Mitchell is an old buddy. We hit the firing range together all the time." Tristan's smirk was smug and uncomfortable, out of place on his usually passive face. She vaguely contemplated how good that smirk would look after her fist was done with it.

"We are not here for your machismo. Are you coming, or do you have other more important plans?"

"Well, if you think it would help, I was going to work on interviews with the support staff. Since you have your rapport built if I recall correctly?"

"Si, perfect. Go. Adios." Abriella shooed Tristan with a soft tch sound before turning to jog up the stairs. It was working out perfectly that she had shaken her partner. Now she could really dig deep into the kid and see if her intuitive prickle had any merit.

She found the two of them sitting side by side in one of the sitting rooms. Who really needed this many sitting rooms, anyway? Theodore was a wreck, and if she weren't here in a professional capacity, she'd have laughed over her burly bear of a best friend's hovering. Always the protective one.

"Agent, Mr. Moreau. How are you this evening?" She winked at Connor with a fleeting smile.

"Who're you?" Theo's eyes narrowed at her, the hazel coloring of his irises paired with the high cheekbones giving him the appearance of a wild cat who trusted her about as much as she trusted her partner, which was not at all.

"Agent Abriella Garcia, FBI." She had her badge out and back by muscle memory alone, a quick flash before she was pulling out the pocket notebook she kept alongside it. "I'm here to ask you a few questions about everything leading up to the press release today.

Connor leaned in even closer against Theo's side, whispering something in his ear that had Theo's body language fractionally relaxing. She made a mental note of the fact that he was wearing Connor's suit jacket, the size clearly too large for Theo's much thinner frame.

Undeterred, she pressed on. "I need to ask you who you remember encountering in the West Wing yesterday. I am sure you've seen the pictures?" She tried to soften her voice and relax her posture. Theo looked close to bolting the room or passing out where he sat.

"I'm not great with the names. There were a lot of people. I know the Vice President was with my mom when we got there, the secretary. A bunch came in after for another meeting. We passed more in the halls after, but I have no clue. I just live here."

"Can you describe any of the people you passed who could have taken the picture of you and your siblings in the hall? The picture from the articles?" It wasn't a compromising picture on its own, the three siblings hugging one another in the halls of the West Wing. Paired with the quotes from "people close to the First Family" about how Theo was going to petition for custody and the President was a negligent mother, they told a different story.

"Suits, ties, uncomfortable shoes. Bunch of white dudes with attitudes, just like everyone else that runs around here." Theo drew his knees up to his chest, hugging the suit jacket around himself as he griped.

"What about at the basketball game? Was there anyone either of you recognized in the audience?" Abriella glanced toward Connor, but he wasn't looking at her. He locked his eyes on Theo, worry etched in his features.

"I would only recognize the other agents. There were four of us on duty. Mitchell, Fornell, and Fitzpatrick, plus me. The rest all looked like a bunch of soccer moms."

"Everyone was taking pictures at the game. Why is this happening? I don't understand why any of this is happening. How bad is it?" Theo's voice, one she had initially read as full of attitude, suddenly sounded weak and vulnerable.

"Smalls, can you close the door?" Connor glanced up at her before jerking his head at the door she was still standing near. Arching her eyebrow, she slid it shut. By the time she turned back around, Connor had pulled Theo in close against his side, arms wrapping around his shoulders with Theo's head tucked under his chin.

"Wait, hold up. Connor Donovan O'Brien. Is this the guy you've been texting?" Abriella's jaw dropped as she put together the clues that had been staring her in the face since she walked in the door.

"God, Abriella, shh." Connor rolled his eyes, a heavy sigh puffing out his cheeks. "Now do you see why I didn't want to tell you?"

"I thought you didn't want to tell me because it was a Grindr hookup, not because it's the First Son! Are you insane?" Abriella pressed her palm to her mouth. Things just got a lot worse if there was actually a nugget of truth to the pictorial evidence. "You've seen the headlines, si? About how you and Theo looked like the perfect little couple cheering for your kids at the basketball game? Half the city is crying for her to resign for being a negligent mother, and the other half is calling you both the poster children for the new American family! Dios mio, Connor!"

Abriella's rapid-fire rant was cut short by a strangled sobbing sound as Theo turned and buried his face against Connor's neck. Connor murmured something to Theo, his soft, slow drawl indecipherable for how quiet it was. With a little nod, Theo shifted, not moving apart from Connor as he finagled a little blue-grey canister out of the pocket of his jeans. He shook it before bringing it to his lips and inhaling. Abriella turned away once she realized what was happening. The kid was hanging on by a thread. Over the years, she'd interviewed witnesses and suspects of all make and model. The signs were clear.

Switching tactics, she closed the distance between herself and Connor, crouching in front of him to make eye contact. "Connor, who knows about you two?"

"No one, honest. I wasn't even sure I had a chance with him until tonight." He snapped his fingers. "And just like that."

"Elias. I told Elias Williams. The Chief of Staff. But he wouldn't. He wouldn't do this." Theo's breathy voice wavered, emotions bubbling just under the surface.

"Are you positive?" Doubt hung on every syllable as Abriella glanced between the two men.

"Absolutely. He's basically family. I've known him for years, before all the political shit."

"How do you know him, Theo? It's important we figure this out. You might not have met under political circumstances, but everything about your life is political now."

"It's not him! My mom met him years ago at some support group for widows of soldiers. It was a grief counseling thing. His kid goes to school with Anna. He's family. He wouldn't do this!"

Abriella inhaled before letting the air slowly pass through her pursed lips. "I know it's hard to believe, but we can't rule anyone out. Someone somewhere had access to the information and pictures that hit the news today—someone who claims to be close to your family. I can't talk to your siblings without your mother's consent. You need to think. Try to remember anything you can."

"Abs, is this connected to what happened on Inauguration Day?" Connor's typically smooth slow molasses accent became edged with something resembling a growl.

Her gaze ping-ponged between Theo and Connor, silence hanging so heavy that she could hear every breath they took. She gambled on the odds, switching to Spanish as she honed her eyes back on Connor. *"Do you trust him? Do you trust this with him because it's not good out there."*

Connor nodded just once. Two decades tied her and Connor together. From the proverbial battlefield of the public school system to the actual battlefield of the combat they'd seen together in the Marines, they'd come to rely on one another's instincts without fail. If he trusted Theo, however improbable it sounded, she had to take that chance.

"Yes. It looks like there's a connection. We're trying to figure out that connection. We don't know the purpose, but someone out there isn't happy about the current administration, and it's more than just chatter on the intelligence lines." Abriella pulled herself back to her feet with a hand on Connor's knee. She gave a little squeeze before she let go.

"What do I have to do to stop it? Are the kids safe?" Theo's wide eyes tracked Abriella's every movement as he spoke.

"Keep doing what you do, but keep your eyes open while you're doing it." She avoided the question about the two younger children. Making promises she couldn't keep wasn't a habit she was trying to start now. "If anything seems off, let me know. Or tell Connor."

She pulled one of her cards from her pocket, setting it on the couch beside Theo before retracing her steps to the door. "And call me later, Biggs. You owe me."

Connor's chuckle in response was subdued but accompanied by his intrepid smile. With a wink, she opened the door and slipped out. She found Agent Mitchell still on duty at the base of the stairs. He acknowledged her presence with a subtle nod.

"Agent Mitchell, correct?"

"That's correct, Agent Garcia." The agent gave her a once-over out of the corner of his eye, remaining otherwise unfazed.

"What can you tell me about Theodore Moreau?"

"Quiet. Keeps to himself. I barely see him. He's good with the kids. They talk about him a lot."

"Is there anything out of the ordinary you've noticed?"

"Other than he rarely leaves, no. No visitors either, except the Chief of Staff, once. Basically lives like a recluse." Mitchell stole another glance in her direction. "I already told all this to Agent Williams. He should still be in the West Wing."

A dismissal if she'd ever heard one, and one she inadvertently had to cede to. Her next destination was the West Wing, hoping to corner the President at the scheduled emergency meeting and see if she could get any closer to untangling this knot. Tristan wasn't hard to find once she made it through the twisting halls and corridors, harassing a young intern with a series of questions back to back in an attempt to overwhelm him. Tristan's interview methods were another thing she didn't like about him, but unfortunately, she had to admit that sometimes his tactics worked where hers did not.

Her arrival gave the intern a chance to recover from Tristan's battering ram as he pulled out one of his cards and handed it to the young man with a crisp "We'll be in touch."

"Get anything good out of your buddies?" Tristan's expression flickered with a smirk.

"We can share notes after. Is Director Fields inside?" She nodded down the hall toward the room they'd agreed to handle together.

"Yeah. Ready for this shit show?" Tristan tugged the lapels of his suit jacket, smoothing his tie down as he started moving along the corridor.

"No, but that doesn't change our fate." She sighed in resignation, falling into stride with Tristan as they headed toward the maelstrom that waited on the other side. They might work together as well as oil and water mixed, but at least they pulled off the illusion of a united front.

CHAPTER TWELVE

Adelaide

Fifteen more minutes remained before Adelaide had to walk into the emergency meeting. It didn't feel like long enough. The Oval Office around her echoed with an oppressive silence, the air weighted as if she were locked in a tomb. For all her time in this space, she'd never felt so overwhelmed as she did at that moment. Her phone dinged on the desk, and she scrambled to check it. She swore under her breath when she checked the notification. Not seeing Theo's name on the screen, she tucked the phone into the breast pocket of her jacket. He hadn't answered her calls, and her texts had gone unread. The sinking feeling in her chest whenever she thought of what he'd said yesterday afternoon returned with a force that left her feeling unmoored and adrift.

A knock at the door focused her attention. Her fifteen minutes of peace were almost over. Her secretary and Secret Service agents joined her as she strode through the hall, making herself taller and forcing her lungs to breathe deeper before she pushed the door to the Roosevelt Room open. All eyes in the room turned toward her with expectant stares and expressionless faces. She didn't bother trying to smile. She didn't feel like smiling.

"Thank you for coming on such short notice. Please, be seated." Adelaide marveled at how her voice could sound so steady despite everything that had happened in such a short period. "First thing, I'd like an update on the protests?"

General Nicolas Siamo stood up from where he'd just sat down, his uniform impeccably tidy and the myriad bars, medals, and pins glittering like the silver streaks in his dark hair. His tawny complexion remained smooth and wrinkle-free, even if he had almost twenty years on Adelaide. He intimidated her, even if she worked hard not to show it. "Madam President, the worst protests in the capital have National Guard presence. Law enforcement from other major cities reported that most crowds dispersed."

"We are continuing to monitor the chatter on the intelligence lines. Our threat assessment is elevated, but I think we've seen the worst of the outcry." Director Luke Fields said, seated across from the General. Blonde hair turning grey, keen eyes, and the typical black suit of the FBI gave him an austere appearance. "Special agents Garcia and Williams are still leading an investigative team to uncover more of the details, but we do not have a conclusive report at this time."

"Is there a clear tie between the events of Inauguration Day and today?" Adelaide asked, mindful to keep her posture upright and her hands folded on the table before her, even if she would rather crawl under said table and pretend none of this was happening.

"We are operating under the assumption that it is a connected incident. The intel we've gathered from various internet communication platforms has indicated as much, but the evidence is not conclusive enough to make an official statement at this time."

"And we don't know who the source is?" Adelaide shifted her gaze from Director Fields to the agents behind him.

"Not at this time, Madam President." Tristan's blue-silver eyes would have been unnerving for their intensity were she not so familiar with his cousin Elias' identical coloring.

"What is the reaction from the Senate, Leader Evans?" Adelaide felt the ghost of a smile cross her lips as she turned her attention toward Aaron Evans. They always laughed about the formal titles when they met privately. Aaron Evans, the Senate Majority Leader, and his brother, Vice President Andrew Evans, were fraternal, not identical twins. Still, the similarities between them would fool anyone into believing they were. They both had the same dark hair, deep blue eyes, and all-American smiles that made Andrew a popular running mate for her presidential campaign.

"Mixed, but this shouldn't come as a surprise. A few from across the aisle are rumbling about an inquiry into the allegations, but I don't think we have anything to be concerned about. We'd never get anything done if the Senate charged after every inflammatory headline." Aaron flashed her one of his boy-next-door smiles before continuing. "And if you'll allow me to speak candidly, we here in this room know you aren't neglecting your children or your duties."

A murmur of agreement filtered through the room. It was almost enough to put her at ease. "Thank you, Senator Evans."

"That does bring us to the response to the public." Andrew leaned forward, his elbows resting on the table's surface. "This is clearly a contentious issue that inflames the American people, and we need to discuss how we will move forward."

"Addressing the allegations made by the news outlets is our first step. I would normally counsel no response to such claims, but these allegations appear to be substantiated by close associates. We must display a unified image of the First Family until the source is determined. If we do not supply the narrative, the press will continue to create one of their own," the Press Secretary said as she leaned over Adelaide's shoulder to place a folder in front of her. Young, fresh-faced, and full of sass, Jessica Brinley was a small but mighty force. Her light brown hair danced over her shoulders, held back by the glasses perched on the top of her head. "I've prepared a statement for you to make in the morning. There's one for Theodore as well."

"No, that won't work." Adelaide shook her head so vehemently that her own chestnut waves tumbled from the clip that had corralled them in place. "There's absolutely no way Theo will be speaking with the press."

"Madam President, unless you both address the allegations, it will just feed the rumor mill." Jessica pressed on, pointing to the folder with a manicured nail. "It's just a short statement, no questions after."

"What if there was another way to show a unified front without public statements in front of the press? Which part are we addressing here?" Adelaide flicked through the papers in the folder, but her vision swam as she tried to make out the words.

"To be completely frank, Madam President, part of the issue is that you have not been seen publicly with your children since you were sworn in on Inauguration Day. The press has documented your youngest children at school and in their extracurricular activities. The photos with you and Theodore from the Inaugural Ball and your campaign photos with all three were some of your best positive press-generating pieces. We need to fight this fire with fire, but you must be the centerpiece." Jessica propped her fists on her hips as her lips flattened into a thin line.

"These are my children, not pawns! We are not using them as puppets for the press." Adelaide pressed her fingertips to her temples as though she could physically stop the pounding of her headache with the pressure.

"Forgive me, Addy, but throughout your entire campaign, we did exactly that," Andrew interjected, his voice level and quiet.

"How dare yo—"

"Last Easter. Anna's birthday party. The soup kitchens. The Pride March. The Fourth of July picnic." Adelaide's heart sank further with every event Andrew threw in her face. "Shall I continue? You ran on the promise of family values and progressive change. Now the people who voted on those promises are reading this story and wondering if it was all a lie."

"Andrew, you know it's different now."

"Yes, it is. It's more cutthroat, vicious, and unforgiving. Give the people something to smile about. Show them the happy family they saw on the campaign trail, even if you have to manufacture it." Andrew's words hung heavy in the air, the silence louder than she'd ever heard.

Adelaide's chest expanded as she drew in a deep breath. "Theo can't handle the press directly. I'll make a statement in the morning. I'll make sure they all come to the State Dinner next week. Elias, can you handle the details for that? I know it's last minute and complicates things with the schedule and the dignitaries."

"Shouldn't you talk to them first? Theo, at the very least." Elias' brow furrowed as he fidgeted with the pen in his fingers.

"Theodore made this mess. He gets to help clean it up." Andrew was quick to supply the accusation. Adelaide's head whipped to the right, her lips parted to retort, but an unlikely source cut her off.

"Mr. Vice President, there is no evidence that Mr. Moreau is complicit in today's press exposé." Agent Abriella Garcia called across the room from her position behind the FBI Director, her posture stiff and her eyes narrowed.

"Be that as it may, he and his mother are victims all the same. If an appearance with the press will repair the damage, I'm sure he'd be happy to help."

"Ms. Secretary, can we make the State Dinner work?" Adelaide could barely recognize her voice. It sounded as hollow as she felt.

"It would be excellent for the optics. We need to normalize the presence of your children in the White House. It'll reinforce the ideals you campaigned with and ease the discontent." Jessica reached out to take the folder from the table. "I'll rework the statement for the morning press pool."

"Thank you. You're all free to go. We can reconvene tomorrow to address any developments." Adelaide rose slowly from her seat, hoping the action would inspire the others to do the same. They had five minutes before she would order them to leave her alone. At least being the Commander-in-Chief had that one small perk.

Little by little, the bodies filtered out of the room, but Elias and Aaron lingered, eyeing one another before approaching Adelaide. Aaron was the first to bridge the gap, gracing Adelaide with another of his characteristic charming smiles.

"Addy, I just wanted to remind you that you're doing an excellent job. I know this has been a hard adjustment for everyone, and my brother was an ass tonight. We're all behind you, even him. This will be another thing we laugh about in a few months." Reaching out, he squeezed her hand in his before letting it drop. "Keep your chin up. It'll all work out."

With a nod toward her and Elias, he turned on his heel and slipped out of the room, leaving Adelaide in relative privacy She could even ignore the presence of the Secret Service agents that were always close.

"Adelaide, you have to talk to him. To all of them. You know he's going to lose it when he hears about the State Dinner. At least give him the illusion of having a choice in the matter." Elias' voice was low as he moved in closer, glancing over her shoulder at the agents lingering against the walls.

"I'm doing the best I can. There's so much to do every day, and when I find the time, he's barely talking to me. I told him the basketball game wasn't a good idea, and look what happened."

"I can't begin to imagine how much pressure you're under, but Addy, you aren't the only one under pressure here. Don't lose sight of that. Please." Elias' hands landed gently on Adelaide's shoulders, and they sagged under the weight as if they represented the pressure of everything that had accumulated throughout her presidency thus far.

"I know how hard the adjustment has been for them. For Theo especially. But he agreed to come here, he agreed to be a part of this, and he agreed to help me. And now I need his help."

"Addy, he agreed to come for the kids. You know that as well as I do. He'd give anything for those kids. He's already given up everything for them. We all sacrifice so much of ourselves to do this work." Elias squeezed her shoulders, his hands gentle. After a brief pause, he pulled her into an embrace, resting his cheek against hers. "But you and I? We're damn near forty years old. Theo's twenty-one. He's been sacrificing himself since your Lawrence died. Please, don't lose sight of that. Don't lose sight of them."

Adelaide sank into Elias' arms, glad for the brief chance to share the burden with someone else. They'd shared so much over the years. Loss and grief had brought them together, but resilience and strength had kept them that way. Though the truth of his words cut deep, his arms held her from falling apart.

"I'm trying. I'm trying, Elias. I don't know if it's enough."

"All we can do is try, Addy. Remember, you're not alone in this. You've never been alone."

Adelaide's eyelashes grew damp with unshed tears. "We'll get through this?"

"We always do. For them."

"For them."

CHAPTER THIRTEEN

Theo

Exhaustion clung to Theo like a weighted blanket as he trudged barefoot into the kitchen, tapping out a text message as he went through the motions of making coffee. Sleep was elusive, even on a good night. He stifled a yawn with the back of his fist as the coffee pot hissed and gurgled, hopping up to sit on the counter and continue his conversation with Connor while he waited for the lifesaving elixir to brew. Their texts were a continual thing now, replies bouncing back and forth whenever they each had a spare moment. The resulting conversations seemed to meander the strangest pathways.

Connor: Hey are you free to talk? Cooking, can't really text.

Theo: Yeah everyone's still asleep.

His phone buzzed in his hand, and he slid his finger across the screen to answer it, muffling another yawn as he brought it up to his ear.

"Morning, sleepy head." Connor's voice sounded tinny through the phone speaker, but the smooth slow drawl that was Theo's kryptonite was instantly recognizable.

"Mornings suck. Why do you sound so awake?"

"I been up for an hour or so now. I usually run in the mornings."

"You're ridiculous. That's an unholy thing to do this early in the day."

"Is this your way of telling me you aren't a morning person?"

"Antithesis of a morning person." Theo's lips curved into a crooked smile as he bantered back and forth over the phone. "Is this one of those opposites attract situations?"

"Hey, about that..." Theo's stomach plummeted with those three words, his nerves instantly leaping into overdrive. They hadn't discussed the events of the evening before the press explosion, though Theo had relived the memory of their kiss at least a dozen times as he tossed and turned all night. But this was it. He'd been nursing this intense infatuation for weeks. Connor might as well have said, "We need to talk." Dozens of different varieties of rejection flooded Theo's mind. Theo was too complicated, too messy, too problematic, too much. He couldn't articulate a response, so he let the silence hang on the line, listening to the clatter and clang of pans and utensils filtering through the phone speakers, trying to picture what Connor was doing instead of imagining the worst.

"Are you there?"

"Yeah, yeah, I'm here. Just grabbing coffee." Theo hopped off the counter and grabbed a mug from the cabinet.

"Look, I'm a pretty straight shooter, so I reckon I'll just come right out with it. I like you, Theo. I really do."

Theo snorted, though it came out as a soft huff of breath. "And here comes the but, right?"

"What, whoa, I mean, yes. I'm incredibly attracted to you. I thought that was obvious. But I'd figured we'd at least work out a proper date. Lord, making me burn my eggs over here."

"What the hell are you talking about?" Theo grabbed a sponge to soak up the coffee he'd managed to spill on the counter while attempting to fill his mug.

"What are you talking about?"

"Oh, I like you, but! It's been fun but! You're really attractive, but!" Theo's voice rose in pitch as he threw the sponge into the sink with more force than was necessary. It made a pathetic squelching sound that had Theo feeling even more ridiculous.

"Wow." Connor sounded earnestly impressed. "You're such a grumpy little shit in the morning."

"I thought you were a 'straight shooter,' Connor. Cut to the chase." Theo wanted this to be over so he could lick his wounds and mourn the loss of the only silver lining that had come out of the last few weeks.

"This conversation is so ridiculous. Drink your coffee and just listen." Clanking and clattering filled the line, and Connor's voice became clearer and sounded closer. "Sorry, I had you on speaker. Anyway, I reckon I maybe went about this sideways, but I get nervous talking about serious stuff. I don't want you to think I'm just some dumb hick, y'know?"

"Connor, you're literally killing me. What in the actual hell are you trying to say? Please." Theo tried to keep the strain out of his voice as he thunked his head against the upper cabinet's door.

Connor laughed his rumbling, rolling thunder laugh before he regained his composure. "Okay, okay. Here goes." Connor took a deep breath, and Theo held his. "I like you, prolly more'n I've liked anyone in a while, and I know this situation's as complicated as all get out, but I think we could prolly be something real good. I reckon what I'm tryin' to say is, even if it is complicated and you maybe don't feel the same thing, I'd like to give it a go if you want that too? I'm not the sort to hookup or be real casual 'bout stuff, and we didn't talk about that sort of thing, seeing as I'm not really good at talking about it."

Theo was dumbfounded. He opened his mouth to reply, but nothing came out.

"Hello? Theo?"

"Connor, are you trying to ask me out?"

"I mean, yeah. I reckon that's exactly what I'm tryin' to say." Connor's voice conveyed a hint of vulnerability that Theo hadn't heard before. He sagged against the counter with a breathy laugh that turned into a burst of giggles he couldn't contain. It was a manic sound as relief flooded through him.

"God damn. Yes. Jesus, you damn near gave me a heart attack. I thought you were about to tell me it was all a mistake!" Theo regained his composure, cradling the phone between his ear and shoulder as he gathered up the coffee mug with both hands.

"Phew. Good lord, I was worried you'd be against it since I can't exactly date you proper when I'm on the clock or anything." Connor's mouth was full, the words pausing as he swallowed before continuing. "But I'm gonna try to make up for that, y'hear?"

"You're fine. I'm the First Son of the United States. If anyone's situation is causing an issue here, it's mine. We can figure it out."

"Yeah, I am pretty fine."

"God. You're ridiculous." Theo's cheeks hurt. He didn't think he could smile this much considering how much of a disaster his life had become. Yet, here he was, standing in the kitchen of the White House in boxer briefs and a baggy crop top while he negotiated a clandestine relationship with his bodyguard over a cup of coffee.

"Aw, crap. I gotta take this call. It's my ma. But I'll be heading over to the castle after. We'll figure out how to grab lunch together."

"Go, it's fine. Finish your breakfast and text me after."

"You drink your coffee, my grumpy little shit. I'll talk to you."

The line went dead before Theo could respond, but he scrunched his nose at the word "my" in Connor's comment, his grin wide enough to cause his eyes to squint as he topped off his mug and made his way back to his bedroom.

His grin fell away instantly as he neared the hallway that led to his room. A pair of voices filtered through the space, and he poked his head around the corner to find two Secret Service agents loitering in the hall outside his room.

"What the fuck? What are you doing here?" Theo's already tenuous grasp on his hair-trigger anxiety swiftly abandoned him. "You aren't supposed to be here unless we invite you. Were you in my room?"

"Easy there, son. Routine security check after the incident yesterday. That's all. I talked to President Montgomery. She gave us the go-ahead." The older agent seemed familiar to Theo, but he couldn't pinpoint a name in his spiraling thoughts. Agent Mitchell beside him was easily recognizable as Anna's primary security detail. Still, something seemed off about this situation, and panic swiftly rose in the pit of Theo's stomach.

The older agent stepped toward Theo with his hand outstretched. Theo, in turn, backpedaled on bare feet, his coffee mug slipping from his hands to shatter on the floor. "Don't you dare! Who are you?!"

A noise behind him caused Theo to pivot in place, hypervigilance making him sensitive to every sound and movement.

"Theo, baby, are you okay?" His mother jogged toward him, still wearing yoga pants and a baggy t-shirt with her chestnut hair loose.

"Please, don't..." Theo choked on the words as he pressed a palm to his racing heart. With a ragged gasp, he pressed on. "Why are they here? Why are they in my room?"

"Oh, honey. This is James Locke and Thomas Mitchell. Agent Locke is the agent in charge of the security detail. They needed to check the residence for security breaches and listening devices." His mom stopped short, her hand outstretched, poised just inches from touching him.

Theo scrubbed his hands vigorously over his face as he let out the breath he'd been holding.

"I'm sorry, I should have said something. I didn't realize they would be here so early. I wanted to surprise you with something, too. Come, baby. Let's go to the sitting room?"

Warily, Theo glared at the agents before slowly following his mother into the nearest of many sitting rooms. Once inside, he snatched up a throw blanket and wrapped it around himself, suddenly aware of how little he was wearing at this impromptu meeting. Tucked into the corner of the largest couch, he enfolded his legs in his arms, cocooning himself in the blanket as he glanced between the agents and his mother.

"Are you okay, baby?" Adelaide moved to sit beside him, her actions slow and deliberate.

"Yeah. I just need a minute. What's going on?" Theo nodded toward the agents, who still stood at attention near the door.

"I had a thought after the incident yesterday, and I talked with Elias after our cabinet meeting. We think it might be good for you to get out a little, to do something fun. I know everything has been such an upheaval and you need some new clothes, a new suit for the State Dinner. Elias' assistant is a fashionista, or so he says, so we thought a little outing to get some new things would be perfect. For your birthday. My treat." Her smile was too bright. Theo didn't miss how she tried to slip the words in without him noticing.

"Hold up, State Dinner? You mean the one on my birthday that I remember saying quite clearly I did not want to attend? The one literally next week?" Theo's face twisted into a scowl despite his best efforts.

"Yes, but you're going out with Elias tomorrow. It'll be fun!" The tone was so chipper and patronizing that Theo wanted to scream. Maybe even break another mug but on purpose this time.

"Thanks, I hate it."

"Well, we've already worked out all the details. Please, just trust me. I know you'll have fun if you give it a chance." She reached out, squeezing his knee with a gentle hand before turning to the agents.

Theo scoffed, the sound muffled and derisive in the back of his throat. "You do remember that every time I leave this damn prison house, some terrible shit happens, right?"

"You know that's just a matter of chance, baby. It's not you. It'll be good for you to get out more. The agents here say it'll be perfectly safe! Isn't that right?"

"Indeed, Madam President. We have two agents who will be shadowing you all day. We won't let anything happen." The agent, who Theo'd just learned was named James, flashed a relaxed smile, his hands clasped behind his back and his posture upright but at ease. Theo thought he was the most beige-looking man he'd ever seen, even in a black suit. Soft grey eyes, pale skin, salt-and-pepper hair in the same haircut every man in the District of Columbia seemed to wear.

"I want Con—Agent O'Brien there. And at the dinner."

"Pardon me, Mr. Moreau?" James' head cocked to the side.

"I want O'Brien on the detail. I know him, and I trust him. He's been there every single time shit went down. I don't know you or him or any of the others. O'Brien or I'm not going anywhere. And that includes the dinner." Theo tried to put extra emphasis and force behind his voice.

"I'm sure Agent Locke can make that happen, baby. Isn't that right, Agent Locke?" Adelaide arched her eyebrow at the older agent and turned a withering gaze on Mitchell, who was trying hard to hide a smirk.

"Consider it done, ma'am."

"And mom, seriously. Stop calling me baby. I'm almost twenty-two." Theo felt a little bolder, riding the high of his win. Lily had told him to set boundaries during one of their weekly meet-ups. She'd be proud of his progress. He held his head a little higher as he crossed the room. Aiming for self-assured, even if he was swishing through the door wearing a throw blanket, he left on his own terms without a word.

CHAPTER FOURTEEN

Connor

By the time Connor got off the phone with his mother, he had to race into the headquarters, already a few minutes late. His mom had been inconsolable, so he was running farther behind schedule than he'd have preferred. She was prone to melodrama, but he'd managed to talk her off the ledge of her latest stressor and hung up with promises to visit over the summer as soon as he could get a decent chunk of time off. His calls to his mother always left him homesick, so he wasn't in the mood for the atmosphere of the Secret Service base.

"Hey, hey, hey, Big Texas! Guess who's got himself a fan club?" Mitchell jeered as soon as he walked through the door.

"Sounds like we have some hero worship going on, big man!" Fornell chimed in, the wad of newspaper he tossed across the room bouncing off Connor's chest with a soft thump. He stooped down to pick it up, smoothing it out to reveal a picture of himself and Theo at the basketball game. It was one of his favorites from the press debacle, him and Theo smiling at one another, unfazed by anything else around them. But he couldn't tell the guys that.

"You gonna tap that? Is that something gay dudes say?" Fitzpatrick snickered as he reached out to bump Fornell's outstretched fist.

Connor tensed, and he knew every emotion was evident in his expression. He'd never been able to mask his feelings well. Some people wore their hearts on their sleeves. Connor wore his as a sandwich board in neon colors.

"Fitzpatrick, that's out of line!" James' voice barked from his desk at the front of the room, startling them all and quieting the chuckles that rippled through the space. "O'Brien, you're with me. Grab your gear."

Connor straightened his spine and flicked a two-finger salute toward James. James was the closest thing to a father figure Connor had since his time in the Marines. While others would be apprehensive over being singled out to meet with the agent in charge of their group, Connor was relieved about the chance to talk with his mentor. He couldn't help but notice Mitchell's scowl out of the corner of his eye as they left the headquarters.

Out in the hallway, they fell into stride with the practiced ease of their training in the service. Like Connor, James had come from a military background, and some habits die hard. As they walked along, he began to worry about the nature of this meeting. Running through the history of his short time on the protective detail, he came up with an impressive list of things that were likely questionable, if not outright, breaches of the conduct code.

"How're you settling in, Connor?" James glanced toward him, never breaking stride.

"I'm loving it, Jim. I reckon protective detail is exactly where I was always meant to end up."

James chuckled, a low wispy sound that softened his severe expression. "You almost didn't get the spot. You're not like the typical agent, son."

"Did I do something wrong, Sir?" Connor turned to the side, briefly making eye contact with James as they continued their walking rounds of the White House.

"At ease, soldier. No complaints so far. If anything, everyone loves you. I'm not surprised about that. No one is." James' hand clapped Connor on the shoulder blade. "I'd venture so far as to say we need more agents like you. You're approachable and pleasant. And you do a damn good job handling the stress of it."

"Thanks, Jim. That means a lot."

"Are you comfortable continuing to work with Theodore? I was worried he would be too much of an asshole for you."

"He's not. People misunderstand him, I reckon."

"Sounds a lot like your situation."

Connor glimpsed toward James again, his brows furrowing. "How do you mean?"

"Big jock, Mister Marine, a footballer from a West Texas border town. You've got that country boy charm, but I see you, son. You're soft, and you feel too much. I can see it all over your face when the boys get going."

"Now, Jim. I ain't soft. I can do the job." Connor couldn't help the defensive note tinging his voice.

"Shut it, O'Brien. That's not what I'm saying. I know you can do the job. You're doing it better than the others. Even if you're playing it as an end-around, it's unconventional, but you're making it work. And Moreau is one of the difficult ones. So I'm assigning you the spot as his dedicated detail. You in?"

"Wait, you're serious?" Connor stopped short in the middle of the hall. "Even with all the stuff in the papers?"

James turned to face him. "Keep your head in the game, keep your name clean, and we might be able to salvage this trainwreck. And the kid trusts you. This presidency is an accident waiting to happen. If it takes some unconventional plays to pull it all together, I'm willing to put my money on you throwing the Hail Mary and actually making it work."

"I'll do my best, Sir." Connor puffed out his chest and squared his shoulders, grinning as he winked at James' amused expression. "I was the QB, after all."

"Get the hell out of here, Connor. You've got a Whisper to chase down."

Connor laughed at Theo's code name. Theodore Moreau had crashed into Connor's world with anything but a whisper. With another salute, they parted ways, and he pulled out his phone as soon as he was sure he was out of sight.

Connor: Hey I'm here. Can we meet up? Where are you?

He continued toward the residence to relieve the agent assigned to Theo's overnight detail. His phone vibrated in his pocket as they debriefed, the urge to pull it out instantly hard to ignore. As soon as the agent had disappeared, Connor nodded toward the remaining detail agents and moved a little further down the hall before sneaking a glance at the screen.

Theo: Yeah I'm upstairs. Can we go for a walk or something?

Connor: Sounds good. Meet me at the stairs

Barely five minutes later, Theo came clattering down the stairs with all the grace of a giraffe trying to take its first steps. Connor tried and failed to stifle his laughter.

"Important meeting, Sir?"

"Yep. Definitely." Theo overemphasized the p in yep, a crooked grin quirking his lips as he pushed the chaotic curls from his eyes.

"Kids tagging along?" Connor tilted his head. Theo was rarely too far from them when they were home.

"Actually, not today. Mom is working from the office upstairs. And I have that important meeting. Let's go. We're late." Theo flashed an awkward wave to the other agents. They made no effort to respond to the gesture.

Theo started down the hall, moving incrementally closer as they fell into sync. He leaned in, his voice barely a whisper. "I have no idea where I'm going."

Connor found the small of Theo's back with his palm, giving subtle direction to their path with gentle pressure. After a while, they'd navigated the corridors and stairways until, at last, they found a sanctuary on the upper floors of the East Wing. Yet another superfluous sitting room availed itself as a hiding place in plain sight. As soon as the door closed behind them, Theo exhaled a sigh that ended in breathy laughter.

"So apparently, we're going shopping tomorrow. I demanded you come, so I'm sorry about that, but also not sorry." Theo suddenly seemed nervous, almost bashful. His hands disappeared into the sleeves of his sweatshirt as he paced the room.

"I reckon it'll be fun. I would have been along anyway. I just got assigned as your dedicated protective detail. Fancy those odds, eh?" Connor replied, closing the gap between them with slow, precise steps.

"Thank God for small blessings. How's your mom? Did the thing with your cousin work out?" He stopped pacing as Connor stepped in front of him, his gaze rising to make eye contact. Connor didn't stop himself when the impulse to brush the dark curls from Theo's brow struck.

"Eh, not really. Ma was upset over it. You can lead a horse to water, but you can't make'em drink. I'd rather not talk about my cousin and rehab right now if that's all right?"

"Sorry, sorry. I didn't mean... I don't know why I'm rambling."

Connor followed the motion of brushing Theo's hair from his eyes, his fingertips trailing down the contour of his cheek and along the line of his jaw. "We don't have to do this, Theo. If you changed your mind, it's all right."

"No! It's not that, I swear. I'm just a mess sometimes. I don't know why. Christ, Connor, no." Theo's hands slipped from within the sleeves of his sweatshirt as he spread them over the expanse of Connor's chest, his touch feather-light over the cotton of the white button-down.

"Theo," Connor murmured, the space between them slowly evaporating. "... breathe."

Theo gasped softly, stealing the breath straight from Connor's lips milliseconds before they came together. His fingers cupped Theo's chin, trying desperately to keep their kiss tender and chaste. Evidently, Theo had other plans. Chaste lasted for mere seconds, their lips parting in sync as the kiss devolved into a feral thing, lips locked and tongues lashing with fervor. When Theo's hands pulled his shirt from the waistband of his pants and slid up over the curve of his spine, he groaned despite his best efforts to smother the sound.

"God damn it, Connor, you can't do that." Theo gasped, his words jumbled as he spoke against Connor's lips. "Do it again."

"Do what, Theo? Tell m—" Connor had no choice but to comply with the order as Theo dipped his head lower, his tongue tracing the pulse point on his throat, just above the shirt collar. Connor's hands flew to the back of Theo's head, his fingertips tangling with the curls. They were even softer than Connor had imagined, long enough to grasp as he balled his fingers into fists. With a little tug, he pulled Theo's head back until he could make eye contact again. Theo's eyelids fluttered open, and Connor was struck with the sudden realization that he had a thing for lush eyelashes and hazel eyes.

"Good Lord, you're gorgeous." Awestruck and overwhelmed by need and want, Connor rejoined his lips with Theo's as they stumble-stepped through the room, collapsing as one on the nearest sofa. Every fiber of Connor's body spontaneously ignited as Theo's legs wrapped around his, thighs parted around his hips as Connor blanketed him against the cushion. Theo's arms coiled around him, one hand sliding over the material of his suit pants and the curve of his ass, the other reaching up toward the nape of his neck, fingernails scratching through the short strands of hair. Pure, unadulterated desire coursed through Connor as he rolled his hips, his moans muffled in the depths of their impassioned kiss.

Theo squirmed underneath him, answering each moan with a groan of his own until he broke the kiss with a ragged inhalation. "Ow, hold up. Stop."

Connor flinched as Theo pulled his hands back to readjust his position on the sofa, unintentionally yanking the earpiece from his ear in the process.

"Shit, sorry! Are you okay?" A brief flash of worry danced over Theo's face as he disentangled the coiled wire from his fingers.

"Yeah, are y'all right? What happened?" Connor searched Theo's face, his own concern growing as he readjusted the earpiece of his radio.

"Your gun. You're hard, but your gun's really hard." Theo dissolved into breathless laughter as he panted, flopping back against the arm of the sofa.

"Oh Lord, I'm sorry." Connor began to laugh, too, until they were both nearly hysterical. "We're ridiculous, eh?"

"Yeah, we really are." Theo sat up a little straighter, tugging at the lapels of Connor's suit jacket to pull him closer. "It's kind of perfect."

Connor nestled against Theo's chest, more mindful of his tactical belt as they settled into a comfortable position on the sofa. Theo's chest became a pillow for his cheek, a shiver running down his spine as Theo nuzzled the hair at the top of his head. "Yeah, it really is kind of perfect."

Theo twined their fingers together on his chest, and they remained like that for hours, intermittently blanketed by comfortable silence and murmured conversation. In spite of the fact that the intense passion had rapidly dissipated, it was somehow the most intimate experience Connor had ever had.

CHAPTER FIFTEEN

Elias

"So how long do we have to pretend this will be fun before we can quit and do something else?" Theo's mutter filtered through the SUV over the hum of the engine. They hadn't even started their excursion, and he was already complaining.

"You're worse than Parker. Your mom said you needed some new clothes. She's paying, so just spend the money, get some nice things for yourself, and I'll get you a coffee as a reward if you're a good boy." Elias glanced back at Theo through the rearview mirror, catching Connor's smirk in his peripheral vision. Having finally met the agent, he instantly understood why Theo was so smitten. He wasn't Elias' type, but there was no denying he was attractive.

"Whatever. I have clothes. She just doesn't like them."

"I don't reckon sweatshirts and Converse work for the image, Sir." Connor chimed in from the driver's seat as he checked the mirrors and flicked the turn signal to take the next right. Elias couldn't see his eyes behind the dark sunglasses, but the grin on Connor's face gave him away nevertheless.

"She doesn't like any of my outfits. The sweatshirts were a compromise as it is."

"Honestly, though. I'm still willing to pay you if you wear the crop top I got you last Christmas to a press junket." Elias turned in his seat to flash a smile at Theo. "Her face was priceless."

"Dude, it was great! Still one of my favorite shirts." Theo shimmied forward in the backseat, leaning over the back of the driver's seat to whisper in Connor's ear. Elias bit back a laugh as he watched the red flush creep up Connor's neck and over his freckled cheeks.

"I reckon that's something someone somewhere would like to see, Sir." Connor stole a glance toward Elias, his hands clenching and relaxing on the steering wheel.

"I take it you listened to my advice then?" Elias gave a subtle nod toward Connor, who was distracted navigating the traffic of the busy side street to find a parking spot.

"Yeah, I'm 'rolling with it,' just like you said." The smile on Theo's face was almost timid as he looked away, worrying at his lower lip with his teeth.

"Good. Good decision. I approve. Slightly jealous, but I approve."

Theo snorted before he stifled a giggle. "Oh, please. As if you couldn't pull the same. Do I have to throw an intervention for you next?"

"Oh, I could absolutely pull. I just choose not to." Elias made a show of tousling his hair, which inspired another fit of stifled laughter from the back seat. Connor appeared amused but kept his mouth shut, even if he seemed ready to burst with the way he shifted in his seat.

"We're here, Sirs. You said we're meeting the assistant in the store, correct?" Connor killed the engine and pocketed the keys, checking all the mirrors and blindspots before turning toward Elias.

"That's right. Were there more agents coming?" Elias unbuckled before reaching for the door. Connor reached out to stop him.

"Not yet, let me come around. The other guys should be inside. I think they wanted to clear the premises."

The driver's side door opened and slammed shut, Connor jogging around the hood of the SUV to open the passenger side door before moving to the rear door. "With me, Sirs."

Elias grimaced as they neared the shop entrance his assistant had told him to visit first. He could hear the distinct voice even through the closed door. He should have sent a disclaimer to the Secret Service. Connor halted their progress as he keyed up his mic.

"O'Brien to Fornell, status?"

After a brief moment, Connor turned toward Elias with a grin on his face, dimples popping at the edges of his smile. "Would your assistant happen to be Caleb Cohen?"

Elias shifted his eyes from side to side, his grin slowly spreading over his face. He definitely should have sent a disclaimer. "That'd be him."

Connor chuckled before he returned his attention to the mic at his wrist. "Mr. Cohen's on the list. Clear to enter with Whisper?"

Another brief pause, and then Connor nodded toward the door to the tailor's shop and followed them through. Inside, Caleb's voice was even louder, the Secret Service agent looking like he wanted one of the clothing racks to swallow him whole.

"I told you, you trussed up hussy! And by the way, you have terrible pores, and your hair is a disaster!" Caleb huffed and turned on his heel, stalking toward Elias with a pinched expression. "I cannot believe I agreed to spend my day off on this, Mr. Williams. My price just went up. Ten frappes. Deal?"

Elias was nearly hysterical. Caleb was a typhoon wherever he went, but he was exponentially powerful with his civilian dress and in his element outside the office. Five feet and five inches of impeccably styled streetwear, slicked back frosted blonde hair, and an attitude that could rival an entire squadron of Secret Service agents.

"Do we have a deal, Williams? I do not have all day. People to do, places to see, blah, blah, blah." Caleb held out his hand, rings and bracelets twinkling in the subdued lighting of the tailor's display room.

"Ten frappes and lunch on me for your troubles, Caleb. And it's just Elias outside the office." They shook hands as if they'd just negotiated an international trade deal. Elias stepped out of the way as Caleb twirled toward a dumbfounded Theo and stunned Connor. He pushed his glasses up, settling them on the pompadour that had reached impressive heights. Elias didn't recognize them and again wondered if they were even prescription lenses or if Caleb simply owned enough designer frames to complement any outfit.

"Is the pasty emo boy my pet today? Mm mm mm, this will be delicious fun. Come along, pet!" Caleb spun on his heel again, the chunky sneaker squeaking on the floor as he minced toward the rear of the store. "Suit first. I think I know just the color for you, you poor disaster."

"Dude, what the hell?" Theo leaned in close, whispering to Elias as he stared in wonder at the force that is Caleb Cohen. "This is your assistant?"

"Yep! He's amazing. Trust the process. His words, not mine." Elias pushed Theo toward the maelstrom of flying fabrics that had consumed the room. Even the other agents took a step back, edging toward the entrance as though they might need to flee the scene. Elias took the opportunity to inch closer toward Connor, Theo now held hostage as Caleb circled him like a cat toying with a mouse.

"It's a pleasure to meet you properly, Connor." Elias kept his voice low to avoid drawing attention to them as they watched the chaos unfold at the rear of the store.

"Likewise, Mr. Williams, Sir." Connor's smile was effortless as he glanced toward Elias. "I've heard the name a few times."

"Just a quick chat, you and me." Elias turned to meet the whiskey-gold eyes that glimpsed at him. "You hurt him, and I will make sure you regret ever stepping foot in DC."

"I beg pardon, Sir?" A fretful expression flickered over Connor's face as his eyebrows bunched together.

"I love that kid like he was my own. His last relationship really messed him up, and if you do the same, I will find a way to make your life hell."

"Wait, did he tell you?" Connor turned his gaze back toward the two men now bickering at the back of the shop.

"I figured it out pretty easy. He hasn't been this happy in a long while. I only had to push a little before he told me who had him all worked up." Elias' cheeks plumped with a smile as he watched Caleb brandish a tailoring pin like a fencing foil.

"Well, Sir, he talks about you a lot. Respects your opinion, something fierce. He doesn't talk much about it, but I know his pa wasn't around, and his stepdad passed, but when he talks about you, he's got that sound in his voice like you hung the stars and moon. I promise I ain't trying to do anything that'd mess this up."

"A word of advice, if I may?" Elias glanced at Connor's profile before returning his attention to the battle of wills that seemed to be taking place over an emerald green jacquard waistcoat.

"Please, Sir. I know you don't really know me, but I promise, I really do like him. Not for all the presidential stuff or any of that. He's special. Real special." Connor's voice was so earnest, all slow drawl and soft-spoken. Elias would have hugged him on the spot if they weren't playacting nonchalant.

"You need to realize that Theo is the last person Theo worries about ever. He's just starting to find his footing. You could steamroll him in a second without even realizing it. And if that happens, I swear on everything holy, I will cut you."

"I figured as much. He slipped and mentioned an internship. He talks about the kids like he's their pa. And I'm always after him about making sure he eats and sleeps and such like." Connor paused, lifting his chin a little higher before he continued. "I might sound all slow molasses when I get talking, but I ain't stupid. And I ain't looking to be some knight come to save the day 'cause I reckon he's stronger'n all of us put together. I want to be with the grumpy little shit 'cause he's something real special. All due respect and all."

Elias tried to contain his laughter and lost the battle. He quickly corralled his reaction with a cough. "Yeah, you've got my seal of approval, Connor."

"It's good he's got you." Connor chanced another glance toward Elias before turning his eyes back to the scene unfolding before them. From their position, it appeared as though Caleb had won the battle, judging by Theo's slumped shoulders and the frenetic activity of Caleb fitting the garments with pins and chalk lines.

"Maybe you can help me with something since you're on the inside?" Elias lowered his voice even further, conversing in conspiratorial whispers. "The State Dinner next week is the last thing Theo wants to do for his birthday, but he's doing it anyway. I want to steal him the day before and give him a chance to get out and act his age for a night."

"I reckon that's a great plan. He's twenty-one going on forty sometimes." Connor's lips pursed as Caleb got closer to Theo, playing with his hair and readjusting the suit jacket.

"He doesn't have many close friends, but I'd like to have him and anyone you think you can trust for dinner, drinks, something. I have the space at my place and Parker can spend the night with Tristan and Becs. I know a night out on the town is out of the question, but I think we can figure out how to make it work. He doesn't do well with crowds anyway. Can you make that happen from your end?"

"I suppose I know some people who can come. I can handle the security and get him where you need him without much fuss."

"I'd like to invite Caleb, too. I think that guy creates a party wherever he goes." Elias ventured, pointedly avoiding Connor's sidelong glance.

"Caleb, your assistant, at your house, for a party?"

"Don't you judge me, O'Brien. I could blow your cover in two seconds flat."

It was Connor's turn to lose the battle against his laughter. He cleared his throat, pressing his fist to his grin before dropping back into parade rest. "I reckon I don't have much room to talk. And now that you say it, I can picture it. Silver fox meets aggressive twink. I think I read that trope a couple of times now."

"And that's your cue to shut up, Connor." Elias swiftly elbowed Connor's side as Theo, now freed from the suit of pins, scurried back toward them.

"I will not get my hair cut, Caleb. You won on the suit, but you aren't touching the hair!" Theo ducked behind Connor's larger frame, his scowl poorly hiding the grin that lingered under the surface. "He's got a gun, and I can make him shoot you!"

"Girl, you wouldn't dare. I'd haunt your fine ass so fast, your mama would need to hire a priest." Caleb quipped in response.

Connor's eyebrows shot toward his hairline as he glared down at Caleb, lips pursing in displeasure.

"Oh, baby bear, calm down. He's not my type." Caleb's light green eyes rolled so hard Elias was worried he was about to have a seizure or faint.

"Oh yeah? What is your type, then?" Theo asked as he slid back into view, taking up his position beside Connor.

"Refined, and fine, and aged like a great wine," Caleb emphasized his words with a wave of the hand toward Elias. "Like him, but, you know, less straight."

"Wow. Bold of you to assume I'm straight, Caleb. I thought you were more progressive than that." Elias couldn't keep the smirk off his face.

Caleb's jaw dropped, and the three burst into laughter as he went silent for the first time all afternoon. They made quite a motley crew, but the laughter that filled the room felt just right despite their differences. Or perhaps because of them.

CHAPTER SIXTEEN

Lily

LILY STOOD ON THE doorstep of the impressive home with the landscaped yard for longer than she should have, the agents parked on the street likely watching her stand there like a fool. She had no clue what she thought when she accepted the invitation to this dinner party. When Connor had, quite literally, barged into her office with a sunshine grin and an address on a Post-It note begging her to come for Theo's not-so-surprise party, she had a hard time saying no. So here she was, with a cake stand in hand, staring at the doorbell like it might electrocute her when she pushed it. Inhale. Exhale. Press.

She heard the chiming sound from deeper inside the house and tensed in anticipation. She wasn't expecting the Chief of Staff to open the door. Especially not wearing chinos and a fluffy sweater and no shoes.

"Um, hi. I'm Lily, here for... uh." she stammered before freezing, entirely out of her element and unable to process the fine art of socializing outside the office.

"Oh! Lily, yes! Theo's mentioned you a couple of times now! Come in, come in!" Elias was effusive and genial, reaching out to take the cake stand before stepping out of the way. "Everyone's in the dining room. You'll hear the noise."

She toed her ballet flats off and smoothed her hands over her blouse, suddenly even more nervous about what she'd gotten herself into. The noise was unmistakable, voices jockeying for supremacy in a room just off the foyer. Compared to her minimal apartment, the midcentury modern aesthetic of this seemingly sprawling house felt like something from a magazine. The dining room was another Better Homes & Gardens spread come to life as she edged through the open archway.

The occupants of the room stole her attention first, though. She was used to seeing everyone in a particular wardrobe in an official capacity. In their street clothes, she felt like she was seeing total strangers. Despite that, she did know everyone around the table. Whether that was a good thing or not was yet to be determined.

"Lily! You came? Oh my God, yes!" Theo jumped up from the table and scampered, actually scampered around the table. He flung his arms around her with a peel of laughter that could only be described as a giggle, and the scent of wine on his breath as he kissed her on the cheek explained his demeanor in an instant. The laughter was infectious as she and everyone else in the room joined in. Instead of his typical baggy sweatshirt style, he was dressed in skinny jeans and a bright blue crop top with a little ghost screen printed on it, proudly proclaiming "Boo Thang" in bold yellow lettering.

Lily managed to untangle herself from Theo's embrace and swept her gaze around the room, shy all over again as she gave a little wave. Connor looked completely different in his jeans and USMC t-shirt instead of the black suits she always saw him in. Abriella perched on the edge of the table beside him, her suit likewise missing and replaced with a fitted cocktail dress in a lush purple paisley pattern that was doing delightful things to the athletic curves of her frame.

At the head of the table, though, was the guest who Lily was least expecting. Caleb Cohen. Staring at her wide-eyed and slack-jawed, his appearance unlike the one she remembered when she'd first met him years ago.

"Caleb? You're here too?" Lily blurted the words before she could stop herself.

"Wait, y'all know each other already?" Connor's words drawled, his accent pronounced, likely to be blamed on the wine glass he clutched in his massive grip.

"Yes."

"No."

"I mean, sort of?" Lily tried to recover.

"Ish." Caleb's eyes darted toward her, pleading.

"College. We volunteered at a soup kitchen together." Lily flashed Caleb a smile, aiming for reassurance. He looked intensely uncomfortable over the fact that she, his therapist from years ago, had suddenly walked into the room at a birthday party. Soup kitchen or LGBT outreach program, same thing, almost. She was a volunteer. Him, not exactly.

Caleb visibly relaxed as the conversation returned to its previous volume, Theo sprawling in his chair beside Connor and the three bickering over the last of the cheese on the board in front of them. Elias slipped into the room like a hero coming to save the day with more cheese, another bottle of wine, and a fresh glass for Lily. She took the remaining seat, coincidentally beside Abriella's perch on the table, and began picking at the plentitude of appetizers that covered the table.

"I think Connor and Theo have been at this for a couple of hours now, si?" Abriella's whisper startled her, suddenly drifting over her ear.

"Apparently so. I've never seen them so..."

"Obnoxious? Yeah, I'm a little stunned. I've seen Connor wasted before, but he never giggled. It's a little sickening." Abriella grinned down at her before clinking their glasses together in a toast.

"Oh, stop, it's cute." Lily returned the tiny toast before settling into the chair, her attention bouncing from one conversation to the next as everyone resumed talking over one another. Without warning, Theo gasped and slapped his fingers on the table.

"Eli! Do you have that game from last Christmas?"

"What? Clue?" Elias' amused smile brought out the faint creases at the corners of his eyes.

"Yes! That one. We should play it! It's like my favorite thing." Theo listed to the side, whispering with zero volume control in Connor's ear. "I'm amazing at Clue!"

Abriella reached over Connor to ruffle Theo's curls, grinning ear-to-ear as she did. "Maybe you were once, but you'll be playing against a doctor, an FBI agent, a Secret Service investigator, and two policy negotiators this time, mi amigo. Good luck. You will need it."

Elias leaned back in his chair, the furnishing precariously balancing on two legs as he pulled the game board out of the credenza against the wall. "You say that now, Miss Abriella, but you don't know what Theo does for a living, do you?"

"Pssh, he makes websites. I'm not scared."

"Actually, websites are just what I do now! Before that, it was like, so much more complex. You're going down!" Theo's words dissolved into giggles as he perched his chin on Connor's shoulder.

Abriella slid off the table and into the chair, not-so-subtly scooting it toward Lily as Caleb worked on clearing a space at the table for the board game. Lily arched her eyebrow as she glanced toward the side, trying not to smile.

"How do you know everyone?" Lily whispered, leaning in closer and catching a whiff of jasmine perfume.

"Connor and I went to school together in Texas. And the Marines after. And then DC. I only just met the others recently. You?"

"Theo and I became friends recently. Connor demanded I come tonight. He was rather emphatic about it." Lily gathered up the cards and scoreboard sheet, covertly palming them in her hand as she put the purple game piece she'd claimed on its square.

"He's like a puppy with a bone when he gets something in his mind. I love him for it." Abriella adjusted the hem of her cocktail dress and leaned over the table, everyone suddenly growing serious as the game began. Never would Lily have pictured herself at a dinner party playing a game she hadn't seen since middle school with a bunch of grown men and a particularly attractive woman, but here she was.

Even in their tipsy state, Connor and Theo managed to turn studious as they bowed their heads over their cards and squinted at the board in turn, each of them taking turns and surreptitiously marking their little papers with the tiny pencils from the box. Even Lily got into the game, not realizing the tip of her tongue had poked out the corner of her mouth, as it was prone to do when she concentrated. She noticed only when she caught Abriella's glances out of the corner of her eye. Her interest had the subtlety of a car horn. Lily found she didn't mind too much, also blaming that on the wine.

After a few rounds of everyone rolling, maneuvering, and calculating the board, Theo abruptly declared that he knew who the murderer was. Rumbles of discontent and jeering came from Caleb and Elias, but they quieted down as Theo cleared his throat.

"It was YOU, Colonel Elias Williams Mustard! In the salon, with the gun!" he proclaimed, looking smug and self-assured, a far cry from the typically quiet, brooding, anxiety-ridden man who usually sat in her office. And he was infinitely more lively than the relaxed, almost shy version she got to see when they met up to swap recipes and discuss the Great British Bake-Off. This Theo was exactly what you'd expect when you say 'twenty-one-year-old.' Lily was stunned.

After a brief conference between the players and the revelation of his answer being correct, Abriella brought her fist down on the table with a scoffing sound.

"How? How did you guess that?! Did you cheat, birthday boy?" Abriella narrowed her eyes as she pointed a finger at Theo. "You cheated!"

"No, honestly, I used to accuse him of the same thing until he explained the reasoning behind his answers. His brain is wired for some bizarre logic coder witchcraft." Elias grinned as he collected the cards and pencils from the table, Caleb jumping up to help but mostly getting in the way. Lily caught his eye over the table and quirked an eyebrow in a silent, unspoken question. Caleb only answered with an eye roll. A warmth spread in her chest to see him doing so well. The last time she'd met with him, he was a shell of a boy, lost and floundering with too many traumatic life experiences packaged into one body.

"Cay, you want to help clear the table while I get the cake? Lily brought cake." Elias packed the board game into the credenza, grabbed empty plates, and used napkins. Lily shrank as all the eyes in the room turned toward her.

"Lily! You didn't have to!" Theo cried out with a smile, pulling himself upright from where he'd settled against Connor's shoulder.

"Yes, I did. It's your birthday, Theo. Birthdays call for cake." She reached her hand across the table and smiled as Theo grabbed it, squeezing once before letting go.

Connor leaned back in his chair, brow furrowing as Abriella slipped from the room without a word. With a shrug, he kissed Theo's temple and slid to his feet, grabbing up more plates and platters from the table as Caleb returned from depositing the first load of dishes in the kitchen. Lily opened her mouth to offer her aid, but Connor cut her off as he made a tch sound and winked.

Once the two left, she was alone with Theo and took the opportunity to scoot closer. She looped her arm over his shoulders and squeezed in an awkward side hug, surprised when he leaned into the embrace.

"Are you drunk, Theo?" Lily kept her voice soft as she rested her cheek atop Theo's curls. He was flushed and warm, his arms loosely wrapped around her waist.

"No, not drunk. Tipsy. Will you stay for the movie?" he murmured, wiggling in place to finagle his inhaler out of the pocket of his jeans while maintaining contact in their surprisingly long hug. Lily wasn't sure what to make of the unexpected snuggling.

"What movie? It better not be a horror film." Lily couldn't stop the impulse to press the back of her fingers against Theo's brow as he took a quick dose of the inhaler and snuck it back into his pocket. Her lips flattened as she heard the faintest wheeze when he exhaled. "Hey, are you feeling all right?"

"Yeah, of course. I'm fine. Really." Theo grinned up at her as he sat up straighter. "And no, not a horror. It's a rom-com, but queer. It's perfect for tonight since I think pretty much everyone here is queer. Not sure about Abri—"

Lily and Theo both looked up as Connor trundled into the room, dragging Abriella by the hand as she spluttered what could only be swear words in Spanish. He pointed to the nearest chair to Lily's right and nodded without saying a word as Abriella sat and folded her arms over her chest with a huff.

"Abriella, are you gay like all of us, or are you the resident ally?" Everyone went silent, Elias and Caleb stopping short in the archway, and they all turned toward Theo with mouths agape.

"Okay, maybe slightly more than tipsy. I'm so sorry. I didn't mean... I don't know why I asked that." Theo dropped his face into his hands, the flush of his cheeks turning into a full-body blush of mortification.

Abriella's laughter burst from her lips as she fell from the chair, clutching her stomach as Connor followed suit, laughter bringing tears to his eyes. Even Lily couldn't stifle her giggle. Before long, the entire room was in hysterics.

"Dios mio, Connor, he is perfect for you! Never let him go." Abriella climbed back into the chair, aiming for graceful but falling short. "Si, Theo. If you must know, I am part of Misfit Island, the Rainbow Brigade edition."

The laughter continued as they each grabbed a slice of the cake before Elias herded them into a family room filled with couches, chairs, bean bags, and numerous toys in fancy baskets. Their levity persisted throughout the movie, with giggles and commentary floating back and forth until the credits rolled. It was one of the best evenings Lily had experienced in months, surrounded by a bizarre collection of new friends she didn't have just hours earlier.

CHAPTER SEVENTEEN

Theo

WARMTH COCOONED THEO, HIS entire body heavy and relaxed. He didn't want to move, but a persistent murmuring pulled him from his slumber, realization gradually replacing his semi-conscious state. He tried to sink deeper under the weighted blanket of sleep, but the murmuring became more insistent until he surfaced, eyelids fluttering open, dazed and confused.

"Mn, m'tired. Lemme sleep." He tried to burrow back into the bed, only to realize he wasn't in a bed at all.

"C'mon, my grumpy little shit. The guest room will be more comfortable." Connor's voice finally cut through the fog, and Theo giggled as he blindly reached for Connor, pulling him closer by the shirt.

"You're here. Come to bed."

"No, you come to bed. You're on the couch. Let's get you comfortable," Connor replied, his voice tinged with stifled laughter. With a grunt, he pulled Theo's body from the couch, despite the stubborn reluctance to move.

"Fine, fine. You're ridiculous."

"Yeah, you like it, though." Connor turned his back to Theo's front and crouched down. "Here, jump up."

"Huh?" Theo's sleep-blanketed mind remained slow, taking a moment to realize what he had meant. "Oh... I'm too heavy."

"Good Lord, do you have to argue everything? Just jump up already." To his credit, Connor had the patience of a saint, and Theo begrudgingly complied, looping his arms around his shoulders before hopping up on the count of three. As soon as he latched onto Connor's frame, he couldn't remember why he'd argued in the first place, the position ideal for nuzzling his neck, ear, and hair. He smelled like woodsy cologne, and the faint remnants of cedar aftershave combined with an indescribable aroma that was purely Connor.

"God, babe... you smell so damn good I just want to lick you." Theo's words came out muffled, his lips rasping against the velvet skin behind Connor's ear.

Connor stumbled a half step before continuing up the stairs, choking back his laughter as he crept across the landing and toward the second story. "You can't say stuff like that. Do you want me to drop you? Shh!"

It was Theo's turn to laugh, the giggle buried in the juncture of Connor's neck and shoulder. "M'gonna learn everything that drives you wild. Everything."

With a nudge of his foot, Connor pushed the guest room door open. He slipped into the darkened space, the glow of moonlight filtering through the sheer curtains of the window and illuminating the simple furnishings in an ethereal silver light. Another soft grunt came from within Connor's chest as he hefted Theo onto the mattress like he was weightless. Theo gasped, reaching his hands out instantly toward Connor.

"C'mere, stay," he murmured, sitting up as Connor moved toward the door.

"I'm staying. I wanna close the door."

Theo stripped his shirt off, balling it up and tossing it at the back of Connor's head, grinning as Connor turned back around.

"Such a brat. I swear if we hadn't drunk as much as we did..." Connor crept toward the bed, the low lighting casting his dimples in dark shadows. Theo had to work hard to resist the urge to bite each one.

"Jesus, just get over here. Now. Please?" Were he not utterly distracted, he would have cringed at how whiny he sounded.

Connor descended on him with a surprising amount of grace and fluidity for someone with such a large, muscular frame, his hands bracketing Theo's head on the mattress and his lips hovering inches from Theo's own.

"I don't want to get your hopes up, but I don't like to fool around if I been drinking or you been drinking." Connor's voice wavered, his lips drawing closer as he exhaled a soft sigh. "I know it's ole fashion or whatever, but I just can't. I just... I want it to mean something when we... y'know. M'gonna kiss the hell out of you, though, if that's all right?"

"God, yes, please. You're killing me!" Theo pulled insistently at the nape of Connor's neck, trying to close the gap between them. Connor chuckled as he dipped lower, the shape of his smile mirroring Theo's own as their lips finally met. Slow and lazy, their mouths danced together in the now familiar rhythms of their kiss. His hands wandered over the contours of Connor's back, tracing the fluid lines of the musculature until he found the hem of the t-shirt with his fingertips.

They parted long enough for Theo to pull the shirt from Connor's body, and they were at last skin-to-skin. He felt like he was burning up, the languid kiss incensed by desperate hands eagerly attempting to memorize the intricacies of the landscape beneath each of their fingertips. Breathless, he tore his lips from Connor's, mouthing the line of his jaw and down his neck, soft groans reverberating through the room all the reward he needed for his efforts.

"Killing me. You're killing me with those sounds." Theo lowered his lips, nipping at the delicate skin over Connor's collarbone.

"Ah! Shit, Theo... damn it!"

Theo arched his back, rolling his hips against Connor's, the denim of their jeans stretched taut as they desperately sought friction against one another's bodies. Theo whimpered. Connor moaned. Their hands flew in a flurry as their limbs entwined. Everything was a blur of yes and need and want and more until Connor pushed himself up, gasping for air as he stared down at Theo with desire so intense they both trembled.

"I... I can't. Not like this. I didn't bring anything."

"Me neither. Fuck! Just let me touch you? No sex, just... please, Connor?" Theo's chest ached with each inhalation, his head swimming for the need of oxygen.

"Yeah. Good Lord, yes." Their knuckles knocked together in the tight confines between their bodies as they raced to undo the buttons and zippers of their jeans, lips seeking lips once more as they freed themselves from the restrictive garments. Theo groaned again, rising to meet the downward pressure of Connor's undulating hips, their lengths sliding against one another with the delirium-inducing sensation of velveteen steel. He tried to reach between them, but Connor batted his hand away with a throaty growl that sent a shiver through every electric fiber of Theo's body.

Theo's whimper died in Connor's mouth as Connor wrapped his hand around both of their cocks, the rough texture against sensitive skin overwhelming Theo's senses. Their movements synchronized almost seamlessly, Connor's weight blanketing Theo as their sweat-slick skin caressed together with each unified rolling motion. Theo was swept up in the fluidity of their bodies, so intensely close and yet not close enough, his nails scratching at Connor's back in desperation to bring him closer, their tongues desperately seeking out the hidden secrets of one another's mouths.

Too much and not enough, Theo tore himself from the kiss with an arch of the back, his head driving deeper into the pillow as he groaned, stars and sparkles glittering at the edges of his vision.

"Babe, oh God, babe, don't stop... I'm close." Theo's voice was a ragged whisper that ended in a moan as Connor redoubled his efforts, grip tightening till it was nearly unbearable.

"Come for me. Come with me. Theo, please!" Theo had never heard Connor so utterly undone. Each syllable tore away at every last restraint Theo had until he was freefalling through space, the delirious plummet of ecstasy whiting out his vision as he tried to silence his cry against Connor's throat. Connor did the same in mirror, his voice vibrating through the pulse point on Theo's neck as a molten heat spread between their bodies.

Connor collapsed on top of him, their bodies trembling as the waves of their shared orgasm washed over them. Theo tried to drag air into his lungs, a flicker of panic starting to rise as he fumbled with clumsy hands for the pocket of his jeans. He couldn't reach, the pants pushed down too far over his thighs during their impassioned writhing. With a gentle push, he tried to roll Connor to the side.

"Sorry. I need..." he mumbled, the words dying on his lips as he struggled. Connor's face fell, worry etched over his features as he shifted his weight to the side and propped himself upright on his elbow.

"Oh Lord, did I hurt you? Theo, m'sorry."

"No. No." Theo managed to dig his inhaler from the pocket of his jeans, shaking it before he brought it to his lips. It burned at the back of his throat, the familiar medicinal taste washing over his tongue as he exhaled. He draped his free arm over his eyes, embarrassment rising as he tried to concentrate on regaining control over his labored breathing.

"Sorry. I'm sorry." Theo released a shaky breath before taking another dose of the medication, shoving the canister underneath the pillow that cushioned his head. "I'm sorry."

"Hey, shh. Theo, look at me."

Peeking one eye out from under his arm, Theo reluctantly met Connor's worried gaze.

"Was it something I did?" Connor's voice came out as a hushed breath.

"No. I'm sorry. I ruined the mood." He gasped softly as Connor grabbed his discarded t-shirt and gently wiped at Theo's stomach.

"Pssh, that was the best sex in years. Are y'all right?"

"Yeah, I'm fine. Really. Some days are worse than others. Exertion doesn't help on bad days. I'm sorry." Theo tried to turn away, his nerves fueled by the shame and the stimulants in the medication.

"Teddy, baby..." Connor turned Theo's face back toward himself with tender fingertips against his jaw. "Just breathe."

He nestled back into the pillow facing Connor, watching as he finished cleaning them both up with the t-shirt before tossing it to the side and pulling the comforter over them. Theo wiggled closer to Connor's warmth, the broad expanse of his chest becoming the ideal pillow. "Sorry again."

"Stop apologizing. You're making it a bigger deal than it needs to be. Y'need to breathe. I don't care if you have to use your inhaler in the middle of sex, before, after. I don't care. You tell me if y'need to stop. You do what y'need. I'll still be here. You ain't gonna shake me that easy."

"Can you call me that again?"

"Huh? Call you wh—oh, Teddy?" Connor nuzzled the top of Theo's head, coiling an arm around his shoulders to tuck him in closer.

"I like it. No one's ever called me that before."

"Well, I reckon sometimes you're a grumpy bear, but I think deep inside you're a teddy bear. At least, I see you that way."

Theo laughed, the sound breathy and soft, as he swirled his fingertips through the faint smattering of chest hair running between Connor's pectoral muscles.

A comfortable silence fell over them as they explored one another with delicate touches and tiny kisses wrapped up under the blankets. Theo counted the deep, relaxed beat of Connor's heart as his eyelids grew heavier.

"Connor?"

"Mm?"

"I really like you a lot."

"Well, I mean, if you gotta know, I reckon I'm pretty smitten m'self."

"You're ridiculous. I'm being serious," Theo huffed softly.

"I know. Don't gotta be such a grumpy little shit."

"I'll always be a grumpy little shit." Theo nipped at Connor's chest, grinning as he squirmed beneath him. "But I can be your grumpy little shit."

Connor cupped his chin, tilting Theo's head to make eye contact. The features of his face were silver-limed by the moonlight, and Theo forgot how to breathe for a moment as he tried to commit the image to memory.

"I reckon I'd like that more'n anything. Calling you mine," Connor whispered, the words feather soft against Theo's lips.

"You say that now, but get back to me in a month. You might change your mind."

"Who's being ridiculous now?" Connor pressed tiny kisses to Theo's nose and cheeks.

"I think you like it." Theo sighed, resting his cheek back on the cushion of Connor's chest. Exhaustion slowly crept over him, weighing down his limbs.

"You're right. Because I really like you, too."

Theo smiled, impressing a kiss upon the center of Connor's chest before wiggling closer. Serenity washed over them both under the blanket of the moonlight, and Theo sank into the gentle rise and fall of Connor's sleep-patterned breathing, the rhythmic lull of his heartbeat soothing him to sleep.

CHAPTER EIGHTEEN

Connor

THE RISING SUN POURED through the sheer curtains, cutting rays of golden light through the dust motes in the air. Inspired by this surreal, dreamlike illumination, Connor allowed himself the indulgence of imagining this could be his future. Shifting carefully under the weight of the comforter, he nestled closer to the warmth of Theo's body beside his. He curled closer in response, a soft mumble breaking the silence of the early morning hour.

As Connor gradually awoke, he realized the room wasn't entirely silent. Honing his attention, he could hear the faint rattle of Theo's breath with each inhale and exhale. Internal debate raged in Connor's mind. Theo was not a morning person, and he was tempted to let him rest longer, but the way Theo's chest rose and fell in shallow, patternless little gasps won out.

"Theo? Theo, wake up." Connor lifted his hand to brush the curls from Theo's brow, his concern growing as his fingertips skated over the sweat-damp skin. "Theo. Hey."

"Mnnf, stop. M'tired."

"Baby, y'all right?" Connor spoke a little louder, trying to coax Theo into wakefulness.

"Tired. Stop." Theo burrowed deeper under the covers, his arm sliding over Connor's chest. He wasn't just warm. Every point of contact between their bodies felt hot to the touch.

"Baby, hey. You need to wake up."

"Why? Stop. Please?" Theo's whimper compounded Connor's growing worry.

Connor took matters into his own hands, sitting upright before physically dragging Theo into a seated position, the grumbles and complaints laced with prolific, albeit muffled, cursing. Sleep soft, disheveled, and scowling, Theo was adorably cranky in the morning.

"Hello, handsome. Here." Connor kissed Theo's temple as he reached under the pillow, searching for the inhaler before handing it over. "Take this. I'll go find coffee."

It didn't take Connor long to dress and find the kitchen, rummaging through the cabinets to find the coffee. Elias' entire life seemed made for a label maker promotional, the tiny white tabs directing Connor through the process of starting the brew. While he waited for the machine to sputter and hiss, he pulled out his phone, scrolling to Lily's contact card to send her a text.

Connor: Hey. It's Connor from the party last night. Text me when you get this.

He didn't have to wait long for a reply, the phone buzzing on the counter as he filled two mugs with steaming hot black coffee.

Lily: Hi! How're you?

Connor: Good. Theo's gonna kill me. I think he's coming down with something.

Lily: You're probably right on both counts. I'll text him. Subtly lol

As Connor neared the top of the staircase, Theo's raised voice filtered down the hall. He paused outside the door, uncertain whether to give him privacy or reenter the room.

"I'm not lying! I feel like shit, mom... You're kidding, right? You really think— Oh, for Christ's sake!"

Connor considered knocking, but juggling the two mugs made it impossible, so he crept through the gap in the doorway as quietly as he could.

"Whatever... No, I won't watch my tone! You— Okay, thanks for nothing." Theo tossed his phone on the foot of the bed, wiping tears of frustration from his eyes with the corner of the comforter. "She hung up on me."

"I'm sorry, Theo. How can I help?" Connor padded through the room, extending the mug of coffee as he drew closer.

"I don't want to go tonight. I just want to sleep," Theo mumbled, trying to regain his composure as he cradled the mug in two hands. Connor's heart tied itself in knots over how morose he looked.

"If you aren't feeling well, you need the rest. I'm sure she'll understand."

"Yeah, not happening. She said I have to be there. Presidential order."

Connor didn't know what to say to that. His mom was the chicken soup and hovering type. The kind of mother who made demands he stay in bed at the slightest sign of a sniffle, not the type of mother who demands appearances at State Dinners to welcome foreign dignitaries. All he could do was offer his support, so he sat beside Theo on the edge of the bed, tucking him under his arm as Theo slumped against his side.

"I reckon we can head back to the White House in a bit. I have to help with the preparations for tonight. You can try to rest more, yeah?" Connor nuzzled Theo's hair, the curls tickling his nose.

Silence blanketed the room as they finished their coffee and packed their overnight bags, slipping through the quiet house and into the SUV hidden in the garage. The drive through the early morning traffic was just as silent. Connor's concern bloomed in his chest with each moment that passed.

··········

Much later in the day, as the sun sank lower on the horizon, Connor finally rejoined Theo. If it weren't for the dark circles under Theo's eyes, the greyish tint on his already pale skin, and the tight clench of his jaw, Connor would have been breathless with awe. The perfectly tailored dark emerald suit hugged Theo's lean frame, and the gold floral embroidery on the waistcoat underneath brought out the unique coloring of his hazel eyes. Theo was stunning, even in his exhausted state.

Connor wanted to run across the room and scoop Theo up in his arms to whisk him away, but he resorted to standing as close as he could without raising suspicion, murmuring quiet reassurances whenever he could. It would be a painfully long night, especially for Theo. Anna and Toby seemed to sense the tension in the air, flanking Theo with a level of diligence that would rival any of the Secret Service agents stationed around the room. Toby's cobalt blue suit complemented Anna's baby blue dress. Were it not for the terse expressions on their faces, they'd look like little porcelain dolls.

The evening dragged on and on, from press lines to dinner, music, and mingling, the younger First Children disappearing sometime between the meal and the dancing. The Chancellor of Germany's visit was a big deal, but neither he nor Theo cared about that, their eyes finding one another as often as they could. Every time Connor caught a glimpse of Theo trying to sneak away or sit down, President Montgomery appeared with another introduction, press photographer, or acquaintance. The exhaustion radiated off Theo in waves, visible in every flickering smile and feeble handshake. Connor's worry skyrocketed, his eyes tracking every movement on high alert.

That was how he managed to jump into action as soon as Theo's knees buckled, swooping in to catch him before he could fall to the floor. The motion was so instantaneous that Connor could use the momentum to escort Theo to the nearest exit, if it could even be called escorting, given that he held up most of Theo's body weight. Connor cringed as he caught the flash of cameras nearby, speeding up to escape the eyes of the crowded room. Fellow agents, trained to respond in times of crisis, appeared out of nowhere, easing Connor's escape route and shutting the door behind them as Theo's body finally gave out.

"Medical to the Lincoln room. Whisper down." Mitchell's familiar voice broke through the chaos in stereo from behind Connor and over the radio. Connor fell back into his bare-bones combat triage training, loosening the collar of Theo's shirt to check his pulse. The rapid-fire staccato of the elevated pulse was stark in contrast to Theo's shallow, patternless breaths. He'd seen action overseas, but never had Connor been this close to panicking during a medical emergency.

"Make room, make room!" A pair of emergency responders that had been on standby in the medical unit for additional coverage of the evening's events strode into the hallway, the circle of agents standing guard parting to allow them access. Connor shimmied out of the way but refused to put any distance between himself and Theo. The chatter over his earpiece was infuriating, and the paramedics moved too slowly. He wanted to shake them, to beg and plead for them to help, but somehow managed to keep himself restrained.

A hand on his shoulder dragged his attention away. James stood behind him, leaning in closer as he squeezed his hand on Connor's shoulder.

"When they have to transport, you stay with him. Miss Ward is en route. She'll go with you. She's the primary medical contact on his file and on the clock tonight."

"Anderson to Med One, standby for transport." Connor's heart sank as the paramedic spoke into his radio, his partner attaching an oxygen mask to Theo's face with practiced ease. So far, the agents had managed to keep the crowd mostly at bay, but people started filtering into the hallway in dribs and drabs. Connor wanted to throw himself over Theo's body, desperate to hide him from the prying eyes. He hadn't moved since he hit the floor, the lifeless sprawl of his limbs turning Connor more and more inside out with every passing second.

Movement caught Connor's eye as another medical responder jogged toward them with a stretcher, Lily keeping pace beside him in her white coat with a tablet and handful of files clutched to her chest. Connor was never more thrilled to see someone he barely knew. The paramedics efficiently transferred Theo's motionless body onto the stretcher. He felt the visceral tightness in his chest as they buckled the straps over Theo's torso and legs, whisking him away as soon as he was secured. Connor grabbed Lily's elbow as he followed them, trying to translate their back-and-forth medical jargon.

"Lil, what's going on?" Connor kept his voice quiet as they zipped through the halls toward the underground garage where the ambulance was waiting.

"His oxygen levels are low. Dangerously low."

"Well, no shit, he passed out." Connor's worry became evident in the inflection of his voice, and he grimaced at his harsh tone. His grumpy bear was wearing off on him. "Sorry, sorry. Is he going to be okay?"

"Connor, I don't know. We'll learn more at the hospital." Lily squeezed his forearm before climbing into the passenger seat in the front of the ambulance, pulling out her cell phone as it rang. "Yes, this is Dr. Lilien Ward. I'm with the patient en route. I have his medical history. Male, age twenty-two, with severe asthma. I'm sending his medication information now."

Connor lost track of her conversation as he squeezed into the back of the ambulance, trying to stay close but simultaneously out of the way as the sirens wailed and the vehicle sped out of the parking garage. The paramedics continued to converse in a back-and-forth volley of words that Connor had a hard time following. Combat field medicine and emergency transport lingo didn't share many similarities.

"Shit. I keep blowing the veins. Anderson, switch."

Watching the medical responders work together was like watching a choreographed dance as they swapped seats in the back of the speeding ambulance. The paramedic, named Anderson, retrieved a fresh IV kit, reaching over Theo's body to grab his other arm. Connor found himself subconsciously leaning forward to concentrate alongside the paramedic. He felt relief on a physical level as the man placed the IV on his third attempt and hooked up a bag of fluids, leaning back to take another reading on the pulse oximeter clipped around Theo's limp finger. Both of Theo's forearms were already blossoming with angry bruising from the failed attempts. The emergency responder radioed in the information as the ambulance pulled into the hospital, driving around to a smaller entrance beside the emergency room.

Connor jumped from the back of the ambulance as soon as the doors opened, a flurry of nurses and attendants waiting as the stretcher came out next. A black SUV pulled alongside them, the tires chirping on the asphalt. Two more of his fellow agents joined the group, the entire ensemble swiftly jogging into the private entrance. So many words flew back and forth as paramedics updated doctors and Lily consulted with nurses. Connor, who prided himself on his level head in emergencies, was overwhelmed.

Once they reached their destination, the stretcher that carried Theo was wheeled into a room, a hand landing on the center of his chest as he tried to follow. The young nurse glared up at him, firmly planting her feet as Connor tried to push past her.

"No, you stay out here."

"He's the Presi—"

"President's son. I'm aware. You stay outside the door."

Connor opened his mouth to protest, but all he could manage was an anguished sound. The nurse's face softened a fraction, the expression so fleeting he almost missed it.

"Sir, it's your job to protect him from physical danger. It's our job to save his life. Stay here, and let us do that."

All he could do was watch as the nurse went into the room and shut the door behind her. Connor had never felt so helpless in his life. He sagged against the wall, his forehead pressed to the cold surface, and exhaled a breath that sounded dangerously close to a sob.

CHAPTER NINETEEN

Adelaide

FLOATING ADRIFT IN A sea of silk dresses and dark tuxedos, Adelaide desperately searched for anyone who could tell her what was happening. Still, everywhere she turned, more people vied for her attention. Like a pinball machine, everything felt too loud, too bright, and too chaotic. When she finally found a familiar face, she latched on to his arm, excusing herself as she moved through the crowd with the man in tow.

"Aaron, thank God you're here. I don't know where my son went." She kept her voice low, the perpetual smile plastered on her face a mask she'd learned to wear early in her political career. "I'm sorry to pull you away, but I need you to find Agent James Locke. I don't know what's going on or where he is."

"Theodore? I saw the agents pulling him out of the room not long ago. Everyone was gossiping as they do." Aaron's smile was likewise a thing of practice as he nodded and raised his glass of champagne in greeting to passersby and acquaintances.

"What did you hear?" Adelaide kept moving through the guests, a meandering path to nowhere to avoid being stopped again. She held up an index finger as the German Chancellor beckoned her from his seat. She was a terrible host for her first State Dinner.

"Gossip. Purely speculation, I am sure. Let me find your agent and bring him. We'll figure it out." He leaned in and brushed his lips over her cheek, which would have seemed out of place were it not for the fact that she'd had dozens of men do the same thing throughout the night.

They parted ways, the crowds swallowing Aaron's figure as she returned to her guest of honor. He'd been a needy guest all evening long. Still, she had a duty as the evening's host, and that duty was to ensure the leader of Europe's largest economy and the third largest exporter of the globe was entertained. In truth, she was barely paying attention to his terrible jokes. Bordering on tactless and tone-deaf, his gregarious personality was loud and abrasive, but he'd at least honored her request to leave the politics till their scheduled meetings tomorrow. Nevertheless, she indulged yet another attempt at stand-up comedy, giggling on cue so he wasn't left laughing at his own jokes like a fool.

"I hear it was your son who is drunk tonight. My lady love tells me she see him dragged from this room. Too much champagne?" Christof Bahrenburg guffawed before toasting nothing at all with a raised glass. "It is because you pick a Frenchman for his father with that name. Not strong like German men."

"Actually, the last name was mine, Chancellor, dear. Surely you are not calling the ancestors of the President of the United States weak?"

"Ha! Never, pretty girl. You know I like my jokes, always my jokes," he retorted, leaning closer before he continued. "It is a shame you can not find strong German man to teach your children to behave."

Adelaide chose the high ground and ignored the comment, glancing over her shoulder to search the shifting bodies for any signs of Aaron and James. Relief brought a genuine smile to her face as she saw the pair striding toward her.

"Oh ho, so many friend tonight. Introduce me!" The Chancellor was persistent, she had to give him that much.

"This is Senator Aaron Evans and Agent James Locke. Gentleman, allow me to introduce Chancellor Christof Bahrenburg." She paused long enough to let them shake hands before cutting in again. If Christof continued his jokes, she'd never have a chance to talk to James. "Please pardon us. Matters of state and all. No rest for the weary. I'll be back!"

The room was impossibly crowded, and she was becoming increasingly frustrated. They managed to find a secluded corner with the assistance of stoic agents who created a physical barrier to deter more needy guests from interrupting. If she were lucky, she'd have a few moments to get the report.

"Madam President, we didn't want to interfere or cause more of a scene. Theodore's been transported to Bethesda Naval Hospital. I have agents and a White House medical staff member with him." James angled himself to create a huddle with Adelaide and Aaron, who remained at her side. She was thankful for the presence, if only because it hid her gasp from eyesight.

"What do you mean? What happened?" She reached out to grasp Aaron's forearm before her knees gave out.

"I don't have a full status report, but it appears he lost consciousness due to low oxygen levels. They won't share the medical details with anyone not on the list. HIPAA laws." James rested his hand on Adelaide's shoulder, swirling his palm in a gentle circle. "I'm so sorry, Madam President."

"I have to go. I need to be there. Can you get me there?" The weight of her guilt crushed her. When he called this morning, she'd assumed he was just hungover and trying to get out of the appearance. He even looked hungover when he showed up at the residence that morning before locking himself in his room without a word.

"Addy, you can't leave the State Dinner." Aaron's words were a whisper in her ear as he shifted his arm to settle around her waist.

"Can't Andrew take over? Aaron, it's my son," she pleaded, her voice raspy on the edges.

"You can't leave the Chancellor of Germany with the Vice-President on the first diplomatic event of the presidency. Do you know what a nightmare that would cause?"

"Ma'am, is there someone else who can go in your stead? Senator Evans is right, not that it's my place to interfere with politics. Logistically speaking, we can't spread our security any thinner, and transporting you out of the White House requires an entire motorcade.

Her thoughts tornadoed, a whirl of chaos that she tried desperately to calm. Her son was in the hospital, and she was stuck in a room full of foreigners and the who's who of Washington, DC. Finally, inspiration stuck as she heard a familiar laugh amongst the revelers.

"Elias! Get Elias. Now."

"The Chief of Staff? Addy, are you sure that—" Aaron wasn't able to finish the sentence before she interrupted.

"He's one of Theo's emergency contacts. I made sure he was on the list."

James nodded, splitting from their huddle in search of his target. People were beginning to whisper and glance not so subtly toward where they stood behind the Secret Service agents. She feigned a smile. Time slowed to a crawl as she drowned in a living nightmare. Although she waited for Elias, it was Andrew who came forward instead.

"Adelaide, what's the issue? Christof is waiting, you still haven't spoken with most of the Congressmen, and we have many campaign supporters here," he murmured in a voice tinged with annoyance.

"It's Theo. He's in the hospi—"

"Every time something goes wrong, it's his name I hear first. We talked about this!" Andrew hissed.

"We're not doing this here, Andrew. Go to the supporters. I'll be done in a moment and handle the others."

Aaron's arm tightened almost imperceptibly around her waist. "She's right, Andrew. It's not the time. Unified front, remember?"

Adelaide fought against the suspicion she'd picked the wrong brother as her running mate, locking eyes on her Vice-President with an expression she hoped gave the appearance she would not broach the topic in the middle of a room full of delegates and socialites.

Andrew made a sound halfway between a scoff and a snort, shaking his head as he turned away from them. As soon as he was out of earshot, Aaron whispered in her ear. "I'll talk to him. Just keep your head on your shoulders."

She didn't have a chance to express her appreciation as Elias joined their impromptu meeting in the corner of the room, his eyebrows furrowed as he wove through the vigilant agents around them.

"Addy, the agent said you needed to speak with me on an urgent matter." Elias greeted Aaron with a slight nod before stepping into Adelaide's space.

"Elias, thank God! It's Theo. He's in the hospital."

"Wait, what happened? I just saw him earlier." Elias' voice rose with surprise, his eyes going wide.

"I don't know. I need you to go to him. I can't leave. Can you go?" Adelaide lowered her voice further in an attempt to get Elias to do the same.

"Of course, but I have to call a taxi. I've been drinking."

"One of my agents can take you, Sir." James beckoned with a swift gesture, already moving toward the nearest exit.

"Elias, call me as soon as you learn something." Adelaide's voice threatened to break. "Please?"

With a nod, Elias polished off the last of his champagne and jogged to catch up with James, setting his glass on a side table as he passed. She watched him leave, and another pang hit her heart. No matter what she did, she disappointed someone somewhere. She stole a brief moment to shut her eyes, breathing deeply to try and settle the swirl of emotions.

"Everything is going to be all right, Addy," Aaron murmured, his tone soft and reassuring.

"You can't say that because we don't know anything."

"You're right. I'm sorry. But we'll get it figured out. He's where he needs to be, and you are where you need to be. Shall we?" Holding his arm out, Aaron flashed a camera-ready smile. She curled her hand over his forearm with a murmured thanks. She didn't think she'd have the stamina to navigate the quagmire of the social gathering without someone to lean on. By the time they reached Christof's table, she had mustered enough of a poker face to resume her socially obligated duties as host.

"Madam Montgomery, you finally make time for your guest!" His laughter was too big for his lanky body. With all his sharp angles and contrasts, Christof looked as abrasive as he acted.

"When duty calls, we must answer, Chancellor. Such is the way for those of us in our positions." Adelaide donned her most convincing smile and prayed that it looked genuine, even if smiling was the last thing she wanted to do.

"Duty to country or family, Madam President?"

"Ah, ah, ah. We promised no politics at parties."

"He never listens. So stubborn." A willowy blonde, all pale skin and delicate features, sashayed around the table, kissing the air beside Adelaide's cheeks. Gisela, the Chancellor's fiancee, wore the most stunning evening gown Adelaide had ever seen, the jewel tones of the batik silk dark against the porcelain complexion. A flash of inferiority complex reared its head. Despite the price tag of Adelaide's emerald green velvet gown, a model she was not.

"Where are your babies? One minute here, and then they are gone," Gisela cocked her head to the side, and Adelaide couldn't help but envision an overeager cocker spaniel.

"Oh, resting. It's such a long night for children." Aiming for cavalier, Adelaide made a vague gesture with her free hand as though she weren't actively worrying about whether or not her child was all right.

"I am sure they miss their mother. I could never be away from my babies like this when we have them, isn't that right, Christof?"

"So right, my love. Children, they need their mother." The Chancellor shifted his position, propping an ankle atop the opposite knee. "Wouldn't you agree, Senator Evans?"

Aaron, to his credit, never let his smile waver. "I do, and I would go so far as to say they need more than just their mother. As the adage goes, it takes a community to raise a child."

The last thing Adelaide needed right now was a foreign dignitary calling her parenting choices into question. Dread and uncertainty sank deep into her bones, but she somehow found the strength to laugh at all the right spots, nod when needed, and add meaningless commentary to the conversation. Determined to put on a good show, she entertained her honorary guests. Anyone on the outside looking in would be none the wiser to the turmoil that consumed her as she balanced a delicate foreign relationship and her yearning to be doing anything but that.

CHAPTER TWENTY

Abriella

STACKS OF PAPER THREATENED to avalanche off Abriella's desk, tenuously held in place by Post-It notes and half-empty cups of coffee. Behind the chaos, two laptops stood at attention, their screens displaying a running feed of internet chatter with keywords pinging in the margins. With a heavy sigh, she sat back in the uncomfortable chair, pressing her fingertips to her eyes to ease the ache. Over the last week, ever since the State Dinner debacle, the backchannels and social media boards had grown increasingly active, and the more they talked, the easier it was to find connections and keywords.

Unfortunately, those threads all pointed to something increasingly worrisome. Murmurings of unease shifted into virtual shouts, death threats and calls for violence rising to an uproar. Between the articles in the newspapers and the theories from the gossip magazines, various groups on the FBI watchlists had loosely gathered under the same banner. That call to arms wanted everyone to take aim at the current administration, particularly Theodore Moreau. She got another alert on one of the laptops and reluctantly clicked on the notification.

While skimming the most recent posts on one of the more disturbing internet communities, Abriella's stomach flipped and churned. More vile threats of violence and graphic plans to kill the President's son skated over the screen as she slid her finger over the track pad. With another exhalation, she logged the latest usernames and sent them to the technical department for tracing. It would lead them nowhere, as all the other reported users had, but they had to be thorough. Jargon like VPNs, satellite redirects, and ghost computers was mysterious to her.

Still, she got the gist of the meaning behind how these groups were hiding their identities and locations.

Resigned, she closed both laptops and tried to make some sense of the papers before pulling out her personal cell phone. She needed a break from the darkness and depravity that was the viper's nest of the right-wing extremist community. She unlocked the screen and pulled up the text thread she had with Connor.

Abriella: How's he doing today?

The bouncing ellipses appeared on the screen mere seconds after she sent her message, and she turned away from the chaos of her desk to put space between her and the nightmare of what her work had thrust upon her.

Connor: Better. He's sleeping now. They'll send him home tomorrow if his O2 levels stay stable overnight.

Abriella: And how are YOU feeling?

Connor: Still fine. They want me to stay on the full course of the antibiotics though.

Abriella: That's what you get for fooling around with the First Son.

Connor: Worth it. ;)

A bubble of laughter erupted from her lips before she could stifle it. Despite everything going on, he still had a sense of humor. Abriella, on the other hand, became increasingly tense and paranoid the further she got into investigating the threats. Shadows started looking like ghosts everywhere, so she couldn't help her suspicion over the vast difference between Theo's reaction to the MRSA bacterial pneumonia and Connor's. Theo had been hospitalized for a week after nearly dying. Connor barely registered a low-grade fever three days after Theo was admitted. And no one else at the party the night before Theo's hospitalization had any symptoms or detectable bacteria load at all.

Her logical brain could write it off as a result of the preexisting condition Theo had, but the part of her brain determined to make connections and find answers was convinced that something was amiss. The paranoid side of her brain was also to blame for the way she nearly jumped out of her seat when she heard a knock on the corner of her desk. She spun around in the chair, only to come face to face with Tristan.

"We should leave now if we want to make it through the traffic and get to the meeting on time." Tristan's stack of tidy files irritated her when she compared it to the disarray on her desk.

"Si, yes. We can discuss the report for the President in the car." Abriella stood slowly, wiggling into her suit jacket before collecting the most important papers from her desk and tucking them into a manilla envelope. At least if they had work to discuss in the car, they'd be less likely to bicker.

....

After nearly an hour, between the traffic and waiting outside the Oval Office, they were finally seated across from Adelaide Montgomery. Abriella was on high alert as she waited for Tristan to start talking. He'd demanded that he take the lead in discussing their latest developments with the President. While she hadn't wanted to yield, she eventually gave in, worried over how much of a disaster it would turn into. Tristan was hardly a master of social skills.

"Madam President, thank you for your time. We'll try to make this brief." Tristan cleared his throat before rifling through the topmost folder. "I understand you've been staying up to date on our daily briefings as well as the DHS reports, but we'd like to discuss the finer points and ask for your insight."

"Of course, and thank you both again." Adelaide looked like exhaustion personified but still managed to keep her expression pleasant yet unrevealing.

"Aside from the elevated security threat, we've narrowed down several groups to continue monitoring. Have you seen that list?" Tristan's eyes briefly lifted from the stack of paper, the icy silver blue color giving Abriella chills. Likely, she needed to see a professional about her paranoia issues.

"Yes, but I'll take a copy of your list for my records. If I understand correctly, this is predominantly inspired by rhetoric from the Neo-Nazi groups?"

"That is the most likely source, correct. We've yet to identify the leader." Tristan held out the sheet of paper.

"The right-wing supporters of the movement refer to him as the Son of the Wolf. Is that something that sounds familiar on a personal level?" Abriella cut in, resulting in a withering look from Tristan.

"No, it doesn't. And you have nothing to go on?" Adelaide skimmed over the list in her hand before setting it face-down on the couch beside her.

"No, but I did want to discuss something I unearthed recently. I didn't include it in the written reports as a matter of discretion." Tristan's fingertips leafed through the papers in a second folder, producing a police report and mugshot that Abriella had never seen before. She sat up straighter, trying to keep the puzzled expression from her face.

"Are you familiar with this man?" He held out the paper for Adelaide to read.

"I..." For the first time ever, Adelaide looked shaken, albeit only briefly, before she resumed her unrevealing expression. "I wouldn't say familiar, no. I've met him once or twice."

"In what capacity?" Tristan asked as Abriella tried to glance at the paper, but he tucked it back into the folder so quickly she couldn't see anything.

"He and my son dated very briefly a couple of years ago. It wasn't a serious relationship. Why?"

"Some of our specialists have identified his IP address on one of the channels in question, and I am concerned that he might still be in contact with your son." Tristan paused, letting the silence hang heavy in the air with an expressionless gaze.

"What leads you to believe that?" Adelaide's voice carried an edge of wariness.

"The personal nature of the information being disseminated on the various message boards is recent, and the likely source is someone within your circle. This is, so far, the only personal connection we've been able to find."

Abriella clenched her teeth, her fingertips going white around the edges with how hard she was grasping her envelope of paperwork. Tristan hadn't shared any of this information with her. She hadn't seen anything in the reports from the technical specialists. She didn't even know who they were talking about. Every time she had pored over the evidence, she could find not a single connection, and none of their searching of Theodore's communication devices had resulted in contacts outside the people closest to him.

"Thank you for the update, agents." Adelaide abruptly stood, gathering the papers from the couch and hugging them against her chest. The dismissal in her motions was evident.

"Of course, Madam President. We will schedule another meeting if we discover any more information." Tristan gave a crisp nod before turning toward the door, leaving Abriella to follow him.

She caught up to him in the hallway, the West Wing a hive of busy clerks and assistants chasing after government officials. She snapped her hand out to grab the sleeve of Tristan's suit jacket before he could continue any further.

"Williams, what the hell was that?" she barked, trying to keep her voice quiet.

"That was me doing my job." Tristan slowly turned his eyes toward her, his eyebrow rising incrementally.

"None of what you just said is substantiated, or it would have made it into the daily briefings. We would have heard something. We'd have a suspect. So again... What. The. Hell. Was. That?"

"The IP address came across my desk yesterday. I recognized the name from Theodore's background check. The one we had to run months ago. If your head were in the right place, you'd have found the connection too." The challenge in Tristan's voice inflamed her temper.

"That's bullshit, and you know it. One instance of an IP on a public website matched to a relationship from years ago does not a suspect make. It's barely even credible, let alone actionable." She had never been good at volume modulation, so her words echoed off the walls, earning them a few sidelong glances.

"That's your opinion, but mine is that we have a link, and the President needed to know it. Especially if the insider is her son." Tristan shrugged her hand off his sleeve with a jerky motion.

"You made a huge accusation against her child to her face with zero evidence. Have you lost your mind? Did you clear this with the Director?"

"I did not. We're running an active investigation on credible threats, and with you taking point, we aren't getting anywhere. I know you live inside O'Brien's ass, and Theo's right there with you." Tristan's index finger jabbed Abriella's shoulder. "You're the one who is compromised, so you'll have to forgive me for picking up the slack."

"Oh, fuck you, Tristan! You know Theo didn't do this as well as I do. Nothing, absolutely NOTHING, points to him!" Abriella slapped Tristan's hand away. "Don't you dare accuse me of not doing my job right. Don't you dare."

Tristan was about to respond. His eyes narrowed in thinly veiled anger when a pair of Secret Service agents appeared on either side of their argument.

"Everything all right here, Agents?" James, the agent Abriella remembered from the various meetings they'd sat in on, flicked his eyes back and forth between the two of them.

"This is the last straw, Williams. You fucked up and went off the book, and you know it. When we get back, I'm putting in your transfer papers. I'm done with you," Abriella uttered the words through clenched teeth.

"I was wondering when you'd pull that crap. You've hated me for no reason since the day we partnered up." Tristan's smirk inspired thoughts of violence in her.

"No reason? Ha! I haven't liked you since you talked all that diversity hire bullshit on the firing range with your little groupies, pendejo. I should have reported you then. But I didn't. My mistake." Abriella made a shooing motion with the manilla folder in her hand. "Now get the fuck out of my face. I'll get a taxi back to the office."

It was apparent when the realization hit Tristan, his typically passive expression shifting into a slack-jawed look of surprise. Abriella seethed, her shoulders tight and her teeth gritting almost painfully. The pair of Secret Service agents looked just as tense, their bodies poised to intervene at any moment.

"Mitchell, walk Agent Williams out." James' voice was even-toned and quiet. Tristan remained blissfully silent, handing her the folders before he turned and walked down the hall, the second Secret Service agent walking beside him. James' posture relaxed once they were out of sight.

"Everything all right, Agent Garcia?" James beckoned her to follow with a slight jerk of his head, leading her down a different hallway. She appreciated the effort, even if it was a self-serving one meant to avoid further conflict.

"Yes, I apologize for the disruption," she replied, trying to regain her composure by smoothing her hand over her blouse. Rattled and still fuming, she landed short of composed.

"It happens. We've all been there. My ex-wife served me the divorce papers in the East Wing a couple years back. Had to call the maintenance guys in to fix the dent I left in the plaster." James flashed a smile that could almost be called sheepish. "I'll give you a ride to the office. I'm off soon and live out that way."

Abriella murmured her appreciation as they navigated the halls and exited into the parking area, maneuvering through the sea of black SUVs. James' vehicle was meticulously clean inside, but Abriella noticed a photograph sticking out from under the sun visor. A young girl, no older than sixteen. The family resemblance was easy to see.

"Your daughter?"

"Yes, that's my Jessie."

"She looks just like you." Abriella was glad for the distraction of small talk. "Does she live here in DC?"

"Minnesota. Minneapolis, specifically." He plucked the picture from the visor and handed it to Abriella. "She's a good girl. Straight As, active in all sorts of sports."

Abriella took a closer look at the picture, which turned out to be printed on regular copy paper. The pixelated image was less detailed up close, but the resemblance between James and her was still evident. She handed the paper back with a soft smile. "You must be so proud."

He nodded, carefully tucking it back under the visor before starting the car. Once they were on the road, the small talk died out. Abriella took the opportunity to pull her phone out of her jacket pocket. She had a new text notification.

Connor: Miss your face. Dinner at my place soon?

Abriella: SI! I demand BBQ

Connor: *thumbs up*

Abriella: Are you two at discussing the exes status?

Connor: That subject change gave me whiplash. Good thing I'm already at the hospital.

Abriella: hahaha funny. Y or N?

Connor: Y, why?

Abriella: Deets plz

Connor: You're being weird.

Abriella: It's my duty as honorary sister to make sure there is no dangerous baggage.

Connor: Nope. All good.

Abriella: You sure sure?

Connor: Yeah. No contact. Clean break. We're good. Stop being weird.

Abriella: Never. I worry because I care.

Connor: You worry because you watch weird true crime shows and work for the FBI

Abriella: Fair. Just be careful. ILY <3

Connor: Love you too Smalls

CHAPTER TWENTY-ONE

Theo

THEO NEVER THOUGHT HE'D consider the White House his home, nor did he think he would find himself in a position to be happy about returning there, but a week in the hospital had a way of changing his perspective.

Climbing out of the passenger seat of Connor's government-issue SUV was a struggle, every inch of his body aching and fatigued as if he'd run a marathon and not lain prone for the last seven days. Or was it eight? He spent so much of the last however many days unconscious that time had become an amorphous thing. Nevertheless, he was glad to be home. His muscles were weak and his hands shaky, partly from the seriousness of his brush with death and partly from the flood of steroids that the doctors had continually pumped through his system. Thankfully, Connor came around the front of the car and stepped in to lend Theo support.

"Straight to the residence, my Teddy?" Connor's voice was calm and soothing as he nuzzled Theo's hair and peppered his forehead with stolen kisses before they left the parking garage.

"Actually, mom said I had to come see her as soon as I got back." Theo leaned into the affectionate touches, reveling in the solidity of Connor's presence. "I guess that counts for something, yeah?"

Theo tried to mollify Connor's sudden peevishness with little kisses on his cheeks. He'd had some choice words about the lack of communication between Theo and President Mom during their stay in the hospital. Hours of unstructured time spent sharing personal stories revealed the closeness between Connor and his mother. Theo had even answered Connor's phone once while he was sleeping, resulting in an hour-long conversation with the southern belle in which they'd swapped email addresses and phone numbers to share recipes. Recalling the conversation gave Theo cautious optimism over the impending conversation with his mother as they made their way through the halls of the White House.

They didn't have to wait very long before the door to the Oval Office opened, which sparked a needling glimmer of hope in Theo's heart. Despite their penchant for arguing and disputes, Theo missed his mom. He'd missed her for a long time, if he were being honest with himself, but never more keenly than he had when he woke up scared and struggling to breathe in a hospital bed.

He wasn't expecting to walk into the room and find it full of other White House officials in addition to his mother. Connor stepped a fraction closer as Theo skimmed the familiar faces. The Vice-President stood beside his mother in front of the desk. Connor's boss and mentor, James, stood off to the side. Elias was there with an armload of folders, looking harried. Unsure what to do, Theo waved and looked back toward his mother.

"Hi, mom," he ventured, his voice cracking with the nerves inspired by the unexpected.

"Theo. I'm glad you're doing better." His mother gestured to one of the couches at the center of the room. "Come sit."

Doing as President Mom told him, he glanced back at Elias with a questioning expression, to which he received only an uncertain shrug.

"Theodore, I have some questions for you." She sat across from him and folded her hands on her lap. The hairs on the back of Theo's neck stood up.

"Is everything okay, mom?"

"Have you been in contact with Timothy Wilkes?"

"Wh— You mean Taz? No, of course not." Theo's brow furrowed, the question about his ex-boyfriend coming out of left field.

"Have you been in contact with any reporters or individuals outside our contact list?"

"No. I have some clients I work with, but you know who they are. What is this about?"

"I wish I could believe you." Adelaide's voice wavered for a moment before she sat up straighter. "They tracked one of the photographs leaked to the press back to your computer, Theodore."

Theo's heart rate began to climb. "What the hell are you talking about?"

"Watch your tone when you are addressing the President of the United States, son." Andrew quipped in an icy tone from nearby.

"No, seriously, what the hell are you talking about? Why the hell would I do that?"

"I don't know, Theodore. I was hoping you could explain it to us."

Elias stepped forward, holding up his hand. "Addy, just a second, where is this coming from?"

"Not now, Elias." Adelaide gave him a warning glare before turning her eyes back toward Theo, still waiting for an answer to a question that made no sense to him.

"Mom, I wouldn't do that. I have no reason to do that. I'm the last person who would do that. Hell, half the time they post anything, it's about ME!" Theo punctuated the last word with a sweep of his hand, the sleeve of his sweatshirt falling to reveal the bruising left behind from countless rounds of IV antibiotics, fluids, and steroids.

"We also discovered a connection between Wilkes and the groups starting the protests and riots. I cannot ignore the similarities between your recent behavior and when you and he were together." Adelaide's face grew stony. Her lips pressed together in a flat line.

"None of this makes sense! None of this. What are you talking about?" The rising anxiety made it impossible for Theo to sit still. He jumped to his feet, Connor appearing beside him with a steadying hand as he listed from the sudden dizziness of standing too quickly.

"You've become angrier, more erratic, resentful, and you're influencing Anna and Toby with your attitude." Adelaide rose to her feet in turn, her gaze unrevealing and locked on Theo's stunned expression.

"And you think that's because I'm suddenly secretly conspiring with my shitty ex-boyfriend to, what exactly? Make my own life hell?"

"We all know you don't want to be here, son. I think maybe it's time we all listened. You can stop the temper tantrum before more people get hurt." Andrew folded his arms over his chest, looking almost smug. Theo wanted to punch him right in the jaw.

"Mom, this is ridiculous! You can't actually believe this shit." Theo turned back to his mother, eyes pleading. "I wouldn't do this, mom. I wouldn't."

"Andrew is right. You told me you didn't want to come here, but I forced your hand for the kids. I didn't realize you would stoop so low to try and ruin everything we've worked for." She shook her head, pushing the hair back from her face with a shaking hand. "What do you want, Theo?"

"Want? All I've ever wanted is you! That's it! I just wanted a normal family, a normal life, and my mom! But I would never, NEVER do something like this." Theo's voice rose, the pain in his chest growing with the rising intensity of his emotions.

"I have done everything for you. For them. Everything! How dare you!" Her temper flared. The crushing realization that Theo was the only one who inspired her angry outbursts hit him.

"You've done everything BUT be our mother! And now you have the nerve to accuse me of conspiracy? Are you absolutely insane?"

"Don't you dare speak to me that way!" Adelaide stepped forward, the anger radiating off her posture.

"What? With the truth? You're pissed because you know it's true! Lawrence died, and you just fucked off to save the world and assumed I'd be there picking up the pieces at home like I always did!" Theo couldn't stop the flood of words falling from his lips. Over a decade of built-up resentment broke through the carefully constructed dam and came pouring out. "I was devastated when he died. You forget he was my father too! Closest I ever had to one. And you just checked out and left me at home with a six-year-old and a fucking baby while you campaigned to be the next hotshot DC darling!"

For a moment, time seemed to freeze as a flicker of hurt passed over his mother's face, and Theo's heart sank. His lips parted to apologize, the guilt swiftly rushing in to drown out the anger, but he didn't have a chance to utter a syllable of regret. Her hand whipped out and Theo was shocked by a sudden, sharp pain blossoming over his cheek as she slapped him across the face.

Chaos enveloped the room. Connor jerked Theo backward and positioned himself as a physical barrier between him and his mother. Elias' armful of files fell to the floor in a whirlwind of loose papers as he rushed forward. Theo thought he might have heard him shout his mother's name, but the blood rushing through his ears suspended him somewhere above reality. James reached out and dragged his mother farther away from where Theo stood in stunned silence, his hand shaking as he cupped his cheek in bewilderment. His mother started shouting again, and it took all of his willpower to hone in on the sound and absorb the words being said.

"—want you out! Get out! I don't care where you go, but get out!"

"Adelaide! Stop! Think about this!" Elias' voice cut through the noise as he reached out to touch her shoulder.

"No, I want him out!" Her angry glare turned back toward him, tears streaking down her face as she pointed toward the door. "You wanted out, so GET OUT!"

A hollow, empty feeling settled in Theo's core. He opened his lips to speak but closed them when nothing came out. Again, his lips parted. Again, they closed. He could think of nothing at all to say that would convey the depths of what he was feeling. He took a step back and then another one as the weight of everything his mother had just said threatened to bring him to his knees. He stumbled, turning toward the door to catch his fall before tearing it open and sprinting through it. Offices and hallways became an indistinct blur as he fled.

Arms appeared around his waist and chest, arresting his flight and inspiring his fight response. He writhed and twisted, but the arms around him tightened. Words filtered through the rushing of his pulse and the breathless, aching wheeze of his panting. A honey-smooth drawl whispered low in his ear.

"Teddy, baby. Theo, it's me. I've got you."

Theo fell backward against Connor's chest, his hands grasping at Connor's forearm where it lay across his chest. The strength in Connor's arms was the only thing holding him up as the tears came, hot and fast. He could barely breathe through the sobs that ravaged his aching chest, his already weary and battered body threatening to collapse were it not for Connor's steadfast presence holding him up.

"I've got you. I'm here." Connor's whispered words were a litany, a prayer, repeated over and over until Theo's sobs gradually subsided enough that he could speak.

"Why d-did... what d-do I..." Theo's words stopped short, his breathless stutter proving futile in communicating the rush of panicked thoughts in his head. He turned, bringing himself face-to-face with Connor before clinging to the fabric of his button-down. Connor wrapped his arms tighter around Theo's frame, his whispered words soothing him with the repetition.

Theo wept, even as James approached while clearing his throat. "Connor, take him upstairs, help him get his things. Get him somewhere safe. We'll figure it out, but get him somewhere safe. This'll blow over, but you need to help him out now."

"Yes, Sir. Thank you, Jim." Connor nodded, his chin nuzzling the hair of Theo's head as he did so.

"Of course, son. We'll figure it out." Theo felt a gentle hand squeeze his shoulder before footsteps retreated down the hall. He choked back another sob.

"I don't know where to go."

"You're coming with me. I've got you." Connor pressed a kiss to Theo's temple before shifting their position to head toward the residence.

Theo's tears flowed with renewed intensity with the realization that the kids weren't home and wouldn't be for hours. He wouldn't even have a chance to see them. His reality began to shift and distort like a Salvador Dali painting, and he was the subject. Disconnected, he floated somewhere above the real world, as if disembodied and watching himself go through the motions of stuffing clothing and toiletries in a backpack as Connor grabbed his laptop and personal effects.

He only snapped back to awareness as he emptied his nightstand. Sobs ripped through him, the pain in his chest excruciating as he pulled out the framed photograph of himself and his late stepfather. Eight years old and so full of joy, sharing cotton candy on a summer's day. It was all too much, too intense, too painful. He clutched the picture to his chest, a lifeline to keep him from drowning, as Connor pulled him to his feet and grabbed the bags before guiding him through the halls. Theo couldn't see through his tears, so he didn't get the chance to look back, for what might be the last time, at the place that had finally become home.

CHAPTER TWENTY-TWO

Connor

WHEN IMAGINING THE FIRST time he had a boyfriend move in with him, Connor had always thought the circumstance would be vastly different from the one he found himself currently in, but he wouldn't change it for anything.

The first few days were rough, not because they weren't compatible, but because of the shocking events in Theo's life. He spent the first twenty-four hours in bed. On the second day, Theo made it to the couch, where he binge-watched baking shows Connor had never seen. By day three, he started putting the pieces of himself back together, poking around the apartment and unpacking his bags. Slowly but surely, he picked himself up, and things only improved from there.

Early in the process of resurrecting himself, Theo got an email from his mother's assistant with paperwork. They thought it would be for the best if he turned down the protective detail usually afforded to the family of the President. Change of address forms for the health insurance were also attached. After discussing it with Elias, they decided it would be best if no one knew where he was, so they listed his address instead of Connor's one-bedroom in Logan Circle. The unfortunate side effect of these forms was that Connor had to return to the White House after they'd finally settled into a routine.

"Are you gonna be all right here all day?" Connor stabbed his fork into the Chinese food container with a vengeance, his worry growing as the night went on. Tomorrow was his first day away from the apartment since the day everything had imploded.

"I don't need a babysitter, Con. I'm a big boy." Theo clacked his chopsticks in the air before Connor's nose.

He bit at the chopsticks with a laugh before settling backward on the couch. "You know what I mean. It's been a lot. I reckon that has to stick with you."

"Yeah. I'm fine, really," he replied, returning his attention to his lo mein. "And I mean actually fine. Maybe it'll hit me eventually, but this is good. I'm good. Thanks again for letting me stay."

"Of course. I mean, I'd hoped eventually we'd get here. Maybe not quite so fast, but I reckon it all works out."

"If it's too fast or whatever, I could stay with Elias." Theo's eyes were locked on the carton of food, his shoulders slowly tensing as he squirmed on the couch.

"Teddy, baby. Look at me." Connor waited for eye contact before he continued. "Why wouldn't I be okay with my boyfriend moving in?"

Theo grinned, albeit shyly, his cheeks growing rosy. He didn't answer. He didn't need to. They finished their take-out in comfortable silence, the now-familiar British accents of the baking show a soothing background noise. Connor had put a moratorium on all news broadcasts. Theo didn't need to see the reports about the increased protests against the current administration's handling of domestic affairs. Eventually, the television screen asked them if they were still watching, signaling the end of the evening. Theo gathered up the empty cartons and beer bottles, stooping to kiss Connor's brow as he did so.

"Go. I'll be right in once I clean up."

"You better hurry, or I'll come looking." Connor swatted playfully at Theo's ass before disappearing into the bathroom, silently berating himself as he went. He'd been trying so hard to keep his hands to himself. Theo's emotional state had been vulnerable and shaky the first few days, and Connor was mindful to keep the topic of intimacy off the table. Theo didn't make it easy, not with the way he arrived at Connor's home, and seemed to fit as though he were always supposed to be there.

He brushed his teeth and washed his face, grinning over the two toothbrushes in the holder and Theo's collection of toiletries beside his on the vanity. It was so domestic, such a small thing, but it turned Connor's stomach to liquid. That cliché warm fuzzy feeling grew more intense when Theo joined him at the vanity, squeezing into the small space and smiling at Connor in the mirror as they got ready for bed.

Behave, behave, behave, Connor thought to himself as he finished up and slipped back into the bedroom, stripping down to his boxer briefs before sliding into the bed. He tried not to stare as Theo did the same. He failed, of course. In vain, he ran through a mental checklist of foolish things to distract himself from the image of Theo climbing into his bed nearly nude. He needed to grab milk tomorrow. Coffee, too. Maybe stuff for baking. He was almost successful in his endeavor until Theo slid in closer and draped himself over Connor's torso, their legs tangling together.

"Have I told you how much I love this?" Theo's voice was soft and husky, a muffled yawn tickling the hair on Connor's chest.

"I reckon it's prolly one of my favorite things about having you to myself, my Teddy." Connor gently carded his fingertips through Theo's hair, untangling the loose curls and gently massaging the nape of his neck.

"I never want to leave." Another yawn caused Theo's jaw to pop, and he laughed, a breathy sound that dusted over Connor's skin with a sensation that made him shiver.

"You ain't ever leaving. Got it?"

"Mm, good. I love— it. Here. With you." Theo buried his face against Connor's chest, squeezing his eyes shut. Connor's, meanwhile, had grown wide in the dim half-light of the streetlamps outside filtering through the small window. His chest ached with a smoldering warmth that felt too big for his body. They both pretended to sleep until sleep eventually came for Theo, leaving Connor with a tumbling tornado of thoughts and feelings he couldn't dare articulate. Exhaustion was the only thing that put him out of his misery.

Misery turned to torture the following morning as Connor woke to find himself spooning Theo's lean frame, their limbs still tangled together. The early light of dawn colored the room in a magical rose glow, Theo's soft sleep-patterned breathing the only sound disrupting the silence. It would have been peaceful were it not for the ache in Connor's groin. He went from drowsy to wide awake as he was struck with the sudden awareness of his erection pressed against the contour of Theo's ass nestled against his lap.

Cautiously, he tried to disentangle himself from their intimate embrace, but Theo stopped him, grabbing Connor's forearm where it crossed over his chest and rolling his hips even closer. Try as he might, he couldn't stifle the muffled groan that slipped from his lips. This was torture. Pure and simple torture. His breath caught in his throat as Theo rolled his hips again, a soft whimper escaping his lips as he did so.

"Don't go. Need you." Theo's voice was husky and quiet, still tinged with sleep in the early morning light.

"Jesus, Theo. You're gonna kill me." Connor spoke the words against the back of Theo's neck. The shiver that ran through Theo's body inspired him to trail a line of kisses and gentle nibbles along the sensitive skin behind Theo's ear.

"Need you, babe." Theo reached backward, his fingertips sliding over the back of Connor's head with a feather-light touch. The sensation caused a keening whine to escape Connor's throat, a sound that would have been embarrassing if he weren't already wholly undone.

"God, baby. You sure?" Connor instinctually responded to another roll of Theo's hips with one of his own, the friction simultaneously too much and not enough.

Theo whimpered again. It was the most delicious thing Connor'd ever heard, and he licked a long line up the side of Theo's neck as though he could eat the sound. "Yes, Con, please?"

"Nightstand."

Theo stretched, rummaging through the drawer, the vacancy left behind sending a shiver through Connor's body. Theo pressed a bottle of lube into Connor's hand before he rolled over, peppering kisses over the contours of Connor's face. It wasn't enough for him. He sought Theo's lips, morning breath be damned. Their lips parted, tongues dancing together as they squirmed and writhed under the tangle of the sheets to rid themselves of their boxers. Connor pushed Theo flat on his back, holding him in place with kisses meandering down his chest and stomach. The taut musculature of Theo's lean frame became the canvas for Connor's tongue as he explored the body he'd desired for so long.

Pausing to squeeze some lube onto his fingers, Connor returned to Theo's body, his mouth continuing its descent as Theo's legs fell open. Need inflamed him, his lips closing around the head of Theo's cock as he slipped his slick fingertips lower, the swirling motion of fingers and tongue together bringing a cry to Theo's lips. He wanted to ravage the man squirming in his bed, desire coursing through every fiber of his body, but he forced himself to go slow, introducing a lube-slick finger into the tight confines of Theo's ass.

"God, fuck, babe, yes. Please, I need you!" Theo's hands flew to Connor's head, fingers combing through the short strands as he dug his heels into the bed, squirming all the while. Connor trembled with the restraint needed to pace himself. A second finger joined the first, Theo's groan driving him even wilder. He sucked Theo deeper into his mouth, cheeks hollowing as he glanced up over the length of Theo's torso. Theo looked unhinged, mouth agape and eyes sparkling with need.

"Condom?" Connor broke away from Theo's cock long enough to utter the single word before returning with renewed vigor, working a third finger into the tight clench of Theo's ass.

"Expired. I checked yesterday. Connor, please. I need you." Theo's back arched, his breath coming in shallow gasps as he scratched at Connor's shoulders. "Please, please, please. I need you now."

"You sure? My last test came back negative, but if y—"

"Same. Now shut up and fuck me."

Evidently, Theo was bossy in bed. It thrilled Connor on a primal level he didn't realize appealed to him so much. He grabbed the bottle of lube again, pulling his fingers from inside Theo's body to apply a prodigious amount of the substance to his length. Snapping the bottle closed, he tossed it aside before crawling up Theo's body like a predator advancing on his prey. Theo was a writhing mess beneath him, his limbs wrapping around Connor's body as they aligned. Connor captured Theo's lips in an impassioned kiss as he pressed the head of his cock against Theo's ass, breathing in his muffled groan.

Somehow, he managed to restrain himself, slowly easing his girth into the slick-hot rapture of Theo's ass. He broke their kiss, groaning low in his chest as he pressed his forehead to Theo's. "Jesus, baby. So good. You feel so good."

Theo gasped, his body rippling with a shiver. Incoherent mumbles fell from Theo's lips as he clung tighter. Connor could feel the sharp sensation of his nails pressed into the muscles of his shoulders as he finally, blissfully, sank the length of his cock into Theo's body. Stilling, he looped his arms under Theo's shoulders to hold him closer. "It's so good, baby. You feel amazing."

Another gasp precipitated a desperate whining sound as Theo writhed beneath him. Not only was he bossy, but apparently, he had a praise kink, too. Connor couldn't hold back any longer. Gradually, he pulled back before grinding in, his hips meeting the synchronized roll of Theo's. Painstaking movements built insidiously into a rhythm as instinct took over. Connor chased every move, their bodies growing slick with sweat and easing the fluid motions of hips meeting hips.

"Just like that, baby. Good Lord, Theo, yes... it's so good. You're so perfect." Connor's voice took on a feral, growling quality as he increased the pace of his thrusts, the elusive edge of orgasm taunting him.

"Connor, Connor, please... don't stop!" Theo's back arched as he tried to finagle his hand between their bodies. Pushing himself up with one hand, Connor swatted Theo's hand out of the way before grasping the velvet steel of Theo's cock in his fist. A new need overwhelmed Connor as he matched the pace of his fist with his hips. He was close but singularly focused on ensuring Theo came first.

"Please, baby. I need you to come for me." Connor's words were breathless and plaintive. "I'm so close, baby. Come for me. Let me feel you come."

Theo lasted only seconds longer. Every muscle in his body seized, the clench around Connor's cock nearly too much to handle. With a desperate cry, Theo's orgasm tore through his body, come spilling over Connor's knuckles and onto the span of Theo's stomach. A wanton groan broke free as Connor thrust harder, chasing the shuddering spasm of Theo's orgasm with his own. He continued to thrust, pursuing the liquid heat pooling deep inside Theo's body. With one final thrust, Connor collapsed, his arms bracketing Theo's head as he swept in for a kiss, their breathless panting making it a short one.

He flopped onto his side, pulling Theo against his chest as he rummaged around under the pillow. With a breathy laugh, Theo shook the inhaler before taking the medication, his limbs sprawled bonelessly over the mattress.

"Yeah, that took my breath away, too." Connor grinned, nuzzling Theo's sweat-damp hair.

"You're ridiculous," Theo groused, wiggling in closer to nestle tightly against Connor's body. "But yeah, that was fucking amazing."

"You're perfect." Connor's grin grew even wider as Theo shuddered against him. "I reckon you like that, eh?"

"Shh. No. Shut up." Theo, already flushed from their lovemaking, grew even rosier.

"Never. I like it."

"You're so ridiculous."

"I think you love it."

"Mm. I do." Theo stretched, just about to get more comfortable, when the clang of Connor's alarm shattered the euphoric bliss. Connor groaned.

"Have fun with that. I'm not getting up." Theo giggled, actually giggled, before nipping at Connor's collarbones. With a mutter, Connor pulled himself out of bed. He'd deny any accusation of swaggering into the bathroom.

CHAPTER TWENTY-THREE

Lily

LATE AGAIN, LILY BURST into the office of the White House medical unit, her bag clutched to her chest as she stopped to catch her breath and smooth her skirt. Dr. Desai laughed, pulling his glasses from the bridge of his nose as he shook his head.

"Lovely girl, how often must I tell you that a few minutes is not the end of the world? We are very relaxed here." He leaned over the desk, winking with a bright grin. "I won't tell your boss."

"Oh, Anand," she laughed with a roll of her eyes. "You are too precious for this world."

"So I have been told, lovely girl. Go, get yourself settled. We can go over more paperwork and read some of the journals."

Lily retreated into one of the back rooms she'd claimed as an office space, donning her white coat and taking a moment to neaten her frazzled appearance. She dug the plastic storage container from her bag and returned to the main office, but Dr. Desai wasn't alone when she got there.

"Connor? Er, Agent O'Brien, I mean." Lily smiled at the misstep, glancing toward Dr. Desai at the desk.

"Hey, Miss Ward. I reckon I need to bother you if you have a moment?" Connor straightened his suit jacket, although it appeared to be already straight, his weight shifting from one foot to the other before he flashed a smile that highlighted the dimples on his cheeks.

"Of course. Is everything all right?" Lily slid the container of cookies onto Dr. Desai's desk, earning her another wink and a brilliant grin. Mango shortbreads. One of his favorites.

"Just a bit under the weather, as it were. Can we?" With a nod, he indicated the door leading deeper into the medical ward.

They walked in silence toward one of the smaller examination rooms, Lily going through a mental checklist of the things she wanted to check. Connor had quarantined alongside Theo in the hospital. She worried the infection had returned, given how resistant this particular strain was to most traditional antibiotics. Once the door latched behind them, she went to the cabinet to grab her instruments.

"Sorry, Lil. I'm actually fine, I just wanted to talk to you private like and I reckoned this'd be the easiest way."

Cocking her head to the side, she turned to face him with a puzzled expression. "What do you mean?"

He beckoned her closer, away from the door, before answering in a whisper. "I didn't want to call. And I wanted privacy. Nothing more private than a medical room."

"Why, though?"

"Did you hear anything about why Theo had to move out?"

"Just gossip in the dining room downstairs. I texted Theo, but he hasn't answered. I assumed he was resting." She paused, arching her eyebrow. "As he should be, after all."

Connor stifled a chuckle, leaning back against the exam table with his arms loosely crossed over his chest. "Always so serious, Lil."

"What's this about?" Lily perched her hands on her hips, eyeing Connor up and down as he shifted into a more comfortable position.

"You ever been up to the residence?"

"You mean the upper floors? The president's home? No. We aren't allowed up there." Lily flapped her hand to the side in a vague gesture. "I tried to bring something for Theo once, and I thought the agent was going to shoot me. So I texted him, and we met up here."

"You sure?" Connor's expression was unrevealing, a true feat given how animated he generally was.

"Connor, why would I lie about that? I have never been there. I've barely been outside the medical unit, just to get lunch or dinner in the mess hall downstairs."

"Theo's a friend to you?"

"Yes, Connor. He's basically my only friend. What is this about?" She started to get stressed, her anxieties rising as the peculiar conversation continued.

"Full confidentiality, all right? We need to keep this between us." Connor's voice was even quieter than before. "Theo's staying with me, but we didn't tell anyone except Elias. They said he leaked one of the pictures to the press, which we know is bullshit."

Lily gasped, her eyes going wide.

"Sorry, I don't usually cuss. As soon as we got back to the apartment, he took his computer apart and everything. Like fully apart. There's pieces stuffed in all the drawers. He keeps his phone off most of the time. Even had me grab him a burner. He's sort of freaked, and it's freaking me out."

"Could it be some sort of virus? On the computer?" Lily's clinical brain went into diagnosis mode, trying to make sense of the things he said.

"I asked him what he thinks happened, and he just shrugged. I don't want to press, but something's not right. I was there in the room when she told him to leave. It's not adding up."

"Wait, she told him to leave? Everyone I heard gossiping about it said he left after he got out of the hospital. That he went somewhere to recover, some said rehab, but you know how the gossips are." She pulled her braided hair over her shoulder, fidgeting with the end as she tried to unravel the mystery.

"Yeah, I saw those articles in the newspapers, the rehab ones. I won't let him watch the news at home. He doesn't need more of that crap." Connor wiped his hand over his mouth, his typical smile replaced by the thin line of his lips pressed together. "He didn't leak any pictures, that's for sure. It's not like him. And it doesn't make any sense. His ma was right pissed, though, and told him to get out. It was a whole blow-up. Real ugly."

"Good God, what a nightmare..." She was stunned by the development, shaking her head slowly as it all processed. "Do you think...?"

He glanced up at her, brows bunching together.

"Do you think someone did it or that they're lying? Maybe not lying. Maybe false information?" Refusal to believe the worst had her latching on to anything.

"I don't know, Lil. I reckon I won't ever know, but something ain't adding up." Connor's shoulders were hunched, making his large frame seem much smaller. She stepped forward on impulse to hug him, not entirely surprised when he returned the affection.

"Is there anything I can do? I'm not FBI or CIA or some fancy acronym, but if there's anything I can do to help, you'll let me know?" She tightened her embrace for good measure before stepping back.

Connor's smile made a reappearance as he winked. "Now, now. You do have a fancy acronym, Miss Lilien Ward, MD."

She giggled, the sound almost too loud in the small room. His chuckle faded out with a soft sigh.

"Just try to keep an eye on things. Maybe you'll see something or hear something. I don't even know what to do, but two eyes are better'n one, I reckon."

She dipped her head, a halfway nod as they moved toward the door in unison. Connor stopped short in the hallway when the sound of conversation registered from the main office. With a squaring of his shoulders, Connor continued his progress, slipping through the door just ahead of Lily. Agent James Locke smiled, giving Connor a little salute that he returned in kind.

"You gonna be all right, son?" James turned his gaze toward Connor's face with a hopeful expression.

"Oh, sure, boss. Right as rain in a few days, I reckon."

Lily had to think quick. With a curt nod to Connor, she smoothed her white jacket and tried to look professional. "It's common with large doses of antibiotics like that, but I expect it'll clear in a few days if you get to rest and stick to a proper diet. Otherwise, as long as you pace yourself, you should be fine for work."

To his credit, Connor thought just as quickly on his feet as she did. "I'll try the yogurt trick. I never thought of it. Thank you, Dr. Ward."

James grimaced, a hissing sound of sympathy passing through his teeth. "Oof, that makes sense now. They had you pretty dosed up, son."

"Hazard of the job, I reckon!" Connor's southern boy charm was back in full force as he grinned, and Lily briefly wondered how much of his effusive demeanor was a facade. She tucked it away as a mental note for later study.

"And yes, thank you, Dr. Ward, for looking after our boys. Above and beyond the call of duty." James turned toward her, laying a hand on her shoulder with a subtle squeeze.

"She's my best. I would not be able to do this work without her." Dr. Desai stood behind the desk, coming around to position himself beside her with a delightful little chortle.

"She reminds me so much of my Jessie girl. Sweet and smart." James' soft grey eyes crinkled as he smiled.

Lily hated every second that passed while the attention was on her. Not sure what else to do in response, she gave a nod, readjusting the stethoscope to sit more evenly around her neck. Eventually, the two agents fell into stride together, heading for the door. Connor reached his arms backward in a motion that looked as though he were going to clasp his hands behind himself, but before he did, he formed a heart shape with his fingers and thumbs. Lily bit down hard on her lower lip to stifle the bubble of laughter that threatened to spill out.

Not even ten minutes later, she felt her phone vibrate in her pocket. Surprised, she pulled it out to check the screen, only to find a message from Connor there.

Connor: Dinner @ the same place tomorrow. 7 pm

Lily: Sounds good

Connor: Bring cake please ;)

Lily: lol of course <3

She smiled at the screen before tucking the phone back in her pocket. She liked this unexpected new circle of friends she'd suddenly stumbled into. It was foreign to her but exciting nevertheless. If she concentrated on that, she didn't have to think about the cryptic meeting she had with Connor. It was easier that way.

••••••••••

The following evening, she found herself on Elias' doorstep, the cold winter winds buffeting against her as she waited. She hadn't even thought twice when she rang the doorbell this time. Elias opened the door within moments, swiftly pulling her in from the inclement weather and pushing the door closed behind her, latching the lock and deadbolt in rapid succession.

"Lily, I'm glad you could make it. We're in the kitchen. Let me grab that for you." Although warm and genial, Elias carried an air of fatigue that had been absent the last time she had been invited to his home. He still wore the suit pants and button-down shirt she assumed he'd had on earlier at the office, though the tie, jacket, and shoes were missing, and the top two buttons were undone. She shed her winter boots and coat, the aesthetic of her pencil skirt and blouse oddly matching the business casual attire of her host.

In the kitchen, another example of Better Homes & Gardens awaited. Farmhouse table in the breakfast nook, a granite island with barstools that matched the chairs at the table, rich wooden cabinetry, and stainless steel appliances. She felt out of place. Everyone from the last gathering loosely assembled around the kitchen in similar states of dressed-down work attire, save for Theo. Perched on Connor's lap, he wore a USMC sweatshirt that looked like it was about to swallow him whole. Still thinner than he had been before his stay in the hospital, but with a healthier glow to his cheeks, the improvement in his condition brought a wave of relief to her.

"Theo, it's so good to see you!" Lily moved toward them, kissing Theo's cheek before stepping into a conversational arrangement around the island. "Abriella, Connor, Caleb. I'm happy to be here."

"Hey, Lil. Glad you could come." Connor reached around Theo to grab a bottle of beer off the table.

"Is there an occasion? You said I should bring cake. Please don't tell me I'm missing a birthday." Lily skated her eyes around the room.

Abriella laughed, a bright melodic sound as she padded toward the fridge on stockinged feet. "No, no birthday. Relax. Beer or wine?"

With another quick glance around the room, she noticed everyone was drinking from bottles of beer, that fact making up her mind for her. "Beer, if it's not a problem."

Abriella grabbed two before closing the fridge with her hip, popping the tops with a twist. She slid in beside Lily at the island, handing the beverage to her before clinking the tops together. Elias returned with a stack of pizza boxes, and Lily berated herself over missing the fact that he'd left the room in the first place. Caleb stepped out from the fringes of their group to help Elias with the pizzas. Quiet fell over the room as they tore into the boxes, mouths too full of sauce and cheese to converse. Like wolves on a kill, the feast was decimated in record time, with three whole pizzas disappearing to leave a pile of greasy plates and napkins in their place.

Caleb cleared the garbage off the island and brought the cake into view, swirling a knife in the air with a flashy whirl. "So, now that we're all here in one place, are we thinking mole, moles, rats, mice, some other type of dirty vermin? A snake in the grass? Murder in the White House? I know we aren't all here just to admire my new haircut. Even if it is amazing."

Theo's eyes shot toward Caleb as his jaw fell open. Lily's snapped to Connor with a look of surprise. Connor's gaze shifted toward Abriella, who was glancing everywhere at once as Elias pinched the bridge of his nose with a look that screamed 'too old for this shit.'

"Smooth, Cay. Ten out of ten for delivery." Elias plucked the knife out of Caleb's hand, occupying himself with cutting the cake.

"Eli did you... how could y—" Theo's words wavered as he shrunk into Connor's loose embrace.

"Bold of you to assume I would do that, Theo. Cay came to me with his suspicions. That's why I invited you all here tonight." Elias pushed the slices of cake across the island toward each of them, aromas of cinnamon, vanilla, and buttercream wafting up to replace the scent of pizza still lingering in the air. Pride swelled in Lily's chest as everyone fought over the silverware to dig into the treat she'd baked, even if her nerves were still fraught with tension. She had the vague sensation of feeling like a side character in a James Bond movie as their evening turned into an espionage thriller over dinner and dessert.

"What suspicions?" Abriella leaned her forearm on the island, tucking into her dessert as she stared ahead at Caleb.

"Well, it goes like this. I was in my delicious Armani with chinos, pretty much looking plain and basic, so no one was paying attention to little old me. I was off on my merry way to deliver some files to Miss President, and the secretary was gone, so I was just going to leave them inside the Oval Office, as one does." Caleb paused, whether to breathe or for dramatic effect, she wasn't sure. "But before I could do that, I heard these creepy whispers from the hallway. Being me, the smartest one in the room, I ducked under the secretary's desk because who doesn't love some good tea?"

"Cay, spit it out," Elias spoke with the patience of someone who had practice dealing with a small child. Lily tried to hide her grin behind a bite of cake.

"So bossy. I love it." Caleb fanned himself as he continued. "I listened from the desk as the creepy whispers came closer, and I heard some guy talking about how the plan had worked perfectly. Something about how if it went as they hoped, she'd be out by summer. Talking about Whisper being gone, Wombat and Wiggle or something on lock down."

"Wiggle and Willow," Connor interjected, his jaw flickering with visible tension.

"That's what I said. Don't interrupt." With a flourish of his hand, Caleb bowed. "Anyway, that's the story of how I became a superior spy and will be at your services to continue such work because, ew, the creepy whisper dude? Bad news bear, and it's really killing the vibe."

Silence fell on the room like a funeral pall as everyone looked from one person to another around the island. No one knew what to say. Lily wasn't sure if there was even anything that they could say. The air suddenly felt colder, and she impulsively inched toward Abriella beside her. It did little to ease the chill that crept up her spine.

CHAPTER TWENTY-FOUR

Elias

"YOU KNOW THE DEAL." Elias kept his voice quiet as he and Caleb traveled the short distance from the Chief of Staff's quarters to the Oval Office. "Do. Not. Choose. Violence."

"You offend me with your lack of confidence in my ability to be chill." Caleb flashed him one of his characteristic crooked smiles. "I'm wearing my chill pants today."

"You don't own chill pants. There's literally nothing about you that is chill, Cay."

"So, are you saying my pants are hot?" Elias felt the nudge of his shoulder, their height difference apparent in the act. "Compliment heard, boss man."

"I have so many regrets right now. Stay here. Stick to the plan." Elias stepped into the secretary's office outside the Oval Office, parting ways with Caleb and heading toward the door. "She's expecting me. I'm the three o'clock."

He only had to wait a moment after knocking before Adelaide called from within. Steeling himself, he pushed the door open and slipped inside, closing it behind himself before he took in the surroundings. So much cream and gold decor. Adelaide stood out like a sore thumb in the center, seated on one of the couches at the center in a black suit and blush-colored blouse.

"Elias, come sit," she murmured as she motioned toward the couch across from hers. Lunch sat abandoned on the table in between. What was with this family and not eating whenever they were stressed?

"How're you holding up, Addy?" Elias broke protocol and chose to sit beside the President instead of opposite. If they were going to have this talk, he needed them on even footing as they'd always been during the challenging discussions.

"Mm. Next question."

"Addy," he scolded in a tone remarkably like the one he used when Parker refused to eat his dinner.

Adelaide exhaled a long suffering sigh. "I'm making it work. It's been rough."

"Will you let me do my job, then? You've got such a bottleneck on everything. Surely there's something more I can be doing. And if not me, someone else. Anyone."

"You think I haven't thought of that? I can trust only so many with most of this, and I still have to make the final call. I trust you, I do. But I need you to focus on what I've already given you. And it just feels like everyone needs something all the time." She sank back into the cushions of the couch with a huff. "How's he doing?"

"Have you asked him that question yourself?" Elias countered, not wanting to play middleman in the Moreau-Montgomery family any more than he already was.

"That's not a fair question. He probably wouldn't answer anyway," she glowered, picking at invisible dust on her pant leg.

"You are going to have to be the one to make the first move this time. You know it as well as I do."

"Not this time. Not after what he did." Adelaide sat up, grabbing a file from the stack on the table in front of them. "Here's the proposal you sent the other night. I've signed and sealed it."

"Addy, stop." Elias took the file and set it out of the way before taking her hand in his. "Are you sure it was him? Where did you get the information?"

"I'm not doing this with you, Elias." She pulled her hand away with a sharp jerk. "I know you're trying to advocate, but I wouldn't have done what I'd done if the evidence wasn't credible."

"I think you need to look at this objectively. At least consider the possibility he's telling you the truth. Please?" Elias wasn't above begging, his voice taking on a pleading tone.

Adelaide hunched forward, her elbows landing on her knees and her head propped up in her hands. "Stop. Just stop. I can't discuss this with you, and there's nothing I can do about it now. He'll be happier with you. What's done is done, and I can't take it back. He can't change what he did, and I can't change what I did. Just drop it!"

Her shoulders quaked, a small sob escaping her lips before she shifted her hand to cover her mouth. Tentatively, Elias laid his hand between her shoulder blades. "Addy, it's never too late when it comes to family. Please, just think about it. Have someone else look into it. Do something. Anything."

With a nearly imperceptible nod, she straightened, wiping her hands over her cheeks as she recovered her composure in the remarkable way she'd always managed. Elias knew the depths of how intensely she felt things, having witnessed innumerable volatile or emotional moments over the years. Still, she always managed to dig deep and find a way to appear calm and in control.

"Does he hate me, Elias? Tell me the truth," she whispered, turning her face toward him. Despite her practiced mask, the heartbreak and devastation lingered just beneath the surface.

"You're his mother. You know him better than anyone. I think you know best the answer to that question."

Her lips parted as if to reply, but a sudden cacophony came from just beyond the door. Caleb's voice was distinctive, even through the barrier. Elias grabbed the file from beside himself before standing. He tried to smile at Adelaide, but the expression fell flat. "I believe my time is up."

No sooner had he said the words than someone knocked on the door. She sighed again, a weighted sound, before calling out to invite whoever it was into the office. Elias was surprised to see Senator Aaron Evans. He wasn't surprised to see Caleb hot on his heels with a harried-looking Secret Service agent following close behind.

"Sir, you need to wait outside. Sir!"

Elias realized after the fact it was the same agent from the night of the blow-up between Adelaide and Theo.

"He's with me, Agent Locke. We were just on our way out." Elias moved through the room, resting a hand on Caleb's shoulder.

"Yes, and I was having a riveting discussion with the Majority Leader about his recent success on the Senate floor. So bipartisan. And dressed so well!" Caleb patted Aaron's arm with a mischievous smile. Elias was ninety-nine percent positive he saw the Senator's eye twitch.

"Give me a call soon, Addy. We'll talk more." Elias waved with the folder in his hand, turning Caleb toward the door as he fluttered his fingertips over his shoulder.

"Bye, Miss President! Lovely blouse! And see you soon, Mr. Senator! We should totally grab coffee!"

Agent Locke took up the rear, more or less escorting them from the Oval Office before closing the door. "I'll walk with you, gentlemen. Fornell, take the door."

The younger agent nodded and stepped into position, his hands loosely clutching the lapels of his jacket as he assumed guard duty outside the office. As the trio stepped into the hallway of the West Wing, James moved to walk abreast with them.

"How's the kid doing, Mr. Williams?" James glanced over Caleb's head at Elias as they made their way back to the offices of the Chief of Staff.

"He's fine. Doing well, all things considered."

Caleb, thankfully silent, glanced swiftly between Elias and James before busying himself with the government-issue phone in his hands. He suspected he wasn't actually handling the mountain of emails their office fielded every day.

"Good, good. I'm glad to hear it. He was pretty wrecked the other day, but I know you two are close, so he's in a good place." James flashed a smile toward him, his stride slowing as they neared the door to the office suite.

"You could say that. Anything else I can help you with today? Mr. Cohen and I need to get back to this." Elias waved the folder back and forth while nodding toward the door.

"No, just wanted to check on Theo. I know how rough it is when kids fight with their parents. Can't help but feel a little paternal about the whole thing." James nodded to Elias and Caleb in succession before stepping out of the way. "Enjoy the rest of your afternoon, gentlemen. And give my regards to the First Son."

Elias and Caleb stood frozen in place as the agent traced his steps back down the hall. Once he turned a corner, they continued past the office door and made the loop around the perimeter of the West Wing, Elias mindful to keep his longer stride in check to keep pace with Caleb's.

"Okay, so did she spill the tea? Who are we looking at?" Caleb stooped over the folder in Elias' hand, their huddle giving any passersby the impression they were in deep discussion over the paperwork within as they walked together.

"Nothing. She's still being stubborn about the whole thing. Which doesn't make sense."

"Unless they're actively investigating. I know you planned to ask her to think objectively. I'm going to ask you to do the same. Is there a chance he might have done it? Devil's advocate; maybe I heard about an office pool or something unrelated." For all his flashy persona and constant humor, when Caleb was serious, he became even more intimidating.

"I'm going to stop you there because you don't know Theo as I do."

"I know he's like your weird cousin-brother-son without the incest, but we must consider all the angles here, El." Caleb's eyebrows rose as he gave Elias a somber look.

"Even outside the family situation, also please never say that again, he's too smart to get caught doing something as stupid as sending incriminating evidence from his own laptop. I'm not kidding when I say he's got computer skills I can't even comprehend, let alone put into words." Elias lowered his voice even farther as they rounded another corner and continued their circuit of the hallways.

"So theoretically, if he were going to start a riot in the press, he wouldn't use his own computer. Do we think one of the other kids could?"

"Think about what you just said. Just for two seconds."

"I mean, it sounds insane, I know that. We need to keep an open mind here, El. This is a massive clusterfuck we're poking at here. I want to protect our asses."

"Fair. And appreciated. But I think we can rule out the kids." Elias sidestepped into another hallway as they changed course in their circle of the West Wing. "Which leaves the scarier option of someone working against them from the inside."

"Which is a whole shit show I'm not sure we're equipped to deal with. Who are we thinking?"

"I don't know, Cay. It seems unfathomable to me. Entirely." Elias pinched the bridge of his nose with a sigh.

They grew quiet as they passed through a busier section of the corridors, but once they were free again, Caleb nudged Elias' shoulder with his own. "Weird how the Speaker of the House showed up right after us. Weird connection, that. What with the VP and all."

"Fair point. Aaron and Andrew are an interesting pair. Remind me to tell you about the campaign trail when we aren't here." Elias grinned down at Caleb beside him. "Drinks at Loco's? We can cut out early and conspire over margaritas before I have to get home to relieve the babysitter."

"Mm mm mm, girl. You are speaking my language." Caleb's crooked smile was brighter at the mention of margaritas, even if they were planning their rendezvous to discuss the potential for a political conspiracy theory. Elias couldn't help but wonder if politics was the right career path for him in the end.

CHAPTER TWENTY-FIVE

Theo

HOT WATER COURSED OVER Theo's back, his already buzzing nerve endings overwhelmed by the flood of sensations running through him. Connor gazed up at him, his cheeks hollowed into dimples as he milked the last of Theo's climax from his overwrought body. Had he not just come, he'd be close again from the sight. They were insatiable. Theo had become an addict chasing a high, and Connor was just as voracious. If ever there was a silver lining to life falling apart at the seams, it was this.

Theo dragged Connor to his feet, diving in for a kiss as they switched spots under the shower head. He chased the taste of himself over Connor's tongue like a starved man, his hand shifting lower to clasp Connor's erection in a tight fist. Finding the right pace had become intuitive. He dropped to his knees, their gazes never parting as Theo took Connor into his mouth to revel in the salt-brine taste of precome before the sluicing water could wash it away. The sounds Connor made when Theo ran his tongue around the crown should be illegal for how deliciously pornographic they were.

Inspired, emboldened, and insatiable, Theo slipped his free hand between Connor's legs, gently cupping his balls and allowing the pads of his fingertips to pass with a featherlight touch deeper into the crevice of his ass. Though Connor's eyelids had slid partially shut, they swiftly snapped open as soon as Theo circled the tip of his index finger over the tight pucker.

"Can I?" Theo's words were breathless and soft as he pulled off long enough to voice the question before resuming his ministrations, tongue pressing firmly against the underside of Connor's cock as he sucked it deeper into his mouth.

"Yes. Yes, good Lord, yes, baby!"

The awestruck desperation in Connor's reply sent a shiver down the entirety of Theo's spine. He had thought Connor was loud before, but it couldn't hold a candle to the rising inflection of his open-mouthed groan as he gently slid a finger into his ass, the muscles clenching tight. Theo was on a mission and he knew, judging by the sounds coming from his boyfriend, that he didn't have long. The mission was inevitably a success. As soon as his fingertip passed over Connor's prostate, he felt Connor's hands fly to the back of his head, fists balling in his hair with an almost-too-tight grip that served only to incite Theo's dedication.

"Jesus. Fuck. Baby! Oh, God, don't stop!"

Connor lasted mere moments, the punch-drunk moan of his orgasm echoing through the tight confines of the bathroom. The vision of his boyfriend's eyes screwed tight during the crescendo of climax was one of Theo's favorite things, and the intensity of this particular orgasm had Theo truly convinced they'd both discovered a new obsession to fuel their sexual appetites.

Even showering afterward was an act of intimacy for them as they exchanged tender touches and shampooed one another's hair, stealing kisses and murmuring praises back and forth against the soundtrack of the water cascading over the tile. These quiet moments between the two were a salve, a balm, dulling the hurt, pain, and worry that was quick to return once Connor stepped through the door to head to work. The alarm Theo'd set cut their shared shower short. It was a necessary evil if Connor ever expected to be on time for work these days.

"When you retire, we're going to have an entire day spent in the shower at least once a week." Theo nibbled the line of Connor's collarbones as they rinsed the last of the soap from their skin before stepping out into the steamy bathroom.

Connor's smile was brilliant, his dimples on full display. "I reckon I like the sound of that, baby."

"Your shirt's on the back of the door. I pressed it yesterday. And I packed the leftovers for your lunch." Theo paused, his head tilting as he watched Connor run the towel over his legs.

"Is it bad that I love when you talk dirty to me like that, Teddy? Being all... domestic-like."

"You shut up. Now," Theo groused, tossing his towel at Connor's cheeky grin.

"Yes, my grumpy little shit."

"I can find a way to shut you up. Don't test me."

"Promises veiled as threats. I love it."

Laughing, Theo pushed Connor out of the way in search of clothing, throwing on a pair of boxer briefs and jeans before disappearing into the kitchen to make coffee. Today promised to be a long one. The coffee pot hissed and sputtered as the coffee brewed, allowing Theo's thoughts to wander. Hands wrapping around his waist startled him out of his stupor.

"Sorry, baby. I thought you heard me," Connor murmured as he brushed a kiss over Theo's neck. "Y'all right?"

"Mmhm. Yeah. Just thinking."

"Penny for your thoughts?" His palms were warm and rough as they skated over Theo's bare stomach to pull him closer.

"I really like this. Here. With you. I feel like I should be more upset than I am. It's confusing." Theo settled his hands over Connor's, resting backward against his frame.

"That makes sense, but if I can speak frank, I think it's long overdue. You living your life for you. And it's okay to be happy about that."

"I am. I really am." Theo's smile faltered a little as the coffee pot beeped. "It's a twelve-hour shift today, right?"

Connor nodded as he let go and moved to pour them both coffee, Theo's in a ceramic mug and his own in a travel mug. Theo hated the twelve-hour days, but at least it wasn't one of those marathon shifts where he had to stay late for events or meetings. He felt pathetic and needy, already missing him before he'd even left the house.

"Don't forget lunch. And take a scone for breakfast. And text me when you can. On the burner."

"Want me to bring dinner home tonight? It'll be late-ish."

"Sounds great. We'll figure it out when you get closer to quitting time."

Connor swept in and planted a firm kiss on Theo's lips, breaking it with a comical 'mwah' sound and another brilliant grin. "I'll text when I get in, Teddy. Be good."

Connor was out the door with a wink as Theo called, "Drive safe!" down the hall and shut the door. Sighing, he rested his forehead against the flat plane. "Love you."

He took his time with the coffee, refilling it twice as he ran through the mental checklist of everything he planned to tackle today. His nerves ramped up over the prospect, and the caffeine was not helping at all. But he was determined. He washed the mug and put it back in the cabinet, rinsing out the coffee pot and setting it up for tomorrow morning. He tidied the kitchen and started a load of laundry. Next on the list was the part he'd been putting off.

Back in the bedroom, he pulled his backpack out from under the bed and checked the contents. With a nod, he finished dressing. He grabbed his baggiest black hoodie from the back of the closet and pulled on his Converse. Layering the larger shirt over another sweatshirt to ward off the chill of late winter, he finished the look with a pair of Connor's sunglasses. Theo'd discovered the man owned half a dozen pairs of sunglasses, but they all looked the same to him. Large, dark, and official. Just what he needed. He hefted the bag onto his shoulder, stepped out of the apartment, locked the door behind him, and stuck the spare key into his shoe.

It was cold and grey outside, the sidewalks busy with the impending lunch hour. Connor lived in a trendy neighborhood full of life and color, explaining why his apartment was so small. The nearness of the metro station was part of the convenience.

Theo managed to navigate the process of getting a rail pass and slipped onto the first train that stopped at the station without incident. He found a seat with ease. Dressing like a sloppy degenerate came with numerous benefits he'd learned early in his mother's political career. Most importantly, people leave you alone if you look unapproachable. He needed that more than ever now. As the train rattled into motion, he grabbed his old cell phone from his backpack, powering it on for the first time in days. He ignored the notifications, even if their presence made his skin prickle with rising anxiety.

It didn't take him long to search through his contacts, jotting the phone number on the back of a business card from his backpack before powering it off again. He stashed it back inside his bag, but not before slipping it inside the blackout case. Every second he was out, his paranoia climbed higher. The next time the train stopped, he melded with the passengers exiting the car and glanced around the station to get his bearings. He knew most of the stops by heart after so many years in DC.

Outside, his breath visible in the air before him, he stepped into the wake of a group of college students walking down the street. Their carefree antics and chatter kept him grounded as they continued along the sidewalk until Theo finally saw the flyer he was looking for in a store window. Ducking into the corner store, he found a place in line and waited his turn. The headlines from the stacks of newspapers and magazine racks taunted him every torturous second he had to stand there.

"Presidential Polls Lower Than Ever - Will the Presidency Survive the Riots?"

"Protests Continue Nationwide: Domestic Nightmare Turning International"

"Too Soft to Tango? Rumbles of Discontent from Montgomery's Cabinet"

"Insider Secrets: Senate Members Discussing Potential Consequences"

"First Son MIA - America's Dirty Little Secrets Revealed"

The tension crawled up Theo's spine as he stepped up to the counter. He tossed a package of chewing gum he'd grabbed randomly on the counter and reached for his wallet. "One of the pay-as-you-go phones and a $20 card for it, please."

The middle-aged man behind the plexiglass had a look of boredom on his face as he blandly repeated the total back to him. With a whispered swear, Theo checked the cash in his wallet before reluctantly pulling out his debit card. *Don't read the name, don't read the name.* Theo chanted the mantra to himself as the cashier finished the transaction and handed over the receipt and items. He made a mental note to hit the next ATM he found as he fled the store, which suddenly felt too claustrophobic.

Outside, he took three deep breaths, the chill of the air causing his chest to seize with renewed tightness. Glancing both ways, he darted across the street and jogged into the nearest coffee shop before digging out his inhaler. The warm air helped ease his breathing, the medication burning his lungs nevertheless. The last of his cash went to purchasing a black coffee before he set up shop at a small table in the farthest corner, his gaze flicking toward the door as he set up the phone.

He stalled by checking his other phone, firing back a reply to Connor's string of texts. They bantered back and forth, discussing dinner options and exchanging flirtatious promises, the familiarity and safety of it giving Theo the courage to pull the business card out of his backpack. He pulled up the text message app on the new phone, punched in the number, and typed out his message.

Theo: Hey Devil. I need to borrow a cup of sugar for the angel food cake.

He set the phone face down on the table and focused on his coffee, measured breathing exercises keeping the anxiety at a smolder as he waited. Fifteen minutes later, the phone vibrated.

2026572231: Angel food cake is my favorite. Meet me @ the treehouse @ 2

Theo finished the dregs of his coffee and packed his bag. If he left now, he'd have enough time to visit an ATM and manage the metro system before he needed to be at the meeting spot. His nerves were wrecked, but he pressed onward in his mission.

....

The treehouse wasn't at all a treehouse. The tavern on the outskirts of one of the poorer neighborhoods in DC was primarily empty save for a few die hard stool warmers who spent more time here than anywhere else. It was dark, and most of the light fixtures were missing light bulbs to hide the grime that clung to the surfaces and hid in the corners, the place looking exactly like he had remembered. Theo bypassed the bar entirely and sat at a hightop in the corner, his gaze once more trained on the exit as he pulled the sunglasses off to see better in the dimly lit space.

A rush of cold air swept through the room as the door opened, the breeze momentarily alleviating the scent of stale beer and neglect from the air. A tall man in tight jeans and a puffy coat crossed the room, pushing the hood off his head as he approached the table where Theo sat waiting. The tension in Theo's neck and shoulders increased exponentially with every step the clean-cut, all-American-looking brunette took toward him.

"It's been too long, Angel."

"Hey, Taz. This isn't a social call."

"I figured as much. What can I do for you?" Taz pulled the stool closer before climbing onto it, his knee bumping against Theo's under the table. It made his skin crawl.

"Did you do it?"

"Do what? You'll have to be more specific, Angel."

"The press leaks, the gossip magazines, the internet chatter on the boards. Was it you?"

"Fucking hell, you're serious right now?" Taz leaned back as if Theo had just struck him across the face.

"They said you got traced back to the sites. I swear to God, if this is some bullshit to try and make my life hell, you won. I just need you to stop. You made your point, but it's getting out of control, and I will blow your shit up so fast, Taz, I swear."

"Wow. Wow, I know I'm an asshole, but wow. I'm not trying to 'make your life hell' sugar. You know exactly why my IP was flagged on those sites. It's the same reason as when we were together. I'm not doing shit for or against you. Flattered, though."

"Yeah, you are an asshole, but I just needed to be sure you weren't an even bigger one. Shit's been going crazy, and I don't know what to do." Theo rubbed the back of his neck with a sigh. "Pretty sure they got into my computer, so I bricked it.

Same with my phone. Under normal circumstances, you're the last person I'd ask for help, but I really need help."

"And why exactly should I help you? You text me on the emergency line two years after we broke up, accuse me of rolling around in the swamp, and then ask for my help." Taz scoffed as he crossed his arms over his chest. "Tell me one reason I should."

"It'll likely involve pissing off the same Nazi freaks and supremacists you always like to piss off?" Theo tried for humor, the waver in his voice causing the attempt to fall short.

"Okay, so it's not fair that you bring my kryptonite to the bartering table, but I'll give you a pass because you're cute as shit with those doe-eyes right now."

"Taz, focus. I'm not here to flirt with you. I need to use your cave. Can you help me? I'm serious, I'm really worried about what's going on."

"Now? Or... what are we looking at here for a timeframe?" Taz pulled out a folded-up index card, skimming the minuscule writing with a quick back-and-forth motion of his eyes.

"This weekend probably. I can text you and let you know. I'm bringing people with me to help." Theo grabbed his backpack, swinging it onto his shoulder with a fluid motion.

"People? I hate you. You're the worst."

"You don't hate me. But I get that it's a lot. I wouldn't ask if it weren't serious, Taz." Theo mustered up the humility he needed to continue. "Please? I'm scared for them."

"You should be scared for yourself, Theo. Have you seen the shit they're saying in the swamp?" Reaching out a hand, Taz nudged Theo's chin with the knuckle of his index finger. "Why do you think I'm trying so hard to blow their shit up?"

"Yeah, I got the gist of it. I need to figure out who's doing this before it's too late."

With a heavy exhalation, Taz stood up with a terse nod. "Text me to iron out the details, but brick the phone before we meet."

Theo rolled his eyes but mumbled his thanks as he crossed through the dingy barroom. He was just about to push through the door when Taz called out.

"Hey, Angel! It was good to see you."

Theo escaped through the door and down the street in rapid time, his nerves finally reaching the point of becoming unbearable. The metro ride home was torture. Walking the short distance from the station to their apartment felt like a marathon. When he reached the third floor, panic clawed at his throat and made breathing difficult. It was a miracle he could pull the key from his shoe and make it into the apartment before he collapsed in a ball against the door as soon as it closed. He needed to get himself together before Connor got home, or else he'd have to confess that panic attacks had become a routine part of his daily life.

CHAPTER TWENTY-SIX

Connor

PROTECTIVE DETAIL FOR THE First Family, since they had strong-armed Theo into turning down his personal protection, could only be described as torturous boredom. James was right, after all. With the rising threat against the administration and First Family, the children were pulled out of private school and primarily worked with private tutors in the residence. Connor had been relegated to standing watch over the tutors or standing guard outside the residence when on duty. Occasionally he went on rotation in different areas of the White House, but he'd already exhausted his ability to occupy his time with constructing mental to-do lists.

Today was a tutor oversight day, leaving Connor listening from the door as Toby's instructor begged him to do anything. Anna's teacher coaxed her into doing at least part of the assignments, all the while fielding the young girl's attitude. The Montgomery children were on the verge of an insurrection of their own. Connor couldn't blame them. He had his own choice words for Madam President, not that he'd ever share them aloud. At least tutor days brought some excitement to his shift.

"Actually, ma'am, I don't have to color the picture. The answers are there. You can shove the crayon up your nose for all I care!" Anna pushed the box of crayons off the table, crossing her arms over her chest with a huff.

"Fine, fine. How about we switch to the reading? You enjoy reading." The poor tutor was no more than twenty-two and very much in over her head.

"I finished the book last night. It sucked. No one kissed, and the boys were all dirty." Anna stood up, pushing the chair in before curtseying, somehow making the movement look like what sarcasm sounds like. "Since we're done here, I'm going to paint, and you can go now."

Connor glanced toward Toby at the other end of the dining table. He barely concealed his smirk, slumping in his chair and wearing headphones under the hood of a baggy sweatshirt. If he were a betting man, he'd put money on it being one of the ones Theo had left behind. Unlike Anna's school work, Toby's sat unfinished in a stack before him. The middle-aged instructor sitting beside him pushed the pile closer to Toby.

"Come on, kid. You'll get grounded again if you don't do something." The man's mellow voice took on a pleading tone.

"Already grounded. What's another week? Not like I can go anywhere." Toby shrugged, grabbing a sheet from the stack of papers. The instructor's face lit up like a child about to blow out their birthday candles. It crumbled again when Toby folded it into a paper airplane and sent it flying across the room.

"Oh em gee, Toby, make me one!" Anna squealed in delight before climbing into the chair beside her brother. He talked her through making her own airplane with soft-spoken patience, the two children utterly ignoring the tutors. Soon, the mountain of unfinished assignments littered the floor in the form of paper airplanes. Once they had completed their arts and crafts project, Toby took Anna by the hand, and they left the room without a word. Connor flinched when he heard the bedroom door down the hall slam shut.

Connor's heart hurt to see the kids in their mutinous state. The basketball game had become a distant memory that felt like a different lifetime. He recalled the face paint and pompoms. The cheering and smiles. He still had a copy of the picture of Theo, Toby, and Anna saved on his phone. Now, they were shut off from the world and pushing everyone who came close away, the orbit of their relationship spiraling closer in a protective impulse to avoid drowning under the weight of their mother's job. Standing watch from the doorway, Connor waited for the tutors to finish cleaning up the dining room before he escorted them through the hall and down the stairs that led to the private residence, turning them over to another agent who would see them the rest of the way to the administrative building parking lot.

Alone at the base of the stairs, Connor could pull out his phone to text. Theo's texts were few and far between today, and he found himself juggling renewed concern over his well-being. Theo usually put on a good poker face, but Connor knew him better than he probably realized. The evidence of his shaky mental health was littered all over the apartment in insidious clues that Connor pointedly avoided bringing attention to. It was obsessively clean, neurotically organized, and locked up tighter than Fort Knox. He usually returned home to find the blinds drawn, windows locked and every light in the house on. The volume on the television in the living room was loud enough to be heard from every room of the apartment.

Connor had made the mistake of not texting Theo as soon as he'd parked the car one night, eager to get upstairs. Upon entering the apartment unannounced, Connor had startled Theo so much he'd dropped a mug of tea on the floor. He had to force Theo to leave the room so he could clean it up, lest Theo cut himself for how badly his hands were shaking as he scrambled to pick up the broken ceramic pieces. The fact that Theo wasn't texting as much as usual shouldn't be a red flag, but things were complicated, and this break in the pattern made Connor's senses tingle with alarm.

He shot off a series of casual texts with a few simple, innocuous questions before pocketing his phone as he heard footsteps echoing farther down the hall. Texting on the job was technically against the rules, but he hadn't gotten caught so far. He hoped to keep it that way. He gave a lazy salute as James rounded the corner.

"Evening, boss."

"O'Brien, how are you?" James closed the distance between them, clapping his hand on Connor's shoulder before falling into parade rest. Once a military man, always a military man.

"Reckon I'm doing well. How 'bout yourself?" Connor mimicked James' pose instinctively.

"Hanging in there. I wanted to talk with you about your performance lately."

Connor's blood went cold, a wash of nerves instantly flooding his system. Performance talks were the job equivalent of being called to the principal's office. He made a point to straighten his spine and square his shoulders with a crisp nod.

"At ease, son. I know the last couple of weeks have been rough. Hell, the last couple of months. I'm not here to tear you a new one. But you've seemed a little more off than usual, and I want to check in. Are you all right?

"Yeah. I reckon I'm just readjusting to the scene. Guard duty on quarantine is different from detail on the kids. What do y'all need me to improve on?" Connor skimmed his eyes over his mentor's familiar, fatherly face. Slight crow's feet and a dusting of grey hair made him look older than he was, the flash of his easy smile reassuring Connor's nerves.

"You've bounced since you hit the ground and made the best of every pivot and swerve—no need for improvement. Just keep your head in the game, soldier. Because you're pivoting again come Monday."

Connor's eyebrows shot upward. "Wait just one second there, Sir. What do you mean?"

"We're transitioning you into the President's protective detail. She knows how good you were with Theodore. He spoke quite highly of you. And you're wasted potential here on babysitting duty." James glanced up the stairs before focusing on Connor's slack-jawed expression.

"Sir, are you sure? I'm flattered, but I reckon I just wasn't expecting that."

"I discussed the transfer with her, and we both agree it'll be for the best. You're young and new to the detail, but you've got the military background and the ability to act quick on your feet. We want you on the team before she takes her first overseas trip. It's going to be a shit show with so little lead time."

Connor's brain reeled with the onslaught of information. Presidential detail. Overseas trip. Working directly with the woman who crushed his boyfriend's heart to pieces. He couldn't formulate a response.

James chuckled, reaching out to squeeze Connor's shoulder in a paternal gesture. "I know it's a lot, so I've arranged your schedule to give you off this weekend to let loose and get your head on straight about it. You'll be good for the team. Everyone already loves you, so it'll be great for morale. Report Monday, and we'll get you set up to shadow one of the guys, so you don't feel overwhelmed."

Connor nodded, still unable to utter a response. The lump rising in his throat prevented it. With another salute, James disappeared down the hall, whistling a carefree tune as if he hadn't just thrown Connor a curveball. He checked his watch and realized he still had another two hours before his relief showed up. It was too much time to sit with his spiraling thoughts. He pulled out his phone and prayed for a reply from Theo to occupy his careening brain.

Theo: I miss you. I need your help with something. We can talk when you get home.

Connor's eyes turned into saucers as he read the text. Maybe he should have been more specific in his prayers for a reply because this was the last sort of text message he needed right now.

Connor: OK you're freaking me out what's wrong?

Theo: Shit sorry I realized how bad that text sounded as soon as I sent it

Connor: Still freaking out

Theo: Sorry, sorry. I have to see someone this weekend and I need you to come with me

Connor: Are you okay though?

Theo: Yeah, promise. Can't text details. Sorry!

Connor was about to reply when the bouncing dots appeared on the bottom of the screen again. He waited, but they stopped. He started typing his reply once more, but the ellipses reappeared. Once more, it disappeared. His thumb flew over the screen with a sigh to type out his response.

Connor: Still freaking a little. I'll be home soon <3

Theo: I miss you babe. See you soon. <3 <3 <3

Everything pressed in with a renewed intensity that drove Connor's nerves through the roof. He prided himself on his calm, collected demeanor, but even mountains crumbled, and he definitely felt like he was crumbling. He briefly found himself worrying that he couldn't pull it all off. Self-doubt was a tricky slope, so he swiftly reeled in his thoughts and directed them elsewhere.

He decided he'd take control of the rest of the night. At least he'd have that much to credit himself with. He switched to the browser app on his phone, cheating his torso away from the cameras he knew lined the hall, and set about wasting the last hours of the shift with his newest mission. Online shopping became a surprisingly efficient distraction, particularly when he could schedule a pick-up time. His mood was infinitely better by the time he checked out and the last half hour of his shift buoyed him with the knowledge that he'd achieved peak boyfriend while still on the clock.

By the time his relief showed up, Connor had already started jogging down the halls to make his way to the headquarters. He ditched his radio on the charger, flashed a wave to the guys loitering, ignored their invitations to grab beers, and sprinted to his car. It was only a short time later that he waited in the store's parking lot as the young cashier loaded the bags into the backseat, the impulse-buy bouquet of roses filling the cabin with the cloyingly familiar floral scent. He'd ordered dinner from a nearby restaurant. Another peak boyfriend decision. Theo had confessed once that his ultimate guilty pleasure comfort food was macaroni and cheese, and a little internet research had revealed this restaurant had won awards for their macaroni dish.

Parked on the street outside their apartment building, Connor pulled out his phone and texted Theo to let him know he was coming up. Juggling all the bags took some careful orchestration and a lot of grunting. By sheer force of will, Connor managed to lock the car, get into the building and climb three flights of stairs, albeit with prodigious amounts of perspiration and a sketchy moment involving overbalancing. He resorted to knocking on the door with his foot.

The look on Theo's face when he pulled the door open was worth all the fuss. Surprise shifted into amusement, which then transitioned into joy and the glisten of tears Theo insisted weren't there. He unburdened Connor's arms, moving farther into the small apartment kitchen with the groceries and goods. Connor watched with smug pride as Theo unpacked the bags with vigor. Aside from the groceries and supplies they needed, there were scented candles, wine, roses, and snack food galore. The throw blanket was a bonus Connor hadn't realized would bring so much happiness.

Connor pulled Theo in close as he lost the battle against his tears. "Y'all right, baby?"

"Yeah. I just really freaking love you."

They both froze in place. Gently, Connor pulled back, carefully tipping Theo's chin upward to make eye contact. His eyes were wide and petrified.

"Love you too, my Teddy. Just in case it weren't obvious."

Theo crumbled into a fit of tearful giggling. Connor raced to wipe the tears away with his thumbs, his own cheeks aching from the wattage of his smile. For a moment, wrapped in the cocoon of Theo's arms, Connor reveled in how intense joy could feel. Maybe everything would be all right after all.

CHAPTER TWENTY-SEVEN

Abriella

DARKNESS HAD DESCENDED ON Washington DC hours earlier, the headlights of the weekend traffic glistening off the damp, slush-covered street as Abriella jogged between the cars. Her heavy winter boots clunked on the sidewalk as she stomped off the worst of the sludge, pressing the call button on Connor's apartment building before blowing her hands to bring them much-needed warmth. Late winter always brought with it such irregular weather patterns.

"C'mon up, Smalls." Connor's voice crackled over the intercom, the door buzzer granting her respite from the late-night dampness and chill. She trotted up the stairs to his floor, unzipping the puffy jacket and tearing the beanie off her head. He was waiting for her outside the door on the third floor.

"Hola, Biggs. Como estas?" Abriella leaned in to press a kiss on her best friend's cheek. His expression was stressed.

"Eh. C'mon in." Connor held the door open for her, latching it behind them once they entered the small space. Theo stood off to the side, flashing a little wave before shoving his hand back into the pocket of his zipper-up hoodie. Tension filled the air of the apartment.

"Dios mio, who died?" Abriella glanced between the two men, noting the unusual distance between them. Typically attached at the hip, tonight they looked like lost ships passing in the night.

"I couldn't explain over the phone. We need to go see a guy, apparently. Over in East Anacostia." Connor became agitated, aggressively kneading the back of his head. "Did you get the information?"

Abriella slowly nodded as Theo appeared to shrink into the folds of the baggy sweatshirt. "Si... who are we going to see?"

Connor scoffed, the sound more breath than vocalization. He pivoted on his heel and disappeared into the bedroom, leaving Theo looking broken and small.

"He's a computer guy. He can help us get more information, and I need his systems." Theo's voice cracked as he looked over his shoulder toward the bedroom, where she could hear a commotion of dresser drawers opening and slamming shut.

"Who, Theo?" Abriella slowly crossed her arms over her chest, arching an eyebrow.

"My ex. I went to see him the other day to figure out if he did what my mom had said and to set this all up." Theo pulled his hands from his pockets, his fingertips pulling at the frayed edges of his sleeves.

Abriella grimaced, squinting her eyes closed. "And... you told him after?" Connor's temper tantrum started to make a little more sense.

Theo hopped onto the counter, pulling one knee up to his chest before resting his forehead on it. "I couldn't exactly tell Connor before I did. And I couldn't call Taz directly. He wouldn't have answered, nor would he have said anything over the phone if he did. He's paranoid about listening devices."

"Dios mio, Theo. Really, we have to go to this man?" Abriella gathered her hair into a loose bun at the top of her head, pulling the beanie over it with a sigh.

"Yes. I need a secure system. He's got the software I need. We need to figure this out, and we can't exactly go to anyone on the inside if we don't know. It's the best I can think of. I'm sorry."

Theo thunked his head back against the cabinet, his eyes staring up at the ceiling as another heavy exhalation parted his lips.

"It is not a bad idea. Connor, he's just..." Abriella tried to find the right word, gesturing aimlessly with her hand. "He feels too much, especially if he cannot fix the problems. You should not have gone alone. But you are right, he probably would not have let you go if he knew. Always a hero. This is why we love him, si? I will talk to him."

Theo murmured his thanks, his teeth worrying at his lower lip. It already looked chapped, red, and cracked. He'd likely been chewing on it for hours. Abriella tousled Theo's messy hair as she walked through the kitchen and farther into the apartment. Connor was still making noise in the bedroom. She knew exactly what she was about to walk into.

"Mi sol," she crooned, knocking on the doorframe before stepping into the room. Connor was busy at the dresser, his gun cleaning kit spread out over the top as he fussed over the firearms disassembled in a precisely organized fashion. She recognized most of them as his personal pieces, although the agency-issue Glock was also in the lineup.

"Hey, Smalls," Connor muttered, deftly reassembling one of his handguns and reloading the clip before holstering it. He moved on to the next with meditative ease.

"Tell me why you are angry, and I will tell you why you are being loco." Abriella stepped forward, resting her palm on the center of Connor's back before rubbing slow circles over the tense musculature.

"I'm mad because it was a stupid idea. I'm pissed off because it's his ex. I'm livid because we have to go there tonight." Connor's fists momentarily clenched before relaxing as he moved on to the next firearm spread out over the top of the dresser.

"And what do we do about it?" She kept her voice quiet and soothing, hoping to take the edge off of Connor's temper. He rarely got mad, but when he did, he smoldered like a hot coal ready to ignite with the slightest breath.

"Ain't shit I can do about it." Connor slammed a clip into the gun in his hand with vigor, the clang of the piece sliding into place too loud in the small bedroom.

Abriella pulled the gun from Connor's hand with a sigh, grabbing the holster from nearby before sliding the firearm into position and snapping the button on the leather restraint. "You will shoot your foot if you do not calm down."

"Everything about this was a bad idea. IS a bad idea." Connor switched gears, packing up his cleaning kit as he huffed and muttered under his breath.

"It is not actually a bad idea. I do not want to be this person, but right now, you need someone to tell you that you are being too much."

Connor snorted again, yanking open the topmost dresser drawer to toss the cleaning kit inside beside the orderly piles of socks and boxers. He slammed it closed, leaning down to pull the bottommost drawer open with the same intensity. Half of it was occupied by a locked safe. "Maybe. But this, this... shit is too much!"

Connor sat back after locking his firearms away, a small pistol in its holster still sitting on the top of the dresser.

"Si, it is. But you are pointing your anger at the wrong person this time. Didn't you tell me his mother's anger already crushed him?" Abriella combed her nails through Connor's hair as his shoulders sank. Her words hit a sore spot of realization.

"Ahh, shit." He sighed, rubbing the heels of his hands over his eyes before standing upright. He grabbed the pistol, sliding it into the waistband of his jeans, nestling the piece in the hollow at the small of his back. "Guess I gotta fix that."

"Si, and then we have to see a man about a computer. Muy loco." Abriella stepped back, moving toward the bathroom. She'd give them a few minutes to iron out their lover's spat before she barged in again. Thankfully, the bathroom was much tidier now that Theo had moved in. Connor wasn't inherently a messy person. In fact, he was far cleaner than most of the men she'd bunked with in the Marines and during her training in the Bureau, but the space was legitimately pristine now. She fussed over her appearance in the mirror to buy time.

Connor had told her to dress in civvies, civilian dress. Her puffy winter coat and plain t-shirt looked out of place when she was used to wearing her suits and blouses. Her jeans did lovely things for her ass, though. She turned to admire the profile in the mirror. Once she heard laughter filtering through the small apartment, she grew confident that all was well on the homefront and they could get on with their mission.

Once outside, Theo stepped into the lead, guiding their trio through the streets and the metro station. He bought them metro cards with cash, and they slid into the next train just a few minutes later. Theo collected the index cards he'd asked them to fill with phone numbers and email addresses of anyone they suspected, even tenuously, of being involved before he held out a strange black bag and asked for their phones.

"It's a blackout bag. Like a faraday cage, sort of. Hard to explain," Theo murmured, sealing the bag and avoiding their puzzled expressions as he stashed it in his backpack. "Do you have your badges?"

Abriella and Connor both nodded, the confusion evident in their expressions.

"Okay, I have to open the door between the cars, and if anyone tries to stop me, just... flash the badges?" Theo glanced between them both with a hopeful expression. He resembled a puppy, all wide eyes as he tilted his head. Connor breathed a heavy sigh.

Abriella's confusion mounted even higher as Theo sent a text message on a cheap burner phone. He pulled a roll of duct tape out of his bag and skulked to the door at the rear of the train car, muscling it open with a grunt before slipping through the narrow space and letting it slam closed behind him. Curious passengers glanced up, but one older woman seemed particularly displeased. She reached up to the call button on the side of the car. With an eye roll, Abriella pulled her credentials out, flipping the leather booklet open to flash the FBI badge. Mollified, the older woman huffed, her nose angled upward with a derisive expression.

Once Theo returned, phone missing but duct tape still in hand, he grabbed the backpack and nodded toward the station indicator. "We have to transfer at the next stop."

Another two transfers brought them east of the Anacostia, where they finally exited the metro and hit the streets. It was darker here, the streetlights spaced farther apart, more burnt out than not. It wasn't inherently a dangerous neighborhood. Just poorer, with fewer government funds filtered into the infrastructure than in other parts of DC. Theo navigated the streets with a familiarity that piqued her curiosity. He ducked through a broken section of chainlink fencing around a parking lot, holding it open for her and Connor before they disappeared further into the dark.

A short, sharp whistle cut through the chilly air before a tall man in a puffy coat, not unlike Abriella's, stepped out of the shadows. Theo stopped short, his hand landing on Connor's stomach to halt him in place. "Do you have a cup of sugar I can borrow?"

"Sure do, Angel Cake. I see you brought the other ingredients." The man, dimly lit in the vacant parking lot, gave Connor and her a once-over before turning his attention back to Theo. "Did you brick them?"

"Yeah, the phones are in my bag, and I sent the burner on a train ride. Can we get out of the cold?"

With a soft huff, the man beckoned with a jerk of his head, ducking into an alley. A stray cat taking off in the opposite direction sent a trash can flying with a loud clatter. Abriella's nerves were ready to ignite, tension slowly growing in every fiber of her muscles. They walked through a maze of dark alleys and empty lots before the mysterious stranger unlocked a padlock on a pair of hurricane doors at the rear of a tall building, shooing them into the darkness below before joining them and slamming the metal doors closed. He secured the interior doors with the padlock before pulling out a hefty keychain and unlocking an obscene amount of padlocks and deadbolts on the door at the base of the stairs.

Beyond the door lay a bizarre world of blue light and buzzing. The air bit Abriella's lungs with a startling chill that didn't make sense until she saw that the basement was a giant walk-in refrigerator. Computer monitors hung from the walls, sometimes stacked two high in places. What she believed were server racks stood at the center of the space, but it was conjecture at best. Beside her, Connor had the appearance of someone who was just about to be hit by a truck, struck mute and wide-eyed. Theo, on the other hand, jumped into action.

"Taz, this is Con and Bella. Bella, you work with Taz on those IPs and usernames I asked you to bring. Con, babe, come over here and help me backtrace the schedules. Taz, I have the numbers and email addresses. You want me to plug them in, or will you do it later?"

"Wait, Angel, you downgraded from asshole computer genius to meathead jock? I'm disappointed." Taz gave Connor a look up and down with a smirk. Abriella was about to give the man a piece of her mind, but Theo cut her to the chase.

"It's an upgrade. The fucking lottery jackpot. Another word, and he'll shoot you while I piss on the server deck and fry everything. Now, work." Theo snapped his fingers, already seated on a rolling stool as he bounced between two computer monitors, typing rapidly on either keyboard as he shifted back and forth. "Also, you still write shit scripts."

Overwhelmed, Abriella stepped toward where Taz had set up in front of another bank of monitors. She pulled out the slip of paper where she had covertly transcribed several of their watchlist suspects' information. Everything about this was seven different levels of illegal, and Abriella prayed to Mother Mary that the ends would justify the means. She made the sign of the cross over her chest before handing over the paper. Taz mumbled questions as he plugged the information into a screen that looked rudimentary at best, the blocky text and strange commands he input making little sense as she gave him what information she had. Before long, a separate monitor off to the side began displaying little beacons and arcs over a map of the globe in white on black, a network of lines criss-crossing in real-time.

"Angel, what's the command prompt for the time zone filtering script you wrote?"

"Backslash happy hour hoes, all one word." Theo didn't even look at the keyboard as his eyes bounced between screens.

Abriella giggled, squinting at one of the monitors Connor was watching. Rather than a map of the globe, this one displayed DC and the tristate area surrounding it, overlapping circles filled with small blinking beacons coming to life as Theo typed with a machine-gun clatter of keys.

"Babe, grab the hard drive out of my bag, please?" Theo glanced to the side as Connor rummaged through the backpack. "Thin black plastic rectangle in the front pocket."

"Ahh, yeah. Knew that." Connor made a soft chuckling sound as he handed Theo the hardware, glimpsing toward Abriella with a dazed expression. She had to stifle another giggle as Taz called her attention back to him with a slew of questions.

"Taz, I'm dumping my drive on the closed system. Don't touch the J drive. I'm quarantining it."

"Roger."

The chatter died out as Theo and Taz continued bouncing between monitors and rolling between keyboards, the constant buzz of refrigeration units and computer fans filling the space with a perpetual cacophony of whirring. Taz gave a little whoop that startled them all.

"Ha! One of them is active now! Let me take care of that...." Taz slid farther down the bank of computers, plugging in a few phrases that made no sense to Abriella before smashing the enter key with a triumphant crow. "Boom! Suck it, Nazi!"

Theo shook his head, trying to stifle a smile as he beckoned Connor closer, quietly murmuring as he pointed at the screen that displayed a bar graph with spikes rising and falling over the span. As Taz rolled back toward Abriella, she leaned in.

"What did you do? With the Nazi?"

"I hit the site he was on with a remote DDS overload to crash their servers. It's a temporary obstacle, but I like fucking with them."

Behind her, it was Theo's turn to whoop. "Bingo! Okay, my computer wasn't remotely hacked. Someone did send something, but it was while we were out. Must have overridden the password with a bootable thumb. But I know for a fact I wasn't there during this timestamp. So that narrows the field to someone physically on the premises."

Connor's face looked flushed, and Abriella arched her eyebrow in a silent question. He shook his head with a cheshire grin, and she realized she didn't want to know exactly what they were doing 'out' during the time in question.

"All right, kiddies. The scripts are all running, we're mining the data, and now I need you all to get the hell out of my cave." Taz clapped his hands three times before shooing them toward the door. "I'll contact you on this when we have something."

Theo tried to catch the cell phone Taz threw, fumbling it before Connor managed to scoop it out of the air. He escorted them to the door, once more unfastening what looked like a dozen locks before climbing up to the hurricane doors. He pulled up a camera app on his phone, a night vision display of the outside popping up on the screen before he unlocked the padlock. They had barely climbed through before it slammed closed behind them. The air felt almost warm compared to the refrigerated room they'd just left. Nevertheless, she felt a shiver run down her spine as they silently trudged into the darkness, retracing their footsteps through the maze of the city. Bone-aching exhaustion washed over her as the gravity of what they had dug themselves into finally hit home.

CHAPTER TWENTY-EIGHT

Adelaide

THE SITUATION ROOM NEEDED to be much larger, Adelaide decided, winding her way through the mass of bodies to collapse in her seat at the head of the table. The wall opposite her held a bank of monitors and live feeds, news broadcasts, and virtual meetings, but the one at the center was where she trained her attention. Within a few moments, the display flickered to life, and her caller's face appeared on the screen, pixelated as the delay caught up.

"Madam Montgomery! You look so good, so healthy! Thank you for taking my call!" Cristof bellowed, the audio not quite synced with the video of the German Chancellor.

"Good evening to you, Chancellor. I'm glad we could sit down to talk." Adelaide straightened in her seat, mindful to practice the air of authority she had worked on in the bathroom mirror during one of her many sleepless nights.

All around her, officials, assistants, and cabinet members arranged their legal pads, ready to take notes and keep the meeting on track.

"Yes, it is unfortunate we must have this call under these circumstances. I understand your economy is not thriving with all this disruption. It is affecting my economy, pretty girl. So now your peoples' discontent has become my peoples' discontent." The Chancellor leaned back in his chair, lazily spinning back and forth as he steepled his fingertips. "What are we going to do?"

"Everything we can, Chancellor. As we have been." Adelaide glanced toward James, who stood off to the side, waiting for his terse nod before she continued. "How are the plans for our visit? I look forward to addressing your people as I intend to address mine."

"Oh, wonderful! Very wonderful! We have much cuisine and culture to share with you, pretty girl. Gisela is buzzing! You will have grand time in Germany!" Cristof's laughter crackled the speakers for how loud it was.

"Excellent. The rest of our advance team flies out tonight. I trust everything will run smoothly, even if it is such a last minute plan."

"Of course, of course. Very safe here in Germany. I look forward to watching your address tonight, pretty girl!" With a wink, the German Chancellor leaned forward, and the screen froze as the call disconnected, his garish expression highlighted for a moment before the picture cut out.

"Five more of my team are on the first flight out after your address, ma'am. We fly out tomorrow morning once we get the all-clear from them. It's an unprecedented timeframe but I'm confident we'll make it work." James nodded toward Connor, the agent he'd insisted would be an excellent fit for her new team. When she looked at him, all she could recall was the expression on his face the day he pulled her son out of harm's way. Out of her way. The memory was a sharp dagger to her chest.

"Perfect, Agent Locke. And security for tonight?" Adelaide tore her gaze away from the dirty blonde agent in the corner, sweeping her eyes around the table at the busy officials taking notes.

"We've dispatched National Guard to assist the Secret Service uniformed division and local law enforcement, Madam President." General Siamo tapped the end of his pen against the table with a staccato rhythm. "That should keep the violence in check."

Adelaide shut her eyes, slowly counting out her exhale before resuming. "Jessica, you have the speech for tonight written? I'd like to review it and make notes again."

The Press Secretary pulled a folder from beneath her stack, sliding it down the table toward Adelaide. "Yes, ma'am. We've addressed every single one of the protestor's concerns in detail. I'm waiting for the Majority Leader to review a copy before we finalize it."

Aaron waved a similar-looking folder over his head from the far end of the table. "We can go over it together at lunch. I've skimmed it, but I have a few comments to help calm the Senate floor."

Adelaide dipped her head in assent as Andrew cleared his throat. "I'd also like to address the people after your departure. I've had my team mirror some notes in my own address. We need to reassure the American people about the continuity of leadership while you are overseas, considering how volatile everything has become."

With a roll of her eyes, Adelaide fluttered her fingers. "I'm visiting one of our strongest allies, not dying. But if you think it will help, by all means."

"All due respect, ma'am, yes, it is just a diplomatic visit, but the tension on the ground is a hair-trigger right now. We don't want to take any risks." Andrew's challenge brought a murmuring of whispers to the assembled group, forcing Adelaide to hold up her hand for silence.

"Asked and answered, Andrew. Give the address, but clear it with my office before we leave tomorrow."

Adelaide glanced around the table again, checking each person's gaze to see if anyone else had any other complaints or concerns. She stalled when Elias raised his hand. "Yes?"

"We've had several individuals approach the office requesting emergency funds for the healthcare sector. I don't think this one can wait until you return, Madam President."

Adelaide's eyebrows bunched together in the middle. "Regarding what, exactly?" She tried to go through the daily briefings in her head, but she hadn't noticed anything from the Health and Human Services sector. Granted, her daily briefings had become so long that she struggled to get through their contents in one sitting.

"Outbreaks of MRSA have hit colleges and public schools in major metropolitan cities up and down the eastern seaboard. This is in addition to the increase in hospital-based infections. Emergency rooms are becoming overloaded, and the specialized antibiotics needed to treat this particular strain are much more expensive." Elias' expression became grim.

Adelaide's body shivered with a sudden chill. "This is the same one that—" She couldn't finish the sentence, her eyes widening as she stared at Elias.

"Yes, ma'am. The same type of infection that put your son in the hospital. It's extremely contagious and highly deadly." Elias's emphasis on the words 'your son' felt weaponized, and the strike hit her right where she assumed he had intended.

Adelaide rubbed her palms over her face. "Can your office write something up? Can I release funds with an executive order?"

She caught a glimpse of Andrew nodding beside her as Jessica reached over to grab her folder. "We can arrange it for the address this evening. I'll get the information from the Chief of Staff and add it to the speech."

"Thank you, everyone. We'll be in touch with each of your offices within the hour to finalize everything." Adelaide crossed her arms over the table, the slight smile on her lips wavering.

The officials and administrative assistants began filtering out of the room as Aaron came over to squeeze her shoulder. "We'll meet in the Oval Office to discuss the speech notes for tonight. What can I get you for lunch?"

She glanced up, his smile warm and reassuring. "Just coffee. I'm not very hungry, and there is a lot to do. I'll be there in half an hour."

"Soup and a sandwich it is!" Aaron winked as he pivoted in place and strode from the Situation Room, his assistant trailing after him as Adelaide's stepped out of the periphery of the room.

"Madam President, I've sent all the information about the travel arrangements to your iPad, and your bags are packed. Your speechwriter is still working on the address for the German people. We don't have the full itinerary for your stay until the advance team reports back."

"Thank you, Darla. Anything else?" Adelaide sluggishly stood up at the table, smoothing out the creases in her suit pants with a sigh.

"Just a few things about the children." The young assistant fidgeted with the iPad in her hands, reluctant to continue.

"And those things are?"

"Tobias is still refusing to do any of his assignments. Annalise did some of them for him. Her tutor also put in her two-week notice this morning. Would you like me to prepare a list of replacements for you to review when you get back?"

"Damn it. Yes. And a list of instructors to replace Toby's tutor. Has he said anything about why he is refusing to do the work?"

Darla shook her head, her round eyes magnified by the glasses perched on her nose.

"I'll try to talk to him tonight— wait, no. I don't have time. Shit!" Adelaide pinched her lower lip, tugging at it as she wracked her brain for a solution. "Ask Elias if he can speak to Toby as a personal favor for me. He might be able to get through to him."

With a silent nod, Darla tapped her notes on the iPad before excusing herself from the room. Adelaide gathered her things, nodding to the agents who lingered, waiting for her next move. She'd become deaf to their radioed communications about her movements over time, but their presence was always a shadow.

As they continued down the hall, she glanced back toward James. "Agent Locke, who is on the second wave advance team?"

"That'd be O'Brien, Fornell, Fitzpatrick, Jenk, and Lewis. Five more total. The other five will stay with you at the address and fly out tomorrow morning if everything goes according to plan."

"Do you have the manpower to increase the security for the children while we're out of the country?" Adelaide glanced toward Connor, who walked just behind them.

"We can make it work. Better to be safe than sorry." James flashed her a warm, effusive smile. "Hard to balance the work, I bet, but we'll make sure your babies are safe, ma'am."

"Do either of you have children, agents?" Adelaide stopped, turning to better face the two men who lived in her shadow.

"No, ma'am," Connor muttered, his hands clasped behind him as soon as they came to a halt.

"Eh, one day, son. You'll be a great dad. Best thing I ever did." James playfully punched Connor's shoulder, the younger agent's cheeks growing just a shade rosier. He turned back toward Adelaide. "I have a daughter, ma'am. She lives with her mother. My pride and joy."

"So you can understand the importance of ensuring my children remain safe, yes?" Adelaide cocked her head, studying James' face.

"Ma'am, I know it better than you can imagine. I'd do anything for my Jessie. So yes, I understand. And I promise you, nothing will happen to your babies. My men are on it."

Adelaide inhaled a deep breath. "And Theo?"

"He's laying low, ma'am. We have officers check the neighborhood when we can spare the manpower." James shrugged, a breath parting his lips. "There's only so much we can do when they turn down the protective detail."

"Yes, I understand. I just worry." Adelaide glanced between the two agents once more before continuing down the hall.

"It's what we parents do. We worry about our babies. Everything'll work out, ma'am." James reached out, resting his hand on her shoulder with a gentle squeeze. It was a small gesture, but more than she'd received in days as the self-doubt mounted higher with every passing day in her presidency. It did very little to assuage her fears.

CHAPTER TWENTY-NINE

Theo

THEO PACED BACK AND forth, the small footprint of the apartment not affording him much distance as he wore a path through the open floor plan kitchen and sitting room, occasionally passing through the kitchen and into the bedroom. A vaguely circuitous route that left him little to occupy his mind. He peeked through the blinds to the street below, but Connor's parking spot was still empty. With another heavy sigh, he began his circuit again.

Ten minutes later, the phone in his pocket buzzed. He pulled it out, and his heart leapt to see Connor's text announcing his arrival home. He tried not to imagine how much he resembled an eager golden retriever as he bounced on his toes, waiting to hear his boyfriend's footsteps outside the door. As soon as the footsteps drew near, Theo whipped the door open and lept into Connor's arms, the momentum causing him to stumble as he scrambled to catch Theo's frame.

"I don't want you to go." Theo didn't give Connor a chance to reply, their lips colliding in a passionate kiss that bordered on desperation. Theo was desperate. He had no shame about it, not at that moment. With a gasp, he delved his lips lower, mouthing at the spot just above the collar of Connor's shirt. The one he knew drove him wild. "How long do we have?"

"Half an hour... God, baby..." Connor moaned, a low vibration in his throat that Theo chased with his tongue.

"Mm, good." Theo wrapped his legs tighter around Connor's hips, his hands grabbing at handfuls of hair and clothing as he resumed kissing him as though it would be the last time they did so. "Inside, inside!"

Connor's laugh was a rumbling bass note that Theo could feel thrumming through his electric nerve endings. Connor grabbed Theo's ass in both hands with a heft, trudging through the apartment door before kicking it closed behind them. Five long strides brought them through the small kitchen before Connor tossed Theo onto the mattress, descending to rejoin their lips together, tongues swirling as desperate hands yanked and tugged at the garments that stood in the way of their inflamed desires.

"Jesus, baby, you're gonna kill me," Connor grunted with the effort it took to flip Theo over and pull him up to his knees, blanketing his arched back as he fumbled with the belt at his waist. Every second felt too long, but at last, their pants were pushed more or less out of the way, Connor leaning to grab the lube from the nightstand.

"I need you, babe. I need you so bad." Theo shifted his knees farther apart, arching his back even more, his hands grabbing bunches of the comforter.

Theo's posturing had the desired effect, just as he knew it would. This wasn't about tender ministrations, doting affections, or marathon lovemaking. Desperation fueled them both as Connor pressed the head of his freshly lubed cock against Theo's ass, thrusting with one slick motion before collapsing over Theo's back with a guttural groan.

"God, yes! Babe... yes. Don't stop!" Theo's words came out as a wail that devolved into a soft, keening whine before shifting into a nearly perpetual moan.

"You feel so damn good." Connor's voice was husky and raw as he began moving his hips, the pace instantly set to no-nonsense as he reached a hand around to grab Theo's cock in a tight grip. The need coursing through them made for a quick and dirty act of passion, Theo's hand reaching up to grab a fistful of Connor's hair as he bucked against every thrust. There was no way he was going to last long with this onslaught.

"Babe, d-don't stop!" Theo's gasping pants were ragged and patternless, the sweat-damp forehead pressed against the nape of his neck pulled closer with another tug of the short hair on the top of Connor's head. "Fuck, close... m'so close."

"That's right, baby. Come for me, Theo. Come for me." The growling groan at the end of his plea sent a shiver through Theo's body as he became utterly overwhelmed. Orgasm tore through him, electric hot and intense, his chest collapsing into the mattress beneath them. It was too much—too much and not enough.

"Connor! Connor, babe, come. Let me feel you, please?" Theo's voice rose in pitch, his moans turning to cries as Connor's pace quickened. With one more profound jerk of his hips, Connor buried himself deep in the recesses of Theo's body, the intensity of his climax bringing inarticulate open-mouthed groans to his lips.

Time slowed and then completely stopped as they froze there, stupefied by the intensely carnal act of mutual pleasure that had just eclipsed reason. Gradually, the breathless gasping slowed to a calmer pace, and Connor pushed himself upright, easing from within Theo's ass before collapsing on his back beside him.

"Hell, baby. Y'all right?" Connor peeked sideways, searching Theo's face with a flicker of concern. He looked absolutely wrecked, and it made Theo's heart race.

"Yes. God damn, Con. You're beautiful. I love you." Theo shifted his weight, sprawling over Connor's chest to dive in for another kiss. Pulling back, he grabbed Connor's cheeks in his hands, searching the depths of his whiskey-gold eyes with the pupils blown wide. "You have to promise me you'll come back, okay? You'll be safe, and you'll come back."

Connor's lips parted with a breath as he reached up to cup Theo's cheeks in return, gently stroking his thumbs over the cheekbones. "I'll be back before you know it, my Teddy. I promise. He pulled Theo down, their kiss tender in contrast to the wild passion that had just consumed them. They traded kisses back and forth, wrapped up in one another's arms, till they both reluctantly pulled away.

"You have to go soon?" Theo tried to keep his voice from cracking, but the prospect of Connor leaving had his anxiety ratcheted up to nearly unbearable levels. He hated, despised being such a wreck over something so simple as a work trip.

“Yeah, I reckon. I don’t wanna.” Connor pressed a kiss square on the center of Theo’s forehead, rolling him over before descending for another kiss, their tongues lingering in a dance of unspoken promises.

“Your bag’s by the door. Please drive safely. Text me if you can.” Theo begrudgingly loosened his grip, sprawling on the bed as he watched Connor straighten his disheveled appearance.

“I will. I love you, baby. I promise I’ll be back before you know it.”

“Love you too, Con. I’ll be here waiting.”

He couldn’t bring himself to walk Connor to the door, opting instead to roll over and bury himself in the comforter. He waited until he heard the door close before he let himself cry.

··········

The room was pitch black when Theo finally stirred, an incessant beeping dragging him from his sleep into wakefulness. He blindly groped for his phone, checking the screen with bleary eyes, only to realize it wasn’t his phone making the sound. He always turned his volume off and remembering this had him sitting up straight in the bed in one fluid motion. He dug through the nightstand drawer and pulled the phone out, his eyes skimming the screen flooded with notifications.

2027328071: The cake is done.

2027328071: lmk you get this

2027328071: urgent before the cake burns

2027328071: omfg answer the phone

Just as he was about to type a response, the phone in his hand started ringing. With a shaky finger, he answered the call.

“Hello?”

“Finally. I’ve got some shit you need to see. Get on the green line heading north. I’ll find you.

“Okay, just gimme like ten min—“

Theo rolled his eyes as he tossed the phone to the side. “Or just hang up.”

He slid out of bed with a soft grunt, his body aching in all the right places as he straightened out his clothes and pulled his backpack from under the bed. He'd have loved a chance to shower, but apparently, he didn't have that luxury. He layered another sweatshirt over the one he already wore, grabbing a pair of sunglasses out of habit as he packed up his bag and left.

The air was crisp outside, just damp enough to be cold. The streets were empty, and the metro far less crowded than usual, allowing Theo the ease of slipping into a seat on the green line train without a fuss. He settled into a slouch, his bag perched on his lap and the sunglasses allowing him to obsessively check the other passengers and exits at every stop. Taz flopped into the seat beside him twenty minutes later.

"Hey, Angel."

"Sup?"

"Nice shades." Taz smirked as he pulled a tablet out of his satchel, bringing the screen to life with a quick tap of the passcode. The privacy screen protector made it impossible for Theo to see what it revealed until Taz slid it into his lap. He scrolled through the screencaps, pausing to absorb the details before skipping to the next one.

"So this is what it looks like?" Theo murmured, glancing up to catch Taz' gaze.

"Yeah, one of our guys slipped up. I was able to slide in a tracker through his email. I've got the live feed running back at home. But this looks like one of our guys if you check the location map. The dummy phone is showing up around the area of the White House pretty regularly. I can't narrow the location down any further than that."

"Yeah, I see that. Any idea who?" Theo pressed the button on the side of the tablet to lock the screen before tucking it into his backpack.

"You're gonna have to ask your boy about that one. He can help us corroborate the locations with the timestamps."

"It'll have to wait. He's out of state for a bit." Theo resumed his slouch, huddling closer to Taz so the other passengers couldn't overhear their voices on the train.

"Any way you can get in touch with him on a secure line?" Taz assumed a similar position, the two of them looking more like junkies or dealers than young guys trying to unearth a conspiracy within the highest levels of the government.

"I can try. But it's sketchy with where he's working right now. I don't wanna risk it. Let me see what I can do, and you keep tracking the data. Maybe we can figure it out before he gets back." Theo pushed himself up from the seat as they neared the next station. "And thank you. Really. I mean it."

"Don't worry about it, Angel. We'll get to the bottom of this. Just stay safe out there." Taz stood, nudging Theo's chin with the knuckle of his index finger. A wistful smile flickered over his lips as they departed the train together, simultaneously flashing a wave to the other before parting ways. Something about it seemed so final, different than the last time. It sent a shiver down Theo's spine. He attributed it to his nerves as he found his way to the platform for the southbound line that would bring him back home.

Exhaustion dulled his senses, as did the fact that he was returning to an empty apartment. Living in a constant state of elevated anxiety brought a level of tension to every scenario, the low-level thrum of adrenaline perpetually coursing through his body. Maybe he was finally collapsing under the pressure. Perhaps he was adapting to the new normal. Whatever it was, he missed the fact that someone had gotten off the train when he did and back on the southbound line one car ahead. He also missed the stranger in the dark hoodie getting off at his stop near Logan Circle. Near his home.

He only sensed something was off when the stranger's footsteps drew closer behind him as he left the metro station. Adrenaline flooded Theo's system with renewed intensity as he honed in on the sound of the footfalls. It took every ounce of willpower not to take off sprinting. He wouldn't lead whoever this was straight to his doorstep. Outside the station, he turned in the opposite direction, keeping his breath as even as he could despite the panic swiftly rising in his chest to wrap icy claws around his throat.

It didn't matter in the end. More footsteps joined the ones already tailing him, the staccato rhythm of their increased speed finally inspiring him to run. If they were going to take him down, he'd make sure they did it on camera. With a desperate prayer, he ran into the nearest intersection as they finally closed the gap. One pushed him from behind as another man grabbed his sweatshirt to reel him back. A third tore the backpack off his shoulder so violently, it sent a shockwave of pain through his body. Four men in dark hooded sweatshirts and ski masks pushed him back and forth like a ping pong ball, laughing and jeering. The tallest man in the group grabbed Theo by the throat, pulling him in close to hiss in his ear, his breath scented with whiskey and tobacco smoke.

"Quit playing big boy games, little brat. Mommy would be so sad if your head ended up on her desk."

Theo couldn't breathe, his fingers desperately clawing at the man's hand around his throat. Tears streaked down his face. Car horns blared from every direction in the intersection, but the sound of the men howling like depraved wolves blocked out every other sound. When the chirp of a police cruiser's sirens cut through the air, he finally pulled free from the iron grip around his throat. Adrenaline fueled his flight as he took off into the night, the strangers disappearing in the opposite direction. He ran, breathless and blind, through the city streets until he couldn't run any farther, dragging himself through the door of the first 24-hour establishment he could find.

The air of the laundromat was damp and hot. It barely registered as Theo sprinted into the corner of the room, collapsing against the wall and pulling his knees up to his chest. He only moved when he needed to use his inhaler. With his eyes trained on the door and the canister clutched in his fist, he huddled there until dawn colored the horizon. At least in the daylight, the monsters in the dark seemed a little less frightening.

CHAPTER THIRTY

Connor

BEING ON THE ADVANCE team for a President's international visit was ten times more stressful than Connor had initially assumed. Especially since they usually had weeks to coordinate, not days. He'd barely slept on the flight, and as soon as they had boots on the ground, they hadn't stopped moving. Between security checks, meeting with the German security teams, checking the transportation routes, and clearing the venues, their team was overburdened, understaffed, and overworked. The advance teams typically had a lot more time to work, but they were trying to do the work of dozens men with half the manpower in half the time.

Connor's natural leadership and charisma unintentionally made him the go-to for their operation. Despite being out of his element and exhausted in ways he hadn't experienced since his deployments with the Marines, Connor and the team managed to run the procedures and set up their headquarters with half an hour to spare before they received word that Airforce One was approaching and preparing for descent. The entire event resembled organized chaos on every level, with calm exteriors hiding the stress levels of the agents as the orchestrated complex safety protocols and the well-oiled procedures needed to transport the President around the city and from venue to venue with minimal risk.

Running on fumes and adrenaline, Connor finally got a chance to crash nearly forty-eight hours after he left American soil. Staggering into their bunk room, he texted Theo a series of jumbled messages that he didn't bother checking for typos or autocorrect fails before finally collapsing face-first into a bed to grab a few blissful hours of exhausted, dreamless sleep. Unfortunately, with how understaffed they were, the hours were not nearly enough. He grumbled and groaned as a fellow agent shook him awake, barely pulling himself from the mattress before his coworker collapsed in his place.

Connor pulled out his phone as he trudged to their headquarters in search of coffee, a frown twisting his features when he discovered that Theo still hadn't replied. He sent another volley of texts, calculating the difference in time zones, before switching to call. It went straight to voicemail. His nerves instantly skyrocketed. Switching back to his contacts, he pulled up Elias' number and went straight for a phone call.

"Williams speaking."

"Elias, it's Connor. Have you heard from Theo?"

"Oh, hey. Sorry, I'm so used to answering work calls. I talked to Theo a couple of days ago. Maybe two or three? What's up?"

"His phone's off. He hasn't texted."

A moment of silence hung over the line.

"Wait, you're on the trip, aren't you?" Elias' voice crackled over the line, the sound hollow and tinny through the phone speaker.

"Yeah, and I haven't heard from him since I left. It's probably nothing, but—"

"No, I'll swing over on my way home from the office. I'll text you."

"Thanks, Elias."

"Anytime, Connor. I'll let you know. Stay safe."

With a beep, the line went dead, and Connor pocketed his phone, heading into the hotel room they had set up as their command base to find coffee and a distraction from his fears. He was due back on the rotation in an hour. He would be on Airforce One with the rest of the advance team as soon as the dinner event scheduled for this evening wrapped. He willed the time to go faster, but it dragged slower with each click of the minute hand on his watch.

The evening became a blur as he relieved the agent on close protective detail, assuming his spot near the President as she wined and dined and played political hardball. Her address to the nation went well, but the address to the German people went even better. She seemed carefree and happy, laughing with the German Chancellor's fiancee over fancy hors d'oeuvres and champagne.

Connor's anger began to pool low in his stomach, insidiously replacing the fear that clung to him like a miasma.

Despite how the hours dragged, they were finally en route to the airport, the motorcade whisking over the tarmac toward the jet that waited at the ready. Already refueled and running, Connor and the rest of the team assembled in formation to move the President from the back of the limousine to the plane's stairs with practiced ease. She stumbled as she took the first step, her high heels mixed with champagne making her a little unsteady on her feet. Connor jumped into action, appearing with an arm outstretched to see her safely up to the top and into her quarters on the plane.

"No, stay. I wanted to talk to you, Agent O'Brien." Adelaide tugged his sleeve as he tried to step back toward the door.

"Ma'am? I don't think that's—"

"Shhh, you're being ridiculous—it's just a little talk. Nothing scandalous. After all, you're gay. I'm a straight woman. Don't argue." Adelaide hiccuped with a little giggle as she propped herself up on the desk of her private office in the jet. Connor bristled with defensiveness.

"Ma'am, I don't reckon I ever actually mentioned that, and that still don't make this right."

"You didn't. James told me. He's so nice, isn't he? He talks so highly of you. I can see why Theo picked you. Is he happy?" Adelaide bent down to unbuckle the high heels from her ankles, the motion nearly sending her to the floor as the plane began to move.

Connor swooped in to prevent a fall, steadying her shoulders as she struggled with the shoes. "Who, ma'am?"

"My Theo. Is he happy with you?"

"I'm sorry, Madam President, but I reckon I really need to go. I'll get your Miss Darla to come get ye situated." Connor's head swam, his pulse pounding in his ears.

"Connor. Can I call you Connor? You're being ridiculous. I'm not mad. James isn't mad. We think it's so cute. I just want Theo to be happy. Is he happy?"

Adelaide looked up at him with wide, earnest eyes, her slightly intoxicated state revealing the hopefulness behind her question.

"I ain't one to speak for others, but I reckon yes, ma'am." The urge to flee the room grew exponentially with every moment that passed.

"It's good he has you. You can keep him safe. Don't hurt my baby, okay? Don't hurt my baby. He's such a good boy." She listed to the side, bracing one palm on the desk as the plane banked in the air, pointing them toward home.

"Ma'am, I think you should lay down. We'll be home before you know it." Connor fretted over whether to try and get her to the bedroom or settle for the couch.

"You have to make sure he eats. He always does that for everyone except himself. He's so ridiculous like that. But if he's going to live with you, you have to make sure now because I'm not there. I wasn't there." Another hiccup turned into a sniffle as she wiped her eyes with her fingertips.

"He's with Elias Williams, ma'am." Connor froze, every hair suddenly standing on end.

"Oh, stop lying. James already told me, silly. He told me right before we left. It's so perfect."

Connor keyed up his mic without a second thought, already moving toward the door. "O'Brien to Fitzpatrick, I need you and the President's assistant in the private office."

As soon as the agent and Darla walked through the door, Connor sprinted down the plane's length before diving into the Secret Service bunk. It was cramped and narrow. Ignoring the confused expressions on his fellow agents' faces, Connor grabbed the satellite phone off the receiver, pulling out his phone to skim through the list of contacts. He punched in the number, his foot anxiously tapping as it rang and rang before finally clicking over to voicemail.

"James! I don't know what in the name of hell is going on, but you call me back!"

Connor slammed the phone down before picking it up again. He scrolled further through his contacts, typing the next number in before waiting with growing impatience. This call rang only three times before the line picked up.

"Williams speaking."

"Elias, did you find him?"

"No, Connor. I'm still at the office."

"Good, stay there. Wait for my call!"

Again, Connor slammed the phone down, scrolling through his contact list with increasingly shaky hands. The agents around him slowly backed away, slipping through the door one by one as Connor became even more volatile. The following number on his list answered after two rings.

"Hello?"

"Lily! It's Connor. Are you at the White House?"

"Yes, why?"

"Stay there, just... stay there. Don't leave the medical unit."

"Connor, what's—"

He didn't have time to explain, so he hung up instead. Now that the remaining agents had fled his presence, Connor slammed the door to the bunkroom closed, wedging a chair under the handle before returning to the satellite phone and switching to the encrypted line. Elias thankfully picked up much faster.

"Connor, what the hell is going on?"

"Did you tell anyone where Theo was staying?"

"No, just you and I know. Even your friends still think he's staying with me. Parker tells everyone at school his fun uncle is living with him. I promised him a puppy to keep up the charade."

"James knows. He told the President. The only way he would know is—"

"Shit," Elias all but breathed the word.

"Yeah. Can you get into the residence where the kids are?"

"Addy put me on the list. I'm supposed to get Toby to do his homework."

"Lil's in the medical unit. I need you to get those kids out of the residence and into her office. I don't care how. Just get them out and get a locked door between them and the Secret Service. At least until we figure this out."

"Connor? Stay safe."

"You too, Eli."

With another click, the line went dead. Connor dialed the next number by heart. It was one of only three he had committed to memory. The phone rang long enough that it almost switched to voicemail.

"Smalls, where are you?"

"Connor?" Abriella's voice lowered as he heard the sound of a door closing in the background.

"Where are you?"

"I'm at the office. Are you okay?"

"Theo's MIA. I think I have a lead on the insider. I'm stuck over the Atlantic. Do you remember how to get to where we went with Theo that night?"

"Si, of course. You think I would go into creepy alleys without making sure I memorized the path?" Connor could almost hear the eye roll in her voice.

"You need to get there. Now. See if Theo is there. Get the guy to help us."

"Connor, this all sounds muy loco. What is going on?"

"James knows where Theo lives, and now Theo is missing," he hissed, keeping his voice low.

"Pendejo... I'll go now. Call me when you land!"

Connor clicked the phone off and back on, dialing another number he knew by heart.

"O'Brien residence!"

"Hey, mama." Connor's voice wavered.

"Connie! Oh, by gosh, it's so nice to hear your voice!"

"I don't have long, but I just wanted to tell you something. Ye know that guy I been talking about?"

"Theo! Oh, he's so wonderful. Y'know, he sent me the sweetest text just last week."

"Yeah, he's pretty perfect. I just wanted to let you know that I reckon he might be the one. If'n anything happens, you remember that, mama."

"Connie, baby. You in a pickle?" His mother's voice grew serious as Connor clenched his hand around the phone.

"Fixin' to be."

“Well, you a smart boy, and you been in plenty of pickles. But I’ll see you and that boy this summer, just like we planned, y’hear?”

Connor smiled, even as his eyes grew misty. “Reckon that sounds like a plan, mama. I love you, ole gal.”

“Love you too, Connie. Now go get yourself out of that pickle.”

CHAPTER THIRTY-ONE

Elias

WALKING DOWN THE WHITE House halls suddenly carried an ominous weight of apprehension as Elias followed the familiar path toward the residence. The last time he'd been in the private section was for the pizza party. It seemed like a lifetime ago. He deliberately slowed his pace, carefully checking his breathing and trying to calm himself. He did not pride himself on his acting skills, but he needed to pull this off.

"Evening, gentlemen!" He waved, smiling at the agents stationed at the base of the stairs. He had no clue who they were, let alone if he could trust them. Not with the suspicions that had been creeping up on him for weeks and the panicked calls he'd just received from Connor. "The President should have mentioned I'd be stopping by. Williams. Elias Williams. All right if I head up?"

"One of us will have to escort you, Sir." For lack of a name to differentiate them, Elias dubbed the shorter one Agent Tweedledee in his head.

"Is that really necessary? I promise she asked me to come to talk to the kids. It'll be better if you stay here. Nothing to worry about." Elias performed an Oscar-worthy act as he flashed a casual smile and hooked his thumbs on his belt.

"Orders, Sir. I can walk you up." Agent Tweedledum turned with military precision on his heel, climbing the stairs two at a time.

"If you just call the agent in charge, he can explain. Really." Elias chased after the man as they ascended the staircase together.

"Agent Locke isn't in tonight. Protocol is protocol."

"Oh, he's off? Must be nice, eh?"

The agent glanced back at Elias with a look of scorn. "He's unwell. Called in two days ago. You have half an hour." The agent nodded toward the nearest sitting room turned dance hall. Reggaeton music played at a decibel he confidently assumed was too loud for children's ears. The agent barely left enough room for Elias to squeeze through the door. This show of macho territorialism made him roll his eyes.

Inside, the music was even louder. He couldn't even be sure where it came from. Toby and Anna sat face to face on the floor, but Anna saw him first. She leapt to her feet and ran toward him with a squeal. He barely had time to catch her as she flew into his arms.

"Uncle ELI!" Her embrace cinched painfully around his neck. Now or never. He brought his hand to the back of her head, holding her close so he could whisper in her ear.

"Baby girl, listen. This is serious. Don't let go of me. Do exactly as I say," he murmured as he knelt beside Toby. The music thumped impossibly loud, but if he leaned in close, they could both hear him. Barely.

"I need you both to act super sick. The sickest ever. We need to get to the medical unit. I have a friend there. I need you to trust me."

"Eli, what's going on?" Toby narrowed his eyes, wariness written on every feature of his face.

"Precaution. Just in case. You take my hand, and you don't let go. Promise me you won't let go." Elias squeezed Anna tighter to his chest, her body trembling as she pressed her arms around his neck.

"Uncle Eli, you're scaring me." Her tiny voice broke his heart.

"I know, baby girl. We need to get somewhere safe where no one will bother you guys while we figure some stuff out." Elias grunted with the effort it took to stand up while holding Anna. Once he found his feet, he reached out a hand to Toby. His eyes were wide, his grip tightening as he pulled himself up, not letting it loosen as Elias took a breath to bolster his nerves.

Four long strides had him back at the door. The agent on duty stood squarely at the center of it, his hands clasping the lapels of his suit jacket. Elias found himself playing a game of chicken on foot. “Move. They’re sick. I’m taking them to the medical ward.”

“No, you aren—“ The agent broke off with a grimace as Anna abruptly started screeching at the top of her lungs.

“I want my MOMMY!” She took a deeper breath before continuing to scream. Elias thought his head would pop. “I don’t FEEEEL good! MOMMY!”

The agent backpedaled, keying up the mic tucked inside his jacket. “Jenkins to base, medical alert. Wiggle and Willow on the move to the med unit.”

Elias took full advantage of the space afforded by the agent’s retreat, his long legs carrying him down the hall toward the stairs as he hauled Toby by the hand behind him.

“Good job, baby girl. Keep it up.” Elias mumbled, even if he could barely tolerate the intensity of her screams in his ear. Toby took up the banner of their cause, faking sobs as they clattered down the stairs. He probably looked like a kidnapper, save for the agents following behind them. He felt rather like a strange hero in a telenovela.

More agents appeared behind them, filtering in as they crashed through the White House, Anna’s shrieks echoing off the high ceilings. Elias poured sweat with exertion and fear. Part of him wondered if he wasn’t being shot at simply because he held Anna like a human shield against his chest. A sobering thought considering everyone on his heels was armed.

By the time they made it to the medical unit, sweat had drenched Elias’ suit, and Anna’s throat rasped with every screech. Toby had gone from fake crying to genuinely crying. They were a mess, staggering into the medical unit to find Lily anxiously wringing her hands in the main office.

“Sick. Very sick. The sickest. Room?” Elias gasped the words, positioning his body as a barricade in the office door to prevent the crowd of agents from filing in after him for as long as possible. Lily reached out, grabbing Anna from his arms.

“Right this way!” Lily perched the little girl on her hip, reaching out a hand for Toby.

“Eli, are you coming?” Toby glanced up at him, his tear-stained eyes hauntingly familiar. So many nights, Elias had sat with the Montgomery family as they all wept over lost loved ones. Toby's face transported him back to that time, and his chest ached with the memory.

"I'm gonna be right here. Go with Lily. She's Theo's friend, okay?" Elias squeezed Toby's hand before letting him go. Lily scooped up the boy's other hand, pulling him through the office and deeper into the medical unit. "Do what you need to, Lily!"

"Sir! You need to get out of our way!" A brusque voice cried out behind him, and he turned in place to face a cadre of agents, some with weapons pulled. Shit got real. Fast.

Elias put his hands up on impulse. "Officers, er… agents. The kids are sick. They need the doctor. I'm just protecting the kids. We're on the same side!"

He wondered how true the words were, even as he uttered them. He couldn't hold back the Secret Service in the middle of the White House, but he stood his ground nevertheless.

"Step away from the door!" One of the agents advanced, and every instinct in him made him take a step backward into the office. "FREEZE!"

He shut his eyes, fully expecting to hear the sharp report of gunfire. What he heard instead could have been a choir of angels for how much joy it sparked.

"Freeze, or step away? God, you guys don't know what you want. Straights, am I right?" Caleb's voice cried out over the hair-trigger tension of the hallway, agents moving out of the way as he walked toward the medical unit with Tristan Williams on his heels. Behind them trailed Elias' lawyer and the Director of the Secret Service, the latter barking orders for the men to put their guns away.

Elias nearly collapsed with relief, his hand reaching out to hold himself up against the doorframe. "Caleb, I think you just saved my life."

"A-yup. Is it a bad time to talk about a raise?" Caleb ducked around another agent before wrapping his arms around Elias. He returned the embrace as though his life depended on it. It might very well have.

"What's the meaning of this?! Where's your supervisor?" The Director scanned the assembled agents with a withering look.

"He's sick, Sir. We're just protecting the First Family."

"Who's running point in his stead?"

The silence became a palpable presence in the room. Elias leaned down, his voice hushed against Caleb's ear. "What are they doing here?"

Caleb slowly shrugged, looking anything but cherubic as a crooked smile brought a dimple to his left cheek.

"I asked you a question, Agents!"

"Mitchell was, Sir, but he left a little while ago."

Elias' lawyer sidled closer, her high heels clicking on the floor. "Mr. Williams, I'm here to discuss the emergency issue your assistant called about, but this doesn't seem like a good time. Are you all right?"

"Yes, Melissa. Sorry, we must have gotten our wires crossed." Elias chanced a glance at Caleb, who found his cuticles suddenly captivating.

"I'll have my secretary bill you. Do you want me to draw up paperwork for a civil suit? Unlawful pursuit? Pain and suffering? We can discuss it over lunch. Call me." She handed him a business card as if he didn't already have a dozen copies of the same card.

"I want all of you back at your posts immediately! I'm the supervisor until we figure out this clusterfuck. NOW!" The Director hadn't stopped berating the agents the entire time. Somehow, Elias' shocked system had momentarily stopped registering the words.

Tristan replaced the lawyer as she sashayed away, an agent scurrying after her to escort her from the White House. Order slowly but surely returned to the hallway as more agents skulked back to their posts like chastened children.

"You good, cuz?" Tristan nudged Elias' shoulder with his own, the smirk on his face betraying how utterly bizarre the entire scene must have appeared.

"Yeah, just a misunderstanding, I'm sure." Elias chuckled, running a hand through his hair. Still sweat-damp, it stood up on end.

"Honestly, you should blame your assistant. He called me squawking about kids. I thought something happened to Parker." Tristan jerked his chin toward Caleb, who returned the gesture with a flick of his manicured middle finger.

"Cay?" Elias turned his gaze toward Caleb, an eyebrow slowly arching.

"There was a lot to unpackage in your message. I figured backup would be helpful. So I called everyone I could think of on your contact list. Not my fault you don't have a lock on your phone." Caleb shrugged again as if it was the simplest thing in the world.

Elias grew concerned he was on the verge of a mental breakdown as he started laughing. He tried to stifle it, but it only made the situation worse. Hysterical, he braced his hands on his knees, breathless from the uncontrollable laughter. Nothing made sense to him anymore. He laughed, cried, and finally sank to his knees outside the medical unit of the White House.

CHAPTER THIRTY-TWO

Lily

LILY HANDED OVER THE last of her stash of cookies to the two children sitting on the examination across from her with a smile, glad they had finally stopped crying and were actively indulging in the treats. Not entirely sure about the protocol of bribing children with sweets, she'd gone with her gut. It worked perfectly.

"Uncle Eli said you're Theo's friend. Did he teach you about the emotional support cookies?" Anna chirped, picking apart the cookie and popping each piece into her mouth with a shower of crumbs.

"We became friends over a mutual love of emotional support cookies. These ones are caramel macchiato." Lily peeked over at Toby, smiling again in an effort to reassure the wary-looking child. "Do you like them?

"Yeah. Theo's are better. He makes them crunchy for me." Toby mumbled, pushing the last cookie into his mouth. He had been slow to start, but once he settled down, he'd consumed five of them so fast she worried she'd have to perform the Heimlich.

"He makes mine gooey." Anna wiggled, flicking crumbs off her lap with intense concentration.

"You're his friend. Why'd he run away?" Toby's glare was a remarkable mirror of the same surly disposition she'd first encountered when she met Theo, the family resemblance finally clear despite how different the younger siblings appeared.

"He didn't run away. Is that what you think happened?" She knew her eyes had gone wide with surprise over his statement.

"No one told us anything. I heard mom arguing with someone on the phone. She was bitching about him not being around. He hasn't called. He just left."

"Toby, you can't say bitching because it's miso-gonist!" Anna smacked her brother's shoulder with an open hand. "That means against women, and I'm a woman, so you can't say that!"

"Misogynist, Anna." Toby gently pushed back at her, rolling his eyes as he continued. "I'm not against you or any other women."

"Theo didn't run away, guys. He had to leave for a little bit, and he misses you both a lot. He has been somewhere where he can't use his phone very much, but I can send him a message if you'd like?" She lowered her voice to a whisper. "We can be like spies on a secret mission. I'll bring your message and come back with the reply."

"Oh em gee, like in that movie! Okay, okay, you gotta tell him Princess Stabby got all As and that the weird agent totally fell for the trap I set, so I'm basically a Top Secret Agent, and that's why I have a codename of Princess Stabby, and that we're gonna catch the bad guy but on the video and we'll send it to like... CNN and ABC and EFG and... Toby, what's the other one?"

"Anna, shh!" Toby's hands shook as he grabbed his sister, clapping a hand over her mouth.

"Guys, what weird agent?" Lily's skin prickled as she slowly deciphered the little girl's ramblings and Toby's panicked reaction. "You have to tell me this story so I can tell Theo. He'd want to know this story."

"Mr. Mitchell. He's always around all the time. Anna's been sleeping in my room since Theo left. We've been hearing him whispering in the hall like he's on a radio or something. So Anna set up traps like in that old Home Alone movie." Toby lowered his hand from Anna's mouth, tucking his hands in his oversized sweatshirt in a motion that was identical to Theo's anxious habit.

"A-yup! I'm a Top Secret Agent now." Anna puffed her chest out with a proud salute. "I put my craft paint on the cookie trays in the hall and took all the lightbulbs out, and I made tripping wires with the Christmas lights from over my bed, and he fell in the dark. He said the nastiest curses, and I got super in trouble with mommy and the maids, but they didn't believe me that it was the creepy whisper agent."

Lily placed a hand on each of their knees. "Can you remember anything he said when he was whispering? It's important, guys, so try to think really hard and remember."

Toby leaned forward, warily glancing at the door. "It was like code words. Wiggle and Willow, those are our code names. He said something about how he was gonna need more juice to get the job done. It was just weird stuff."

"Super weird. I was too scared to go to sleep, so we were going to stay up all night. This is why we had the music so loud upstairs." Anna picked at a raised red bump on the back of her hand, something Lily only noticed as the motion brought her attention to it. She snapped her hand out to stop Anna's scratching.

"Anna, how long have you had that bump? It looks itchy." Lily carefully pushed the sleeve of her sweater up, revealing several more small red dots peppering her skin.

"I don't know, Miss Lily. Maybe since this morning?" Anna shrugged, pointing toward her legs, "I think maybe it's like chicken pox. I heard that was something kids used to get?"

"Toby, do you have any red spots too?" Lily let go of Anna's hand, stepping over to the cabinet on the wall to grab a pair of latex gloves after rubbing sanitizer over her hands and arms.

"Not as bad as Anna's spots. She probably used too much bubble bath again." Toby pushed the sleeves of his sweatshirt up to his elbows. Tiny bumps dotted the undersides of his arms.

Lily closely examined each of their arms before grabbing a thermometer from the cabinet. She aimed it at Anna's forehead first, waiting for the beep before she checked the reading. 99.7. She turned to Toby, clearing the thermometer before taking his temperature. 100.1.

She grabbed the sanitizer again, squirting her hands liberally as she considered her options. She didn't have time to reach a decision, though. A sharp knocking caused all three of them to jump in unison. The door between them muffled the voice that called out, but she recognized it nevertheless.

"Lily, it's Elias. You can open the door now."

"Uncle ELI!" Anna's shriek caused Lily to jump again. The poor girl's voice would be ruined come morning for all her screeching.

Lily held up an index finger with a smile. "Let me talk to Elias while you two stay snug in here. We'll be right back, okay?"

Anna deflated, flopping dramatically over Toby's lap. His fingers combed through her hair, his expression unrevealing as he hawkishly watched Lily's departure. She slipped through the door, closing it behind herself before turning to the small group of people in the hallway. Elias stood beside a tall man in a crisp black suit.

"Who're you?" Lily bristled, not allowing her hand to fall from the doorknob.

"Carl Moore, Director of the Secret Service." He dipped his head, glancing over her shoulder at the door. "I've come to see that the children are returned to the residence."

"I don't know if that's the best idea, Director. They aren't well." Lily glanced toward Elias. "Both have a fever and skin irritations. I am concerned it might be a case of MRSA. Their brother also had the infection."

Elias did a double-take, his mouth hanging open. "Wait, you're serious?"

Carl gave them both a look, his mouth growing thin. "You're both treading a very fine line here. The stunt you pulled tonight almost got you shot. The President is due to land any minute now. I'd like to know what is happening before she arrives."

"I'm being serious. They aren't well. And I'm not letting them out of my sight." Lily pulled herself up straight, milking all five feet and six inches of her height for what it was worth.

"Me neither." Elias shifted forward, positioning himself in front of the door beside Lily. He had a full six inches on her. Together, they made an imposing pair.

"Sir, with all due respect for your station, I'm not sure what the show is about. You can return to the residence with the children if you want. You're one of the few with approved access. The President has you listed as their guardian in absentia." Elias' brows shot skyward.

"Oh, well... that makes it easier." Cocking his head, he continued. "Why wouldn't the agents let me see them earlier?"

"I'm not at liberty to discuss, Sir."

Lily and Elias glanced at one another simultaneously. Bolstering herself with a deep breath, she turned back toward the Director.

"You need to get different agents. For the kids, I mean. Not the usual ones." Her knuckles went white where she gripped the doorknob. "And we're waiting for the President. Because she needs to decide on their treatment before I'll clear them to leave the premises."

Carl passed a hand over his mouth with a muffled sigh. "I'm not at liberty to discuss the assignments of the agents, but I'll see what we can do. The President's expected to arrive within the hour."

Lily's body vibrated from top to toe with nervousness, but she held her chin higher, her bravado surprising for how anxious she was challenging the Director. Nevertheless, the kids were her patients, and she would let no man, regardless of title, get in the way. Patient advocacy was the only thing she ever found a backbone for.

"Very well. You can wait in the main office while we see to the children. Sir." She jerked her chin up higher for added emphasis. "Privacy laws. I'm sure you understand."

Carl exhaled in exasperation as he turned on his heel, striding toward the front of the medical unit with a mutter. As soon as he was through the exit, Lily exhaled the breath she hadn't realized she had been holding since she finished her speech. Elias pretended to clap his hands, mindful to keep the sound muffled.

"Stay right here, don't let anyone in the door. I have to run to the med room. I think we have some prescriptions on hand. I don't want to wait longer than we already have in their treatment. You're guardian in absentia. Do you consent to the treatment?" Lily had made it halfway down the hall as she spoke.

"Yes, Lil. Of course. Just do what you need to keep them safe." Elias shooed her, standing more squarely in front of the door.

She jogged the rest of the way and hastily pulled ointments, antibiotics, and fever reducers from storage before racing back to the examination room. As soon as she returned, she checked the exits before leaning in closer, the sensation of being a covert operative rising as she did so.

"Something's not right, Elias. The kids said one of the agents was sneaking around the residence and whispering. It might be the same person Caleb heard. We need to tell the President."

"Lil, I think you're right. Connor called me from Airforce One. Theo's not answering any of his calls. He said something about one of the agents. It's all chaos. I don't know what to do." Harried and exhausted were the only way Lily could explain Elias' appearance. The descriptors also worked to describe how she currently felt. With a tiny sigh, she nodded.

"We do one thing at a time until we have to do the next thing. Let's get back to the kids." They entered the room together, the brightening of the children's expressions giving her hope that perhaps everything would be all right if they took it all one step at a time. Together. It was better than facing it alone.

CHAPTER THIRTY-THREE

Theo

SHOCK AND PARANOIA DID strange things to rational thought and the passage of time, but Theo eventually mustered the courage to return home. Having no identification, money, or cell phone limited his options. Threats loomed around every corner and in every sideways glance. There was no one he could trust, least of all his own judgment. Nevertheless, the desire for safety brought him to the place that had become home.

After wandering for who knows how long, head aching and body drowning in fatigue, he needed a shower, food, and more than a few seconds of sleep. As he rounded the corner, the now-familiar block he called home stretched before him like a beacon in the darkness. The hair on the back of his neck stood up as he walked closer to the entrance of their apartment building, but the constant clamor of alarm bells in his head had desensitized him to the sensation. Singularly focused on getting somewhere safe, he bent down and pulled the key from his shoe. The beep of the access code to the building sang a siren song promising salvation. The metallic click of a firearm's safety disengaging before the barrel pressed against his spine erased all hope he had left.

"Scream, and you die. Now show me the love nest, boy." The familiar voice ran through his body with the shock of an explosive device.

He swallowed the swiftly rising bile churning in his empty stomach. Terror left him frozen until James pushed the gun harder against his spine. "Now."

The fear that had left him frozen now pushed him through the motions on autopilot as he muscled the heavy door open. Each step up the three flights of stairs became harder and harder to climb. His hand violently shook as he tried to fit the key into their door. Eventually, it slotted into place. With a quick twist, the sanctuary of home became tainted by the violation of an intruder as James shoved him into the apartment so hard he fell to the ground. One, two, three kicks to his stomach had him dry heaving as he tried to curl around himself. The door slammed shut. The chain lock rattled into place. The deadbolt thunked with an ominous finality that had Theo's heart sinking.

He tried to stifle his groan as he attempted to push himself upright, but the pain coursing through him made it impossible. James advanced like a rabid animal. With disheveled hair and crazed eyes, he resembled a possessed man. Theo didn't have time to react before the barrel of the gun slammed against the side of his head, and everything went dark.

He became aware of the noise first once consciousness returned. Dishes breaking alongside the incessant mutterings of a deranged man. Theo tried to move as his eyelids fluttered open, but the sharp bite of metal against his wrists stopped him short. Handcuffs held him in place, looped around the pipes under the kitchen sink. Disoriented and floating somewhere above reality, Theo took stock of his situation from a detached place, making the whole experience surreal. He ached from head to toe. Nausea threatened to overwhelm him at any moment. Somewhere, a low groan punctuated the noise of James' destruction of the apartment. The realization that it was his own voice startled him at the same time that it caught James' attention.

"Good morning, princess." His sneer made Theo recoil as far as his bonds would allow him.

"Wh-what are you doing?"

"Where did you hide the evidence? I know you've been sneaking around playing detective, you little shit. Where is the rest of it?!" James tore open another cabinet, the pots and pans clattering to the floor with a crash that made his already throbbing head pound even harder.

"There's nothing. I don't have anything. I promise!" Theo flinched as James reeled on him, landing another kick on his prone torso.

"Liar! You lie! My guys saw you sneaking around playing telephone tag! They have your bag with the fucking computer pieces and the tablet!"

"I swear, I don't know anything! Just let me go, please?" Theo sobbed, the act causing pain to tear through his body.

"No, no, no. The plan isn't finished. You ruined it. Everything's ruined, but I can still fix this. I can fix this. We can make this work." James turned and disappeared into the bedroom. Although the distance muffled the noise, James' path of destruction continued.

Theo painstakingly shimmied in place, contorting himself despite the excruciating pain the movement caused until his feet found purchase against the baseboard of the cabinets. The metal links of the handcuffs squeaked against the piping. Theo leveraged himself and yanked. He yanked again. Gritting his teeth, driven by the instinctual fight or flight response, he pulled a third time, every muscle in his body taut with the effort. Something snapped in his wrist, sending a searing pain up his arm, but this time, the pipe snapped too. Water sprayed from the busted piping with a hiss.

He staggered to his feet, breathless and fueled by adrenaline alone, before sprinting to the door. His right hand dangled uselessly, but he flipped the deadbolt, fumbled the chain lock, and whipped the door open. James' shouting followed close behind him, but all he could process were the words *run, run, run* on repeat in his primal mind. As his captor barreled after him like a runaway train, he clattered down the stairs as fast as his feet would carry him. Close, closer, too close. In a last-ditch effort to get help, Theo smashed the fire alarm on the wall before James tackled him to the landing.

With a feral sound, James grabbed Theo by the back of the shirt and his hair, hauling him to his feet before roughly manhandling him down the last flight of stairs. He shouldered the door to the street open, jerking Theo with him. Outside, pedestrians gave them a wide berth, the fire alarm clang echoing between the buildings as residents came filtering out. Theo cried out, incoherent shouts of help and please jumbling together as James dragged him, kicking and screaming, to the dark SUV parked on the curbside. Theo tried to resist, but James managed to shove him into the backseat of the car, flashing his badge at the gawkers with a smile as he held Theo face-down against the upholstery.

"Caught the burglar."

Theo's cries dissolved into sobbing as the fight drained out of him. Breathing became more difficult with each gasp he took. He vaguely registered James unlocking the handcuffs long enough to clip the ring around the door handle before he pulled his weight back. When the door slammed shut, Theo gave it a weak kick, the glitter dust sparkles on the fringes of his vision alerting him to his rapidly depleting oxygen levels. He needed to switch gears in his effort to survive.

The car dipped as James plopped into the front seat. Inhale. He flicked on the emergency light clipped above the rearview mirror. Exhale. The engine rumbled to life as James turned the key. Inhale. Motion made Theo's stomach twist, dizziness descending with renewed vigor. Exhale.

Moving slowly, he shifted his newly freed hand toward the front pocket of his jeans. Every movement sent razors of pain through his arm. His vision went dark at the edges. Despite the clawing burn of his broken wrist, he pried the inhaler from his pocket, nearly fumbling it as his fingers refused to move the way he wanted them to. *Theo, breathe.* Connor's voice in his head coached him through the motions. Eyes scrunched tight, he brought the inhaler to his lips and depressed the canister by sheer force of will, breathing the medication in as deep as possible. *You need to breathe, baby.* Again, he gasped as another puff of the inhaler relieved the tightness in his chest.

"You're really making it hard for me to find a reason to keep you alive, you little bastard." James' muttering from the front seat floated on the edges of Theo's awareness as he concentrated on the methodical deep breaths he needed. "She needs to pay. I'll make her regret everything." The car lurched forward as James pressed down harder on the accelerator.

"I don't... know what... you're talking... about."

"If she hadn't run for all these offices, I'd still have my fucking family! It's all her fault!" James smacked the steering wheel with the heel of his palm as he continued shouting, punctuating each word with a strike. "It's all her fault!"

Hopelessness crushed him more every minute they drove, the flash of passing streetlights combined with the emergency flasher on the windshield illuminating the car with macabre pulsing strobe lights. "None of this makes sense, James, please!"

"All your mother talked about! For years! Women this, women that! Taking back their power! Living life on their terms! Equality! Justice!" James jerked the wheel, his driving becoming more erratic the further they went. "My wife wouldn't have left me if it weren't for all that bullshit! She wouldn't have taken my little girl away!"

It still didn't make any sense. None of it made any sense. Theo tried to brace himself in the backseat, but every jerk of the SUV sent shockwaves through his battered body.

"Why me?! What does any of this have to do with me?"

"She destroyed me." The tires screeched as the vehicle came to an abrupt stop. "So I'm going to destroy her."

The flashing lights flicked off. The engine cut out as James turned the keys and pulled them from the ignition. The world became darker. Theo had no clue where they were. The back door opened, jerking his arm by the handcuffs attached to the handle. James fiddled with the key and then hauled Theo from the car. Never had he ever in his life experienced so much pain. Even if he dared to fight back, he wouldn't have had the energy.

"Come on, bastard. You've caused enough trouble for one night." James dragged Theo like a rag doll through doors, dark hallways, and down a flight of stairs. Helpless to do anything but go where James forced him to, he staggered until his back pressed against a wooden beam. A shriek left his lips as James struck the loose end of the handcuffs around his wrist, cinching the metal bond tight around the swollen joint. His knees buckled, splinters from the wooden beam barely registering against the intensity of his suffering as he slid to the floor.

"Now shut the fuck up and let me concentrate," James muttered as he circled the room, flicking on light switches and computer monitors before grabbing a roll of duct tape. He pulled a section loose before tearing it off and stretching it over Theo's mouth.

The tape muffled his sobs as he took in the surroundings. Illumination from the harsh fluorescent lighting overhead revealed dozens, no, hundreds of campaign posters, pictures, news articles, and magazine covers that wallpapered the basement walls. A complete overhead view of his mother's political career.

Pictures of him, Anna, and Toby mingled with print-outs of surveillance photos of a teenage girl that looked remarkably similar to James. Throughout this montage, Theo found symbols and images familiar to him only because of Taz' obsessive campaign to take down right-wing extremists and neo-Nazis. Calls to embrace traditional family values. Rhetoric about liberal agendas destroying the fabric of society. Replicas of Hitler's propaganda posters.

The computers scattered around the room were open to some of the same sites they had mined for information. In the corner, against a backdrop of more neo-Nazi banners, stood a stool, and on top of it sat a black leather wolf mask. A camera perched on a tripod faced the vignette. Cold dread settled in the pit of his stomach. They'd finally uncovered the identity of the Son of the Wolf. And now Theo was trapped inside his den.

CHAPTER THIRTY-FOUR

Connor

Connor had never been more thrilled that Airforce One had priority at the designated landing zone, but time still dragged torturously slow. Abandoning his post wasn't an option. Not when the Director of the Secret Service had taken over the supervisory role at the White House. The information filtered through his earpiece in dribs and drabs with no clear sign of what had caused the switch in leadership. At least the kids were safe. If only he could say the same about Theo.

The drive from the plane to the White House proceeded slowly, but at last, they were in the garage and out of the cars. His earpiece nearly blew up with reports as soon as they announced Wish was back on the premises.

"Madam President, a moment." Connor jogged to catch up to her. "You need to report to the medical unit. The kids are there."

Adelaide didn't bother questioning it. Connor had to continue jogging to keep pace as she tore through the halls. The agents behind them did the same until a cacophony of thundering feet echoed off the walls. Connor tried to reach for the door, but she beat him to it, pushing it open so hard it smacked against the wall with a loud bang. The Physician to the President tumbled in after them as she called out for her children.

"Mommy, mommy!" Anna squealed from deeper inside the medical ward.

"Wait, Anna!" Lily entered, following in the wake of the tornado known as Anna.

Toby and Elias appeared behind them, with Caleb and Parker tucking in beside Elias. The room suddenly became overcrowded as Adelaide pulled her two youngest children closer and snapped her gaze toward Lily.

"What's the meaning of this? What's going on? Why are they here?"

"Addy, first things first, Lily thinks the kids have MRSA. Skin, not pneumonia like Theo's. I gave her the green light to start them on treatment." Elias edged forward to stand at Lily's side.

"The cream is stinky, but I like how it feels. You should try it for your wrinkles!" Anna coiled her arms around Adelaide's waist, giggling as she squeezed her mother tight.

Caleb stifled a snicker. Scanning the room, Connor was struck by how stressed and tired every single one appeared. He likely had to include himself in that observation.

"And the other thing?" Connor hinted toward Elias while casting a sidelong glance over his shoulder.

"You weren't wrong to call me, Connor. Toby, tell your mom what you told Miss Lily, okay? She's here now, and she's going to listen. We're going to fix this." Elias bumped Toby's shoulder with a gentle nudge of his fist.

"Mom, Anna and I are too scared to go back to the house with the agents. One of them was sneaking around. He's the one who set off all of Anna's traps she got in trouble for. I'm not making it up, okay?" Toby jerked his chin higher, narrowing his eyes as he folded his arms. "We wouldn't lie about stuff like that."

Connor's head swam as he reached out to brace himself with the nearest wall. "When was this, Toby?"

"Last week and then again the last few nights. We were going to try and stay up all night long and get a video of it on mom's tablet tonight, but Elias came, and we all ran here."

"It was awesome, mom! I had to pretend I was sick, so I screamed and screamed, and no one yelled at me to stop. But then Miss Lily said we were actually sick." Anna had yet to loosen her grip on her mother's waist.

Adelaide stood with her mouth agape before finally blurting, "What the hell is going on here?"

Connor pulled his wrist to his mouth before keying up the mic. "O'Brien to Director Moore."

"Go for Moore. Line 5."

Connor switched the channel on his radio before continuing. "Do we have a location on Agent James Locke?"

"Negative. Report to headquarters for debriefing."

"All due respect, Director Moore, but I can't. Find Locke. It's an emergency." Connor flipped his radio off before pulling the earpiece from his ear and disentangling the wire from his sleeve. He tossed it on the desk. "Madam President, I need to go find your son. Do not let these kids out of your sight."

"Connor, what can I do?" Elias reached out to stop Connor's departure, worry etched in the lines of his exhausted face.

"Stay with them. Lily and Caleb too. Everyone stays together. I'll call you." Like a switch had been flipped, Connor resorted to his Marine mentality. His singular focus became finding Theo. He'd deal with the rest of it when he had to. He made sure the remaining agents had directives to stick with the group before taking off down the hall, his cell phone already dialing Abriella's number as he ran straight into Director Carl Moore.

"Agent O'Brien, explain yourself!" The Director grabbed Connor's shoulders as he tried to step around the muscle mass blocking his exit.

"I reckon Agent James Locke's the mole, Sir. And now he's missing. So is the First Son. So I'm going to go do my job, if it pleases." Connor jerked out of the Director's grip, speaking into his phone as he did so. "Abs, one second. I'm on my way."

"Why wasn't any of this reported to me?" The Director's face turned a vivid shade of red.

"I only just put the pieces together earlier on the plane. He told the President some things he shouldn't have known, and it all sort of clicked. I called the people I had to. Now, I'm going." Connor almost slipped away before Carl grabbed his arm.

"I'm sending a uniformed division to his home address. Find the kid and report back. I presume your vehicle still has a radio, at least?"

Connor nodded, albeit begrudgingly.

"Good. We don't fly rogue. Stick to the book; I might let you keep your job."

Connor didn't need to be told twice. He sprinted down the hallway, bringing the phone back to his ear.

"Dios mio, Connor. Where are you?" Abriella's voice came over the line in a torrent. "Everything is loco. I have Taz with me. Where ARE you?"

"I'm heading to my apartment. Can you meet me there?"

"We're already on the way." In the background, Taz cried out. "Shut up. I'm not going to crash. Was it him, mi sol?"

"Yeah. He's MIA. Someone's been sneaking around the residence too. Just get there." During their brief conversation, Connor made it to the garage, tossing the phone in his suit pocket before fishing out his keys. The engine's rumble had barely kicked over before he had the car in gear. With a flick, the emergency lights flashed in sobering shades of color that made everything more intense.

Instinct took over, the evasive driving skills he learned in the agency academy finally finding practice in a real-world situation as he weaved in and out of traffic, skirting along the shoulder of the road at every intersection. A commute that generally took almost half an hour in regular traffic was cut in half as he drifted around the corner of his street. His body jerked as the vehicle's front end jumped up the curb before screeching to a halt. His interpretation of parallel parking violated numerous ordinances.

Deep, measured breathing punctuated the pounding of his feet as he flew out of the car and toward the apartment building. He punched in the access code by muscle memory, his keys in one hand and his gun in the other. Bounding up the stairs two at a time, he reached the third floor and nearly careened into the building superintendent.

"Connor! You have ironic timing. We had a complaint on the first floor about a leak. I thought it was the vacant apartment on two, but it's coming fro—"

"Don't. Touch. Anything." Connor stepped around the dazed man, holding his gun upright with his finger poised over the trigger. He crept toward his apartment door, the fact that he was running procedure at his home not quite registering through the flood of adrenaline. A thin line of light was visible around the edges of the frame. He nudged the door with his foot, repositioning his firing arm to swiftly duck into the room with a sweeping motion.

The main room was empty. And completely destroyed. Connor moved carefully over the linoleum, water seeping into his shoes, before he stepped into the bedroom, clearing the space before moving on to the bathroom. Every room was empty, but the destruction was everywhere.

"Shit! God damn it!" Connor holstered his gun, returning to the kitchen to find the building superintendent staring in horror at the wreckage.

"Go! Pull the security tapes! I'm calling the cops. Go!" Connor swept his gaze over the room to try and make sense of the crime scene his life had become. Shattered plates covered the floor. Hot water hissed out of the broken pipe under the kitchen sink. He stepped back to get a clearer picture. A small pool of dried blood inside the entryway caught his eye as his heart sank into the pit of his stomach. Connor had enough presence of mind to leave the crime scene before his guts turned inside out. He held himself up against the wall as he retched, dread filling his now-empty stomach.

Wiping his mouth on his shirt sleeve, he tumbled down the stairs in a clatter of wet shoes over textured tile before bursting into the damp chill of the late night. He jogged to his vehicle on the sidewalk, the lights still flashing as he yanked the door open and pulled the radio toward himself. He ran through the dial on the box before keying up the mic.

"This is Special Agent Connor O'Brien to base. I need an APB on James Locke. Suspected kidnapping, assault, home invasion. Whisper is MIA, presumed injured, and medically sensitive. I need forensics to 143 Locklan Street, Apt 3C. Over."

"Director Moore, copy. Stay on the scene. Over."

Connor clicked the receiver back into place before racing back into the building and up the stairs. His breath came hard and fast by the time he got into the apartment, carefully avoiding the majority of the evidence as he went back into his bedroom. Their bedroom. Theo's things lay scattered amid his own on the bed they'd shared, and it took every ounce of willpower he had not to throw up again. He found the gun safe lying against the wall, a hole punched through the sheetrock above it. He pulled out his key ring and unlocked it. The firearms went into the waistband of his pants alongside his government-issue Glock before he grabbed a spare clip and shoved it into his pocket.

It only took minutes. Back outside, Abriella's SUV had nosed in beside his. The two sets of flashing emergency lights dueled for supremacy in the darkened street. She sprung from the car and sprinted toward him.

"Biggs, is he there?"

"No, Abs. He's gone." Connor glanced over her shoulder toward the car. Taz sat wide-eyed in the passenger seat. "Does he have anything?"

"Si, one of the cell phones. He has the locations. Come on!" Abriella grabbed his sleeve, and they jogged to her car. Connor hauled himself into the backseat as Abriella hopped into the driver's seat. The vehicle was in motion before he even had the door closed.

"Look, Theo's gone, and we need to find him. Show me what you got."

"I have a general location but not an address. Does this look familiar?" Taz craned his torso in the passenger seat, holding out a tablet with an overhead map on the screen. A circle ringed the center of the image. Connor sucked in a breath as recognition of the neighborhood hit him.

"You done gotta be shitting me!"

"What? What is it, Connor?!" Abriella snapped her eyes to the rearview before returning them to the road. Her knuckles were white where she gripped the steering wheel to dart around the cars ahead of them.

"I know that area. I've been there before." Connor swore again, striking the ceiling of the vehicle with his fist before reaching over the center console to Abriella's radio unit. He turned the dial to the right channel and grabbed the receiver. "Special Agent Connor O'Brien to base. We're en route to the residence of Thomas Mitchell. Requesting back-up. Over."

The receiver slotted back into its clip with a soft click as the crushing realization that they might be too late threatened to swallow him whole. The vehicle dipped and swerved and careened around corners like a rollercoaster, but it might not be enough no matter how fast they went. All he wanted to do was keep Theo safe. All he had done was fail.

CHAPTER THIRTY-FIVE

Adelaide

MORE CROWDED THAN EVER, the Situation Room buzzed with chatter, making it impossible to pick out any single conversation. Her advisors were up in arms over the presence of so many new people, especially her children. Elias had Toby tucked under his arm behind her. The doctor, Lily, who had treated all three of her children, stood in the corner with Anna and Parker. The Vice President stood at the opposite end of the table, his brother taking up the space to Adelaide's right. It was standing room only between the Director of the Secret Service, FBI, CIA, and Homeland Security, plus all their assistants.

Everyone juggled cell phones, radios, tablets, and paperwork as assistants raced back and forth between screens and printers. The monitors along the wall showed a mixture of live traffic feeds and news broadcasts of protests that had broken out around many of the major cities along the eastern seaboard. Adelaide cleared her throat. No one paid her any attention. She coughed louder. Still, no one shifted their focus. Finally, she brought the palms of her hands down on the table with as much force as she could muster.

"Everyone STOP!"

All eyes turned toward her as if she'd grown three extra heads. Gathering her tenuous composure, she stood a little straighter, sweeping her eyes over the faces surrounding her.

"One at a time, I need you to tell me what we are working with here. Please. You first, Director Moore." She pointed at the Director of the Secret Service.

"We are attempting to locate James Locke and Thomas Mitchell for questioning. James is not at home. I have agents en route to Thomas Mitchell's residence," Carl replied, momentarily pausing with a distant look as he listened to his radio. "They're about fifteen minutes out."

"Fields," Adelaide snapped as she swung her pointed finger toward Director Luke Fields of the FBI.

"Madam President, our investigators are trying to backtrace the numbers and email addresses of the suspects. We should have a full report within the hour. Our forensics team is sweeping the crime scene as we speak. We have a squadron of agents en route to the Mitchell and Locke residences."

"You." The CIA Director's name eluded her. Pointing worked regardless.

"Our analysts are monitoring the chatter on the dark web. The individual who calls himself the Son of the Wolf has put out a call to arms to initiate the plan. Groups are assembling at tourist attractions, college campuses, and government facilities in five major cities, including DC. We do not have specifics about the motives or plan." With a nod toward the bank of screens, he continued. "We have narrowed down the identity of the leaders in three of the five cities and are working with local law enforcement units to apprehend them."

"Patten, you next." Adelaide rubbed her hands over her face before nodding toward the Director of Homeland Security.

"We've escalated the threat advisory nationwide. Our headquarters is in communication with the local branches in each of the five cities to orchestrate a joint effort with the agencies on the ground. We've debriefed them to expect violence and prepare for the most likely acts of domestic terrorism."

A moment of quiet fell over the room before it was interrupted by Lily as she softly cleared her throat and murmured, "Ma'am, if I may?"

Startled, Adelaide turned in place to cast the timid girl a questioning glance. The room bristled all around her with tension.

"Sorry, sorry. I heard from a friend at a research lab in New York City. It's one of the places worst hit by the MRSA outbreak. The strain is a genetic match to the one your son and numerous officials recently had. I checked the CDC database. The other four cities on the news are also hotspots for the outbreak." Lily tucked her hair behind her ear, swiftly scanning the faces around the room.

"And? What does this have to do with anything?" Andrew snapped, a scowl playing over his features.

"Sir, emergency rooms and hospitals in these cities are already struggling with overcrowding and strained resources. If the genetic makeup of the strain is the same in DC and New York, there's a chance it's also a match to Philadelphia, Miami, and Charlotte." Lily squared her shoulders, elevating her chin as she did so. "I believe there's a connection here. You should tell the agencies to be on the alert for a biological element. Masks and gloves, at the very least."

Adelaide glanced at Anna and Parker standing beside Lily. She turned her eyes toward Toby. All three of her children with the same infection.

"She has a point. We can't ignore the evidence. Alert your people." Adelaide turned back toward the table, snapping her fingers. The Directors spoke into their respective radios and cell phones to convey the news.

"Wait, patch it through! Put it on the screen!" The Director of the CIA shooed his assistant toward the bank of monitors on the wall.

The younger man rushed to do as instructed, one of the screens going blank before an image straight out of Adelaide's worst nightmare flashed to life. The room gasped in unison. Anna screamed behind her. Toby clapped a hand to his mouth to stifle a sob.

"No. No, no, no!" Adelaide cried out as her knees nearly buckled. Aaron caught her fall with an arm around her waist. Lily grabbed Parker and Anna by the hands and rushed them, sobbing, from the room. Elias tried to hide Toby's face against his chest, but he struggled against the act.

All the while, Adelaide stared in horror at the image of her Theo on the screen. Her sweet baby boy. Despite the blood smeared over the side of his face and the haggard appearance, she would never miss that it was her son who kneeled on the floor in the video feed, held upright by a man in a black leather wolf mask. The background filled with symbols of hate made it worse. But the most chilling part of the image was the machete held to her son's throat.

"Turn it up! Max, are you guys tracing this?" The Director of the CIA spoke to the assistant and on the phone simultaneously as the younger man fumbled with the controls. The speakers crackled to life.

"—for too long! Now it is our turn! Rise up against these false promises, these immoral beliefs! Fight against the poison that is tearing families apart! President Montgomery, you are not the role model this country needs! You are a serpent! A liar and temptress! Just as Eve destroyed the promise of paradise for mankind, you are destroying the vision of this country! So we will destroy you! And we'll start with your bastard son!"

"TURN IT OFF!" Adelaide screamed, clapping her hands to her ears as tears streamed down her face. They continued to flow even as she scrunched her eyes tight. Wrenching free from Aaron's hold on her waist, she scrambled backward until her back hit the wall. Gravity pulled her to the ground.

Chaos erupted around her, bodies jostling for position at the bank of monitors and around computer screens. The sound from the speakers cut out as people grabbed headphones and earbuds. Aaron stooped down next to her, murmuring reassurances that became static in her ears. Toby's wailing cut above the noise before Caleb managed to drag him out of the room. Elias slammed the door closed behind them.

"Aaron, get her out of here! I'll take over." Andrew stepped into her spot at the head of the table, firing directives left and right. Her vision swam in technicolor hues, blurry from the tears that flowed freely down her cheeks. Numb. She was numb from head to toe as she tried in vain to wipe her eyes. She forced her gaze back to the screen on the wall, forced herself to focus on the last image of her baby boy still alive.

Aaron managed to pull her to her feet despite her resistance. He maneuvered her closer to the door, whispering quietly in an attempt to mollify her. The numbness consumed her until it suddenly disappeared. Like a bubble around her had popped, the chaos rushed back in full force.

Andrew's voice bellowed over the room. "Aaron, I'm enacting the 25th Amendment! Someone get General Siamo on the line. We're declaring martial la—"

"No, you are not!" Adelaide tore herself from Aaron's grip before reeling on her Vice-President with every ounce of pain, anger, and devastation that coursed through her veins. "I am the President of the United States, and I am not going anywhere!"

Adelaide stalked toward the head of the table, stopping just inches from him. She faced down her Vice-President, her running mate, the man she had called friend. And she was not prepared to back down. So much sacrifice had led her to this place. Perhaps the greatest sacrifice of all. But she would not let her child suffer in vain, nor would she allow anyone else to take over, push her aside, or manipulate her into decisions she did not want to make. James' betrayal. Andrew's conviction. Her own misguided dedication. They'd all led to this moment.

"Step aside, or leave. I am the Commander-in-Chief," she snarled, Andrew taking a step back with a shocked expression. She turned toward the table, spreading her palms on the surface to brace herself. "Someone get me a radio. Updates. Now!"

One of the Secret Service agents pulled his radio off and slid it over the table to her. Paperwork still warm from the printer appeared on the table. A tablet skated to a halt near her hand. With a deep breath, she took one last glance at the image of her son on the screen before diving into the emergency response team. She'd taken up this work to make the world a better place. To honor a dream her late husband had made the ultimate sacrifice for. And now she would make sure she finished the job. For her children.

CHAPTER THIRTY-SIX

Abriella

"TAKE THE NEXT RIGHT!" Connor called from the backseat of the SUV, his hand reaching over the center console to point toward the next street. Abriella jerked the steering wheel, the tires squealing on the pavement before they regained traction. Taz' face adopted a sickly shade of green in the passenger seat beside her.

"You vomit in my car, I shoot you," she muttered through clenched teeth, pressing down harder on the accelerator.

"Left up ahead! Duplex on the right-hand side." Connor pulled back before his hand reappeared, holding a pistol in front of Taz. "Ever shot a gun?"

"What the... no!" Horrified, Taz recoiled. "Dude, what the hell?!"

"Flick the safety on the side, point it, pull the trigger." Connor waved the gun with a beckoning motion. "Take it, Taz!"

"You guys are nuts," he muttered, reaching out to take the gun as if it would go off any second.

Again the tires screeched as she stopped in front of the building Connor had described. The poorly lit street revealed a run-down exterior with an unkempt plot of patchy dead grass partially covered in slushy snow. A black SUV sat in the driveway before the garage door on the right-hand side of the building. Connor pushed the back door open and took off in a sprint toward the building. Abriella unleashed a string of irritated swear words in Spanish before jumping out of the front seat. Sirens echoed in the distance.

"Taz, stay! Connor, stop!" Abriella tried to catch up, but the man was on a mission. "Connor!"

He didn't reply, bounding up the steps of the right-most stoop before squaring his feet. If he were determined to dive in head first, covering him would be the least she could do to hopefully prevent catastrophe. Connor kicked the door just below the handle. The frame splintered as the door whipped open. A rapid pop, pop, pop that echoed off the buildings lining the street followed the bang of the door. Gunfire. Abriella impulsively spun to take cover as Connor did the same in a mirror of her motion.

"Mitchell! Drop it!" Connor hollered, his gun held upright before himself as he rested his back against the wall.

"Fuck you, O'Brien! So sick of you and your golden boy bullshit!"

Connor met Abriella's gaze across the short distance that separated them, and they nodded once in unison. She pivoted first, bringing her firearm horizontal with the ground to fire off three rounds into the darkness of the entryway. A return volley answered her shots as she returned to cover. Connor followed suit, another three shells exploding from the barrel of his gun. She timed her movements with his, darting out to keep the pressure on the shooter inside the building. They were firing blindly into the dark, trusting their instincts and the deafening crack of each gunshot that answered theirs.

Connor hissed beside her. A quick glance reassured her he hadn't gotten shot in any vital organs. Adrenaline pumping, she spun back into the doorway. She fired off one shot and then another, but her third shot went wide as a searing pain blossomed in her shoulder. Connor called out to her, but the ringing in her ears drowned out the words. She assumed he asked if she was good, but she couldn't be sure, so all he got in response was a grunt. It would be a miracle if they made it through the night.

She swore again, a relentless barrage of colorful words and phrases in her native language, as Connor barged through the door, pulling a second firearm from the waistband of his pants. He pressed forward in the wake of a maelstrom of back-to-back gunshots. Rational thought made her hesitate. Loyalty drove her forward. He'd always had her back. Now it was her turn. She ducked through the door and took up position behind him, angling her firearm to cover even as the movement sent a burning, throbbing wave of pain through the left side of her body.

The blitz attack worked, despite the probability that it wouldn't. A crash of furniture alerted them to the shooter's location as he attempted to flee. With a swift, practiced movement, Abriella tracked the movement, and on the exhale, she pulled the trigger. Their attacker went down with a grunt. Tossing one of his firearms to the side, Connor leapt like an animal, like a man possessed, grappling with the man before swinging his hand down to land a series of blows to the assailant's face.

"Where is he?! Where?"

The only response was a wheezing, gurgling exhalation followed by an eerie silence as the man went still. Their heavy breaths filled the silence. Time froze momentarily, a strange limbo of inactivity after a life-or-death flurry of activity. Their heads snapped up in unison as a muffled cry rang out from outside. Connor reared back, scrambling to stand before racing back to the front door. As they got closer, they could hear the shout again, clearer this time.

"D-Don't move, or I'll sh-shoot you!"

They flew through the door and down the steps in a flurry, following the sound to the narrow space that separated the buildings. Taz stood at the mouth of the alley, his hands quaking as he held the gun in front of himself. Connor sprinted to him, Abriella right behind. Her shoulder throbbed more with each beat of her heart. The sirens were closer now. Overhead, the staccato thump of helicopter blades cutting through the air filled the night with a persistent thrum that grew louder with each passing second.

Connor and Abriella flanked Taz, each aiming their firearms into the darkened recesses of the alley. The scene resembled something from a horror movie. Theo appeared to be nearly unconscious, if not wholly unconscious. His frame was limp as a wolf-masked man held him up with an arm around the throat, positioned as a shield between the trio and his captor.

"Let him go, James! It's over!" Connor's voice was ragged, echoing into the alley plaintive and desperate as he shifted his grip on the gun. "Look, I'll put it down. Just let him go."

"One more move, and he's done, Connor." The ominous warning froze Connor in his tracks. The helicopter overhead switched directions, flying over the buildings. The flash of a spotlight briefly illuminated the alley like a lightning flash. It disappeared as quickly as it came before backtracking. The beam of light shone down, and suddenly it was day-bright.

"Drop your weapon! There's nowhere to go!" Abriella repositioned her grip on the gun, the pulsating pain causing her hands to tremble. Taz shook even harder.

Theo's body tensed as he inhaled. Relief flooded her system. She wasn't sure if he was alive until he took that desperate, gasping breath. Connor leveled his weapon higher, taking aim.

"Theo, baby. You need to breathe." Connor barely exhaled the words, the softest whisper into the night. The emotions hanging in the air sent chills up her spine.

Another slight rise and fall of his chest showed he'd heard Connor's words. In slow motion, a sequence of events played out like freeze-frames from a movie. Abriella caught the faint tell in James' hand, the slightest shift in the tendons as his finger tensed on the trigger. Connor let loose a desperate cry of "No!" that was lost to the blare of sirens as emergency vehicles flooded the street behind them. Taz hit the ground as police shouted freeze and stop and get on the ground. Abriella's finger squeezed the trigger as Connor did the same. Two shots fired in unison, a single pop crashing through the air. James' head rocked back as he began to fall, and a third gunshot rang out. Together, James and Theo collapsed.

Slow motion sped up in the aftermath. Abriella sank to her knees as if she had deflated. Connor fell forward, a sob escaping his lips as he dove toward the two bodies on the ground. Law enforcement officers raced into the alley, calling out orders and commands that turned into a jumble of incoherent shouting. Colors, lights, and flashes of images in freeze frames raced around her in a blur as her vision grew dim and fuzzy. Someone jostled her, and then too many people were touching her. She opened her mouth to call for Connor, but nothing came out. More lights, more shouting. Too many bodies. *Connor!* She couldn't yell, but in her rapidly approaching delirium, she figured he'd come to her if she thought it hard enough.

A chill crept over her body as she fell backward. Maybe someone pushed her. Her shoulder didn't hurt anymore. Bizarre thoughts began to flit in and out of her mind as the sensation of floating washed over her. She had always assumed Heaven would be warmer, like a spring day in Texas. Brighter, too. Not this cold, clinging darkness.

"Hold on, Smalls. I'm here." Connor's voice blanketed her with the warmth she was missing. That didn't make sense. Unless he was dead too. Maybe they were all in Heaven together. That would be fitting. She tried to reach out to him, if only in her mind. And then everything was finally blissfully silent.

··········

The silence didn't last long enough. Nor did the brief respite from the pain. A bloodcurdling scream woke her from the best sleep she'd had in months, and when she sat up straight in the bed, the pain that tore through her shoulder and chest inspired a flurry of curses to pour from her lips. *Not dead after all.* The matter-of-fact thought helped explain the strange scene before her.

"Shh, I'm here, Teddy. Y'all right. Just breathe, baby." Connor's familiar drawl cut through her clouded thoughts as she blinked, bringing the dimly lit room into focus.

"Lie back, mi corazon. Ignore them." An even more familiar voice coaxed her back into the bed. Things made less sense the more time she spent conscious.

"Abuela?" Her voice croaked, and she grimaced.

She shifted to her side, the tight sling holding her arm in place, tugging uncomfortably around her torso. She reached out her good hand, the bony fingers of her grandmother wrapping around it with a gentle squeeze. Behind her grandmother's familiar face, she spied Connor sitting upright in the bed beside hers. She blinked three more times before the form of Theo curled up against his chest came into focus.

"What is happening?" Abriella sputtered, trying to make sense of it all.

"You had a surgery. But this pendejo say he will not leave you or him. Many men in black like the movie flash badges, so you must share this room. I was scare they will take my memory with the flashy, si?" Her grandmother waved a slipper at Connor before resting it in her lap. Abriella laughed. She imagined that the slipper had been waved at many people.

"Sorry, Smalls. You know how it goes. I ain't leaving your side." Connor had the decency to at least look sheepish. His hands never stopped rubbing small circles on Theo's back.

"Did we get him?" Abriella relaxed back into the cushion of the mattress, squeezing her grandmother's hand again, just to be sure it wasn't all imaginary.

"A-yup. Two in the head." Connor winked at her over the top of Theo's head. "Good shot, Smalls."

She huffed, her eyelids suddenly growing heavy against her will. "Good riddance."

Fingertips combed through her hair as her eyes slipped closed. Soft words floated over her, the familiar song her grandmother had sung since her earliest memories coaxing her back to sleep. Everything, at least for now, was all right.

CHAPTER THIRTY-SEVEN

Lily

LILY READJUSTED HER GRIP on Parker's hand, giving it a little squeeze as they waited for Elias to finish talking to the young woman at the nurse's station. The atmosphere reminded her of the struggle of so many years of clinical rotations. Introversion and the chaos of hospitals hadn't been a good mix then, but today's visit was important. Container of cookies in hand, she smiled at the little boy tucked close to her side.

"Are you excited to see uncle Teo, Miss Lily?" Parker glanced up at her, returning the smile with a gap-toothed one of his own.

"Of course I am. Miss Abriella too."

"Come on, you two. We got the all clear." Elias strode across the distance that separated them. "Room four-oh-three. Visiting hours await!"

"Remember, Parker. We have to be calm and gentle with our friends, okay?" Lily gave his hand another squeeze. A case of the wiggles slowly replaced his shyness at the promise of seeing Theo. It warmed her heart.

"Yeah, super calm 'cause uncle Teo has injuries. But dad said he was gonna be okay and would love one of my hugs. I'm d'best hugger."

"That you are, my man." Elias grabbed Parker's free hand as they went down the hall.

Ambient light from the windows illuminated the shared recovery room, hushed conversation filtering through the door as they carefully pushed it open.

"Hey, guys. It's just us." Elias eased the door open further, and the trio stepped through in single file.

"Uncle Teo!" Parker tore himself from their hands, running across the room to crash into the side of the hospital bed where Theo sat tucked against Connor's chest. She grimaced as he flinched.

"Parker, easy!" Elias swiftly stepped forward to scoop up his son in a fluid, practiced motion. "Calm, remember?"

"Sorry, Teo. I am just really happy to see you. Can I hug you now?" Tears glittered at the corners of the little boy's eyes. Theo's mirrored his, the emotions playing over his expression as he nodded. Lily crept around the periphery of the room to slide in beside Abriella's bed.

"You look ready to kill the next person who walks in the room, Abriella. How are you feeling?" Lily smiled, leaning in to brush a kiss over Abriella's cheek.

"Tired, sore. I want to go home and eat a pint of Ben & Jerry's in my own bed. This is bullsh— bull. This is bull." Abriella glanced at Parker in the neighboring bed as she censored herself. Too busy petting Theo's curls, he hadn't noticed the slip. Elias and Connor, meanwhile, smothered snickers. They were all just overgrown children.

"It's not ice cream, but I brought cookies. Vanilla latte. Theo's recipe." Lily popped the top of the container and held it out.

Abriella's smile was radiant as she grabbed two. "How are you so sweet, Lil? I thought Connor was sweet, but you take the cake. Don't give him any lessons. I can only handle so much sugar, si?"

"We have to counterbalance your spice, Bella." Lily averted her eyes with a grin as the warmth crept over her cheeks.

Abriella's eyes rolled as she laughed, carefully shifting her arm in the sling around her neck before sinking back into the pillow. "I have to keep things exciting. Otherwise, we would all be bored to tears."

Lily brushed the hair from Abriella's forehead with another smile. "So true. I'm just glad you're all right. Don't be stubborn. Us doctors know what we're talking about."

"So much fuss. You are almost as bad as my Abuela. I can send you away like I did her." Abriella waved the last of her cookies at Lily with a stern expression that dissolved into a smile.

"You wouldn't dare. And I can pull rank. I'm his physician, after all!" Lily darted in to plant another kiss on Abriella's cheek before ducking out of the way with a cheeky grin. Having people she was comfortable enough to relax around was a new feeling but one she wouldn't trade for the world.

She slipped around the periphery of the room again, this time sliding onto the edge of Theo's bed as Elias traded places with her to sit with Abriella. Theo met her eyes over the top of Parker's head, tears still clinging to his lashes despite the small smile that quirked his lips.

"How are you holding up, Theo?" Lily pressed her palm to the back of Theo's hand where it lay on Parker's back.

"I'm... not okay. But I think I will be?" The honesty in his reply was striking. He'd spent so long trying to convince her he was fine that she didn't know what to make of the shift.

"You will be. I promise. We're all here with you." Lily caught Connor's gaze as he nuzzled at the messy curls on the top of Theo's head.

"Baby, I'm going to go stretch my legs and grab something to eat while you talk with Lil. Y'all need anything?" Connor gently eased himself from the bed, a difficult feat for how entwined he was with Theo's frame.

A chorus of no filled the room. Connor stretched and tried to silence the groan as he worked the stiffness out of his back before he trudged from the room with one last glance toward Theo. Lily watched the exchange with her head cocked. Once the door was closed behind him, she turned back toward Theo.

"Yeah. He's not okay, either. Don't tell him I said anything. I feel guilt—"

"No. Nope. Shut it, Moreau," Abriella barked from the neighboring bed. Evidently, her approach was the tough-love variety.

"Guilt is a normal feeling. You've all been through a lot. We all have been. It's okay not to be okay. At least you are all alive to feel this way. It'll pass. And then we'll all be okay." Lily gently cupped Theo's cheek, brushing away a tear that had fallen free from his lashes with her thumb.

"Probably not the right time to bring this up, but we don't have much longer. Your mom wanted me to tell you that you can come back to the White House when you get out. And to apologize that she hasn't come to visit, but they didn't want to risk the press swooping in on her heels." Elias tousled the hair on the top of his head before smoothing it back down. Lily caught the way Theo's whole body tensed out of the corner of her eye. Even Parker sensed it, carefully wrapping his arms around Theo's waist before settling against his chest.

"I don't think I'm ready. I miss the kids, but... I don't know if I'm ready. Connor and I were talking about getting a smaller place somewhere else in the city. I don't want to leave him. I'm not ready to deal with mom. I don't know. It's a lot."

"Nah, screw that. You guys can move in with Park and me." Elias jerked his thumb over his shoulder in the direction of the door. "Including him. You can't go back to the apartment. And I don't blame you for not wanting to go back to the White House. I wouldn't."

Theo blinked. Parker sat up so fast Lily almost thought he had been shocked.

"Oh em gee, Teo, you can be like my roommate! Like camp! We can watch movies. We can get polishes on Amazon if dat's okay with dad. Please say yes. Dis is even greater den a puppy!" Parker wiggled in place so hard she put a hand out just in case he vibrated himself off the bed.

"I'll talk to Connor and see what he says, okay?" Theo brushed a finger under his eyes to catch the new-fallen tears. "Thanks, Eli. I mean it. Sorry, I don't know why I keep cryi—"

"No. Nope. None of that, Moreau!" Abriella barked once more with a stern look. Lily burst into a fit of giggles. She was like a guard dog trying to keep self-deprecating thoughts out of the room.

Theo huffed, but the faint smile playing over his lips made her smile in response.

Lily leaned over Parker to kiss Theo's forehead. "Can we do dinner and movie nights? I promise I'll bring a cake if you say yes, Elias."

Abriella perked up at the mention of cake. "Dios mio, Lily. I think you are trying to make us all fat. And I, for one, am completely all right with this."

Connor eased himself back into the room as they all dissolved into soft laughter. His eyes darted around the room with a wary look.

"Con, babe. Eli has something to tell you." Theo reached out his arm as Connor approached, the plaster cast constricting the movement of his fingertips as they hooked around Connor's outstretched hand.

"Smooth, Theo. Smooth." Elias grinned before turning his eyes toward Connor. "Theo said you two were looking for a new place once you're sprung from here. Don't. I have too much space, and you guys are welcome to it."

"Wait, you mean..." Connor boggled, his eyes going wide as his brows jumped toward his hairline. "I mean, I reckon it's an amazing offer, but we can make it work, Sir. Even if I do get kicked off the force, I can find something. Theo can work from home once the cast is off."

"Babe, breathe. We don't have to decide today. Let's talk it over." Theo winced as he shifted on the bed to accommodate Connor's frame. Lily coaxed Parker to herself with a cookie to give them more space as they resumed the entangled position she had found them in when they first entered the room.

"Biggs, this is when I jump in to say you are being loco. You need a place to stay, and my apartment is a man-free zone. Sorry, not sorry. Stay with him."

"Even if it's just temporary. My door is always open to Theo and, by extension, you. You're all kind of stuck with me now." Elias cracked a smile that made him look twenty years younger than he was.

"And me. I needed new people to feed cake to. It works out perfectly in my master plan." Lily squished Parker against her chest as he leaned in for a hug. He was surprisingly affectionate for a child who was initially so shy with her, something she attributed to a form of trauma bonding until he flashed her another boyish grin.

"Yeah, you too, Miss Lily. Dad says your cakes are best. And you're one of my friends now because you're uncle Teo's friend and uncle Teo's husband's friend, so you have to come too. And I'm gonna make Caleb come and be dad's husband too, and Miss Abriella is gonna come, and dis means I'll have more friends forever!"

Everyone in the room collectively sputtered. Elias pinched the bridge of his nose as Abriella cackled. Connor's cheeks turned three shades redder, and Theo pressed his palm to his face with a snicker. Parker, on the other hand, appeared utterly confused.

"Dis is d'best plan. You're all just being silly now." He folded his arms over his chest with a small sniff. "You're just mad dat I'm d'smartest."

"Yeah, I reckon you might be, Parker. I guess that settles it?" Connor nuzzled Theo's temple, whispering in his ear so low Lily couldn't make out the words even though she sat right beside them.

"If you're sure, Eli, then yeah. Thank you. I really appreciate it," Theo replied with a grin, shifting himself into a more comfortable position as Connor carefully tugged him back into a reclined position in the narrow hospital bed.

"We. We really appreciate it," Connor interjected with a grin. "Thanks, Elias."

Abriella rolled her eyes again before dramatically groaning. "Get me out of here. They are obnoxious. Theo, you've ruined my best friend!"

"Don't be jealous, Smalls," Connor quipped as he fussed over the blanket. A smile played over Lily's lips as she watched the two of them. Connor had always hovered in Theo's orbit, but now he did so with such intensity she wondered if she'd ever see them not attached at the hip.

"Since you're all here, Elias... can we borrow your place for another birthday party next week? It's Connor's birthday. Lily already volunteered for cake duty." Abriella pushed herself back into a sitting position. The woman never seemed to sit still. Lily exhaled, marching around the room to push her back into the pillows.

"You need a keeper, Abriella. Rest, remember that part of the doctor's orders?" Lily muttered as she checked the dressing on Abriella's shoulder. "You had surgery. Rest. Or you'll never get out of here."

With another roll of her eyes, Abriella whined, "Si, Mami. So serious."

"I'm all for another house party. How old, Connor?" Elias swatted at Connor's foot where it hung off the side of the bed.

"Twenty-eight. Y'all don't need to make a fuss. It's been a helluva couple months." Connor's nose scrunched as he tightened his arms around Theo's torso, who tried to stifle a whimper. "Shit. Sorry, baby."

"Theo, you've ruined him completely. He never cussed this much before." Abriella nearly sat up again until Lily cast her a severe look. They were all incorrigible. "And we are celebrating your birthday, so shut it."

"You're all ridiculous. And I love you for it," Theo mumbled, a smile sneaking over his lips as fresh tears burgeoned on the fringes of his eyelashes. Elias swooped in to grab Parker before he could pounce on Theo again.

"That settles it, then. Next weekend, party at our place. Park, wanna head to the dollar store for embarrassing party hats?" Elias plucked the boy up and perched him on his hip.

"Dat's perfect, dad. And we need to get snacks. And decorations. Stickers too! And juice." Parker scrunched his eyes as he pushed his glasses higher up his nose. "I'm gonna be in charge of dis party. We need a pinata. And balloons."

One by one, they all dissolved into laughter, which left Parker scowling. Lily reached out to poke his nose with a smile.

"It's going to be the best party, Parker. Don't forget birthday candles, okay?" She leaned in to kiss his cheek. Emboldened, she made a circuit of the room to do the same to everyone else. By the time she'd finished, her eyes were threatening to spill over. Never had she been adopted into a friend group so quickly, and the fact that she'd almost lost them all hit her as she took one last look around the room before slipping out. The echoes of everyone calling out "love you, Lil" caused a sob to bubble over as she left.

CHAPTER THIRTY-EIGHT

Elias

ELIAS GLANCED INTO THE rearview mirror at the motorcade of vehicles crowding his street once he parked the car in his garage. As the door slowly closed, he lost sight of the chaos. He caught Theo's gaze from the passenger seat. Wide-eyed with visible tension in his jaw, he had the appearance of a frightened child, something Elias could only empathize with. He still hadn't broached the topic of what exactly happened, but he'd seen enough over the live stream to know it wasn't good. The way Connor hovered like a protective guard dog only served to reinforce his belief that the kid had been through hell.

"Are you sure you're up to visitors? It's been a long day already. I'm sure they'd understand." Elias reached out his hand as slowly as he could, palm upturned. Theo still flinched at the movement.

"It's fine. I'll be fine. I want to see the kids." Although his smile was thin and wavering, it appeared genuine enough. Theo reached out to squeeze Elias' hand before pulling away to open the door and slip out. He made it to the door leading into the house before he froze. Connor climbed out of the backseat in a matter of seconds as Elias reworked the expected timeframe for Theo's adjustment period yet again. The tension in his jaw made his teeth ache.

"Come on, Park. Let's get inside before Anna gets in. Remember, you guys need to stay super calm, okay?" Elias rechecked the rearview mirror, smiling as he met Parker's eyes.

"Yes, dad. Calm. I'll keep Anna calm. She's hyper." Parker fumbled with his seatbelt before tumbling out of the car. Elias' smile grew incrementally wider as he watched his boy slide in close beside Theo with a sideways hug.

Inside the house, they shed their shoes and jackets, the entryway suddenly more cluttered than it had been in a while. The idea of his oversized home finally feeling lived in gave him the morale boost he needed. Elias shooed the trio into the family room with a grin.

"Welcome home, guys. I'm going to get dinner in the oven. Let me know when you're ready for the influx."

Theo rubbed a hand over his face before nodding. He and Parker disappeared into the family room without a word while Connor texted the agents in the motorcade outside.

"Hey, you good, Connor?" Elias stepped in closer, resting a hand on the younger man's forearm. He'd barely been speaking for days now whenever Elias had gone to visit them in the hospital. Once they'd discharged Abriella, Theo finally crumbled, and Connor became a shell of himself.

"Yeah, I reckon. I think this is too soon, but he says he can handle it."

"I mean you. How are you, Connor?" Elias squeezed Connor's forearm before dropping his hand back to his side.

"I'm angry. Livid. Confused. Mostly angry. But I'll live." Connor shrugged, scratching at the bandage Elias knew was wrapped around his upper arm. "I know it ain't nothing like what he went through, but… I'm just mad at it all."

"We can talk later, once everyone's gone. I think you need to talk to someone." He exhaled a sigh when a knock came from the front door. He was inclined to agree with Connor on this. It was too soon. But they didn't have a choice as Adelaide, Toby, Anna, and two Secret Service agents Elias had never seen entered the foyer.

Connor instantly bristled. "Names, badge numbers. Now. You both stay right there outside that door." Adelaide's nod in assent had the cowed agents skulking back through the door before Connor rushed in to ensure it was locked and deadbolted.

"Uncle Eli!" Anna's squeal rang out, shrill and excitable, although they'd seen each other near-daily since the incident.

"Hey, Anna-Banana. I'm glad you're here. All of you." Elias stooped down to hug the girl, squeezing her tighter than necessary. "Remember what we talked about, okay? You gotta stay calm. You and Parker both, okay? Theo's in the family room with Parker. Connor will take you guys."

Even though Anna was the most outwardly excited, it was Toby who strode through the foyer with the purposeful intention of a young man on a mission. Elias reached out a hand to stall Adelaide's movement.

"Addy, give them a couple minutes."

"Elias, I—"

"No, Adelaide. He's barely holding it together. Don't." Despite his best intentions, he couldn't keep the edge out of his voice. As much as it wrenched his heart to see her crushed expression, the wait was necessary.

"He's still mad at me." Adelaide followed, compliant and crestfallen, as Elias led her into the kitchen. "Hell, I'm still mad at me too. I don't blame him."

They fell into silence as Elias moved around the kitchen to prepare dinner. A gourmet chef, he was not. Frozen lasagna and bagged salad mix could only occupy him for so long before he turned toward Adelaide where she stood leaning against the island.

"I don't have any wine. Theo's not allowed to drink on the meds they sent him home with. Apple juice, water, or tea?"

"Water's fine," she murmured, shrinking in on herself as the sound of her three children crying filtered through the distance. Connor appeared in the doorway with a teary-eyed Parker perched on his hip.

"Reckon we could hang out with y'all in here? I think they need some time." Connor glanced toward Adelaide, and the flicker of his tensing jaw was evident as he skirted around the island to stand beside Elias.

"Dinner'll be ready in an hour or so. Park, why don't you run upstairs for a bit and get changed before dinner? Grown-up talk." Elias tousled his son's hair with a smile as he hopped over for a hug. Every instinct told him to shield his little boy from as much as he could, even if he'd already seen so much and displayed the resilience only a child could possess.

"Sure, dad! I'm gonna get my markers too. We can decorate Teo's cast with pictures." And with that, he was off.

"How's the investigation going, Addy?" Elias searched through the cabinets until he found the water pitcher he owned but had never used. Having a house full of guests called for service wear. So did the need to keep himself occupied while everything felt so unsteady.

"Lily was right about the sickness. They found a makeshift lab in Thomas Mitchell's attic. We've kept all of it out of the press, so this is confidential information. The genetic testing has been a match across the board. They were distributing it in some sort of saline solution to the groups. They found traces all over the residence. It's a miracle the casualties weren't higher."

"Wait, the same as what Theo had?" Connor's hand clenched around his water glass so hard Elias was convinced the glass would shatter any moment.

"We suspect they targeted him first. Inhaling the bacteria is different from the topical infection the kids had. I've signed the emergency order to implement a decolonization program for all the locations hit the worst." Adelaide glanced down into her glass, spinning it back and forth between the palms of her hands. "We'd like you back on the job, Connor. I was going to wait until Director Moore reached out, but I just wanted you to know. I made sure he signed off on your back pay. It's the least I could do. Thank you sounds too weak."

"Ma'am..." Connor's jaw dropped, the puzzlement on his expression giving him the appearance of a lost child. Elias' paternal instincts apparently extended to Connor as well as Theo. "I reckon I appreciate it, but I'm gonna talk to Theo before I decide, all due respect, o'course. I just ain't comfortable making decisions without his input first."

Adelaide's eyes grew misty as she glanced at Connor. Elias slipped from the room with a nod to no one in particular. This wasn't his place. He listened at the door to the family room before poking his head in through the opening.

"Hey guys, how's it going?" He aimed for lighthearted and upbeat, falling just short of the goal but smiling nevertheless.

"Look, dad. S'rainbow colors!" Parker brandished a marker before gesturing to Theo's cast with it. Rainbows, indeed. Vivid color covered the entire cast from top to bottom, Anna and Parker laying beside Theo where he sat on the floor, each diligently coloring in every spare space of plaster. Toby sat on the couch just behind Theo, showing him something on his phone with his arms loosely wrapped around his older brother's shoulders.

"That's a good job. It's going to be a little bit before dinner is ready. When you're done coloring, how about we let Theo spend some time with his mom, yeah?" Elias' smile faltered as Theo's face went pale. Their eyes met across the distance.

"Y-yeah. Sure." Theo's chest rose, and fell with a deep breath. "Yeah."

Anna and Parker grumbled before collecting the markers and skipping from the room, the rambling plans for their next adventure echoing as they tumbled through the hall and stormed up the stairs. Toby hadn't moved an inch.

"It's okay, Tob. It'll just be a minute. Go bug Con about the game, yeah? He made me watch it. He's good with sports stuff." Theo craned his head to make eye contact with Toby. Whatever he communicated in the glance must have been reassuring enough. Toby slowly unwrapped his arms from around Theo's shoulders before sliding to his feet. Elias scooted out of the way as the muttering boy stalked toward the door and brushed past. The smile Elias stifled slipped through in a laugh as he turned back to Theo, reaching out a hand to help him off the floor.

"He's so much like you, it's almost scary."

"Yeah, he really is. I feel bad for his teachers." Theo shifted on his feet, scanning the room for something but ultimately glancing back toward Elias. *Slow and steady*, Elias coached himself. Everything was one step at a time now.

"You want me to stay, or you good to do this solo?" Elias kept his voice low, searching the tension-lined hazel eyes that looked up at him.

"I have to do it solo. It's just... weird." Theo glanced down at his feet, the bright purple socks suddenly capturing his full attention. "She's my mom. I love her, but... it's just complicated. It feels like we're strangers now."

"It IS complicated. You don't have to figure it out now. But I think this'll help." Elias gently pressed his hand to Theo's shoulder before continuing. "Everything you feel is valid. Don't you dare doubt that for a second, got it?"

Theo's nod was the only response he got. With a nod of his own, he returned to the kitchen. Adelaide glanced toward him with a questioning glance, and her face lit up when Elias nodded toward the doorway. As she left, he ran an interception on Connor.

"Give them a second, cowboy. Your man's got this," Elias murmured, pressing his hand to Connor's chest with gentle pressure. "He needs this."

"Yeah, but—" Connor's distress etched lines across his face.

"Remember, you're the one who told me you thought he was stronger than all of us put together. Let him do what he needs to do, Connor." Elias let his hand drop as the man's shoulders sank.

"Yeah. I reckon you're right. Gimme something to do before I lose my mind." Connor flashed a grin, a shadow of his normally radiant smile. Elias would take it. Any smile he saw on Connor or Theo's faces these days was a win.

"Help me by setting the table. I'll get the garlic bread in the oven while you two do that." Elias shooed Toby and Connor from the room with armfuls of dishes, silverware, and glasses. Once he was finally alone, he rubbed his hands over his face, shoulders sagging. They were all home now. The daunting process of rebuilding had finally begun. As the tension he hadn't realized he'd been carrying for weeks slowly left him, exhaustion washed in to replace it. They'd get through this—one step at a time.

CHAPTER THIRTY-NINE

Theo

WITH A DEEP BREATH, Theo slipped from the guest room that had become his and Connor's bedroom, compulsively checking the hallway before padding toward the room Elias used as an office during the weekend. He'd been building himself up to this moment all morning long. With another measured inhale and exhale, he knocked on the doorframe before poking his head into the room. He found Elias dressed in the most cliche flannel pajamas he'd ever seen, rocking back in his chair with a scowl on his face.

"Hey, Theo. Everything all right?" His smile returned with the flip of a switch, putting Theo more at ease as he stepped into the room.

"I need to borrow your car, if that's all right. I can get an Uber otherwise." Theo fidgeted with the sleeves of his sweatshirt, resisting the urge to shove his hands in his pockets. He needed to appear calm and collected.

Elias' eyebrows flew up in surprise. "I'm just about done here. I can give you a ride wherever you need to go."

"I kinda wanna go solo. I have some things I want to do. I totally understand if you don't want me to take the car. I can just—"

"It's not about the car. It's about you. You've only been out of the hospital a couple of days, Theo. Are you sure—"

"I'm fine. I want to do this. I need to." Theo rubbed his hands over his face with a heavy sigh. "Please?"

Elias stepped around the desk, moving cautiously in the way that Theo had noticed everyone moving around him lately. It rubbed him all wrong, even if he understood why. Despite his best efforts, he was jumpy and flighty.

"Look, Theo. I get it. But you don't have to prove anything to us, okay?" Elias rested his hands on Theo's shoulders with a gentle squeeze.

"I have to prove something to me. I'm not going far, but I just need to know I can do this. It's important to me."

"I'm not going to tell you no. You're a big boy. Keep your cell close, volume on, and call me if you need me." He squeezed again, adding a little shake for emphasis. "For anything, understood? No man is an island, and I'll be there. Got it?"

Theo's lips quirked into a smile. "Got it, Eli. I'll be back soon. And I'll text you. Do you need anything while I'm out?"

"Actually, if you can grab a gallon of milk and some bread, that'd be great. We're almost out. Take my card."

Theo waved him off, the cast on his arm making the movement comical and stilted. He hurried from the room to the sound of Elias' protests. Obstacle one overcome. Now he was onto the next obstacle.

Once he had his shoes and the new coat his mother had sent him on, he approached the car in the garage like a wary animal. His first solo excursion since the ordeal loomed ominously before him, but he persevered. It took a while to adjust the seat just right. The mirrors took a little longer, the switches frustrating him as his anxiety started climbing. Eventually, he turned the key in the ignition and pushed the remote to open the garage door. Before putting the car in reverse, he pulled out his phone and scrolled through his contact list.

Switching to speakerphone, he tossed the phone in his lap as it rang, navigating the driveway and easing into the street before he was on his voyage. The click of the call connecting gave him something to concentrate on besides the nerves that had his hands shaking on the steering wheel.

"O'Brien residence!"

"Hey, Miss Birdie. It's Theo."

"Oh, well I'll be! How's my boy today?"

"I'm okay. I'm on my way to the store to get some stuff for Connor's birthday party tonight." Theo remained at the stop sign for longer than he needed to, the car behind him beeping the only thing that startled him into motion.

"All by your lonesome?" Birdie's voice over the line was tinny from the speakerphone, but he heard the concern in her tone nevertheless.

"Yeah. I'm going to get stuff to make ribs. If you aren't busy, mind sticking with me? So I get what I need?" Theo tried not to let his voice waver, but the further he drove from their home, the more his anxiety threatened to turn into a full-blown panic attack. He never went an entire day without at least one now.

"I reckon I can do that. I got to make sure you get just the right ingredients for my famous barbeque ribs, after all!"

They chatted back and forth, idle small talk filling the void to keep his racing paranoia at bay until he finally managed to maneuver the car into a parking spot. Once the engine died, he grabbed the phone and turned off the speaker before bringing it to his ear.

"Okay. At the store now." Theo left the rest unspoken. His ribs ached. His chest grew tight. He rummaged around in the glove compartment to pull out a pair of sunglasses. Somehow, Connor's sunglasses hid everywhere, duplicated by some strange magic wherever he spent any time.

"Hey, Theo?" Birdie's words came over the line with a tenderness that left him juggling conflicting emotions in his heightened state of apprehension. "This ain't no thing. And we're gonna make sure our boy gets his birthday dinner."

Theo's laughter bordered on manic as he nodded, despite the fact she couldn't see the motion. More to himself than in response to her comment. Getting out of the car was another hurdle he had to clamber over. But nothing compared to the store itself. He clutched the phone tight to his ear as Connor's mother regaled him with tales of Connor as an awkward, gangly teenager. The conversation became the only thing that kept him moving forward through the weekend crowds.

"Birdie, it's so busy in here," he mumbled into the receiver, stopping dead in the quietest aisle he could find for a chance to catch his breath.

"Well, I reckon it's always busy on the weekends, love. Let's get what we need and get back home. I want to watch the next episode of RuPaul with you while we cook the ribs. Chop, chop!"

"Birdie, you're a lifesaver. Okay, what do I need?" Theo took another deep breath before pushing the cart back into the main aisle, concentrating on the list of ingredients and trying to avoid eye contact with passersby. The amount of recognition he was getting made the nerves worse. He opted for self-checkout once the pointing started.

"Theo, love. You aren't breathing. Gonna need ya to take a deep breath, else I'm gonna have to call Connie, and we're almost done. We don't want that, love. So just take yourself a deep breath and finish up," Birdie coached over the line as a group of people started edging closer to where he stood.

With a shaky gasp, he did as instructed, fumbling the card before successfully tapping it against the reader. Once the receipt popped out, he fled the store. She stayed with him on the phone as he threw everything into the trunk. She waited with him as he climbed into the car and slammed the lock button. She never left him, even as he fell apart in the driver's seat, stifling his sobs with his free hand as he clutched the phone to his ear. Only once his tears had subsided did she break the companionable silence.

"You did it. You did it, Theo. And I'm so proud of you."

"Thank you. For staying with me." Theo sniffed, settling back in the seat before fishing the keys out of his pocket. "It really means a lot to me."

"Oh, pish posh. It ain't no thing, love. Now, text me when you're ready to start cooking so we can watch the next episode. You got half an hour, or I'm calling Connie. Understand me?"

Theo laughed, albeit shakily, before they said their goodbyes and finally ended the call. He texted Elias to let him know he was on his way back before putting the car in gear. The promise of home made the return journey easier.

··········

Once the evening rolled around, with the aid of a Xanax, Theo managed to calm himself enough to help Parker set up all the decorations and put out the spread of food he'd concentrated on all afternoon. He'd beaten Elias back with a dish towel as soon as the smell of barbeque ribs had filtered through the house. Now that everything was ready to go, the three of them waited anxiously in the foyer for the imminent arrival of their guests. Once his phone started chiming with text alerts, he knew the party was about to begin. The chatter of voices approached the door, muffled until Parker flung it open in his excitement. Theo laughed as the host of the night thrust party hats at everyone before they could even cross the threshold.

"Happy bir'day! Happy day! Cay-Cay, you sit with me tonight! C'mon! I got you dis special hat!"

Theo edged out of the way as Caleb, Abriella, and Lily shed their shoes and followed the mighty party planner into the dining room with Elias on their tail. Once the foyer cleared, Connor stepped forward. Theo fell into his arms with a heavy exhalation.

"Missed you, babe. Happy birthday."

"Miss you always, baby. Y'all right?" Connor nuzzled his hair and peppered his face with kisses, pulling him even closer. The pressure ached in his ribs, but he clung tighter, glad for the contact. If he could live perpetually in Connor's arms, he would die a happy man.

"Mmhmm. Your mom helped me make the ribs you like. For your birthday." Theo's words were muddled as he buried his lips in the familiar crook of Connor's neck.

"Wait, you mean THE ribs?" Connor pulled back to search Theo's face.

"Yeah. I went to the store and got everything. We watched Drag Race while they cooked. I love your mom." Theo flashed a lopsided smile before walking backward toward the dining room. "Come before they're all gone. I don't trust Elias. He's been trying to poach them all afternoon."

"Baby, you didn't—"

An explosion of singing cut off Connor's voice, the familiar chords of 'Happy Birthday' filling the dining room around them. His face turned three shades redder, and his smile alone was all the reward Theo needed for the effort. Deadly dimples on full display, Connor turned to him, speechless, before swooping in for a kiss. The hoots and hollers of their friends all around them filled Theo's heart with such profound warmth. For the first time in months, there was nothing that could dull his happiness. It wasn't perfect. Some things were still a struggle, and maybe always would be. But at that moment, wrapped in Connor's arms and surrounded by the friends who had become family, he finally felt like he could breathe.

CHAPTER FORTY

Connor

Three Months Later

The sound of music caused Connor to pause on the sidewalk outside their new apartment building, the familiar, upbeat chords of the bluesy ballad filtering through the open windows on the second floor. His smile grew wider as his partner's even-more familiar off-key voice rose above the sound for the chorus. He jogged up the stoop with renewed vigor and hurried into the building.

"Hey, Carson!" He flashed a wave to the guard at the front desk. They'd only been residents of the building for a week, but the names and faces of the building's security team were well-ingrained in his memory as he strode through the lobby and toward the stairs.

He didn't bother texting before he slid his key into the lock of their home. He didn't need to anymore. By the time he pushed the door open, his grin had his cheeks aching. He nudged the door closed, throwing the deadbolt and locking the knob before slipping into the kitchen to lean against the frame of the open archway. No matter how often he encountered it, the display inside still left him speechless.

The music was even louder inside as Theo danced around the island, belting out the chorus into a makeshift wooden spoon microphone, begging his darling to put his loving hands out. Theo was a terrible singer. Connor never wanted him to stop singing. With a twirl, Theo startled as he caught sight of him in the doorway, his smile a radiant mirror of the one Connor still wore. He reached out to grab Theo's outstretched hand in time to the music, taking up the words in unison as they swayed around the kitchen.

Before long, the song ended and the next began, Theo abandoning his mixing spoon mic on the counter to wrap his hand around the nape of Connor's neck. Singing and dancing led to kissing in rapid succession, breathlessness parting their lips before things could escalate too far.

"Missed you, babe."

"Miss you always, baby. Y'all right?" Connor slid his hands up Theo's sides, traveling under the hem of the baggy crop top to explore the familiar span of skin he'd spent so many nights memorizing.

"Mmhmm. This morning was a little rough, but I'm good. How was work?" Theo murmured the words against the pulse point on his neck, the sensation sending a shiver through his body.

"Same ole, same ole. The kids say hi. We're a go for next weekend's sleepover." Connor hoisted Theo up, setting him on the edge of the counter before stepping between his knees. "What happened this morning? You didn't call."

"Unexpected knock on the door. I handled it okay. I promise I'll call if it gets bad." Theo tangled his fingers in Connor's hair as he spoke. With a gentle tug, he leaned in for another kiss.

Time slowed and then stilled as their mouths joined, lips languidly lingering. No matter how many times they did this, his heart was always left racing. If anything good could come from the disastrous events that colored the early months of their relationship, it was the knowledge of just how precious their time together was. The realization he wouldn't know which kiss could be their last had left an indelible mark on Connor's heart.

Connor's body turned electric as Theo's hands slid down the curve of his back and into the waistband of his pants. With a mind of their own, his hips rocked back, seeking more of Theo's touch and frustrated by the restriction his suit pants imposed on them. Nevertheless, his partner was persistent, taunting him with a too-brief passing touch along the crease of his ass. Minutes turned to moments, the two of them lost in the rising intensity of their passionate kiss and roving hands before the timer on Theo's phone interrupted their affections. They reluctantly pulled apart, though they were still so close that he could feel the curve of Theo's smile against his lips.

"Baby," Connor whined, his hips still rolling and his voice tinged with frustration. "I need you."

"Raincheck, babe. The rest of the cookies have to come out so I can get dinner in. Everyone's showing up in an hour."

Connor tugged Theo's lower lip with a little nip before stepping out of the way. He landed a playful swat on Theo's ass before scampering out of the room with a snicker. From the hallway, he could just make out the sound of Theo's off-key singing resuming amid the clatter of baking sheets. Their apartment was modest enough in size that he could hear him from any room. It was a comforting togetherness that he didn't think he'd ever grow tired of.

As difficult as it had been, starting over turned out to be the best thing for them both. Everywhere he turned in their apartment, displays of the home they were building together came into view. They each had a nightstand. They each had pictures hung on the walls. Shoes in two different sizes littered the floor of the closet beneath the clothing on hangers, one side for him and the other for his boyfriend. Even the bathroom displayed how easily two lives became one and how melding two lives could make both better. With another grin, he turned the shower on, pausing to sniff the new shampoo he found with a sticky note attached. "Try this one. Better for blonde hair. XOXO"

Connor took his time in the shower, allowing the hot water to ease away the stresses of the work day. Taking over the supervisory position on the White House Secret Service had been a considerable learning curve that he was still struggling to adjust to. Still, every day became a little easier and returning home each evening melted away the strain. He toweled off and got dressed but only made it halfway down the hallway before Theo called out from the kitchen.

"Hamper!"

He cackled, backtracking to tidy up the bathroom and dump his clothes in the aforementioned basket, but not before calling out a retort of his own. "Yes, my grumpy little shit!"

Back in the kitchen, he pushed up his shirt sleeves to wash the dishes in the sink, humming along with the song playing on the speaker as Theo finished preparing the rest of dinner. They fell into sync so easily, working together like a well-oiled machine with a fluidity born of intimacy and understanding. Everything flowed so effortlessly.

A sharp knock on the door broke the rhythm. Theo startled, dropping the metal bowl he'd been drying. Connor abandoned the sink, leaving the faucet running as he reached for his hip, only to remember he was not wearing his tactical belt.

He peeked through the peephole on the door, relief flooding his system. "All clear, baby. It's Elias."

Elias grimaced as he slipped through the door, scrunching his nose as he mouthed an apology. They continued into the kitchen to find it empty.

"Sorry. I should have called ahead. I know I'm early. You guys settling in okay?" Elias stepped around the island, dumping bags of snacks on the empty space at the end.

"Yeah, I reckon we are. It's been nice. An adjustment, but nice." Connor resumed cleaning the dishes. "Beer's in the fridge. Everyone else should be 'round in half an hour."

"Where's Theo?" Elias cocked his head over the door of the fridge as he held out a second beer with an unspoken question.

"Bedroom. He just needs a minute. And thanks!"

Dishes washed and beer in hand, Connor ushered Elias into the living room with a shooing motion, calling down the hallway as he passed. "ETA fifteen! Put your pants on!"

"God, you're ridiculous!" The distance muffled the answering retort, but Connor knew full well the eye roll that had surely accompanied it.

"Love you too, baby!"

Elias settled on the couch, trying in vain to smother the smile on his face at their antics. They chatted back and forth to the background noise of ESPN, stifling snickers as Theo entered the room long enough to slide coasters under their beers before disappearing again. When another knock came at the door, it was Theo who called out that he would get it. The controlled chaos that overwhelmed the apartment was an expected and welcome one.

"Ay, this is so cute! Biggs, get your ass in here and help!"

"El, you too! I'm literally wilting!"

"Theo, thank you for having us. I brought cake."

They joined the suddenly overcrowded kitchen, each of them falling into place around the island as bags and boxes plopped on the counters.

"Lord, what is all this?" Connor boggled at the scene.

"Housewarming, mi sol!" Abriella swooped in to press a kiss to his cheek before shoving a bag into his hands. "I brought more pictures for your walls. From high school."

"And I brought candles because we do NOT trust El to pick out scents. He's hopeless." Caleb winked with a crooked grin at Elias.

Lily edged around the room, ducking around elbows and bodies to slide in beside Theo. Connor caught sight of her whispering in Theo's ear before handing him a giant gift bag. Curiosity piqued, he arched a brow at Theo. The smile that lit up his face made Connor's chest ache with adoration.

"Lil! You didn't!"

"I did. It's tradition." Her giggle caught the attention of everyone around the kitchen. With the exuberance of a child on Christmas morning, Theo pulled the gift from the bag with a bright peel of laughter.

They all collectively cheered as Theo held up the board game. They had their own Clue game now. Theo pulled Lily in for a hug, the box sandwiched between them as they embraced. As the chatter of their conversations resumed, he managed to catch Theo's gaze across the distance. In unison, they mouthed "I love you" to one another. Connor reached across the island, bridging the gap between his hand and Theo's outstretched fingertips. With a squeeze, they laced their fingers together and smiled. Despite everything they'd been through, they were all right. No matter what had come before or what might still come in their future, right now, everything was all right.

"We're home, baby."

Acknowledgments

What an adventure! I wrote a damn book… whoa. That didn't happen without a lot of help, though.

Mamacita! There aren't enough words in any of the known languages to express everything that needs to be said, so I'm gonna keep it simple: none of this would be real without you. Love you forever. Love you always.

Linds - For all the late-night indulgence of my scatterbrained obsession over fictional boys falling in love and numerous occasions of talking me off the edge. Ride or die, bish.

Kris - Namaste because your type of creative is a perfect complement to my type of creative and you get it.

Matt - Writing is a lonesome thing, but sometimes you find that je ne sais quoi with another. I went into this hoping for a tribe and ended up with a bestie. Stay fabulous, my friend.

Quinton - Not only did you polish my dumpster fire into something glittering, but the hype game is on point and I'm honored to travel this winding path together.

And last but certainly not least, a shout out to all those who give but never take as well as those who take but never give: thank you for fueling the fire. I promise any resemblance to real persons or other real-life entities is purely coincidental. ;)

The Rainbow Brigade Series

Corruption. Deceit. Lies. Power struggles.

Washington DC is the glittering symbol of American strength, but lurking in the shadows of the night are the secrets that no one wants to acknowledge.

Until a motley group of unlikely heroes bands together, carving out a place to stand together against the forces that aim to keep voices like theirs silenced.

Join the Rainbow Brigade as they work together against the enemies in the darkness, with love and compassion as their weapon of choice.

Book Two Coming Autumn 2023

Illuminate the Night

The Rainbow Brigade - Book Two Autumn 2023

Chief-of-Staff Elias Williams has always been the rock, despite the struggle of being a widowed single father with a monumental government job. Dependable and reliable, he's the glue holding together not only his own life, but the lives of friends and family in addition to the daily operations of the White House's highest offices. But this selflessness and fortitude hide a deep, gnawing loneliness that weighs on his heart. And he's not hiding it as well as he thought he was.

Deputy Chief-of-Staff Caleb Cohen sees it more than anyone else. Working side-by-side with Elias in the White House, this small but mighty force of nature gravitates toward his boss, desperately seeking his warmth and solidity to combat the demons of his own traumatic history. Unfortunately, nothing ever comes easy when working in the White House.

When the shadows of the right-wing rear their ugly head again, upheaval follows in their wake. With nowhere to turn but toward one another, Elias and Caleb band together with their trustworthy friends to fight against these nefarious forces. As the darkness draws closer, it becomes a battle with increasingly dire stakes. Desperation pulls them together, even as the threat of having to make the ultimate sacrifice undermines the foundation of everything they are fighting for.

The City Boys Never Sleep Series

Known for glitz and glamor, NYC is the shining beacon of optimism and hope for millions. The glittering lights of the iconic skyline are the inspiration for countless dreams, drawing them from near and far with the alluring promises of success and happiness.

But this shining facade often hides a darker secret. The hustle and bustle of the Big Apple is a distraction from the gritty, raw, and often hopeless pursuit of perfection. Behind the blinding lights and busy streets, intrepid residents must face their deepest and darkest nightmares before the merciless grind chews them up and spits them out.

Follow the stories of the people of NYC as they dig deep to confront the demons of their own psyche in the pursuit of something real and lasting. Because when night falls in the city that never sleeps, these city boys never sleep.

Checking Out

City Boys Never Sleep - Book One July 2023

Shiloh Corbel is just a simple boy from a small town but when he and his twin brother are thrown head first into the deep end, their status quo is turned upside down. They never even knew their father's name, but a knock on their door early one morning finds them suddenly inheriting a luxury hotel empire, Clueless about how to handle this change of circumstances, they have to figure out how to navigate the fast-paced city lifestyle and the burden of maintaining a successful business while struggling to come to terms with their sordid, secret history.

Trey Guillebaume has been with Talbot & Co Properties for almost a decade, working his way up from bellhop to executive assistant with the grit and determination needed to succeed in this fast-paced industry. When tragedy strikes, his world is turned upside down, faced with the uncertainty of working alongside the Corbel twins and his late boss' grieving wife as they try to keep the dream alive. The weight of it all threatens to crush him, as he tries in vain to deal with his own addictions and demons. Alone.

Forced to work together, Shiloh and Trey find themselves slowly drawn together, even as they desperately try to deny their magnetic attraction. It becomes even harder when the secrets and nightmares lurking in the alleys of their pasts step into the light. As the layers are peeled back, they are left raw and vulnerable, fighting against their demons for a chance to find something real together.

About the Author

Jay Leigh is an author (duh) as well as a voracious reader of primarily M/M romance novels filled with all sorts of goodies like action, suspense, emotions, and spice. Lots of spice.

Plot twist: It's actually just three mischievous raccoons in a trench coat fueled by levels of caffeine known to cause cancer in the state of California. Good thing they live in New York!

Learn more at authorjayleigh.com and on most social media platforms as @jayelle_m

Printed in Great Britain
by Amazon